Three Boys
Or The Chiefs Of The
Clan Mackhai

by

George Manville Fenn

Three Boys
Or The Chiefs Of The Clan Mackhai
by George Manville Fenn

ISBN: 978-93-60468-58-3

Published by

DOUBLE 9 BOOKS

2/13-B, Ansari Road
Daryaganj, New Delhi – 110002
info@double9books.com
www.double9books.com
Tel. 011-40042856

ABOUT THE AUTHOR

George Manville Fenn was a very productive author of novels, a writer, an editor, and an educator from England. He was born on January 3, 1831, in Pimlico, London. He mostly learned on his own; he taught himself Italian, French, and German. During the years 1851–1854, he went to Battersea Training College for Teachers and then became the head of a state school in Alford, Lincolnshire. In the early 1850s, Fenn started to write short stories and pieces for newspapers and magazines. The Old Forest Ranger, his first book, came out in 1856. Afterward, he wrote more than 100 books, many of them for teenagers and young adults. He was one of the most famous writers of his time, and his books were well-liked and read by many people. He also worked as a reporter and writer for Fenn. Among the newspapers and magazines, he worked for was The Boy's Own Paper, which he ran from 1866 to 1874. He worked hard to make children's books better and was a strong supporter of education and reading. The Englishman Fenn passed away on August 26, 1909, in Isleworth.

CONTENTS

Chapter One
The Mackhai of Dun Roe

"Look here, Scoodrach, if you call me she again, I'll kick you!"

"I didna ca' you she. I only said if she'd come ten the hoose aifter she had the parritch—"

"Well, what did I say?"

"Say? Why, she got in a passion."

Whop! Flop!

The sound of a back-handed slap in the chest, followed by a kick, both delivered by Kenneth Mackhai, the recipient being a red-headed, freckled-faced lad of seventeen, who retaliated by making a sharp snatch at the kicking foot, which he caught and held one half moment. The result was startling.

Kenneth Mackhai, the sun-browned, well-knit, handsome son of "the Chief," came down in a sitting position on the stones, and screwed up his face with pain.

"Scood, you beggar!" he roared; "I'll serve you out for—"

"Ken, are you coming to breakfast?" cried a loud, severe voice from fifty yards away.

"Coming, father!" shouted the lad, leaping up, giving himself a shake to rearrange his dark green kilt, and holding up his fist threateningly at the bare-legged, grinning lad before him. "Just you wait till after breakfast, Master Scood, and I'll make you squint."

The lad ran up the steep slope to the garden surrounding the ancient castle of Dunroe, which had been built as a stronghold somewhere about the fourteenth century, and still stood solid on its rocky foundation; a square, keep-like edifice, with a round tower at each corner, mouldering, with portions of the battlements broken away, but a fine monument still of the way in which builders worked in the olden time.

The portion Kenneth Mackhai approached had for inhabitants only the jackdaws, which encumbered the broken stairs by the loopholes with their nests; but, after passing beneath a gloomy archway and crossing the open interior, he left the old keep by another archway, to enter the precincts of the modern castle of Dunroe, a commodious building, erected after the style of the old, and possessing the advantages of a roof and floors, with large windows looking across the dazzling sea.

Kenneth entered a handsome dining-room, where the breakfast was spread, and where his father, The Mackhai, a tall, handsome man of fifty, was pacing angrily up and down.

"Sorry I kept you, father. Scood said there was a seal on the lower rocks, and—"

"The scoundrel! How dare he?" muttered The Mackhai. "To take such a mean advantage of his position. I will not suffer it. I'll—"

"I'm very sorry, father!" faltered Kenneth, crossing slowly toward his frowning elder. "I did not mean to—"

"Eh! what, Ken, my boy?" cried The Mackhai, with his countenance changing. "I've only just come in. Sit down, my lad. You must be half-starved, eh?"

"I thought you were cross with me, sir."

"Cross? Angry? Not a bit. Why?"

"You said—"

"Tchah! nonsense! Thinking aloud. What did you say?—a seal?"

"Yes, father. Scood said there was one, but it had gone."

"Then you didn't shoot it? Well, I'm not sorry. They're getting scarce now, and I like to see the old things about the old place. Hah!" he continued, after a pause that had been well employed by both at the amply-supplied, handsomely-furnished table; "and I like the old porridge for breakfast. Give me some of that salmon, Ken. No; I'll have a kipper."

"More coffee, please, father," said Ken, with his mouth full. "Have a scone, father? They're prime."

"Gently with the butter, my boy. There is such a thing as bile."

"Is there, father?" said Kenneth, who was spreading the rich yellow churning a full quarter of an inch thick.

"Is there, sir! Yes, there is. As I know to my cost. Ah!" he added, with a sigh, and his face wrinkled and made him look ten years older; "but there was a time when I did not know the meaning of the word!"

"Oh, I say, father," cried Kenneth merrily, "don't! You're always pretending to be old, and yet you can walk me down stalking, and Long Shon says you can make him sore-footed any day."

"Nonsense! nonsense!" said The Mackhai, smiling.

"Oh, but you can, father!" said Kenneth, with his mouth full. "And see how you ran with that salmon yesterday, all among the stones."

"Ah, yes! I manage to hold my own; but I hope you'll husband your strength better than I did, my boy," said The Mackhai, with a sigh.

"I only hope I shall grow into such a fine man!" cried Kenneth, with his face lighting up, as he gazed proudly at his father. "Why, Donald says—"

"Tut, tut, tut! Silence, you miserable young flatterer! Do you want to make your father conceited? There, that will do."

"Coming fishing to-day, father?"

There was no answer.

The Mackhai had taken up a letter brought in that morning by one of the gillies, and was frowning over it as he re-read its contents, and then sat thoughtfully gazing out of the window across the glittering sea, at the blue mountains in the distance, tapping the table with his fingers the while.

"Wonder what's the matter!" thought Kenneth. "Some one wants some money, I suppose."

The boy's face puckered up a little as he ceased eating, and watched his father's face, the furrows in the boy's brow giving him a wonderful likeness to the keen-eyed, high-browed representative of a fine old Scottish clan.

"Wish I had plenty of money," thought Kenneth; and he sighed as he saw his father's face darken.

Not that there was the faintest sign of poverty around, for the room was tastily furnished in good old style; the carpet was thick, a silver coffee-pot glistened upon the table, and around the walls were goodly paintings of ancestral Mackhais, from the bare-armed, scale-armoured chief who fought the Macdougals of Lorne, down to Ronald Mackhai, who represented Ross-shire when King William sat upon the throne.

"I can't help myself," muttered The Mackhai at last. "Here, Ken, what were you going to do to-day?"

"I was going up the river after a salmon."

"Not to-day, my boy. Here, I've news for you. Mr Blande, my London solicitor, writes me word that his son is coming down—a boy about your age."

"Son—coming down? Did you invite him, father?"

"Eh? No: never mind that," said The Mackhai hastily. "Coming down to stay with us a bit. Regular London boy. Not in very good health. You must be civil to him, Ken, and show him about a bit."

"Yes, father," said Kenneth, who felt from his father's manner that the coming guest was not welcome.

"He is coming by Glasgow, and then by the Grenadier. His father thinks the sea will do him good. Go and meet him."

"Yes, father."

"Tell them to get a room ready for him."

"Yes, father."

"Be as civil to him as you can, and—Pah!"

That ejaculation, pah! came like an angry outburst, as The Mackhai gave the table a sharp blow, and rose and strode out of the room.

Kenneth sat watching the door for a few moments.

"Father's savage because he's coming," said Kenneth, whose eyes then fell upon a glass dish of marmalade, and, cutting a goodly slice of bread, he spread it with the yellow butter, and then spooned out a portion of the amber-hued preserve.

"Bother the chap! we don't want him here."

Pe-au, pe-au, came a wailing whistle through the open window.

"Ah, I hear you, old whaupie, but I can do it better than that," said Kenneth to himself, as he repeated the whistle, in perfect imitation of the curlews which abounded near.

The whistle was answered, and, with a good-tempered smile on his face, Kenneth rose from the table, after cutting another slice of bread, and laying it upon that in his plate, so as to form a sticky sandwich.

"Scood!" he cried from the window, and barelegged Scoodrach, who was seated upon a rock right below, with the waves splashing his feet, looked up and showed his white teeth.

"Catch!"

"All right."

Down went the bread and marmalade, which the lad caught in his blue worsted bonnet, and was about to replace the same upon his curly red head, but the glutinous marmalade came off on one finger. This sticky finger he sucked as he stared at the bread, and, evidently coming to the conclusion that preserve and pomade were not synonymous terms, he began rapidly to put the sweet sandwich somewhere else.

"I wish you had kept it in your bonnet, Scood."

The boy looked up and laughed, his mouth busy the while.

"Father saw sax saumon in the black pool," he cried eagerly.

"Then they'll have to stop," said Kenneth gloomily.

"Eh?"

"There's a chap coming down from London."

"To fesh?"

"Suppose so. We've got to go and meet him."

"With ta pony?"

"No, the boat; coming by the Grenadier."

"Ou ay."

"It's a great bother, Scood."

"But it's a verra fine mornin' for a sail," said the boy, looking up and munching away.

"But I didn't want to sail, I wanted to fish."

"The fush can wait, tat she can."

"Oh, you!" shouted Kenneth. "Wish I had something to throw at you."

"If she did, I'd throw it back," said Scoodrach, grinning.

"I should like to catch you at it. There, go and get the boat."

"Plenty of time."

"Never mind that; let's be off and have a good sail first, as we have to go."

"Will she—will you tak' the gun?"

"Of course I shall. Take the lines too, Scood; we may get a mackerel."

The lad opened his large mouth, tucked in the last piece of marmalade, and then leaped off the stone on to the rock.

"Scood!"

The boy stroked down his grey kilt, and looked up.

"Put on your shoes and stockings."

"What for?"

"Because I tell you. Because there's company coming. Be off!"

"She's got a big hole in her stocking, and ta shoe hurts her heel."

"Be off and put them on," roared Kenneth from the window. "I shall be ready in a quarter of an hour."

Scood nodded, and began to climb rapidly over the buttress of rock which ran down into the sea, the height to which the tide rose being marked by an encrustation of myriads of acorn barnacles, among which every now and then a limpet stood out like a boss, while below, in the clear water, a thick growth of weed turned the rock to a golden brown, and changed the tint of the transparent water.

Chapter Two
"A Bore!"

"What a bother!" muttered Kenneth, as he left the dining-room, crossed the hall, and entered a little oak-panelled place filled with all kinds of articles used in the chase, and whose walls were dotted with trophies—red deer and roebucks' heads, stuffed game, wild fowl, a golden eagle, and a pair of peregrine falcons. He took a double-barrel from the rack, placed a supply of cartridges in a belt, buckled it on, and then returned to the oak-panelled hall, to pause where his bonnet hang over the hilt of an old claymore.

Carelessly putting this on, he sauntered out of the hall into the shingly path, where he was saluted by a chorus of barking. A great rough-coated, long-legged deerhound came bounding up, followed first by a splendid collie with a frill about his neck like a wintry wolf, and directly after by a stumpy-legged, big-headed, rough grey Scotch terrier, with a quaint, dry-looking countenance, which seemed like that of some crotchety old man.

"Hi, Bruce!" cried Kenneth, as the deerhound thrust a pointed nose into his hand. "What, Dirk, lad!"

This to the collie, which reared up to put its paws upon his chest, and rubbed its head against its master; while the little dog ran round and round clumsily, barking all the while.

"Down, Dirk! Quiet, Sneeshing, quiet!"

The dogs were silent on the moment, but followed close at their master's heels, eyeing the gun wistfully, the deerhound going further, and snuffing at the lock. Being apparently satisfied that it was not a rifle, and that consequently his services would not be required, the hound stopped short by a warm, sheltered place, crouched down, and formed itself into an ornament upon the sea-washed rock.

"There, you can do the same, Dirk. It's boat day," said Kenneth.

The collie uttered a whine and a loud bark.

"Yes, it's boat day, lad. Be off!"

The dog stopped short, and only the little ugly grey terrier followed his master, wagging a short stump of a tail the while, till Kenneth noted his presence.

"No, not to-day," he said sharply.

"Wuph!"

"No. Can't take you. Go back, old chap. Another time!"

Sneeshing uttered a low whine, but he dropped down on the shingle which took the place of gravel, and Kenneth went slowly on along a path formed like a shelf of the huge rock, which, a peninsula at low, an island at high water, towered up from the blue sea an object of picturesque beauty, and a landmark for the sailors who sailed among the fiords and rocks of the western shore.

The scene around was glorious. Where the soft breeze did not turn the water into dazzling, rippling molten silver which sent flashes of light darting through the clear air, there were broad bands of still water of a brilliant blue; others beneath the shelter of the land were of a deep transparent amethyst, while every here and there mountainous islands rose from the sea, lilac, purple, and others of a delicate softened blue, which died away into the faintest film.

Shoreward, glorified by the sunshine, the mountains rose from the water's edge; grey masses of stone tumbled in confusion from a height of four thousand feet to the shore, with clusters of towering pine and larch and groups of pensile birches in every sheltered nook. Here the mountain showed patches of dark green and purple heath; there brilliant green and creamy beds of bog moss, among which seemed to run flashing veins of silver, which disappeared and came into sight, and in one place poured down with a deep, loud roar, while a mist, looking like so much smoke, slowly rose from the fall, and floated away with a rainbow upon its breast.

On every side, as Kenneth Mackhai gazed around from the rocky foot of the mouldering old castle, there were scenes of beauty which would have satisfied the most exacting. Cloud shadow, gleaming sunshine, purple heather, yellow ragwort like dusts of gold upon the mountain side, and at his feet the ever-changing sea.

It was all so lovely that the lad stood as if entranced, and exclaimed aloud, —

"Bother!"

Then there was a pause, and, with an impatient stamp of his foot, he exclaimed, —

"Oh, hang it all! what a bore!"

But this was not at the scene around. Ken had looked upon it all in storm and sunshine ever since he could toddle, and he saw none of it now.

His mental gaze was directed at the salmon stream, the trouty lochs, the moors with their grouse and black game, and the mountains by Glenroe where he was to have gone deer-stalking with Long Shon and Tavish, and with Scood to lead the dogs, and now all this was to be given up because a visitor was coming down.

"Ah-o! ah-o!" came from the water, and a boat came gliding round from the little bay behind the castle, with Scood standing up in the stern, and turning an oar into a fish's tail, giving it that peculiar waving motion which acts after the fashion of a screw propeller, and sends a boat along.

But the boat needed little propelling, for the tide swept swiftly round by the rocky promontory on which the castle stood, and in a few minutes Scood had run the little vessel close beside a table-like mass of rock which formed a natural pier, and, leaping out, rope in hand, he stood waiting for Kenneth to descend.

"Look here, you sir," cried the latter; "didn't I tell you to put on your shoes and stockings?"

"Well, she's got 'em in the poat all ready."

"I'll get you in the boat all ready!" cried Ken angrily. "You do as you're told."

"And where am I to get another pair when they're worn out?" remonstrated Scood.

"How should I know? There, jump in."

Ken set the example, which was followed by Scood, and, as the boat glided off, yielding to the stream and the impetus, a miserable yelp came from the rocks above, followed by two dismal howls in different keys. Then there was an atrocious trio performed by the three dogs, each of which raised its muzzle and its eyes skyward, and uttered an unmusical protest against being left behind.

"Yah, kennel! go home!" roared Kenneth; and the collie and deerhound, after another mournful howl apiece, went back, but the grey terrier paid no heed to the command, but came closer down to the water, and howled more loudly.

"Ah, Sneeshing!" cried Scoodrach.

"Yow—how!" cried the dog piteously, which evidently by interpretation out of the canine tongue meant, "Take me!"

"Will you be off?" shouted Kenneth.

"How-aoooo!"

"If you don't be off, I'll—"

The lad raised his gun, cocked both barrels, and took aim.

The effect upon the ugly little terrier was instantaneous. He tucked his tail between his legs, and rushed off as hard as ever he could lay leg to rugged rock?

Nothing of the kind. He took it as a direct insult and an injurious threat. Raising his stumpy tail to its full height of two inches, without counting the loose grey hairs on the top, he planted his four feet widely apart, and barked furiously, changing his appealing whines to growls of defiance.

"You shall not frighten him," said Scood, showing his teeth.

"I'll let you see," cried Kenneth. "Here, you, Sneeshing, be off! home!"

There was a furiously defiant roulade of barks.

"Do you hear, sir? Go home!"

A perfect volley of barks.

Bang!

Kenneth fired over the dog.

"You shall not frighten him," said Scoodrach again.

He was quite right, for the shot seemed to madden the dog, who came to the very edge of the rock, barking, snarling, leaping up with all four legs off the rock at once, dashing to and fro, and biting at the scraps of lichen and seaweed.

"She says you're a coward, and don't dare do it again," cried Scoodrach, grinning.

"Does he? Then we'll see," cried Kenneth, firing again in the air.

"I told you so," cried Scoodrach. "Look at him. She'd bite you if you wass near."

"For two pins I'd give him a good peppering," grumbled Kenneth, slipping a couple of cartridges into the gun, and laying it down.

"Not you," said Scood, stepping the mast, Kenneth helping him with the stays, and to hoist a couple of sails. Then the rudder was hooked on, and, as the rapid current bore them out beyond the point, the wind filled the sails, the boat careened over, the water rattled beneath her bows, and, as the little vessel seemed to stand still, the beautiful panorama of rocky, tree-adorned shore glided by, Sneeshing's furious barking growing more distant, and dying right away.

Chapter Three
The Guest from London

It was well on in the afternoon when Scoodrach, who was lying upon his chest with his chin resting on the boat's gunwale, suddenly exclaimed, —

"There she is."

The sun was shining down hotly, there was not a breath of air, and Kenneth, who seemed as languid as the drooping sails, slowly turned his head round to look at a cloud of smoke which appeared to be coming round a distant point of land.

Hours had passed since they sailed away from Dunroe, and for a time they had had a favourable wind; then it had drooped suddenly, leaving the sea like glass, and the boat rising and falling softly upon the swell. There had been nothing to shoot but gulls, which, knowing they were safe, had come floating softly round, looking at them with inquiring eyes, and then glided away. They had gazed down through the water at the waving tangle, and watched the shoals of glistening young fish. They had whistled for wind, but none had come, and then, as they lay in the boat at the mercy of the swift tide, the hot hours of the noontide had glided by, even as the current which bore them along the shore, helpless unless they had liked to row, and that they had not liked to do upon such a glowing day.

"I don't believe that's she," said Kenneth lazily. "That's the cargo boat. Grenadier must have gone by while you were asleep."

"While she wass what?" cried Scood sharply. "Haven't been to sleep."

"Yes, you have. You snored till the boat wobbled."

"She didn't. She never does snore. It wass you."

"All right. Dessay it was," said Kenneth, yawning. "Oh, I say, Scood, I'm getting so hungry, and we can't get back."

"Yes, we can. We shall have to row."

"I'm not going to row all those miles against tide, I can tell you."

"Very well. We shall have to wait."

"I can't wait. I want my dinner."

"It is the Grenadier!" cried Scood, after a long look. "I can see her red funnel."

"You can't at this distance."

"Yes, I can. The sun's shining on it; and there's the wind coming."

"How do you know?"

"Look at the smoke. We shall get home by six."

"But I'm hungry now. I shall have to shoot something to eat. I say, Scood, why shouldn't I shoot you?"

"Don't know," said Scoodrach, grinning.

"Wonder whether you'd be tough."

"Wait and eat him," said Scood, grinning.

"Eat whom?"

"The London laddie."

Kenneth, in his idle, drowsy fit, had almost forgotten the visitor, and he roused up now, and gazed earnestly at the approaching cloud of smoke, for the steamer was quite invisible.

"It is the *Grenadier*," said Kenneth; "and she's bringing the wind with her."

"Shouldn't say *she*," muttered Scood.

"Yes, I should, stupid. Ships are shes."

"Said you'd kick me if I said 'she,'" muttered Scood.

"So I will if you call me 'she.' I'm not a ship. Hurrah! Here's the wind at last."

For the mainsail began to shiver slightly, and the glassy water to send forth scintillations instead of one broad silvery gleam.

Kenneth seized the tiller, and the next minute they were gliding through the water, trying how near the duck-shaped boat would sail to the wind.

For the next half-hour they were tacking to and fro right in the course of the coming steamer, till, judging their distance pretty well, sail was lowered, oars put out, and they rowed till the faces which crowded the forward part of the swift boat were plain to see. Soon after, while the cloud of smoke seemed to have become ten times more black, and the cloud of gulls which accompanied the steamer by contrast more white, the paddles ceased churning up the clear water and sending it astern in foam, a couple of men in blue jerseys stood ready to throw a rope, which Scood caught, and turned round the thwart forward, and Kenneth stood up, gazing eagerly at the little crowd by the paddle-box.

"How are you, captain?"

"How are you, squire?"

"Any one for us?"

"Yes. Young gent for Dunroe," said a man with a gold-braided cap.

"Where is he?"

"Here just now. Here's his luggage," said one of the men in blue jerseys. "There he is."

"Now then, sir! Look alive, please."

"But—"

"This way, sir."

"Must I—must I get down?—that small boat!"

Kenneth stared at the pallid-looking youth, who stood shrinking back, almost in wonder, as the visitor clung to the gangway rail, and gazed in horror at the boat dancing in the foaming water.

"Ketch hold."

"All right."

There was the rapid passing down of luggage—portmanteau, hat-box, bag, gun-case, sheaf of fishing-rods, and bale of wrappers; and, as Scood secured these, Kenneth held out his hand.

"Come along," he said. "It's all right."

"But—"

"Look sharp, sir, please; we can't stop all day."

Evidently in an agony of dread and shame, the stranger stepped down into the boat, staggered, clung to Kenneth, and, as he was forced down to a seat, clung to it with all his might. Scood cast off the rope; the captain on the bridge made his bell ting in the engine-room, a burst of foam came rushing from beneath the paddle-box, the little boat danced up and down, the great steamer glided rapidly on, and Kenneth and Scoodrach gazed in an amused way at the new occupant of the boat.

"We've been waiting for you—hours," said Kenneth at last. "How are you?"

"I'm quite well, thank—I mean, I'm not at all well, thank you," said the visitor, shaking hands limply, and then turning to look at Scood, as if wondering whether he should shake hands there.

"That's only Scood, my gillie," said Kenneth hastily. "Did we get all your luggage?"

"I—I don't know," said the visitor in a helpless way. "I hope so. At least, I don't mind. It has been such a rough passage!"

"Rough?" shouted Kenneth.

"Yes; terribly. The steamer went up and down so. I felt very ill."

"Been beautiful here. Now, Scood, don't sit staring there. Shove some of those things forward and some aft."

Scood jumped up, the boat gave a lurch, and the visitor uttered a gasp.

"Mind!" he cried.

"Oh, he's all right," said Kenneth bluffly. "When he has no shoes on he can hold by his toes. Come and sit aft."

"No, thank you; I would rather not move. I did not know it would be so rough at sea, or I would have come by train."

"Train! You couldn't come to Dunroe by train."

"Couldn't I?"

"No."

"Oh!—Are you Mr Kenneth Mackhai?"

"I'm Kenneth Mackhai," said the lad rather stiffly. "My father asked me to come and meet you—and, er—we're very glad to see you."

"Thank you. It was very kind of you; but I am not used to the sea, and I should have preferred landing at the pier and coming on in a cab or a fly."

"Pier! There's no pier near us."

"No pier? But never mind. You are very good. Would you mind setting me ashore now?"

"Ashore! What for?"

"To—to go on to the house. I would rather walk."

Kenneth laughed, and then checked himself.

"It's ten miles' sail from here home, and it would be twenty round by the mountain-road. We always go by boat."

"By boat? In this boat?" faltered the visitor.

"Yes. She skims along like a bird."

"Then—I couldn't—walk?"

"Walk? No. We'll soon run you home. Sorry it was so rough. But there's a lovely wind now. Come aft here, and we'll hoist the sail. That's right, Scood. Now there's room to move."

"Could—could you call back the steamer?" said the stranger hoarsely.

"Call her back? No; she's a mile away nearly. Look!"

The visitor gave a despairing stare at the steamer, and the wake of foam she had left behind.

"You will be all right directly," said Kenneth, suppressing his mirth. "You're not used to the sea?"

"No."

"We are. There, give me your hand. You sit there aft and hold the tiller, while I help Scood run up the sails."

"Thank you, I'm much obliged. But if you could set me ashore."

"It's three miles away," said Kenneth, glancing at the mainland.

"No, no; I mean there."

"There? That's only a rocky island with a few sheep on it. And there's such a wild race there, it's dangerous at this time of the tide."

"Are they savages?"

"Savages?"

"Yes; the wild race."

"Poof!"

"Be quiet, Scood, or I'll chuck you overboard. What are you laughing at? I mean race of the tide. Look, you can see the whirlpools. It's the Atlantic rushing in among the rocks. Now then, come along."

The visitor would not rise to his feet, but crept over to the after part of the boat, where he crouched more than sat, starting violently as the light craft swayed with the movements of its occupants, and began to dance as well with the rising sea.

"I'm afraid you think I'm a terrible coward."

"That's just what I do think," said Kenneth to himself; but he turned round with a look of good-humoured contempt. "Oh no," he said aloud; "you'll soon get used to it. Now, Scood, heave ahoy. Look here, we can't help it. If you laugh out at him, I'll smash you."

"But look at him," whispered Scood.

"I daren't, Scood. Heave ahoy!"

"Take care! Mind!" cried the visitor in agony.

"What's the matter?"

"I—I thought—Pray don't do that!"

Kenneth could not refrain from joining in Scood's mirth, but he checked himself directly, and gave the lad a punch in the ribs, as he hauled at the mainsail.

"You'll have the boat over!" cried the shivering guest, white now with agony, as the sail filled and the boat careened, and began to rush through the water.

"Take more than that to send her over," cried Kenneth merrily, as he took the tiller. "Plenty of wind now, Scood."

Scoodrach laughed, and their passenger clung more tightly to his seat.

For the wind was rising to a good stiff breeze, the waves were beginning to show little caps of foam, and to the new-comer it seemed utter madness to be seated in such a frail cockle-shell, which kept on lying over from the pressure on the sail, and riding across the waves which hissed and rushed along the sides, and now and then sent a few drops flying over the sail.

"You'll soon get used to it," cried Kenneth, who felt disposed at first to be commiserating and ready to pity his guest; but the abject state of dread displayed roused the spirit of mischief latent in the lad, and, after a glance or two at Scoodrach, he felt compelled to enjoy his companion's misery.

"Is—is there any danger?" faltered the poor fellow at last, as the boat seemed to fly through the water.

"No, not much. Unless she goes down, eh, Scood?"

"Oh, she shall not go down chust direckly," said Scoodrach seriously. "She's a prave poat to sail."

"What's the matter?" cried Kenneth, as his passenger looked wildly round.

"Have you—a basin on board?" he faltered.

This was too much for the others. Scoodrach burst into a roar of laughter, in which Kenneth joined for a minute, and then, checking himself, he apologised.

"Nonsense!" he said; "you keep a stout heart. You'll like it directly. Got a line, Scood?"

"Yes; twa."

"Bait 'em and throw 'em out; we may get a mackerel or two."

"They've got spinners on them," said the lad sententiously, as he opened a locker in the bows, and took out a couple of reels.

"Don't—go quite so fast," said the visitor imploringly.

"Why not? It's safer like this—eh, Scood?"

"Oh yes; she's much safer going fast."

"But the waves! They'll be in the boat directly."

"Won't give 'em time to get in—will we, Scood? Haul in that sheet a little tighter."

This was done, and the boat literally rushed through the water.

"There, you're better already, aren't you?"

"I—I don't know."

"Oh, but I do. You'll want to have plenty of sails like this."

"In the young master's poat," said Scoodrach, watching the stranger with eyes which sparkled with mischief. "Wouldn't the young chentleman like to see the Grey Mare's Tail?"

"Ah, to be sure!" cried Kenneth; "you'd like to see that."

"Is—is the grey mare ashore?" faltered the visitor.

"Yes, just round that point—a mile ahead."

"Yes, please—I should like to see that," said the guest, with a sigh of relief, for he seemed to see safety in being nearer the shore.

"All right! We'll run for it," cried Kenneth; and he slightly altered the boat's course, so as to draw a little nearer to the land. "Wind's getting up beautifully."

"Getting up?"

"Yes. Blow quite a little gale to-night, I'll be bound."

"Is—is there any danger?"

"Oh, I don't know. We get a wreck sometimes—don't we, Scood?"

"Oh ay, very fine wrecks sometimes, and plenty of people trowned!"

"You mean wrecks of ships?"

"Yes; and boats too, like this—eh, Scood?"

"Oh yes; poats like this are often wrecked, and go to the pottom," said Scood maliciously.

There was a dead silence in the boat, during which Kenneth and Scood exchanged glances, and their tired companion clutched the seat more tightly.

"I say, your name's Blande, isn't it?" said Kenneth suddenly.

"Yes; Maximilian—I mean Max Blande."

"And you are going to stay with us?"

"I suppose so."

The lad gave his tormentor a wistful look, but it had no effect.

"Long?"

"I don't know. My father said I was to come down here. Is it much farther on?"

"Oh yes, miles and miles yet. We shall soon show you the Grey Mare's Tail now."

"Couldn't we walk the rest of the way, then?"

"Walk! No. Could we, Scood?"

"No, we couldn't walk," said the lad addressed; "and who'd want to walk when we've got such a peautiful poat?"

There was another silence, during which the boat rushed on, with Kenneth trickily steering so as to make their way as rough as possible, both boys finding intense enjoyment in seeing the pallid, frightened looks of their guest, and noting the spasmodic starts he gave whenever a little wave came with a slap against the bows and sprinkled them.

"I say, who's your father?" said Kenneth suddenly.

"Mr Blande of Lincoln's Inn. You are Mr Mackhai's son, are you not?"

"I am The Mackhai's son," cried Kenneth, drawing himself up stiffly.

"Yes; there's no Mr Mackhai here," cried Scoodrach fiercely. "She's the Chief."

"She isn't, Scood. Oh, what an old dummy you are!"

"Well, so she is the chief."

"So she is! Ah, you! Look here, you, Max Blande: my father's the Chief of the Clan Mackhai."

"Is he? Is it much further, to the grey mare's stable?" faltered the passenger.

The two boys roared with laughter, Max gazing from one to the other rather pitifully.

"Did I say something very stupid?" he asked mildly.

"Yes, you said stable," cried Kenneth, wiping his eyes. "I say, Scood, wait till he sees the Grey Mare."

"Yes; wait till she sees the Grey Mare," cried Scood, bending double with mirth.

Max drew in a long breath, and gazed straight before him at the sea, and then to right and left of the fiord through which they were rapidly sailing. He saw the shore some three miles away on their left, and a couple to their right, a distance which they were reducing, as the boat, with the wind well astern, rushed on.

"It's too bad to laugh at you," said Kenneth, smoothing the wrinkles out of his face.

"I don't know what I said to make you laugh," replied Max, with a piteous look.

"Then wait till you see the Grey Mare's Tail, and you will."

"I don't think I want to see it. I would rather you set me ashore, and let me walk."

"Didn't I tell you that you couldn't walk home? Besides, every one goes to see the Grey Mare's Tail—eh, Scood?"

There was a nod and a mirthful look which troubled the visitor, who sat with his face contracted, and a spasm seeming to run through him every time the boat made a leap and dive over some wave.

They were running rapidly now toward a huge mass of rock, which ran gloomy looking and forbidding into the sea, evidently forming one of the points of a bay beyond. The mountains came here very close to the sea, and it was as if by some convulsion of nature the great buttress had been broken short off, leaving a perpendicular face of rock, along whose narrow ledges grey and black birds were sitting in scores.

"See the birds?" cried Kenneth, as they sped on rapidly, Max gaining a little confidence as he found that the boat did not go right over from the pressure of the wind on the sail.

"Are those birds?" he said.

"Yes; gulls and cormorants and puffins. Did you feed Macbrayne's pigeons as you came along?"

"No," said Max quietly; "I did not see them."

"Oh, come, I know better than that. Didn't you come up Loch Fyne in the Columba?"

"The great steamer? Yes."

"Well, didn't you see a large flock of grey gulls flying with you all the way?"

"Oh yes, and some people threw biscuits to them. They were like a great grey and white cloud."

"Well, I call them Macbrayne's pigeons."

"Are we going ashore here?" said Max eagerly, as they neared the point, about which the swift tide foamed and leaped furiously, the waves causing a deep, low roar to rise as they fretted among the tumbled chaos of rocks.

"I hope not. Eh, Scood?"

"Hope not! Why?"

"Because the sea would knock the boat to pieces. That's all."

"Hah!"

Max drew his breath with a low hiss, and gazed sharply from Kenneth to the foaming water they were approaching so swiftly, and now, with the little knowledge he had gained, the lowering mass of rock began to look terribly forbidding, and the birds which flew shrieking away seemed to be uttering cries of warning.

"Hadn't you better pull the left rein—I mean steer away, if it's so dangerous?"

"No; I'm going in between those two rocks, close in. Plenty of water now, isn't there, Scood?"

"Not plenty; enough to clear the rock," was the reply.

"Sit fast, and you'll see what a rush through we shall go. Hold tight."

Max set his teeth, and his eyes showed a complete circle of white about the iris as the boat careened over, and, feeling now the current which raced foaming around the point, he had a strange catching of the breath, while his hands clung spasmodically to the thwart and side.

The huge mass of frowning rock seemed to be coming to meet them; the grey-winged birds flew hither and thither; the water, that had been dark blue flecked with white, suddenly became one wild race of foam, such as he had seen behind the paddle-boxes of the steamers during his run up from Glasgow. There was the perpendicular wall on his right, and a cluster of black crags on his left, and toward these the boat was rushing at what seemed to him a terrific rate. It was like running wildly to their death; but Kenneth was seated calmly holding the tiller, and Scood half lay back, letting one hand hang over and splash amongst the foam.

Hiss, roar, rush, and a spray of spattering drops of the beaten waves splashed over them as they raced on, passing through the opening at a rate which made Max Blande feel dizzy. Then, just as the boat careened over till the bellying sail almost touched the low crags on their left, it made quite a leap, rose upright, the pressure on the sail ceased, the rush of wind seemed to be suddenly cut off, and they were gliding rapidly along in an almost waveless bay, with a deep, loud, thunderous roar booming into their ears.

"What do you think of that?" cried Kenneth, laughing in his guest's astonished face.

"I—I don't know. Is anything broken?"

"Broken? No. We're under the shelter of the great point."

"Oh, I see. But what's that noise? Thunder?"

"Thunder? No. That's the Grey Mare wagging her tail."

"Poof!"

Scood exploded again.

"You are laughing at me," said Max quietly. "I can't help being so ignorant."

"Never mind, we'll show you. I say, Scood, there's wind enough to carry us by if we go close in."

"No, there isn't; keep out."

"Shan't. Get out the oars and help!"

"Best keep out," grumbled Scood.

"You get out the oars—do you hear?"

Scood frowned, and slowly laid out the oars, as he took his place on the forward thwart, after a glance at the sail, which barely filled now.

"She aren't safe to go near," he said sulkily.

"Does she kick?" said Max eagerly.

Kenneth burst into a fresh roar of laughter.

"Oh yes, sometimes," he said, "right into the boat."

Scood sat with the oars balanced, and a grim smile upon his countenance, while Max looked sharply from one to the other, and, seeing that there was something he did not grasp, he sat watchful and silent, while the boat, in the full current which swept round the bay, glided rapidly out toward the farther point, from behind which the thunderous roar seemed to come.

In another minute they were close to the point, round which the tide flowed still and deep, and directly after Max held his breath, as the boat glided on, with the sail flapping, towards where in one wild leap a torrent of white water came clear out from a hundred feet above, to plunge sullenly into the sea.

"That's the Grey Mare's Tail," cried Kenneth, raising his voice so as to be heard above the heavy roar; and the fall bore no slight resemblance to the long white sweeping appendage of some gigantic beast, reaching from the face of the precipice to the sea.

Max felt awe-stricken, for, saving on canvas, he had never seen anything of the kind before. It was grand, beautiful, and thrilling to see the white water coming foaming down, and seeming to make the sea boil; but the perspiration came out on the lad's brow as he realised the meaning of what had passed, and understood Scood's remonstrances, for it was evident that the boat was drawing rapidly toward the fall, and that in the shelter of the tremendous cliff there was not sufficient wind to counteract the set of the current.

Scood gave one glance over his shoulder, and began to row hard, while for a moment Kenneth laughed; but directly after he realised that there was danger, and, leaving the tiller, he stepped forward, sat down hastily, and caught the oar Scood passed to him.

A minute of intense anxiety passed, during which the two lads rowed with all their might. But, in spite of their efforts, the boat glided nearer and nearer to the falling water, and it seemed but a matter of moments before they would be drawn right up to where the cataract came thundering down.

"Pull, Scood!" shouted Kenneth. "Pull!"

Scoodrach did not reply, but dragged at his oar, and for a few moments they made way; then surely and steadily the boat glided toward the fall, having to deal with the tide and the natural set of the surface toward the spot where the torrent poured in.

Max Blande grasped all now, and, ignorant of such matters as he was, he could still realise that from foolhardiness his companion had run the boat into a terrible danger beyond his strength to counteract.

There it was, plain enough: if they could not battle with the steady, insidious current which was slowly bearing them along, in another minute the torrent would fill the boat and plunge them down into the chaos of foaming water, from which escape would be impossible.

"Quick! here!" cried Kenneth in a shrill voice, heard above the deep humming roar of the fall. "Push—push!"

For a few moments Max could not grasp his meaning, but, when he did, he placed his hands against the oar, and thrust at each stroke with all his might.

For a few moments the extra strength seemed to tell, but Max's help was weak, and not enough to counteract the failing efforts of the two lads, who in their excitement rowed short, and without the steady strain wanted in such a time of peril.

"It's no good," cried Scood hoarsely. "She'll go town, and we must swim."

His voice rang out shrilly in the din of the torrent, but he did not cease pulling, for Kenneth shouted back, —

"Pull—pull! Will you pull?" He bent to his oar as he spoke, and once more they seemed to make a little way, but only for a few moments; and, as Max Blande looked up over his shoulder, it seemed to him that the great white curve was right above him, and even as he looked quite a shower of foam came spattering down into the boat.

Chapter Four
Welcome to Dunroe

A cry of horror rose to Max Blande's lips, but there it seemed to be frozen, and he knelt, with starting eyes, crouched together, and gazing up at the falling water. Stunned by the roar, too helpless to lend the slightest aid to the rowers, he felt that in another moment they would be right beneath, when the boat suddenly careened over, struck by the sharp puff of wind which seemed to come tearing down the ravine from which the torrent issued, and in a few moments they were fifty feet away, and running rapidly toward the mouth of the bay.

The first thing Max Blande realised was that he had been knocked over into the bottom of the boat by Kenneth, who had sprung to the rudder, and the next that he had been trampled on by Scood, who had seized the sheet, and held on to trim the sail.

Max got up slowly, and shivered as he glanced at the great fall and then at his companions, who, now that the danger was past, made light of it, and burst into a hearty laugh at his expense.

"Are we out of danger?" he faltered.

"Out of danger! Yes, of course; wasn't any," replied Kenneth. "Had the boat full; that's all. You said you could swim, didn't you?"

Max shook his head.

"Ah, well, it don't matter now! Scood and I can soon teach you that."

"If she couldn't swim she'd ha' been trowned," said Scood oracularly, "for we should have had enough to do to get ashore."

"Hold your tongue, Scood; and will you leave off calling people she?"

"Where would the boat have come up?" continued Scood.

"Bother! never mind that. There's plenty of wind now, and we'll soon race home."

"But we were in great danger, weren't we?"

"N–n–no," said Kenneth cavalierly. "It would have been awkward if the boat had filled, but it didn't fill. If you come to that, we're in danger now."

"Danger now!" cried Max, clutching the side again.

"Yes, of course. If the boat was to sink, I daresay it's two hundred feet deep here."

"Oh!"

"But that's nothing. We'll take you up Loch Doy. It's seven hundred and fifty feet up there, and the water looks quite black. Ha, ha, ha!" laughed Kenneth; "and the thought of it makes you look quite white."

"It seems so horrible."

"Not a bit. Why should it?" cried Kenneth. "It's just as dangerous to sail in seven feet of water as in seven hundred."

"Mind tat rock," said Scoodrach.

"Well, I am minding it," said Kenneth carelessly, as, with the wind coming now in a good steady breeze, consequent upon their being out of the shelter of the point, he steered so that they ran within a few feet of where the waves creamed over a detached mass of rock.

Max was gazing back at the cascade, whose aspect from where they were well warranted the familiar name by which it was known. He could, however, see no beauty in the wild leap taken by the stream, and he drew a sigh of relief as they glided by the next point, and the fall passed from his view, while the thunderous roar died away.

"There!" cried Kenneth; "that will be something for you to talk about when you go back. You don't have falls like that in town."

"She'd petter not talk about it," said Scood. "If the Chief knows we took the poat so near, she'll never let us go out in her again."

"Oh, I don't know," said Kenneth. "It was pretty near, though. I say, don't say anything to my father. Scood's afraid he'd be horsewhipped."

"Nay, it's the young master is afraid," retorted Scood.

"You say I'm afraid, Scood, and I'll knock you in the water!"

Scood grinned, and began to slacken the sheet, for the wind kept coming in sharper puffs, and at every blast the boat heeled over to such an extent that Max felt certain that they must fill.

"You haul in that sheet, Scood, and let's get all we can out of her."

"Nay, nay, laddie, she won't bear any more. We ought to shorten ta sail."

"No," cried Kenneth; "I want to see how soon we can get home. Why, it's ever so much past six now. We shan't be back till late. Don't want to see the Black Cavern, do you, to-night?"

"Oh no!" cried Max eagerly.

"We could row right in ever so far with the tide like this."

Max shuddered. It was bad enough in the open sea; the idea of rowing into a black cavern after what he had gone through horrified him.

"All right, then. Make that sheet fast, Scood, and trim the boat. I'll make her skim this time."

"No," said Scood decisively. "Too much wind. She'll hold ta sheet."

"You do as I tell you, or I'll pitch you overboard."

Scood looked vicious, but said nothing, only seated himself to windward, so as to counterbalance the pressure, and held on by the sheet.

"Did you hear what I said?"

Scood nodded.

"Then make that sheet fast."

Scood shook his head.

"Will you make that sheet fast?"

"Too much wind."

Kenneth left the tiller and literally leaped on to Scood, and, to the horror of Max, there was a desperate wrestle, during which he was in momentary expectation of seeing both pitch over into the sea. The boat rocked, the sail flapped, and a wave came with a slap against the side, and splashed the luggage in the bottom, before Scood yielded, and sat down on the forward thwart.

"I don't care," he said. "I can swim as long as I like."

"I'll make you swim if you don't mind," said Kenneth, seizing the rope and making it fast.

"She'll go over, and you'll trown the chentleman!" cried Scood.

"He won't mind!" cried Kenneth, settling himself in the stern and seizing the tiller; when Max gave vent to a gasp, for the boat seemed to be going over, so great was the pressure on the bellying sails, but she rose again, and made quite a leap as she skimmed through the waves.

"That's the way to make her move," cried Kenneth triumphantly. "Think I don't know how to manage a boat, you red-headed old tyke?"

"Ah, chust wait till a squall comes out of one of the glens, Master Ken, and you'll see."

"Tchah! Don't you take any notice of him. He's an old grey corbie. Croak, croak, croak! Afraid of getting a ducking. You sit still and hold tight, and I'll run you up to Dunroe in no time."

Max said nothing, but sat there in speechless terror, as, out of sheer obstinacy, and partly out of a desire to scare his new companion, Kenneth kept the sheet fast—the most reprehensible act of which a boatman can be guilty in a mountain loch—and the boat under far more pressure of sail than she ought to have borne.

The result was that they literally raced through the gleaming water, which was now being lit up by the setting sun, that turned the sides of the hills into so much transparent glory of orange, purple, and gold, while the sea gleamed and flashed and danced as if covered with leaping tongues of fire.

It was a wondrous evening, but Max Blande, as he clung there, could only see a boat caught by a sudden gust, and sinking, while it left them struggling in the restless sea.

Over and over again, as they rushed on, the bows were within an ace of diving into some wave, and the keel must often have shown, but by a dexterous turn of the tiller Kenneth avoided the danger just at the nick of time, and nothing worse happened than the leaping in of some spray, Scood silently sopping the gathering water with a large sponge, which he kept on wringing over the side.

"There's a puff coming," cried Scood, suddenly looking west.

"Let it come. We don't mind, do we?"

Max's lips moved, but he said nothing.

"I don't care, then," said Scood, pushing off his shoes, and then setting to work to rid himself of his coarse grey socks, as if he were skinning his lower extremities, after which he grumpily began to load his shoes as if they were mortars, by ramming a rolled-up-ball-like sock in each.

"Nobody wants you to care, Rufus," cried Kenneth.

"My fathers were once chiefs like yours," continued Scood, amusing himself by sopping up the water and squeezing the sponge with his toes.

"Get out! Old Coolin Cumstie never had a castle. He only lived in a bothy."

"And she can tie like a mans. It's a coot death to trown."

Scood was getting excited, and when in that state his dialect became broader.

"Only you'll get precious wet, Scoodie," cried Kenneth mockingly. "Never mind; I shall swim home, and I'll look out for you when you're washed ashore, and well hang you up to dry."

"Nay, I shall hae to hang you oop," cried Scood. "D'ye mind! Look at the watter coming in!"

"Then sop the watter up," cried Kenneth mockingly, as a few gallons began to swirl about in the boat.

"Is—is it much farther?"

"No, not much. Can you see the North Pole yet, Scood?"

Max looked bewildered.

"No, she can't see no North Poles," muttered Scood, as he diligently dried the boat.

"Never mind; I can steer home without," laughed Kenneth. "There we are. You can see Dunroe now."

They were just rounding a great grey bluff of rock, and he pointed to the old castle, as it stood up, ruddy and warm, lit by the western glow.

"I—I can't see it. Is it amongst those trees?"

"No, no. That's Dunroe—the castle."

"Oh!" said Max; and he sat there in silence, gazing at the old ruin, as they rapidly drew nearer, Kenneth, after giving Scood a laughing look, steering so as to keep the boat direct for the ancient stronghold, with its open windows, crumbling battlements and yawning gateway, which acted as a screen to the comfortable modern residence behind.

The visitor's heart sank at the forbidding aspect of the place. He was faint for want of food, weary and low-spirited from the frights he had had, and, in place of finding his destination some handsome mansion where there would be a warm welcome, it seemed to him that he had come to a savage dungeon-like place, on the very extreme of the earth, where all looked desolate and forlorn among the ruins, and the sea was beating at the foot of the rocks on which they stood.

In an ordinary way Kenneth would have run the skiff past the castle and round behind into the little land-locked bay, where his visitor could have stepped ashore in still water. But, as he afterwards told Scood, there would have been no fun in that. So he steered in among the rocks where the castle front faced the sea, and, after the sail had been lowered, he manipulated the boat till they were rising and falling in the uneasy tide, close alongside of a bundled-together heap of huge granite rocks, where he leapt ashore.

"Now then!" he cried; "give me your hand." It was a simple thing to do, that leaping on to the rock. All that was necessary was to jump out as the wave receded and left a great flat stone bare; but Max Blande look the wrong time, and stepped, as the wave returned, knee-deep among the slippery golden fucus, and, but for Kenneth's hand, he would have slipped and gone headlong into the deep water at the side.

There was a drag, a scramble, and, with his arm feeling as if it had been jerked out of the socket, Max stood dripping on the dry rocks beneath the castle, and Kenneth shouted to Scood,—

"Get your father to help you bring in those things, and make her fast, Scood."

"Ou ay," was the reply; and Kenneth led the way toward the yawning old gateway.

"Come along," he said. "It's only salt water, and will not give you cold. This is where the fellows used to come to attack the castle, and get knocked on the head. Nice old place, isn't it?"

"Yes, very," said Max breathlessly, as he clambered the difficult ascent his companion had chosen.

"See that owl fly out? Look! there goes a heron across there—there over the sea. Oh, you haven't got your seaside eyes yet."

"No; I couldn't see it. But do you live here?"

"To be sure we do, along with the jackdaws and ghosts."

"Ghosts?"

"Oh yes, we've three ghosts here. One lives in the old turret chamber; one in the south dungeon; and one in the guardroom over the south gate. This is the north gateway."

Max shivered from cold and excitement, and then shrank close to his companion, for the dogs suddenly charged into the place, the hollow walls of the gloomy quadrangle echoing their baying, as all three, according to their means of speed, made at the stranger.

"Down, Bruce! Dirk, be off! You, Sneeshing, I'll pitch you out of that window! It's all right, Mr Blande; they won't hurt you."

Max did not seem reassured, even though the barking dwindled into low growls, and then into a series of snufflings, as the dogs followed behind, sniffing at the visitor's heels.

"Do you really live here?" said Max, glancing up at the roofless buildings.

"Live here? of course," replied Kenneth; "but we don't eat and sleep in this part. We do that sort of thing out here."

As he spoke, he led his companion through the farther gateway, along the groined crypt-like connecting passage, and at once into the handsome hall of the modern part, where a feeling of warmth and comfort seemed to strike upon Max Blande, as his eyes caught the trophies of arms and the chase, ranged between the stained glass windows, and his wet feet pressed the rugs and skins laid about the polished floor.

Kenneth noted the change, and, feeling as if it were time to do something to make his guest welcome, he said,—

"We won't go in yet. Your wet feet won't hurt, and the dinner-gong won't go for an hour yet. I'll take you round the place, and up in the old tower. Can you climb?"

"Climb? Oh no. Not trees."

"I meant the old staircase. 'Tisn't very dangerous. But never mind now. We'll go to-morrow. Come along."

Max thought it was to his room. But nothing was farther from Kenneth's thoughts, as he started off at a sharp walk about the precincts of the old place, talking rapidly the while.

"Why, the sea's all round us!" exclaimed Max, after they had been walking, or rather climbing and descending the rocky paths of the promontory on which the castle was built.

"To be sure it is, now. When the tide's down you can hop across the rocks there to the mainland. You don't live in a place like this?"

"We live in Russell Square, my father and I."

"That's in London, isn't it? I've never been to town, and I don't want to go."

"But isn't this very inconvenient? You are so far from the rail."

"Yes, thank goodness!"

Max stared.

"But you can't get a cab."

"Oh yes, you can—in Edinburgh and Glasgow."

"Then you keep a carriage?"

"Yes; you came in it—the boat," said Kenneth, laughing. "We used to have a large yacht, but father gave it up last year. He said he couldn't afford it now on account of the confounded lawyers."

Max winced a little, and then said, with quiet dignity, —

"My father is a lawyer."

"Is he? Beg pardon, then. But your father isn't one of the confounded lawyers, or else you wouldn't be here."

Kenneth laughed, and Max seemed more thoughtful.

"S'pose you think we're rather rough down here; but this is the Highlands. You'll soon get used to us. There's no carriage, but we can give you a mount on a capital pony. Walter Scott would do for you."

"Is Walter Scott alive? I've read all his stories."

"No, no; I mean our shaggy pony. He's half Scotch, half Shetland, and the rummest little beggar you ever saw. He can climb and slide, and jump like a grasshopper. All you've got to do is to stick your knees into him and hold on by the mane when he's going up so steep a place that you begin to slip over his tail, and you're all right, only you have to kick at his nose when he tries to bite."

Max looked aghast.

"Can you fish?"

"No."

"But you brought a lot of rods."

"Oh yes. Father said I was to learn to fish and shoot while I was down here, as some day I should be a Highland landlord."

"We can teach you all that sort of thing."

"Can you fish and shoot?"

"Can I? I say, are you chaffing me?"

"No; I mean it."

"Well, just a little. Let's see, I'm seventeen nearly, and I was only six when my father made me fire off a gun first. I've got a little one in the gun-room that I used to use."

"And were you very young when you began to learn to fish?"

"I caught a little salmon when I was eight. Father said the fish nearly drowned me instead of me drowning the salmon. But I caught him all the same."

"How was that?"

"Oh, I tumbled in, I suppose, and rolled over in the stream. Shon pulled me out."

"Did he?"

"Yes; Scood's father. He's one of our gillies. Lives down there."

"By that pig-sty?"

"Pig-sty? That isn't a pig-sty. That's a bothy."

"Oh!" said Max, as he stared at a rough, whitewashed hovel, thatched, and covered with hazel rods tied down to keep the thatch from blowing off.

"There won't be time to-night after dinner, but I'll take you down to Shon to-morrow. We always call him Long Shon because he's so little, and we pretend he's so fond of whisky. Scood's a head taller than his father."

"It will be all most interesting, I'm sure," said Max, whose feet felt very wet and uncomfortable.

"I'll take you to see Tavish too," continued Kenneth, with a half-laugh at his companion's didactic form of speech. "Tavish is our forester."

"Forester?"

"Yes; and then I must introduce you to Donald Dhu."

"Is he a Scottish chief?"

"Well," said Kenneth, with a half laugh, "I daresay he thinks so. Like pipes?"

"Pipes? No, I never tried them. I once had a cigarette, but I didn't like it."

"Oh, I say, you are comic!" said Kenneth, laughing heartily, and then restraining himself. "I meant the bagpipes. Donald is our piper."

"Your piper! How—"

Max was going to say horrible, as he recalled one of his pet abominations, a dirty, kilted and plaided Scotchman, who made night hideous about the Bloomsbury squares with his chanter and drone.

But he restrained himself, and, as Kenneth led the way here and there about the little rocky knoll, he kept on talking.

"Donald has a place up in one of the towers—that one at the far corner. He took to it to play in. He composes dirges and things up there."

"But do you like having a piper?"

"Like it? I don't know. He has always been here. He belongs to us. There always was a piper to the Clan Mackhai. There, you can see right up the loch here, and that's where our salmon river empties itself over those falls. See that hill?"

"Yes."

"That's Ben Doy. You'll like to climb up that. It isn't one of the highest, but it's four thousand, and jolly steep. There's a loch right up in it full of little trout."

Boom—boom—boom—boom.

"What's that?"

"That? why, the dinner-gong, of course. Just time to have a wash first. We don't dress down here. That's what father always says to visitors who bring bobtails and chokers. Bring a bobtail with you?"

"I brought my dress suit."

"Then, if I were you, I would make it up into a parcel, and send it back to London. What's your name, did you say?"

"Maxi—Max Blande."

"To be sure! Max Blande, Esquire, Russell Square, per Macbrayne and Caledonian Railway; and we'll catch a salmon, or you shall, and send to your father same time. Come on; run. Hi, dogs, then! Bruce, boy! Chevy, Dirk! Come along, Sneeshing! Oh, man, you can't half run!"

"No," said Max, panting heavily, and nearly falling over a projecting piece of rock.

"I say, mind! Why, if you fell there, you'd go right down into the sea, and it would be salt water instead of soup."

Kenneth laughed heartily at his own remark as they ran on, to pause at the steep slope up to the castle, where the dogs stopped short, as if well drilled as to the boundaries they were to pass, while the two lads once more crossed the gloomy ruined quadrangle and entered the house.

Chapter Five
The Effects of the Sail

"Look sharp! Father doesn't like to be kept waiting. Don't stop to do anything but change your wet things. That's your room. You can look right away and see Mull one side and Skye the other."

Kenneth half pushed his visitor into a bed-room, banged the door, and went off at a run, leaving Max Blande standing helpless and troubled just inside, and heartily wishing he was at home in Russell Square.

Not that the place was uncomfortable, for it was well furnished, but he was tired and faint for want of food; everything was strange; the wind and sea were playing a mournful duet outside—an air in a natural key which seemed at that moment more depressing than a midnight band or organ in Bloomsbury on a foggy night.

But he had no time for thinking. Expecting every moment to hear the gong sound again, and in nervous dread of keeping his host waiting, he hurriedly changed, and was a long way on towards ready when there was a bang at the door.

"May I come in?" shouted Kenneth. But he did not say it till he had opened the door and was well inside.

"Oh, your hair will do," he continued. "You should have had it cut short. It's better for bathing. Old Donald cuts mine. He shall do yours. No, no; don't stop to put your things straight. Why, hallo! what are you doing?"

"Only taking a little scent for my handkerchief."

"Oh my! Why, you're not a girl! Come along. Father's so particular about my being in at dinner. He don't mind any other time."

Kenneth hurried his visitor down-stairs, and, as they reached the hall, a sharp voice said,—

"Mr Blande, I suppose! How do you do? Well, Kenneth, did you have a good run? Nice day for a sail."

Max had not had time to speak, as the tall, aquiline-looking man, with keen eyes and closely-cut blackish-grey hair, turned and walked on before them into the dining-room. The lad felt a kind of chill, as if he had been repelled, and was not wanted; and there was a sharp, haughty tone in his host's voice which the sensitive visitor interpreted to mean dislike.

As he followed into the room, he had just time to note that, in spite of his coldness, his host was a fine, handsome, *distingué* man, and that he looked uncommonly well in the grey kilt and dark velvet shooting-jacket, which seemed to make him as picturesque in aspect as one of the old portraits on the walls.

Max had also time to note that a very severe-looking man-servant in black held open and closed the door after them, following him up, and, as he took the place pointed out by Kenneth, nearly knocking him off his balance by giving his chair a vicious thrust, with the result that he sat down far too quickly.

"Amen!" said the host sharply, and in a frowning, absent way.

"I haven't said grace, father," exclaimed Kenneth.

"Eh! haven't you? Ah, well, I thought you had. What's the soup, Grant?"

"Hotch-potch, sir," replied the butler.

"Confound hotch-potch! Tell that woman not to send up any more till I order it."

He threw himself back in the chair as the butler handed the declined plate second-hand to the guest and then took another to Kenneth.

"'Taint bad when you're hungry," whispered the lad across the table.

Max glanced at his host with a shiver of dread, but The Mackhai was in the act of pouring himself out a glass of sherry, which he tossed off, and then in an abstracted way put on his glasses and began to read a letter.

"It's all right. He didn't hear," whispered Kenneth, setting a good example, and finishing his soup before Max had half done, for there was a novelty in the dinner which kept taking his attention from his food.

"Sherry to Mr Blande," said the host sharply; and the butler came back from the sideboard, where he was busy, giving Max an ill-used look, which said plainly, —

"Why can't he help himself?"

Then aloud, —

"Sherry, sir?"

"No, thank you."

The decanter stopper went back into the bottle with a loud click, the decanter was thumped down, and the butler walked back past Kenneth's chair.

"Hallo, Granty! waxey?" said Kenneth; but the butler did not condescend to answer.

"Much sport, father?"

"Eh? Yes, my boy. Two good stags."

"I say, father, I wish I had been there."

"Eh? Yes, I wish you had, Ken. But you had your guest to welcome. I hope you had a pleasant run up from Glasgow."

"Pretty good," faltered Max, who became scarlet as he saw Kenneth's laughing look.

"That's right," said the host. "You must show Mr Blande all you can, Ken," he continued, softening a little over the salmon. "Sorry we have no lobster sauce, Mr Blande. This is not a lobster shore. Make Kenneth take you about well."

"I did show him the Grey Mare's Tail, father," said Kenneth, with a merry look across the table.

"Ah yes! a very beautiful fall."

The dinner went on, but, though he was faint, Max did not make a hearty meal, for, in addition to everything seeming so strange, and the manners of his host certainly constrained, from time to time it seemed to the visitor that all of a sudden the table, with its white cloth, glittering glass and plate, began to rise up, taking him with it, and repeating the movements of the steamer where they caught the Atlantic swell. Then it subsided, and, as a peculiar giddy feeling passed off, the table seemed to move again; this time with a quick jerk, similar to that given by Kenneth's boat.

Max set his teeth; a cold perspiration broke out upon his forehead, and he held his knife and fork as if they were the handles to which he must cling to save himself from falling.

He was suspended between two horrors, two ideas troubling him. Would his host see his state, and should he be obliged to leave the table?

And all the while the conversation went on between father and son, and he had to reply to questions put to him. Then, as the table rose and heaved, and the room began to swing gently round, a fierce-looking eye seemed to be glancing at him out of a mist, and he knew that the butler was watching him in an angry, scornful manner that made him shrink.

He had some recollection afterwards of the dinner ending, and of their going into a handsome drawing-room, where The Mackhai left them, as Kenneth said, to go and smoke in his own room. Then Max remembered something about a game of chess, and then of starting up and oversetting the table, with the pieces rattling on the floor.

"What—what—what's the matter?" he exclaimed as he clapped his hand to his leg, which was tingling with pain.

"What's the matter? why, you were asleep again. Never did see such a sleepy fellow. Here, let's go to bed."

"I beg your pardon; I'm very sorry, but I was travelling all last night."

"Oh, I don't mind," said Kenneth, yawning. "Come along."

"We must say good-night to your father."

"Oh no! he won't like to be disturbed. He's in some trouble. I think it's about money he has been losing, and it makes him cross."

Kenneth led the way up-stairs, chattering away the while, and making all manner of plans for the morning.

"Here you are," he cried. "You'd like a bath in the morning?"

"Oh yes, I always have one."

"All right. I'll call you."

As soon as he was alone, Max went to the window and opened it, to admit the odour of the salt weed and the thud and rush of the water as it beat against the foot of the castle and whispered amongst the crags. The moon was just setting, and shedding a lurid yellow light across the sea, which heaved and gleamed, and threw up strange reflections from the black masses of rock which stood up all round.

A curious shrinking sensation came over him as he gazed out; for down below the weed-hung rocks seemed to be in motion, and strange monsters appeared to be sporting in the darkness as the weed swayed here and there with the water's wash.

He closed the window, after a long look round, and hurriedly undressed, hoping that after a good night's rest the sensation of unreality would pass off, and that he would feel more himself, but he had no sooner put out the candle and plunged into bed than it seemed as if he were once more at sea. For the bed rose slowly and began to glide gently down an inclined plane toward one corner of the room, sweeping out through the wall, and then rising and giving quite a plunge once more.

It all seemed so real that Max started up in bed, and grasped the head, and stared round.

It was all fancy. The bed was quite still, and the only movement was that of the waves outside as they beat upon the rocks.

He lay down once more, and, as his head touched the pillow, and he closed his eyes, the bed heaved up once more, set sail, and he kept gliding on and on and on.

This lasted for about an hour, and then, as the boat-like bed made one of its slow, steady glides, down as it were into the depths of the sea, it went down and down, lower and lower, till all was black and solemn and still, and it was as if there was a restful end of all trouble, till the stern struck with a tremendous thud upon a rock, and a hollow voice exclaimed,—

"Now, old chap! Six o'clock! Ready for your bath?"

Chapter Six
A Morning Bath

"Yes! Come in. Thank you. Eh? I'll open the door. And—Don't knock so hard."

Confused and puzzled, Max started out of his deep sleep, with his head aching, and the bewilderment increasing as he tried to make out where he was, the memory of the past two days' events having left him.

"Don't hurry yourself. It's all right. Like to have another nap?" came in bantering tones.

"I'll get up and dress as quickly as I can," cried Max, as he now realised his position. "But—but you said something about showing me the bath."

"To be sure I did. Look sharp. I'll wait."

"Oh, thank you; I'll just slip on my dressing-gown."

"Nonsense! You don't want a bathing-gown," cried Kenneth. "Here! let me in."

"Yes, directly," replied Max; and the next minute he went to the door, where Kenneth was performing some kind of festive dance to the accompaniment of a liberal drumming with his doubled fists upon the panels.

"Ha! ha!" laughed the lad boisterously. "You do look rum like that. Slip on your outside, and come along."

"But—the bath-room? I—"

"Bath-room! What bath-room?"

"You said you would show me."

"Get out! I never said anything about a bath-room. I said a bath—a swim—a dip in the sea. Beats all the bath-rooms that were ever born."

"Oh!" ejaculated Max, who seemed struck almost dumb.

"Well, look sharp. Scood's waiting. He called me an hour ago, and I dropped asleep again."

"Scood—waiting?"

"Yes; he's a splendid swimmer. We'll soon teach you."

"But—"

"You're not afraid, are you?"

"Oh no—not at all. But I—"

"Here, jump into your togs, old man, and haul your shrouds taut. It's glorious! You're sure to like it after the first jump in. It's just what you want."

Max felt as if it was just what he did not want; but strong wills rule weak, and he had a horror of being thought afraid, so that the result was, he slipped on his clothes hastily, and followed his companion down-stairs, and out on to the rock terrace, where a soft western breeze came off the sea, which glittered in the morning sunshine.

He looked round for the threatening-looking black rocks which had seemed so weird and strange the night before, and his eyes sought the uncouth monsters with the tangled hair which seemed to rise out of the foaming waters. But, in place of these, there was the glorious sunshine, brightening the grey granite, and making the yellowish-brown seaweed shine like gold as it swayed here and there in the crystal-pure water.

"Why, you look ten pounds better than you did yesterday!" cried Kenneth; and then, raising his voice, "Scood, ho! Scood, hoy!" he shouted.

"Ahoy—ay!" came from somewhere below.

"It's all right! He has gone down," cried Kenneth. "Come along."

"Where are you going?" said Max hesitatingly.

"Going? Down to our bathing-place; and, look here, as you are not used to it, don't try to go out, for the tide runs pretty strong along here. Scood and I can manage, because we know the bearings, and where the eddies are, so as to get back. Here we are."

He had led his companion to the very edge of the rock, where it descended perpendicularly to the sea, and apparently there was no farther progress to be made in that direction. In fact, so dangerous did it seem, that, as Kenneth quickly lowered himself over the precipice, Max, by an involuntary movement, started forward and made a clutch at his arm.

"Here! what are you doing?" cried Kenneth. "It's all right. Now then, I'm here. Lower yourself over. Lay hold of that bit of stone. I'll guide your feet. There's plenty of room here."

Max drew a long, catching breath, and his first thought was to run back to the house.

"Make haste!" cried Kenneth from somewhere below; and Max went down on his hands and knees to creep to the edge and look over, and see that the rock projected over a broad shelf, upon which the young Scot was standing looking up.

"Oh, I say, you are a rum chap!" cried Kenneth, laughing. "Legs first, same as I did; not your head."

"But is it safe—for me?"

"Safe? Why, of course, unless you can pull the rock down on top of you. Come along."

"I will do it! I will do it!" muttered Max through his set teeth, as he drew back, ghastly pale, and with a wild look in his eyes. Then, turning, and lowering his legs over the edge, he clung spasmodically to a projection which offered its help.

"That's the way. I've got you. Let go."

For a few moments Max dared not let go. He felt that if he did he should fall headlong seventy or eighty feet into the rock-strewn sea; but, as he hesitated, Kenneth gave him a jerk, his hold gave way, and the next moment, in an agony of horror, he fell full twenty inches—on his feet, and found himself upon the broad shelf, with the crag projecting above his head and the glittering sea below.

"You'll come down here like a grasshopper next time," cried Kenneth. "Now then, after me. There's nothing to mind so long as you don't slip. I'll show you."

He began to descend from shelf to shelf, where the rock had been blasted away so as to form a flight of the roughest of rough steps of monstrous size, while, trembling in every limb, Max followed.

"My grandfather had this done so that he could reach the cavern. Before that it was all like a wall here, and nobody could get up and down. Why, you can climb as well as I can, only you pretend that you can't."

Max said nothing, but kept on cautiously descending till he stood upon a broad patch of barnacle-crusted rock, beside what looked like a great rough Gothic archway, forming the entrance to a cave whose floor was the sea, but alongside which there was a rugged continuation of the great stone upon which the lads stood.

"There, isn't this something like a bath?" cried Kenneth. "It's splendid, only you can't bathe when there's any sea."

"Why?" asked Max, so as to gain time.

"Why? Because every wave that comes in swells over where we're standing, and rushes right into the cave. You wait and you'll hear it boom like thunder."

Plosh!

"What's that?" cried Max, catching at his companion's arm.

"My seal! You watch and you'll see him come out."

"Yes, I can see him," cried Max, "swimming under water. A white one—and—and—Why, it's that boy!"

"Ahoy!" cried a voice, as Scoodrach, who had undressed and dived in off the shelf to swim out with a receding wave, rose to the surface and shook the water from his curly red hair.

"Well, he can swim like a seal," cried Kenneth, running along the rough shelf. "Come along."

Max followed him cautiously, and with an uneasy sense of insecurity, while by the time he was at the end his guide was undressed, with his clothes lying in a heap just beyond the wash of the falling tide.

"Look sharp! jump in!" cried Kenneth. "Keep inside here till you can swim better."

As the words left his lips, he plunged into the crystal water, and Max could follow his course as he swam beneath the surface, his white body showing plainly against the dark rock, till he rose splashing and swam out as if going right away.

But he altered his mind directly, and swam back toward the mouth of the cave.

"Why, you haven't begun yet," he cried. "Aren't you coming in?"

"Ye–es, directly," replied Max, but without making an effort to remove a garment, till he caught sight of a derisive look upon Kenneth's face—a look which made the hot blood flush up to his cheeks, and acted as such a spur to his lagging energies, that in a very few minutes he was ready, and, after satisfying himself that the water was not too deep, he lowered himself slowly down, gasping as the cold, bracing wave reached his chest, and as it were electrified him.

"You shouldn't get in like that," cried Kenneth, roaring with laughter. "Head first and—"

Max did not hear the rest. In his inexperience he did not realise the facts that transparent water is often deeper than it looks, and that seaweed under water is more slippery than ice.

One moment he was listening to Kenneth's mocking words; the next, his feet, which were resting upon a piece of rock below, had glided off in different directions, and he was beneath the surface, struggling wildly till he rose, and then only to descend again as if in search of the bottom of the great natural bath-house.

"Why, what a fellow you are!" was the next thing he heard, as Kenneth held him up. "There, you can touch bottom here. That's right; stand up. Steady yourself by holding this bit of rock."

Half blind, choking with the harsh, strangling water which had gone where nature only intended the passage of air, and with a hot, scalding sensation in his nostrils, and the feeling as of a crick at the back of his neck, Max clung tenaciously to the piece of rock, and stood with the water up to his chin, sputtering loudly, and ending with a tremendous sneeze.

"Bravo! that's better," cried Kenneth. "No, no, don't get out. You've got over the worst of it now. You ought to try and swim."

"No. I must get out now. Help me," panted Max. "Was I nearly drowned?"

"Hear that, Scood?" cried Kenneth. "He says, was he nearly drowned?"

"I—I'm not used to it," panted Max.

"Needn't tell us that—need he, Scood? No, no, don't get out."

"I—I must now. I've had enough of it."

"No, you haven't," cried Kenneth, who was paddling near. "Hold on by the rock and kick out your legs. Try to swim."

"Yes, next time. I'm—"

"If you don't try I'll duck you," cried Kenneth.

"No, no, pray don't! I—"

"If you try to get out, I'll pull you back by your legs. Here, Scood, come and help."

"Don't, pray don't touch me, and I'll stay," pleaded Max.

"Pray don't touch you!" cried Kenneth. "Here, Scood, he has come down here to learn to swim, and he's holding on like a girl at a Rothesay bathing-machine. Let's duck him."

Max uttered an imploring cry, but it was of no use. Kenneth swam up, and with a touch seemed to pluck him from his hold, and drew him out into the middle of the place, while directly after, Scood, who seemed more than ever like a seal, dived into the cave, and came up on Max's other side.

"Join hands, Scood," cried Kenneth.

Scood passed his hand under Max, and Kenneth caught it, clasping it beneath the struggling lad's chest.

"Now then, let's swim out with him."

"Ant let him swim back. She'll soon learn," cried Scood.

"No, pray don't! You'll drown me!" gasped Max, as he clung excitedly to the hands beneath him; and then, to his horror, he felt himself borne right out of the cave, into the sunshine, the two lads bearing him up easily enough between them, till they were fully fifty yards away from the mouth.

Partly from dread, partly from a return of nerve, Max had, during the latter part of his novel ride through the bracing water, remained perfectly silent and quiescent, but the next words that were spoken sent a shock through him greater than the first chill of the water.

"Now then!" cried Scood. "Let go! She'll get back all alone, and learn to swim."

"No, no, not this time," said Kenneth. "We'll take him back now. He'll soon learn, now he finds how easy it is. Turn round, Scood."

Scoodrach obeyed, and the swim was renewed, the two lads easily making their way back to the mouth of the cave, up which they had about twenty feet to go to reach the spot where the clothes were laid.

"Now," cried Kenneth, "you've got to learn to swim, so have your first try."

"No, no; not this morning."

"Yes. At once. Strike out, and try to get in."

"But I can't. I shall sink."

"No, you shan't; I won't let you. Try."

There was no help for it. Max was compelled to try, for the support was suddenly withdrawn, and for the next few minutes the poor fellow was struggling and panting blindly, till he felt his hand seized, and that it was guided to the side, up which he was helped to scramble.

"There!" cried Kenneth. "There's a big towel. Have a good rub, and you'll be all in a glow."

Max took the towel involuntarily, and breathlessly tried to remove the great drops which clung to him, feeling, to his surprise, anything but cold, and, by the time he was half dressed, that it was not such a terrible ordeal he had passed through after all.

"She'll swim next time," said Scood, as he rubbed away at his fiery head.

"No, she won't, Scoodie," said Kenneth mockingly; "but you soon will if you try."

"Do you think so?" asked Max, who began now to feel ashamed of his shrinking and nervousness.

"Of course I do. Why, you weren't half so bad as some fellows are. Remember Tom Macandrew, Scood?"

"Ou ay. She always felt as if she'd like to trown that boy."

"Look sharp!" cried Kenneth, nearly dressed. "Don't be too particular. You'll soon get your hair dry."

"But it wants combing."

"Comb it when you get indoors. Come away. Let's have a run now, and then there'll be time to polish up before breakfast. You, Scood, we shall go fishing this morning, so be ready. Now then, Max,—I shall call you Max,— you don't mind climbing up here again, do you?"

"Is there no other way?"

"Yes."

"Let's go, then."

"There are two other ways," said Kenneth: "to jump in and swim round to the sands."

"Ah!"

"And for Scood and me to go up and fetch a rope and let it down. Then you'll sit in a loop, and we shall haul you up, while you spin round like a roast fowl on a hook, and the bottle-jack up above going click."

"I think I can climb up," said Max, who was very sensitive to ridicule; and he climbed, but with all the time a creepy sensation attacking him—a feeling of being sure to fall over the side and plunge headlong into the sea, while, at the last point, where the great stone projected a little over the climbers' heads, the sensation seemed to culminate.

But Max set his teeth in determination not to show his abject fear, and the next moment he was on the top, feeling as if he had gone through more perils during the past eight-and-forty hours than he had ever encountered in his life.

"Look out!" cried Kenneth suddenly.

"Why? What?"

"It's only the dogs; and if Bruce leaps at you, he may knock you off the cliff."

Almost as he spoke, the great staghound made a dash at Max, who avoided the risk by leaping sideways, and getting as far as he could from the unprotected brink.

Chapter Seven
Shon and Tavish

The hearty breakfast of salmon steaks, freshly-caught herrings, oat-cakes, and coffee, sweetened by the seaside appetite, seemed to place matters in a different light. The adventure in the cave that morning was rough, but Kenneth was merry and good-tempered, and ready to assure his new companion that it was for his good. Then, too, the bright sunshine, the glorious blue of the sea, and the invigorating nature of the air Max breathed, seemed to make everything look more cheerful.

Before they took their places at the table, the stony look of the Scotch butler was depressing; so was the curt, distant "Good morning, Mr Blande," of The Mackhai, who hardly spoke afterwards till toward the end of the meal, but read his newspaper and letters, leaving his son to carry on the conversation.

"I say, Grant, aren't there any hot scones this morning?"

"No, sir," said the butler, in an ill-used whisper.

"Why not?"

"The cook says she can't do everything without assistance."

"Then she ought to get up earlier—a lazy old toad! It was just as bad when there was a kitchen-maid."

The butler looked more severe than ever, and left the room.

"He's always grumbling, Max—here, have some marmalade."

Max took a little of the golden preserve, and began to spread it on a piece of bread.

"You are a fellow," said Kenneth mockingly; "that isn't the way to eat marmalade. Put a lot of butter on first."

"What, with jam?"

"Of course," said Kenneth, with a grin, as he gave a piece of bread a thick coating of yellow butter, and then plastered it with the golden red-rinded sweet. "That's the way to eat marmalade!" he cried, taking, out a fine half-moon from the slice. "That's the economical way."

"Extravagant, you mean?"

"No, I don't; I mean economical. Don't you see it saves the bread? One piece does for both butter and marmalade."

"I don't know how you manage to eat so much. You had a fried herring and—"

"A piece of salmon, and some game pie, and etceteras. That's nothing. I often have a plate of porridge as well. You'll eat as much as I do when you've been down here a week."

"I hope not."

"Nonsense! Why, it's just what you want. Here, you let me take you in hand, and I'll soon make a difference in you. See how white and thin you are."

"Am I?"

"Yes, horrid! You shall have some porridge and milk to-morrow morning. That's the stuff, as Long Shon says, to lean your back against for the day."

"I don't understand you!"

"Lean it against forwards," said Kenneth, laughing. "Besides, we only have two meals here a day."

"Only two?" cried Max, staring. "Why, we always have four at home!"

"That's because you don't know any better, I suppose. You can have lunch and tea here if you like," said Kenneth contemptuously, "but we never do—we haven't time."

"Haven't time?"

"No. Who's going to come back miles from shooting or fishing for the sake of a bit of lunch. I always take mine with me."

"Oh, then you do take lunch?" said Max, with a look of relief.

"Yes, always," said Kenneth, showing his white teeth. "I'm taking it now—inside. And old Grant's always grumbling to me about having so much to do now father does not keep any other men-servants indoors. Only two meals a day to see to, and we very seldom have any company now."

"I hope Mr Blande is making a good breakfast, Kenneth," said The Mackhai, laying down his newspaper.

"No, father, not half a one."

"Oh, thank you, I am indeed."

"I hope Mr Blande will," said The Mackhai stiffly. "Pray do not let him think we are wanting in hospitality at Dunroe."

"I'll take care of him, father."

"Quite right, Ken. What are you going to do to-day?"

"Take him up to the Black Pools and try for a salmon, and go afterwards with the guns across the moor up Glen Doy, and then right up the Ten after a hare or two. After that we could take the boat, and—"

"I think your programme is long enough for to-day, Ken," said The Mackhai dryly. "You will excuse me, Mr Blande," he continued, with formal politeness; "I have some letters to write."

"How about the deer, father?"

"Shon is packing them off for the South, my boy. Good morning."

The Mackhai walked stiffly out of the room, and Kenneth seized a plate and knife and fork, after which he cut a triangle of a solid nature out of a grouse pie, and passed the mass of juicy bird, gelatinous gravy, and brown crust to his guest.

"I couldn't, indeed I couldn't!" cried Max.

"But you must," cried Kenneth, leaping up. "I'm going to ring for some more hot coffee!"

"No, no, don't, pray!" cried Max, rising from the table.

"Oh, all right," said Kenneth, in an ill-used manner; "but how am I to be hospitable if you won't eat? Come on, then, and I'll introduce you to Long Shon. I'll bet a shilling he has got Scood helping him, and so greasy that he won't be fit to touch."

Max stared, and Kenneth laughed at his wonderment.

"Didn't you hear what my father said? Shon has been skinning and breaking up the deer."

"Breaking up the deer?"

"Well, not with a hammer, of course. Doing what a butcher does—cutting them up in joints, you'd call it. Come along."

He led the way into the hall, seized his cap, and went on across the old castle court, stopping to throw a stone at a jackdaw, perched upon one of the old towers.

"He's listening for Donald. That's his place where he practises. I daresay he's up there now, only we can't stop to see."

Outside the old castle they were saluted by a trio of yelps and barks, the three dogs, after bounding about their master, smelling Max's legs suspiciously, Sneeshing, of the short and crooked legs, pretending that he had never seen a pair of trousers before, and taking hold of the material to test its quality, to Max's horror and dismay.

"Oh, he won't bite!" cried Kenneth; "it's only his way."

"But even a scratch from a dog's tooth might produce hydrophobia," said Max nervously.

"Not with Scotch dogs," said Kenneth, laughing. "Here, Sneeshing, you wouldn't give anybody hydro-what-you-may-call-it, would you, old man, eh?"

He seized the rough little terrier as he spoke, and turned him over on his back, caught him by the throat and shook him, the dog retaliating by growling, snarling, and pretending to worry his master's hand.

This piece of business excited Dirk the collie, who shook out his huge frill, gave his tail a flourish, and made a plunge at the prostrate dog, whom he seized by a hind leg, to have Bruce's teeth fixed directly in his great rough hide, when Kenneth rose up laughing.

"Worry, worry!" he shouted; and there was a regular canine scuffle, all bark and growl and suppressed whine.

"They'll kill the little dog," cried Max excitedly.

"What, Sneeshing? Not they. It's only their fun. Look!"

For Sneeshing had shaken himself free of Dirk, over whose back he leaped, then dashed under Bruce, raced round the other two dogs for a few moments, and then darted off, dodging them in and out among the rocks, the others in full pursuit till they were all out of breath, when Sneeshing came close up to his master's heels, Bruce trotted up and thrust his long nose into his hand, while Dirk went to the front, looked up inquiringly, and then, keeping a couple of yards in front, led the way toward a cluster of grey stone buildings hidden from the castle by a stumpy group of firs.

"He knows where we are going," said Kenneth, laughing, and stopping as they reached the trees. "Hear that! Our chief singing bird."

Max stared inquiringly at his guide, as a peculiar howl came from beyond the trees, which sounded as if some one in a doleful minor key was howling out words that might take form literally as follows:—

"Ach—na—shena—howna howna—wagh—hech—wagh!"

"Pretty, isn't it?" said Kenneth, laughing. "Come away. The ponies are in here."

He led the way into a comfortable stable, whereupon there was a rattling of headstalls, and three ugly big rough heads were turned to look at him, and three shaggy manes were shaken.

"Hallo, Whaup! Hallo, Seapie! Well, Walter!" cried Kenneth, going up and patting each pony in turn, the little animals responding by nuzzling up to him and rubbing their ears against his chest.

"Look here!" cried Kenneth. "This is Walter. You'll ride him. Come and make friends."

Max approached, and then darted back, for, rip rap, the pony's heels flew out, and as he was standing nearly across the stall, they struck the division with a loud crack, whose sound made Max leap away to the stable wall.

"Quiet, Wat!" cried Kenneth, doubling his fist and striking the pony with all his might in the chest.

The sturdy little animal uttered a cry more like a squeal than a neigh, shook its head, reared up, and began to strike at the lad with his hoofs so fiercely, that. Kenneth darted out of the stall, the halter checking the pony when it tried to follow, and keeping it in its place in the punishment which followed.

"That's it, is it, Master Wat, eh?" cried Kenneth, running to a corner of the stable, and taking down a short thick whip which hung from a hook. "You want another lesson, do you, my boy? You've had too many oats lately. Now we shall see. Stand a little back, Max."

This Max readily did, the pony eyeing them both the while, with its head turned right round, and making feints of kicking.

The next minute it began to dance and plunge and kick in earnest, as, by a dexterous usage of the whip, Kenneth gave it crack after crack, each sounding report being accompanied by a flick on the pony's ribs, which evidently stung sharply, and made it rear and kick.

"I'll teach you to fight, my lad. You rhinoceros-hided old ruffian, take that—and take that—and take that."

"Hey! what's the matter, Master Ken?" cried a harsh voice.

"Kicking and biting, Shon. I'll teach him," cried Kenneth, thrashing away at the pony. "I wish he had been clipped, so that I could make him feel."

"Hey! but ye mak' him feel enough, Master Ken. An' is this the shentleman come down to stay?"

"There's one more for you, Wat, my boy. Don't let him have any more oats to-day, Shon," cried Kenneth, giving the pony a final flick. "Yes, this is our visitor, Shon. Max, let me introduce you. This is Long Shon Ben Nevis Talisker Teacher, Esquire, Gillie-in-chief of the house of Mackhai, commonly called Long Shon from his deadly hatred of old whusky—eh, Shon?"

"Hey, Master Kenneth, if there was chokers and chief chokers down south, an' ye'd go there, ye'd mak' a fortune," said the short, broad-set man, with a grin, which showed a fine set of very yellow teeth; "and I'm thinking that as punishment aifter a hard job, ye might give me shust a snuff o' whusky in a sma' glass."

"Father said you were never to have any whisky till after seven o'clock."

"Hey, but the Chief's never hard upon a man," said Shon, taking off his Tam-o'-Shanter, and wiping his brow with the worsted tuft on the top; then, turning with a smile to Max, "I'm thinking ye find it a verra beautiful place, sir?"

"Oh yes, very," replied Max.

"And the Chiefs a gran' man. Don't ye often wonder he ever had such a laddie as this for a son?"

"Do you want me to punch your head, Shon?" said Kenneth.

Shon chuckled.

"As hard as hard, sir; never gives a puir fellow a taste o' whusky."

"Look here, have you broken up the deer?"

"Broke up the deer, indeed? Why, she wass just finished packing them up in ta boxes."

"Come and see, Max," cried Kenneth, leading the way into a long, low building, badly lit by one small window, through which the sun shone upon a man seated crouched together upon a wooden block, with one elbow upon his bare knee, and a pipe held between his lips.

"Hallo, Tavish, you here?" cried Kenneth. "Here, Max, this is our forester. Stand up, Tavish, and let him see how tall you are."

Max had stopped by the doorway, for the smell and appearance of the ill-ventilated place were too suggestive of a butcher's business to make it inviting; but he had taken in at a glance a pile of deal cases, a block with knives, chopper, and saw, and the heads, antlers, and skins of a couple of red deer.

The smoker smiled, at least his eyes indicated that he smiled, for the whole of the lower part of his face was hidden by the huge beard which swept down over his chest, and hid his grey flannel shirt, to mingle with the hairy sporran fastened to his waist.

Then the pipe was lowered, two great brown hairy hands were placed upon his knees, and, as the muscular arms straightened, the man slowly heaved up his back, keeping his head bent down, till his broad shoulders nearly touched the sloping roof, and then he took a step or two forward.

"She canna stand quite up without knocking her head, Master Kenneth."

"Yes, you can—there!" cried Kenneth. "Now then, head up. There, Max, what do you think of him? Six feet six. Father says he's half a Scandinavian. He can take Shon under one arm and Scood under the other, and run with them up-hill."

Max stared wonderingly at the great good-tempered-looking giant, with high forehead and kindly blue eyes, which made him, with his aquiline nose, look as grand a specimen of humanity as he had ever seen.

"She knockit her head against that beam once, sir and it's made her verra careful ever since. May she sit down now, Master Kenneth?"

"Yes, all right, Tavish; I only wanted my friend to see how big you are."

"Ah, it's no great thing to be so big, sir," said the great forester, slowly subsiding, and doubling himself up till he was once more in reasonable compass on the block. "It makes people think ye can do so much wark, and a man has a deal to carry on two legs."

"Tavish is afraid of the work," grumbled Shon. "I did all these up mysel'."

"An' why not?" said the great forester, in a low, deep growl. "She found the deer for the Chief yester, and took the horns when he'd shot 'em and prought 'em hame as a forester should."

"Never mind old Shon, Tavish. Look here, what are you going to do to-day?"

"Shust rest hersel' and smock her pipe."

"No; come along with us, Tav. I want my friend here to catch a salmon."

"Hey! she'll come," said the forester, in a low voice which sounded like human thunder, and, knocking the ashes out of his pipe, he stuck the stem inside his sock beside the handle of a little knife, but started slightly, for the bowl burnt his leg, and he snatched it out and thrust it in the goatskin pocket that hung from his waistband.

"And Scood and me are to be left to get off these boxes!" cried Shon angrily.

"No, you'll have to do it all yourself, Shon," said Kenneth, laughing; "Scood's coming along with us."

"Scood—die!" he shouted as soon as he was outside, and there was an answering yell, followed by the pat pat of footsteps as the lad came running up.

Tavish bent down as if he were going to crawl as he came out of the door.

"Why, you stoop like an old goose coming out of a barn, Tavvy," cried Kenneth, laughing. "How particular you are over that old figurehead of yours."

"Well, she's only got one head, Master Kenneth; and plows on the top are not coot for a man."

"Never mind, come along. Here, Scood, get two rods and the basket. You'll find the fly-book and the gaff on the shelf."

"I have a fishing-rod—a new one," said Max excitedly.

"Oh! ah! so you have," replied Kenneth. "Never mind, we'll try that another day. Can you throw a fly?"

"I think so," said Max dubiously. "I never tried, though."

The big forester stared down at him, as he drew a blue worsted cap of the kind known as Glengarry from his waist, where it had been hanging to the handle of a hunting-knife or dirk, and, as he slowly put it on over his shaggy brown hair, his fine eyes once more seemed to laugh.

"He'll catch one, Tavvy, a forty-pounder, eh?" cried Kenneth, giving the forester a merry look.

"Nay, she shall not catch a fush like that," said the forester.

"Get out! How do you know?" cried Kenneth.

"Oh, she kens that verra weel. She shall not catch the fush till she knows how."

"We'll see about that," cried Kenneth, catching Max by the arm. "Here, Tav, you see that Scood gets the rods all right. I want to introduce Mr Blande to old Donald."

"She will be all retty," said the forester, nodding his head slowly, and standing gazing after the two lads till they were some yards away, when he stopped the nodding motion of his head and began to shake it slowly, with his eyes seeming to laugh more and more.

"She means little cames with the laddie; she means little cames."

Chapter Eight
In the Old Tower

"Father said I was to make you quite at home, Max," said Kenneth, "so let's see old Donald before we go. You have been introduced to the cook by deputy. Come along."

"Who is old Donald—is he a chief?"

"Chief! no. I thought I told you. He's our piper."

"Oh!"

"This way."

Kenneth led his companion back to the great entrance of the ruined castle, through which gateway Scoodrach had gone in search of the rods.

Tah-tah-tah! cried the jackdaws, as the lads entered the open gloomy yard, and half a dozen began to fly here and there, while two or three perched about, and peered inquiringly down first with one eye and then with the other.

Max looked up at the mouldering walls, with their crevices dotted with patches of polypody and *ruta muraria*, velvety moss, and flaunting golden sun ragwort, and wondered whether the place was ever attacked.

"Here's Scood," cried Kenneth, as the lad appeared through the farther arch, bearing a couple of long rods over his shoulder as if they were lances for the defence. "Here, we're going up to see Donald. Is he there?"

"Yes, she heard him as she went to the house."

"All right. You go on to Tavvy. Stop a moment. Go back and get a flask, and ask Grant to fill it with whisky. Tavvy will want a drop to christen the first fish."

"She's got it," said Scoodrach, holding up a flask by its strap.

"Did he give you plenty?"

"She asked him, and Master Crant said he wouldn't give me a trop, and sent me away."

"But, I say—"

"Ta pottle's quite full," said Scood, grinning. "Master Crant sent her away, so she went rount to the window, and got in, and filled it at the sideboard."

"I say, Scood, you mustn't do that!" cried Kenneth sharply.

"Why not? She titn't want the whusky, but the young master tit. Who shall Master Crant be, she should like to know!"

"Well, never mind now, only don't do it again. It's like stealing, Scood."

"Like what?" cried the lad, firing up. "How could she steal the whusky when she ton't trink it hersel? She wanted her master's whusky for the young master. You talk creat nonsense."

"Ah, well, go on. We'll come directly."

Scoodrach went off scowling, and Kenneth scratched his head.

"He's a rum fellow, isn't he? Never mind; nobody saw him; only he mustn't do it again. Why, I believe if father saw him getting in at the window, he'd pepper him. Here, this way."

Kenneth entered another doorway, whose stones showed the holes where the great hinges and bolts had been, and began to ascend a spiral flight of broken stairs.

"Mind how you come. I'll give you a hand when it's dangerous."

"Dangerous!" said Max, shrinking.

"Well, I mean awkward; you couldn't fall very far."

"But why are we going up there?"

"Never mind; come on."

"But you are going to play me some trick."

"If you don't come directly, I will play you a trick. I wasn't going to, but if you flinch, I'll shove you in one of the old dungeons, and see how you like that."

"But—"

"Well, you are a coward! I didn't think Cockneys were such girls."

"I'm not a coward, and I'm coming," said Max quickly; "but I'm not used to going up places like this."

"Oh, I am sorry!" cried Kenneth mockingly. "If I had known you were coming, we'd have had the man from Glasgow to lay on a few barrels of gas, and had a Brussels carpet laid down."

"Now, you are mocking at me," said Max quietly. "I could not help feeling nervous. Go on, please. I'll come."

"He is a rum chap," said Kenneth, laughing to himself, as he disappeared in the darkness.

"Do the steps go up straight?" said Max from below.

"No; round and round like a corkscrew. It won't be so dark higher up. There used to be a loophole here, but the stones fell together."

Max drew a deep breath, and began stumbling up the spiral stairs, which had mouldered away till some of them sloped, while others were deep hollows; but he toiled on, with a half giddy, shrinking sensation increasing as he rose.

"If you feel anything rush down by you," said Kenneth, in a hollow whisper, "don't be afraid; it's only an old ghost. They swarm here."

"I don't believe it," said Max quietly.

"Well, will you believe this?—there are two steps gone, and there's a big hole just below me. Give me your hand, or you'll go through."

Max made no reply, but went cautiously on till he could feel that he had reached the dangerous place, and stopped.

"Now then, give me your hand, and reach up with one leg quite high. That's the way."

Kenneth felt that the soft hand he took was cold and damp.

"Got your foot up? Ready?"

"Yes."

"There now, spring."

There was a bit of a scuffle, and Max stood beside his young host.

"That's the way. It's worse going down, but you'll soon get used to it. Why, Scood and I run up and down here."

Max made no answer, but cautiously followed his leader, growing more and more nervous as he climbed, for his unaccustomed feet kept slipping, and in several places the stones were so worn and broken away that it really would have been perilous in broad daylight, while in the semi-obscurity, and at times darkness, there were spots that, had he seen them, the lad would have declined to pass.

"Here we are," said Kenneth, in a whisper, as the light now shone down upon them. "Be quiet. I don't suppose he heard us come up."

Max obeyed, and followed his guide up a few more steps, to where they turned suddenly to left as well as right—the latter leading to the ruined battlements of the corner tower, the former into an old chamber, partly covered in by the groined roof, and lit by a couple of loopholes from the outside, and by a broken window opening on to the old quadrangle.

The floor was of stone, and so broken away in places that it was possible to gaze down to the basement of the tower, the lower floors being gone; and here, busy at work, in the half roofless place, with the furniture consisting of a short plank laid across a couple of stones beneath the window, and an old three-legged stool in the crumbling, arched hollow of what had been the fireplace, sat a wild-looking old man. The top of his head was shiny and bald, but from all round streamed down his long thin silvery locks, and, as he raised his head for a moment to pick up something from the floor, Max could see that his face was half hidden by his long white beard, which flew out in silvery strands from time to time, as a puff of wind came from the unglazed window.

He too was in jacket and kilt, beneath which his long thin bare legs glistened with shaggy silver hairs, and, as Max gazed at the dull, sunken eyes, high cheek-bone, and eagle-beak nose of the wonderfully wrinkled face, he involuntarily shrank back, and felt disposed to hastily descend.

For a few moments he did not realise what the old man was doing, for there was something shapeless in his lap, and what seemed to be three or four joints of an old fishing-rod beneath his arm, while he busily smoothed and passed a piece of fine string or twisted hemp through his hands, one of which Max saw directly held a piece of wax.

"Is he shoemaking?" thought Max; but directly after saw that the old fellow was about to bind one of the joints of the fishing-rod.

Just then, as he raised his head, he seemed to catch sight of the two lads standing in the old doorway, and the eyes that were dull and filmy-looking gradually began to glisten, and the face grow wild and fierce, but only to soften to a smile as he exclaimed, in a harsh, highly-pitched voice,—

"Ah, Kenneth, my son! Boy of my heart! Have you come, my young eagle, to see the old man?"

"Yes; I've brought our visitor, Mr Max Blande."

"Ah!" said the old man, half-rising and making a courtly bow; "she hurt that the young Southron laird had come, and there's sorrow in her old heart, for the pipes are not ready to give him welcome to the home of our Chief."

"What, haven't you got 'em mended yet?"

"Not quite, Kenneth, laddie. I'm doing them well, and to-morrow they shall sing the old songs once again."

"Hurrah!" cried Kenneth. "My friend here is fra the sooth, but he lo'es the skirl o' the auld pipes like a son o' The Mackhai."

"Hey! Does he?" cried the old man, firing up. "Then let him lay his han' in mine, and to-morrow, and the next day, and while he stays, he shall hear the old strains once again."

"That's right."

"Ay, laddie, for Donald has breath yet, auld as he is."

"Ah, you're pretty old, aren't you, Donald?"

"Old? Ay. She'll be nearly a hundert, sir," said the old man proudly. "A hundert—a hundert years."

Max stared, and felt a curious sensation of shrinking from the weird-looking old man, which increased as he suddenly beckoned him to approach with his thin, claw-like hand, after sinking back in his seat.

In spite of his shrinking, Max felt compelled to go closer to the old fellow, who nodded and smiled and patted the baize-covered skin in his lap.

"Ta bag," he said confidentially, "she isn't a hundert years auld, but she's auld, and she was proke, and ta wint whustled when she plew, but she's chust mended, and to-morrow—ah, to-morrow!"

"Yes; we're going fishing," said Kenneth, who was enjoying Max's shrinking way.

"Chust going to fush," said the old man, who was gazing searchingly at Max. "And she likes ta music and ta pipes? She shall hear them then."

"Yes, get them mended, Donald; we want to hear them again."

"P'raps she could chust make enough music the noo."

Kenneth laughed as he saw Max's horror, for the old man began hastily to twist up the wax end with which he had been binding one of the cracked pipes; but he laid his hand on his shoulder.

"No, no; not this morning. Get them all right, Donald."

"Yes; she was ketting them all right," he muttered, and he began with trembling fingers to unfasten the waxed thread.

At a sign from his companion, Max hurriedly followed him to the doorway.

"We'll go up on the top another time," said Kenneth. "There's such a view, and you can walk nearly all round the tower, only you have to be careful, or over you go."

Max gave a horrified glance up the crumbling staircase, and then followed Kenneth, who began to descend with all the ease of one long accustomed to the dark place.

"Take care here!" he kept on saying, as they came to the awkward places, where Max felt as if he would give anything for a candle, but he mastered his timidity, and contrived to pass over the different gaps in the stairs safely.

"How does that old man manage?" he asked, as he drew breath freely at the bottom.

"Manage? Manage what?"

"Does he always stay there?"

"What! Old Donald? Why, he cuts up and down there as quickly as I can."

"Then he is not always there?"

"Not he. Too fond of a good peat fire. He lives and sleeps at Long Shon's. But come along."

He hurried Max out of the quadrangle and down toward the narrow neck of rock which was uncovered by the falling tide, and then along by a sandy path, which passed two or three low whitewashed bothies, from whose chimneys rose a faint blue smoke, which emitted a pungent, peculiar odour.

Suddenly a thought occurred to Kenneth as they were passing one of the cottages, where a brown-faced, square-looking woman in a white mutch sat picking a chicken, the feathers floating here and there, and a number of fowls pecking about coolly enough, and exhibiting not the slightest alarm at their late companion's fate.

"That's Mrs Long Shon, Max," whispered Kenneth hastily. "You go on along this path; keep close to the water, and I'll catch up to you directly."

"You will not be long?" said Max, with a helpless look.

"Long! no. Catch you directly. Go on. I just want to speak to the old woman."

Max went on, keeping, as advised, close to the waters of the little bay, till he could go no farther, for a rapid burn came down from the hills and emptied itself there into the sea.

"Hillo! ahoy!" came a voice from behind him, just as he was gazing helplessly about, and wondering whether, if he attempted to ford the burn, there would be any dangerous quicksands.

Max turned, to see Kenneth coming trotting along with a basket in his hand.

"Off with your shoes and socks, Max," cried Kenneth.

He set the example, and was half across before Max was ready.

"Tuck up your trousers," continued Kenneth, laughing. "Why don't you dress like I do? No trousers to tuck!"

Max obeyed to the letter, and followed into the stream, flinching and making faces and balancing, as he held a shoe in each hand.

"Why, what's the matter?" cried Kenneth.

"It's—very—chilly," said Max, hurrying on as fast as he could, but managing so badly that he put one foot in a deep place, and to save himself from falling the other followed, with the result that he came out on the other side with the bottoms of his trousers dripping wet.

Chapter Nine
Salmon-Fishing

"You are a fellow!" cried Kenneth, laughing. "Here, what are you going to do?"

"Return to the castle and change them," said Max, as he was about to retrace his steps.

"Nonsense! You mustn't mind a drop of water out here. We're going salmon-fishing. I daresay you'll get wetter than that. Come on."

"I'll put on my shoes and stockings first," said Max, taking out a pocket-handkerchief to use as a towel.

"Get out! Let the wind dry you. It's all sand and heather along here. Come on."

Max sighed to himself, and limped after his guide, who stepped out boldly over the rough ground, hopping from stone to stone, running his feet well into patches of dry sand, which acted like old-fashioned pounce on ink, and from merry malice picking out places where the sand-thistles grew, all of which Max bore patiently for a few minutes, and then, after pricking one of his toes sharply, he stopped short.

"What now?" cried Kenneth, with suppressed mirth.

"Hadn't we better put on our shoes and stockings here?"

"What for?"

"We might meet somebody."

"Well, of course. Suppose we did?"

"It—it looks so indelicate," said Max hesitatingly.

"Oh, I say, don't!" cried Kenneth, roaring with laughter; "you make my sides ache again."

"Did I say something funny, then?"

"Funny! Why, it's screaming. Why, half the people go bare-legged here. All the children do."

"But the things prick one's feet so, and we might meet with poisonous snakes."

"Then let's put them on," said Kenneth, with mock seriousness. "I did not think about the poisonous snakes."

He set the example of taking possession of a stone, and, slipping on his check worsted socks and low shoes in a few moments, to jump up again and stand looking down at Max, who made quite a business of the matter. Kenneth gave each foot a kick and a stamp to get rid of the sand. Max proceeded very deliberately to wipe away the sand and scraps of heather from between his toes with one clean pocket-handkerchief, and to polish them with another.

"Oh, they look beautiful and white now!" said Kenneth, with mock seriousness, as he drew his dirk and stropped it on his hand. "Like to trim your toe-nails and cut your corns?"

"No, thank you," said Max innocently. "I won't keep you waiting to-day."

"Oh, I don't mind," said Kenneth politely.

"There, you are laughing at me again," cried Max reproachfully.

"Well, who's to help it if you will be such a mollycoddle! Slip on your socks and shoes now. I want you to catch that salmon."

"Ah yes, I should like to catch a salmon!" said Max, hastily pulling on his socks and then his too tight shoes. "There, I'm ready now."

Half a mile farther they struck the side of a sea loch, and, after following its shore for a short distance, Kenneth plunged into the heath and began to climb a steep, rugged slope, up which Max toiled, till on the top he paused, breathless and full of wonder at the beauty of the scene. The slope they had climbed was the back-bone of a buttress of the hill which flanked the loch, the said buttress running out and forming a promontory.

"There, we have cut off quite half a mile by coming up here."

"How beautiful!" said Max involuntarily, as he gazed at the long stretch of miles of blue water which ran right in among the mountainous hills.

"Yes, it's all right," cried Kenneth. "There they are half way down to the river."

"Then we are not going to fish in the loch?"

"No, no; we're going to hit the river yonder, a mile from where it enters the sea, and work on up toward the fresh-water loch."

"Where is the river, then?"

"You can't see it. Runs down yonder among the trees and rocks. You can just see where it goes into the loch," continued Kenneth, pointing. "Hillo! ahoy!"

"Ahoy!" came back from the distance; and Scood and the tall forester seated themselves on a great block of granite and awaited their coming.

Tavish smiled with his eyes, which seemed to have the same laughing, pleasant look in them seen in those of a friendly setter, the effect being that Max felt drawn toward the great Highlander, and walked on by his side, while Kenneth took the two long rods from Scoodrach, giving him the basket to carry; and, as they dropped behind, with Kenneth talking earnestly to the young gillie in a low tone, the latter suddenly made a curious explosive noise, like a laugh chopped right in two before it quite escaped from a mouth.

Kenneth was looking as solemn as Scoodrach as Max turned sharply round, his sensitive nature suggesting at once that he was being laughed at.

Tavish evidently thought that there was something humorous on the way, for he gave Max a poke with his elbow, and uttered the one word,—

"Cames!"

A quarter of an hour's rough walking brought them to a steep descent among pines and birches, directly they had passed which Max uttered an ejaculation, for the scene which opened out before him seemed a wonder of beauty.

Just in front the ground sloped down amidst piled-up, rugged masses of rock to a swiftly-flowing river, whose waters were perfectly black in every deep basin and pool, and one rich, deep, creamy foam wherever it raced and tumbled, and made hundreds of miniature falls among the great boulders and stones which dotted the stream. Right and left he could gaze along a deep winding ravine, while in front, across the river, there was a narrow band of exquisite green, dotted with pale purple gentian and fringed with ragwort, and beyond, the mountain rose up steeply, looking almost perpendicular, but broken by rifts and crevices and shelves, among which the spiring larch and pine towered up, showing their contrast of greens, and the lovely pensile birches drooped down wondrous veils of leaf and lacing delicate twig, as if to hide their silvery, moss-decked stems.

"Like it?" cried Kenneth.

"Like it!" cried Max enthusiastically. "It is lovely! I didn't think there could be anything so grand."

"Ferry coot. She knows what is ferry coot," said Tavish, nodding his head approvingly, as he set down a basket.

"Glad you're satisfied!" cried Kenneth; "but we've come to fish."

"To fish?"

"Yes, of course."

"Are there salmon here, then?"

"Yes; there's one in every pool, I'll bet; and I daresay there's one where the little fall comes down."

"What! There?" cried Max, as he looked up and up, till about two thousand feet above them a thread of glancing silver seemed to join other threads of glancing silver, like veins of burnished metal, to come gliding down, now lost to sight among the verdure of the mountain, now coming into view again, till they joined in one rapid rivulet, which had cut for itself a channel deep in the mountain side, and finally dashed out from beneath the shade of the overhanging birches, to plunge with a dull roar into the river nearly opposite where they stood.

"Now then," said Kenneth, "I'm supposing that you have never tried to catch a salmon."

"Puir laddie!" muttered the great forester; "a'most a man, and never caught a fush! Hey! where are ye gaun wi' that basket, Scood?"

"Never you mind, Tavvy. I sent him," said Kenneth sharply, as Scoodrach plunged in among the rocks and bushes behind them, and disappeared.

"I think you had better fish," said Max shrinkingly, "I have never tried."

"Then you are going to try now. Take this rod. Hold it in both hands, so. There, you see there is a grand salmon fly on."

"Yes, I see."

"Well, now, do just as I do. There's not much line out. Give it a wave like this, just as if you were making a figure eight in the air, and then try to let your fly fall gently just there."

Max had taken the rod, and stood watching Kenneth, who had taken the other, and, giving it a wave, he made the fly fall lightly on the short grass beside the river.

"Is this a salmon leap, then?" asked Max innocently.

"No; but there's one higher up. Why?"

"Because I thought the salmon must leap out of the river on to the grass to take the fly."

"Hoo—hoo—hoo! Hoogle—hoogle—hoogle! I beg your pairdon!"

Tavish had burst out into a kind of roar, as near to the above as English letters will sound. Perhaps he was laughing in Gaelic, with a cross of Scandinavian; but, whatever it was, he seemed heartily ashamed of his rudeness, and looked as solemn as a judge.

"Don't laugh, Tavvy," cried Kenneth, to conceal his own mirth. "Why, can't you see that I was making you practise on the grass before letting you throw in the water."

"She mustn't splash the watter," said Tavish sententiously.

"Scare the salmon away. Now then, try and throw."

Max made a clumsy effort; the line whistled through the air, and Tavish gave a violent start.

"She nearly hookit her in the nose!" he cried.

Max stopped short, looking horribly perplexed; but Kenneth urged him on.

"Try again," he said. "Like that, and that, and that. It's easy enough. Try and throw the fly lightly right away from you."

Max tried and tried, but with very indifferent success, Tavish making him very nervous by shaking his head from time to time.

"No, no! not that way; this way!" cried Kenneth.

Max tried again.

"Now she's trying to hook her in the eye," muttered the forester, moving out of range.

"Try if you can throw it a little worse," said Kenneth mockingly.

"I couldn't," sighed Max.

"Try."

Max threw once more.

"There, what did I say?" cried Kenneth.

"Try to throw a little worse; and I did," said Max apologetically.

"And you threw ten times better. He'll soon throw a fly, Tavvy."

"Ay, she'll soon throw a fly," said the forester.

"There; now you shall try and throw one downstream," said Kenneth.

"No, no; I'd rather you would try," cried Max.

"I can try any time. I want you to learn now. Look here! you see those stepping-stones leading out to that big block?"

"What! right out there in the rushing water?"

"Yes; that's a splendid stand."

"She's a coot stand, a ferry coot stand," said Tavish. "She's caught manny a coot fush there."

"But it looks so dangerous," pleaded Max.

"Nonsense!"

"But suppose I fell in?"

"Then Tavvy would fish you out with the gaff. Now don't be a coward. Go out there, and try and throw your fly just over that big rock close inshore. See where I mean?"

"Yes, I see," said Max dolefully; "but I shall never do it."

"You won't without you try," cried Kenneth. "Now go out, and keep on trying to throw till you make the fly fall on the other side of that big block."

"But there's no watter there," said Tavish.

"Hold your tongue. You can't see behind it," said Kenneth. "How do you know?"

"She knows there's no watter there, and if there was it wouldn't hold a fush. You let him throw the flee yonder."

"Am I to fish with a flea?" said Max.

"No, no, no!" cried Kenneth, stamping about with mirth, while another chopped-off laugh seemed to come from below. "Tavvy means a fly. You go on and do as I say."

"But, Master Ken, there shall not be a fush there."

"You Tavvy, if you say another word, I'll pitch you into the river."

The great Highlander chuckled softly, like a big turkey practising a gobble, and took off his bonnet to rub his head, while Kenneth hurried Max on, and stood on the shore, while the visitor walked out over the stones amongst which the river ran and foamed, Max looking, rod in hand, like a clumsy tight-rope dancer balancing himself with his pole.

Kenneth held up his hand to Tavish, who stared wonderingly, and took off his cap to look inside it as if he expected an explanation there, but he put it on again, and stood watching his young master and the visitor wonderingly, as the latter, urged by Kenneth, made an attempt to throw the fly, which fell almost at his feet.

"There's no watter on the far side," muttered Tavish.

Whish went the line again.

"Well done, Max. Go on. You'll soon do it, and catch a salmon," cried Kenneth.

"It's very awkward standing here," said Max appealingly.

"You're all right. Throw away. Get your fly the other side of the stone."

"Phwhat for will she get the flee the other side o' the stane?" muttered Tavish, tugging at his beard.

"Now, another, Max. Go on."

"Noo anither, she says to the puir feckless laddie."

Whizz!

Max made a desperate throw, and, to his own wonderment, the line, with the fly at the end, passed right over the great block of stone lying close to the shore.

"Is that right?" said Max.

"Yes. Bravo! capital! You'll have one. Don't strike too hard if you have a touch."

"Stanes and spates!" roared the great Highlander, leaping from the ground in his excitement. "Strike, laddie, strike! That's gran'! Haud oop yer rod. Keep the point o' yer rod oop. Noo, Master Kenneth laddie, ye shall see what tooks place. Keep oop the point o' yer rod, laddie. Dinna haud on by the reel. Let the fush rin! let the fush rin! Hech! but it does a man's hairt gude to see."

"It's tugging so, it will pull me in," cried Max, whose face was flushed with excitement as his rod bent nearly double.

"No, no; stand fast. Keep a tight line," cried Kenneth, who seemed just as excited. "It's a rare big one, Max."

"Ay, it's a fine fush," cried the forester. "It's nae kelt. Shall I go and help the laddie?"

"No, no, Tav; let him catch it himself. Look how it pulls!"

"But it don't rin. Has she hookit a stane? Na it's a fush, and a gude fush. Dinna be hasty, laddie. I'll be ready wi' the gaff. Let her rin, and—Stanes and spates! did ye ever see the like o' that, Maister Kenneth? She's caught a watter-hen!"

For at that moment, after the rod had bent double nearly, and been jerked and tugged till Max could hardly keep his footing, the invisible fish behind the rock suddenly seemed to dart upward, and, as the rod straightened, the captive to the hook flew right up in the air and fell with a splash on the side of the stone nearest to where Max stood staring at Tavish who waded into the water knee-deep, and with a dexterous jerk of the gaff hook got hold of the captive and dragged it ashore.

"Sure eneuch, it's a watter-hen," cried Tavish excitedly. "Ye've caught a watter-hen, maister, and it's no' a fush. D'ye hear, Maister Kenneth, and did ye ever hear o' such a thing? It's a watter-hen."

"No, Tavvy," cried Kenneth, who had fallen back on the heather, and was kicking up his heels, as he roared with laughter,—"no, it isn't a water-hen; it's a cock." The forester took up the bird he had hooked, and examined its drenched feathers and comb before letting its head swing to and fro.

"Why, its weam's all loose," he cried, "and it's quite deid! Eh, but it's ane o' yer cames, Maister Kenneth. Here," he cried, running to the rock and making a dab with the gaff, which hooked something, "come oot, Scood! They've peen making came o' ye, maister. I thought there was something on the way."

"It's too bad," said Max reproachfully, as Scood, hooked by the kilt, allowed himself to be dragged forward, grinning with all his muscular force, while Kenneth lay back roaring with laughter, and wiping his eyes.

"Yes, it was too bad," he said feebly, and in a voice half choked with mirth. "But never mind; you show him now, Tawy. Make him catch a salmon."

"No," said Max, stepping back and laying down the rod; "you are only making fun of me."

"Nay, I'll no' mak' fun o' thee, laddie," said Tavish. "Come wi' me, and ye shall get a saumon, and a gude ane. Let them laugh, but bide a wee, and we'll laugh at them."

Max shook his head, but the great forester seemed to be so thoroughly in earnest, and to look so disappointed, that, after a moment's hesitation, he stooped and picked up the rod once more, while Tavish took hold of his arm and led him toward another stone, upon which whosoever stood had the full command of a broad deep pool, into which the waters of the river surged and were slowly eddied round and round.

"Now then," said Tavish, making a careful examination of the fly, "ye'll do as I tell ye, and before long we'll hae a bonnie fush."

Chapter Ten
Max's first "Fush"

If Max Blande could have done as he liked, he would have said, "No, thank you, I would rather see you fish," but, with a strong feeling upon him that if he refused to make another trial he would either be laughed at or looked upon as a contemptible coward, he took the long rod, with the line sufficiently drawn from the reel to allow the gaudy fly to hang down by his hand.

"Ye'll tak' haud o' the flee, or maybe ye'll hae the hook in your han'," cried Tavish. "That's richt. Noo ye'll throw the flee richt oot yonner, and keep drawing a little more line frae the reel at ivery cast. I'll tell ye whaur to throw. Noo then, tak' your stan' richt oot on that big stane whaur the watter comes doon."

"But it looks so wet and slippery."

"The watter always mak's the stanes wet."

"But it's dangerous."

Tavish looked at him with astonishment. He could not conceive the possibility of any one seeing danger in going with a spring from rock to rock among which the beautiful river rushed, and his blue eyes opened widely.

"I mean," faltered Max, "that it would be so easy to slip in."

"Oh, I ken the noo," cried Tavish. "Dinna be skeart, laddie. Ye think she'll catch a cold. Hey, but ye needna be feart o' that. The watter comes doon fresh frae the loch, and she wouldna gie cold to a bairn, let alane a bonnie young laird like you."

Max glanced at Kenneth, who was busily tying on a fly and talking to Scoodrach. So, drawing a long breath, he stepped from the bank on to the first stone, after a stride of about a yard, and then stood still, for the water rushing swiftly round him made him feel dizzy.

"Noo the next," said Tavish encouragingly; and, comforting himself with the idea that if he was to fall into the rushing water it seemed shallower farther out than close in-shore, where it looked very black and deep, he stepped out to the next stone, and then to the next, wondering the while that nothing had happened to him. Then on and on from stone to stone, feeling giddy, excited, and in a nervous state which impelled him on, though all the while he seemed to have a tragedy taking place before his eyes—of one Max Blande, visitor from London, slipping from a rock out in the midst of that rushing river, and being rolled over and over in the foam, tossed here, banged there against projecting masses of rock, gliding round and round in smooth black whirlpools, and finally being fished out a mile below, dead and cold, and with his clothes clinging to him.

He was just about to get on to the imaginary scene of his own funeral being conducted in the most impressive manner, when the voice of the forester made him start.

"Gude—gude—gude!" he cried. "Why, ye can leap frae stane to stane as weel as young Scood."

The praise acted like a spur, and Max pressed on over the rest of the rocks till he came to the last, quite a buttress nearly in the middle of the stream.

"Ye'll no' go farther," cried Tavish.

Max did not intend to try, for the next step would have been into the cold boiling water.

"Got one yet, Max?" shouted Kenneth, his voice sounding weak and faint in the roar of the hurrying stream.

Max shook his head without daring to turn, as he stood there with the foaming, glancing water all round, steadying himself, and forgetting all about the object for which he had come, his one idea being that his object there was to balance himself and to keep from falling.

"Noo," shouted Tavish, and his voice electrified Max, who nearly dropped the rod. "That's the way, laddie. Tak a good grip o' the butt and mak' your first cast ahint that black stane. She shall hook a fush there. Leuk, did ye see the fush rise?"

Max was trying to make out among scores the black stone "ahint" which he was to throw his "flee," and in a kind of desperation he gave the rod a wave as if it was a great cart-whip, and threw.

That is to say, he did something, but where the ornamented hook fell, or whether it fell at all, he had not the slightest idea.

"A coot cast!" cried Tavish; "richt for the spot, but not long eneuch. Pull oot some more line, laddie, and do't again."

Max obeyed, trying to repeat his former performance in the same blind fashion, and involuntarily he cast the fly in the very pool the forester had pointed out, the eddy catching it and giving it a swirl round before carrying it out of the smooth black water and then away down-stream.

"There, she will hae the fush directly. See her rise?"

Max made no reply, but let the fly run to the extent of the line, and, without being told, cast again, and looked at Tavish as if to silently ask if that was right.

To his surprise, the forester was dancing about frantically upon the shore, while Kenneth and Scoodrach seemed to be roaring with laughter.

"Have I done anything very stupid?" said Max to himself.

"Ye winna catch a fush like that," cried Tavish; and the next moment Max looked at him in horror, for he came with a rush across the stones, and in the most reckless manner, as if at any moment he must fall headlong into the water.

Nothing of the kind. Tavish was a giant in size, but as sure-footed as a goat, and in very few seconds he was alongside Max, bending down to take his keen knife out of his stocking, and looking fiercely at the fisher.

"What have I done?" Max's lips parted to say, but they did not utter the words, for Tavish had seized him by the jacket, and for the moment ideas of attacks by savage Highlanders made upon peaceful Southrons flashed into the lad's brain and faded away.

"She'll never catch a fush like that," cried Tavish.

"But I did try," said Max in remonstrance.

"She says she did try," cried Tavish scornfully. "Turn roond, she's got ta flee in her pack."

"A flee? Back? Oh, I see!" cried Max, yielding to the pressure of the Highlander's hand, and turning half round.

"Mind. Does she want to co into the watter?"

But for the strong grasp upon his arm, Max would have stepped off the rock and gone headlong, but he hastily found a place for his erring foot, and stood still while a slight slit was made in the back of his tweed jacket, and the salmon fly which had hooked in there was cut loose.

"Why didn't you leave it, Tav?" Kenneth shouted, with his hands to his mouth.

"There, now, she'll co pack. Cast again, laddie. She'll soon find ta way."

Tavish trotted back, and Max stood for a few moments, with his brow wrinkled up, watching the forester till he was back ashore.

"Look, laddie, she's rising," he shouted. "Noo cast yonder ahint that stane."

Max had not noticed the rise, but he grasped now the spot where the fish was supposed to be, and made a dash with his rod, sending the line first, the fly after it, and the top of the rod into the stream with a splash.

"Acain! cast acain!" cried Tavish; and Max threw and threw his fly, never going two-thirds of the way toward the pool, where a salmon was patiently waiting for such good things as might be washed down and into the great hole behind the stone.

As the tyro whisked and waved the rod about, the natural result was that he ran out more and more line, which, thanks to the rushing water, was saved from entanglement.

"It's of no use," he said at last despondently, after nearly overbalancing himself, and feeling very dizzy once more.

The remark was meant for the forester's ears, but the sound drowned it, and the forester shouted,—

"Noo acain, laddie! Get a good grip o' the butt, and send the flee close under the stane; ta fush is there."

Max drew a long breath, and, after the fashion shown him, gave the rod two or three good swishes in the air, the line flying out well behind, and then with all his might he made a tremendous down-stroke, whose effect was to send the fly right across the pool and on to the black stone, where it caught and held on.

"Drop your rod!" roared Tavish. "Na, na, the point, laddie, the point!"

Tavish was just in time. Another moment, and the rod would have all been in the river. As it was, only the point splashed in, and as the line was slackened the hook fell over sideways and then glided slowly down the side of the rock and dropped lightly into the pool, to go gliding round.

Splash!

"Up wi' the rod, laddie! up wi' the point o' your rod, laddie!" cried Tavish excitedly. "She's cot ta fush—she's cot ta fush!"

Max obeyed, and raised the point of his rod, and then felt a tremendous tug, which sent an electric shock through him.

"She's cot him! she's cot him!" cried Tavish, dancing about on the shore and waving the gaff hook he held. "Noo, my laddie, never let the fush rin without feeling your han'."

Max heard the forester's shout, but hardly comprehended his words in the excitement of feeling the fish he had hooked dart here and there from side to side of the black-looking pool, and keeping so tight a line that all at once there was a flash of silver, and a goodly salmon leaped right out of the water and fell with a great splash.

"Ah, she's gone!" cried Tavish, stamping with rage. "Nay, hold on! Let her rin the noo. An' dinna catch haud too tight o' the line."

Max was too confused to obey his instructions, but, fortunately, he did the right thing. For the fish darted away so furiously that the lad loosed his hold upon the line to a great extent, and contented himself by keeping the hard plait close to the rod, so that it was checked a good deal in running through his hand. But all the same the winch began to sing, as, after two or three more darts, the fish dashed off out of the pool and down the stream.

The checking it received was greater than would have been dealt out by an experienced fisher, and the result was that, after darting down about forty yards, the salmon reached another pool, where, after it had sailed round two or three times, there was a sudden cessation of movement, and a dead weight hung at the end of the line.

"She's got the line around a stane," cried Tavish, running over the stepping-stones, gaff in hand. "She'll lose the fush! she'll lose the fush."

"Has it gone?" asked Max rather piteously.

"Let her tak' a grip o' the rod, my lad," said the forester; and, catching the long supple wand from the boy's hand, he stood thinking for a few moments winding in a few yards of the line.

"Nay, she's on safe," he cried, handing the rod back to Max.

"What shall I do now?" said Max nervously.

"She shall play ta fush till she's tired, and then she will use the gaff."

"But I'm tired now."

"But ta fush isna tired, laddie. Wind in, and keep a tight line."

To Max's wonder, Tavish went back ashore, and ran down the bank past Kenneth and Scood, to begin picking up big stones and hurling them right into the middle of the pool, so as to disturb the fish, which lay sulking at the bottom, in spite of the steady strain kept on its head.

Tavish's efforts were, however, unsuccessful, and in his excitement the forester began to abuse the salmon, calling upon it to move.

At last, though, as Max stood upon his tiny rock island with his rod bent, gazing wistfully down at the pool, Tavish sent in a great piece of slaty shale, which fell with a great splash, and then began to zigzag down through the dark water with so good a movement, that it touched the fish on the flank and started it off once more.

"Haud up ta rod! haud up ta rod!" cried Tavish.

"Hooray, Max! you'll have it now," cried Kenneth; and all watched the fisherman now with the greatest interest, as the salmon darted here and there, sometimes with a good stress on the rod, often, in spite of Tavish's adjurations, with a loose line, for when it rushed toward the holder of the butt, Max could not be quick enough with the winch.

Now it was one side of the pool, now close in, and Max's excitement increased till he reached fever heat, and then something happened.

The fish had rushed right up toward him, as if about to seek the upper pool, in which it had been hooked, when, apparently feeling itself free, from the pressure being taken off as Max wound up rapidly, the prize turned suddenly, leaped out, giving the water a sounding slap with its tail, and then darted off down the river.

"Haud your rod up! Haud your rod up!" cried Tavish frantically; but Max did not respond this time, and the result was that there came a sudden snatch, as it were, at the rod, the winch sung for a moment, and as Max tried to stop it, he had his finger pinched.

He had not time to think of that, though, for the next instant there was a sharp snatch and a heavy jerk which drew his arms out, and, before he could recover himself, he lost his balance and went headlong into the pool, while as he rose it was right in the full rush of the stream, which rolled him over, and, after tangling him in his line, before the boy could realise the position, he was being swept away rapidly down toward the sea loch a couple of miles below.

Chapter Eleven
"Twa-an'-Twenty Pun'"

It was a curious sensation, but, in spite of the danger, Max Blande felt no fear. One moment he was below the surface, the next he was in some shallow, being rolled over by the rushing water and carried here and there. He was conscious of catching at the masses of rock against which he struck, but they were slippery, and his hands glided over them.

Now he had his head above water for a few moments, and caught a few panting breaths as, in the wild confusion, noise of the water, and the dizzy, wildering state of his brain, he fought for life. Then the river surged against, and seemed to leap at him, as if to sweep him right away as something which cumbered the easy flow, and proved more manageable than the blocks of stone which broke up the river into a hundred streams.

And all through his rapid progress downward, Max was conscious of something tugging at, and jerking him away whenever he strove to catch hold of the nearest stone, till, what with the scalding, strangling sensation in his nostrils, the deadening feeling of helplessness and weakness coming over him rapidly, all seemed to be darkening into the semblance of a feverish dream, from which he was roused by a fresh jerk.

As soon as he could draw a breath which did not choke and make him cough painfully, he found that he was gazing up in the face of the great forester, who was holding him in some way, as he stood upon a stone, while the water kept on dragging and striving to bear him away.

"Oh, she's cot the puir laddie richt. You come here and tak' a grip o' the gaff handle, Master Kenneth, an' she'll have her oot."

The confusion was passing over, and Max could see more clearly, as Kenneth came wading out through the rushing water to the stone upon which Tavish stood.

"He's all right, Tav," cried Kenneth, whose serious face gradually grew mirthful. "Give us hold."

The forester passed the gaff handle, and, as soon as Kenneth had it tightly, stepped down into the torrent up to his waist, and began to wade.

"Keep a tight haud," he cried.

"I've got him," said Kenneth. "Look here, Scood, here's a fish."

"Ye canna see the fush," said Tavish excitedly. "She wouldna lose that saumon now for twa pun'."

Max was thoroughly awake now to the fact that the gaff hook was through the collar of his jacket, and that the stream seemed to keep on tugging at him, to get him free.

Perilous as was his position, seeming as it did to him that his life depended on the secure hold of the hook in the cloth of his jacket, he could not help feeling some annoyance that Kenneth and the forester should talk laughingly about him, as if he were a fish.

But he had no time to think of self, for Tavish had waded below him, and passed his arm about his waist.

"Got the line, Tav?" cried Kenneth.

"Ay, she's cot ta line, and ta fush is on, but what a sorry tangle she's in, wrapped roond and roond the laddie, and ta most peautiful rod we've cot proke in twa. Here, Scood, come and tak' haud o' ta rod, while we ket him on ta stane."

Scood came wading toward them, holding on by the rocks, for the pressure of the water was sufficient to have taken him off his legs; and now, for the first time, Max awoke to the fact that he was holding tightly to the rod, which had snapped in two just above the bottom joint, and that the stout salmon line was about his body, while the top portion of the rod was some distance away along the line, kept in place by the rings.

"Hae a care, laddie—hae a care!" cried Tavish. "Cot ta rod, Scood?"

"Yes; but ta line's all about him."

"Never mind tat. Noo I'll help ye. Let's ket her on to ta rock."

Max made some effort to help himself, but he was tied up, and he had to submit while the forester lifted and Kenneth pulled him out.

"Noo she's richt," cried Tavish.

"No, no; let's get him ashore."

"Without ta fush!" cried Tavish indignantly. "D'ye think ta laddie would like to lose ta fush aifter a rin like tat?"

He shook his head and thrust his bared arm down into the water, as Max sat shivering on the rock.

"Why, ta line's doon here aboot ta laddie's legs," cried Tavish, rising up with the strong fine plait in his hand. "Noo, Scood, stan' awa. She's richt noo, Maister Kenneth; so rin ashore again, and go below to yon stane. She'll try to bring ta fush in for ye to gaff her there. Or would ta Southron chentleman like to gaff her fush her nainsel?"

"No, no," said Max, with a shiver. "I want to get ashore."

"I wouldn't lose a fush like that for twa pun'!" cried Tavish again; and, as Kenneth stepped down into the water, gaff in hand, waded ashore, and ran downward among the rocks, dripping like an otter, Tavish slowly waded to bank, drawing the line slowly and carefully, and passing it through his hands.

"See him yet, Tav?" cried Kenneth from where he stood out in the stream. "Sure he's on?"

"Ay, she can feel her. It's a gran' fush, Maister Kenneth, but ta whole hundred yairds o' line was rin off ta reel. She wouldna lose ta fush for twa pun'."

As he spoke he manipulated the line very cleverly, drawing it in foot by foot, and then letting it go again as the fish made a rush, but only for the line to be steadily drawn upon again, so as if possible to manoeuvre the captive close to the rock where Kenneth stood, gaff hook in hand, ready to strike.

"Oh, it's a gran' fush!" cried Scood excitedly, as he ceased from freeing Max from the line, and looked on.

For the fish was not yet wearied out, and made a brave struggle for freedom, but, in spite of its efforts and the chances in its favour, the forester only having the line, and no springy rod with its playing power, the end seemed to be drawing nigh. Again and again it was drawn towards Kenneth, and again and again it dashed away, the man letting the line run; but every time he had more line in hand, and the salmon's tether grew more short.

"Hey, but she's well hookit!" cried Tavish; "and she wouldna lose that fush for ten pun'."

There was another rush, and a great bar of silver flashed out into the sunshine and fell with a splash upon a black stone half covered with foam.

"Leuk at that, maister," cried Scood excitedly.

It was a momentary look, for the fish gave a flap with its tail and glided off into deep water, and made a fresh dash for liberty.

There was a steady draw of the line, though, and Tavish waded slowly more in-shore.

"That will do it, Tavvy," shouted Kenneth, as the fish was drawn very close to the rock upon which he stood. "No, he's off again."

"Ay, she's a gran' fush," cried the forester; "and she wouldna lose her noo for fifty pun'."

Away went the salmon, taking out more line than ever this time, the water dripping like a shower of diamonds from the keeper's fingers, as the fine silk plait ran through his hands.

"Can ye set any more free, Scood?" he cried.

"Na; it's a' of a tangly twiss," cried Scood.

"Then we'll hae her the noo. Leuk oot, Maister Ken. She's coming richt."

Tavish steadily drew in the line, and this time the salmon came well within Kenneth's reach.

Max, in spite of his chilly sensations, sat watching intently, the excitement gaining upon him, and, in the midst of a breathless pause, Kenneth was seen to bend a little lower with outstretched hands, to straighten himself suddenly, and then step down into the shallow water and run splashing ashore, dragging after him a glistening salmon right up on to the rugged, grassy shore, where the silvery prize made a few spasmodic leaps, and then lay shining in the sun.

"Hooray!" shouted Kenneth, waving the gaff.

"Hey, hey, hey!" roared Scood, dancing about in the water and splashing Max.

"Hey hi!" roared Tavish, wading toward the rock where Max was seated. "She's a gran' fush, and she wouldna ha' lost her for twa hundert pun'. There, laddie," he continued, as he reached Max, "ye heukit her wunnerful; and ye've caught the gran'est fush this year. She's twa-an'-twenty pun'. Come along."

"How shall I get ashore?" said Max, with a shiver.

"Stan' up, laddie, and get on my pack. Nivver mind a drap o' watter. Maister Ken there's got the whusky, and we'll christen ta fush and troon a' ta colds in ta old kintra."

Max hesitated for a moment, and then, with some assistance, stood up, and let himself be drawn on to the Highlander's back.

"I shall make you so wet," he said apologetically.

"Ant ta whusky'll mak' us poth try," cried Tavish, laughing. "Why, ye're tied up in a knot, laddie, and ye've proke ta pest rod; and pring it along, Scoody lad, and ton't get ta line roond ta stanes."

"I'm very sorry I broke the rod," said Max apologetically again.

"Nivver mind ta rod; it's her nainsel' as can ment any rod. We've caught a wunnerfu' saumon, laddie. She's a gran' fush. There, noo, we'll get ye oot o' the tangle. What is she, Maister Kenneth—twa-an'-twenty pun'?"

"Five-and-twenty," cried Kenneth, as Max was deposited on the grass.

"Na, na; twa-an'-twenty pun'. I ken the size," cried Tavish. "Noo, laddie, stan' still; and you, Scoody, tak' a haud of the reel, and walk roond and roond till ye get all the line, and wind her up as ye go."

Scood took the reel, and went round, releasing Max from the bonds the river had thrown about him in rolling him over and over, after which he forgot his dripping state, and walked to where the salmon lay.

"Ye'll tak' joost a sma' taste, sir, to keep oot ta cold," said the forester, offering the cup from the bottom of the flask to Max, who shook his head.

"Mebbe ye're richt," said Tavish, tossing off the spirit; "it's a fine hailsome trink for a grown man, but—Na, na, Scood, if ye're thirsty, laddie, there's plenty coot watter in the river."

"Yes, don't give Scoody any," said Kenneth.

"Nay, Maister Kenneth, I winna gie him a taste. Ye'll be takkin' a wee drap yersel', I'm thenking?"

"Not I, Tavvy. Now then, it's a twenty-five pounder, isn't it?"

Tavish wiped his mouth with the back of his hand, gazing thoughtfully down at the salmon, after which he laid the butt of one of the fishing-rods beside it, and compared the captive with a nick on the side before drawing a piece of knotted string from his sporran, which had to be taken off and drained, for it was half full of water.

"Nay," he said, as he knelt on one knee, after measuring the girth of the fish with great deliberation, "I said twa-an'-twenty pun', Maister Ken, but I'll gie ye anither pun'. She's three-an'-twenty pun' barely."

"Five-and-twenty, Tavvy!"

"Nay, sir, three-an'-twenty, and not an ounce ower, and the laddie's caught the best fush this year. Noo then, I'm thinking I can show him where there's anither. Ye'll lend her your rod?"

"Oh yes. Here you are, Max!"

"I think I would rather go home and change my wet things," said Max.

"Nivver mind a drap o' watter, laddie. Watter like this winna gie you cauld. Have a gude rin, and then—"

"Not to-day, Tav," said Kenneth. "We're all wet through, so let's go back. Who's going to carry the twenty-five pound salmon?"

"Ta fush weighs three-an'-twenty pun' and nae mair, Maister Kenneth."

"Ah, well, we'll see as soon as we get back," said Kenneth; and back they tramped to Long Shon's bothy, that worthy sitting at the door smoking a pipe, and smiling broadly as he saw his son approaching with the goodly fish, the circulation brought by the walk having chased away the sensation of cold.

"Here, Shon, weigh this fish," cried Kenneth imperiously.

"Ask Tavish," was the reply. "He'll tell you to a pound, sir."

"I tell you I want you to weigh it," cried Kenneth and Shon rose to his feet, to stand not much higher than he sat, and, taking the fish, he bore it into the place where he cut up and packed the haunches of venison. There the capture was hung upon one of the hooks of the steelyard.

"Now, Tavish, look," cried Kenneth triumphantly. "Five-and-twenty pounds if it's an ounce."

"Three-an'-twenty, and hardly that," said Tavish firmly. "Noo, Shon, what does she scale?"

"Twa-an'-twenty pun' an' three-quairters," said Long Shon.

"Oh!" exclaimed Kenneth, in a disappointed tone.

"An' ta finest fush o' the season, laddie," cried Tavish triumphantly. "And noo, if ye winna hae a drappie, go and tak' aff the wat claes, for too much watter is bad for a man, even if the watter's coot."

Chapter Twelve
A Lesson from Max

"Caught a twenty-two-pound salmon, eh?" said The Mackhai, looking up from a letter he was reading.

"He thinks he caught it, father," said Kenneth, laughing; and, as they stood waiting in the dining-room, the boy related the adventure of the day, and how they had, after changing, gone for a long tramp across the mountain slope, and chased the hares. "Well, be civil to him, Ken. Remember we are gentlemen. And even if he is the son of a miserable shark of a lawyer, let his father learn that the Mackhais can do good for evil."

Kenneth stared wonderingly in his father's face. "What does it all mean?" he thought, and he noted the lines of trouble and annoyance deepening as The Mackhai let his eye fall upon his letter once more.

"My father must hate his father," thought Kenneth; "and he is too much of a gentleman to show his dislike to his son. Why does he have him here, then? A stupid, girlish muff of a fellow! One's obliged to laugh at him, poor beggar!"

The Mackhai doubled up his letter angrily, and thrust it into his pocket.

"Did that boy hear the gong?" he said peevishly.

"I don't know, father. Shall I run up to his room?"

"No, certainly not. Treat him as you would any other visitor, but you are not his gillie. Ring, and send Grant."

The bell was touched: the butler entered directly.

"The young gentleman is not down yet, sir."

"Well, I know that," said his master sharply. "Go and tell him we are waiting dinner."

The butler, as he turned, looked as if he would like to give notice to leave on the spot, but he said nothing, and left the room.

"It is a gross want of courtesy!" muttered The Mackhai angrily. "Am I to be kept waiting by the son of a miserable pettifogging scoundrel of a London lawyer? The beginning of the end, Ken, I suppose!" he added bitterly.

"I don't know what you mean, father."

"Wait. You'll know quite soon enough, my boy. Too soon, I'm afraid, and then—"

The door was thrown open by the butler with a flourish, and he stood back holding it wide for Max to enter, looking very thin and scraggy, in a glossy new evening suit, with tight patent leather boots, handkerchief in one hand, new white gloves in the other.

The Mackhai's brow contracted, and Kenneth gave his left leg a kick with his right heel, so as to stop an inclination to laugh.

"I—I have—I have not kept you waiting?" faltered Max.

"Not very long," said The Mackhai coldly; "but we always sit down to meals directly the gong has sounded."

The butler left the room.

"I am very sorry," faltered Max; "but I got so wet for the second time to-day, that I thought I had better have a warm bath."

"Indeed!" said The Mackhai coldly. "Oh my, what a molly!" muttered Kenneth. "My father told me to be careful," continued Max.

"Pray follow out your father's advice," said The Mackhai, "and consider that you are quite at home here."

"How jolly sarcastic father is!" thought Kenneth.

"Thank you," said Max politely.

"While this place is mine, I wish my guests to be quite at their ease," continued The Mackhai; "but you will excuse me for saying that we never dress for dinner."

"No, I thought not," said Max confusedly; "but I made myself so wet, and my other suits were in the small portmanteau, and I've lost the key."

That dinner was hot, but very cold, and Max felt exceedingly glad when it was over. His host tried to be polite, and asked questions about the salmon-catching, but Max spoke in a hesitating way, and as if he thought he was being laughed at, and it was with a feeling of intense relief that he ceased to hear his host's voice, and escaped from the stony gaze of the butler, who, under an aspect of the most profound respect, seemed to glare at the visitor with a virulent look of hatred.

"They don't seem to like me at all down here," thought Max, as they rose from the table.

"I wonder what's the matter," thought Kenneth. "I never saw father seem so severe before."

Just then, looking very stern and out of temper, The Mackhai left the room, and Kenneth, after a moment's hesitation, went after him; but changed his mind directly, and returned to Max.

"I beg your pardon," he said. "Father does not seem to be well."

"I am sorry. I'm afraid he was put out because I kept you waiting."

"Oh, never mind that. I say, we can't go out with you like that, and it's such a jolly night. I don't know, though, if you put on an ulster."

"I think I would rather not go out any more tonight," said Max, hesitating.

"All right. Then we'll go and have a game at billiards. Come along."

This was more to Max's taste, and, after Grant had been summoned to help light the lamps, Kenneth shut the door, chuckling to himself about the big beating he was going to give the Londoner, who, instead of taking a cue, was gazing round the handsome billiard-room at the crossed claymores, targes, and heads of red deer, whose antlers formed rests for spears and specimens of weapons from all parts of the world.

"Are those swords sharp?" asked Max.

"Sharp? Yes, I should think they are. They're the claymores my ancestors used to handle to cut off the heads of the Macleods and Macdougals."

"Used there to be much fighting then?"

"Fighting? I should think there was. Every chief lived in a castle and had a galley, and they used to fill them half full of pipers and half full of fighting men, and go to war with their neighbours."

"It must have been very terrible."

"Not a bit of it. Very jolly—much better than living in these tame times. Come along; you break."

Max played first, and handled his cue so easily that Kenneth stared.

"Hallo!" he said, "you've played before."

"Yes; we have a billiard-table at home."

"Oh!" ejaculated Kenneth, and the big beating did not seem so near. Not that it proved to be more distant, only it was the other way on, for Max played quietly and respectably, keeping up a steady scoring, while Kenneth's idea seemed to be that the best way was to hit the balls hard, so that they might chance to go somewhere.

This they did, but not so as to add to his score, and the consequence was that, when Max marked a hundred, Kenneth was only thirty-three.

"Oh, I say!" he exclaimed, "I didn't know you could play like that."

"I often have a game with my father," said Max. "He always gives me fifty out of a hundred, and he can beat me, but he lets me win sometimes."

Kenneth whistled.

"I say," he said, "your father must be a very clever man."

"Yes," said Max, in a dull, quiet way, "I think he is very clever."

"You don't seem very much pleased about it."

"I'm afraid I'm very tired. It has been such a hard day."

"Hard! that's nothing. You wait till your legs get trained, you won't think this a hard day."

"I'm afraid I shan't be down here long enough for that."

"Oh, you don't know. Let's have another game, and see if I can't beat you this time. Only, mind, none of your father's tricks."

Max started and turned scarlet.

"I mean, you will try."

"Of course," said Max; "I don't think it would be fair not to try one's best."

They played, and Kenneth came off worse.

They played again, and he was worse still; while, after the fourth game, he threw down his cue pettishly.

"It's of no use for me to play you. Why, you're a regular out-and-outer."

"Nonsense! These strokes are easy enough. Let me show you. Look at the things you can do that I can't."

"You show me how to make those strokes, and I'll show you everything I know."

"I'll show you without making you promise that," said Max good-humouredly; and the rest of the evening was spent over the board, which they only quitted to say "good-night" and retire to their rooms; but Kenneth did not go to his until he had been to the butler's pantry, and then to the kitchen, which was empty, the servants having retired for the night, after banking up the fire with peat, which would go on smouldering and glowing for the rest of the night, and only want stirring in the morning to burst into a blaze.

There was something very suspicious in Kenneth's movements as he crossed the kitchen in the faint glow, and a great tom-cat glowered at him as he stole away to the fireside and watched.

At one moment it seemed as if Kenneth was going to the larder to make a raid upon the provisions, but he stopped short of that door, and stood listening, and started violently as a sudden sound smote his ear.

It was the start of one troubled with a guilty conscience, for the sound was only a sharp tack made by the great clock, preliminary to its striking eleven.

"How stupid!" muttered Kenneth; and then he started again, for he heard a door close rather loudly.

"Father!" he muttered, and he ran to the entry and listened again, before going cautiously to the fire, where he suddenly made two or three snatches of a very suspicious character, and hurried out of the kitchen along a stone passage. Then all was silent about the place, save the lapping and splashing of the water among the rocks outside.

Chapter Thirteen
An uncomfortable Breakfast

That same night Max fell fast asleep as soon as he was in bed, for never in his career had he used his muscles so much in one day.

His rest was dreamless, but he awoke as the turret clock struck six, and lay thinking.

It was a glorious morning, for his window was illumined by the sunshine, and he felt warm and comfortable, but all the same he shivered.

For a troublesome thought had come to him, and he lay quite sleepless now, listening for Kenneth's step, feeling quite certain that before many minutes had passed the lad would be hammering at his door, and summoning him to come down and bathe.

He shuddered at the idea, for the thought of what he had passed through—the climb down to the cavern with its crystal cold water, the weed-hung rocks, and the plunge, and the way in which he had been given his first lesson in swimming—brought out the perspiration in a cold dew upon his brow.

"I will not go again," he said to himself. "One ought to be half a fish to live in a place like this."

The banging of a door and footsteps were heard.

"Here he comes!" muttered Max, and by an involuntary action he caught hold of the bedclothes and drew them tightly up to his chin.

No Kenneth.

The sun shone brightly, and he could picture the dazzling sheen of the waves as they rippled and flashed. He could picture, too, the golden-brown seaweed and the creamy-drab barnacles on the rocks which had felt so rough and strange to his bare feet.

Then a reaction set in. It was so cowardly to refuse to go, and Kenneth and Scood would laugh at him, while to his sensitive nature the jeering would be more painful than the venturing into the water.

"But," he argued to himself, "there is no danger in being laughed at, and, on the other hand, they might get me out—they are so reckless—and drown me."

He shuddered, and then he felt ashamed. He wanted to be as brave as the other lads, and he felt that he must seem to them a miserable coward.

"I'm down here, and with the chance of learning all these out-door sports, and I shall try. I will not be so cowardly, and when Kenneth comes I'll go down and bathe, and try to master all this horrid fright."

As soon as he had bravely come to this determination he felt better, though all of a tremor the while, and his agitation increased as from time to time he heard a sound which his excited imagination told him was the coming of Kenneth.

But he did not spring out of bed and begin to dress, so as to be ready when Kenneth came, but lay feeling now uncomfortably hot as he recalled his previous experience in the water, and his terrible—as he termed it—adventure over the fishing, and his being hooked out by Tavish, but all the time he could not help a half suspicion taking root, that, had he been a quick, active lad, accustomed to such things, he would not have been swept off the rock, and, even if he had been, he would have struggled to some shallow place and recovered himself.

"I will try!" he said aloud. "I'll show him that if I am a coward, I am going to master it, and then perhaps they will not tease me and laugh at me so much."

Kenneth did not come, and, in spite of his determination, the boy could not help feeling relieved, as he lay thinking of what a long time it seemed since he came down there, and what adventures he had gone through.

Then there were footsteps, and a bang outside the door.

Kenneth at last!

No; the steps were not like his, and they were going away. It was some one who had brought his boots.

Max lay and thought again about the people he had met,—about The Mackhai, and his haughty, distant manner. He did not seem to like his visitor, and yet he was very polite.

"Perhaps he doesn't like my father," thought Max sadly. "Perhaps—"

Perhaps it was being more at ease after his determination to master his cowardice:

Perhaps it was from the feeling of relief at the non-appearance of Kenneth:

Perhaps it was from having undergone so much exertion on the previous day:

Perhaps it was from the bed being so warm and comfortable:

Be all this as it may, Max Blande, instead of getting up, dropped off fast asleep.

"Max! I say, Max, do you know what time it is?"

Max started up in bed, and had hard work to collect his thoughts, as his name was called again, and there was a loud knocking at the door.

"Yes, yes; coming!" cried the boy, leaping out of bed, and hurrying on his dressing-gown.

"Open the door."

"Yes; I'm coming!"

Max opened the door, and Kenneth rushed in.

"Come, old lazy-bones!" he cried; "look sharp! It's a quarter to nine, and the dad will look dirks and daggers if we keep him waiting."

"I—I'm very sorry," said Max. "I—I dropped off to sleep again. I thought you would come and call me to bathe."

"What was the use? See what a fuss you made yesterday!"

"But I meant to come."

"Well, don't talk, old chap. Look sharp, and dress."

"Yes; but are you going to stay?"

"Of course, to help you."

Max felt disposed to rebel, and thought it objectionable.

Kenneth saw his looks, and spoke out.

"Look here!" he said; "I'll wait for you in the passage, and look out of the window."

"Oh, thank you!" cried Max, and the next moment he was alone.

In a few minutes Max's bell rang.

Kenneth went off on tip-toe, and met Grant, who was coming up-stairs looking rather sulky.

Kenneth said something to the butler, who nodded and went down again, while Kenneth went softly back grinning, and stood looking out of the passage window, giving one leg a kick of delight as he heard Max's bell ring again.

Then there was a pause, and at last the bell rang once more.

"Ten minutes to nine," said Kenneth to himself, with a look of suppressed glee.

Then Max's door opened.

"Ready?" cried Kenneth.

"No. I'm very sorry, but I've rung three times, and no one has come."

"P'r'aps Grant is busy with father. What do you want—hot water?"

"No," said Max. "The fact is, I got two pairs of trousers very wet yesterday, and I sent them down to be dried. They haven't been brought up."

"Oh, is that all?" cried Kenneth. "I'll run and fetch them."

"Oh, thank you!"

Kenneth ran off, and came back at the end of a few minutes, but without the trousers.

"Thank you," said Max hastily. "I'm ashamed to have let— Why, you haven't got them!"

"No," said Kenneth. "Are you sure you sent them down? Grant says he hasn't seen them."

"I gave them to one of the maids."

"It's very strange. No one has seen them. Never mind. Jump into another pair. The guv'nor will be furious if you are late."

"But I've lost the key of my portmanteau, and I can't put on black this morning."

"Oh no, that would never do!" cried Kenneth. "Pop on your knickerbockers."

"I haven't any."

"No knicks! Oh, I say! what will you do? That blessed gong will be going directly."

"Yes. Shall I put on my dress things?"

"No, no, no! You'd make the pater laugh horribly. Here, I tell you what! you and I are about the same size—shall I lend you some of my duds?"

"Oh, if you would!" cried Max.

"All right!"

Kenneth dashed off to his own room, and came back in a minute.

"Here you are!" he cried. "Slip on those socks."

"But I've got socks."

"But they won't do. On with these."

"But—"

"On with them. The gong will go directly."

Horribly scared at the idea of keeping The Mackhai waiting again, Max obeyed, hardly knowing what he did, and then he made a protest as Kenneth held out a garment for him to put on next.

"Oh," he exclaimed, "I couldn't put on that!"

"But you must. You haven't a moment to spare; and it's my best one."

Max shrank, and then yielded, for all at once boom! boom! boom! sounded the gong; and, half frantic with haste and his want of moral courage, the poor boy submitted to the domination of his tormentor, with the result that, five minutes after the gong had ceased, and still hesitating as to whether he had not better stay away, Max followed Kenneth down-stairs, that young gentleman having preceded him two minutes.

"The Mackhai is beginning breakfast, sir," said Grant, as Max came down; and he drew back with a tray full of hot viands, his sour, stony face relaxing into a grin as the shrinking figure of the young guest passed him.

"Good morning, Mr Blande!" said The Mackhai sternly; and then his severe face underwent a change. He was about to burst out laughing, but he bit his lip, frowned, and then in a changed tone of voice said, "Thank you for the compliment, Mr Blande."

"It—it was not meant for a compliment, sir," faltered Max.

"Indeed! I thought you had donned our tartan out of compliment to your host."

"It is an accident, sir," stammered Max, with his face scarlet. "I have lost my clothes, and Kenneth has been kind enough to lend me a suit."

"Oh, I see!" said The Mackhai, as the dogs, which for a treat had been admitted, came sniffing round the shivering lad, who looked pitiably thin and miserable in the kilt, with the sporran hanging down far lower than it should.

"It is a very comfortable dress," said The Mackhai, recovering himself, though, to Kenneth's delight and Max's misery, he could not repress a smile. "There, pray, sit down, the breakfast is growing cold."

Max went to his place shrinkingly, for Bruce, the great deerhound, was following close behind him, apparently examining him thoughtfully.

"Lie down, Bruce!" said Kenneth, and the dog dropped into a couching attitude. "You look fizzing, Max," he said, in a low voice, as his father walked to the window and peered out.

Max gave him a piteous look, and gladly seated himself, seeming glad of the shelter of the hanging tablecloth, for, after examining him wonderingly, Sneeshing suddenly set up his tail very stiffly and uttered a sharp bark, while Dirk shook his frill out about his neck and uttered a menacing growl, which to poor Max's ears sounded like, "You miserable impostor, get out of those things!"

Just then Grant entered with the portion of the breakfast kept back till Max came down, The Mackhai seated himself, and the breakfast began.

As at previous meals, the host was very much abstracted: when he was not partaking of his breakfast, he was reading his letters or referring to the newspaper, leaving the task of entertaining the guest to his son.

"How do you feel now?" said Kenneth.

"Not very comfortable," whispered Max. "May I ask Grant to have a good search made for my things?"

"Oh no, don't ask him now. It puts him out. You'll be all right, and forget all about them soon."

"I—I don't think I shall," said Max, as he made a very poor breakfast.

"Oh yes, you will. I say, if I were you, I'd write up to my tailor to send you down two rigs-out like that. You'll find 'em splendid for shooting and fishing."

Max shook his head.

"Never mind. Have some of this kipper, it's—"

"Ow!" ejaculated Max, dropping his coffee-cup on the table, so that it upset, and the brown fluid began to spread, as the lad sprang back from the table.

"What's the matter?" cried The Mackhai.

"Nothing, sir;—I—that is—that dog—"

Kenneth was seized with a violent fit of laughing and choking, which necessitated his getting up from the table and being thumped on the back by Grant; while Dirk, who had been the cause of all the trouble, marched slowly out from under the table, and stood upon the hearthrug uttering a low growl, and looking from one to the other of the boys, as if he felt that they were insulting him.

"Look here, Kenneth, if you cannot behave yourself at table," cried The Mackhai angrily, "you had better have your meals by yourself."

"I—I—oh dear!—oh, oh, oh! I beg your pardon, father, I—oh, I say, Max, don't look like that, or you'll kill me!" cried Kenneth, laughing and choking more than ever.

"I beg your pardon, sir," said Max piteously. "I'm afraid it was all my fault;" and he looked at the stained cloth.

"There is no need for any apology, Mr Blande. Here, Grant, lay a doubled napkin over this place, and bring another cup. Pray sit down, sir."

Max turned shrinkingly toward the table, but glanced nervously from one dog to the other, and just at that moment, Bruce, who was behind, smelt his legs.

"Oh!" cried Max, making a rush, as he felt the touch of the dog's cold nose.

"Here, Kenneth, I've said before that I will not have those dogs in the dining-room!" cried The Mackhai angrily. "Turn them out."

Kenneth hastily obeyed, the dogs marching out through the French window, and then sitting down outside and looking patiently in, as dogs gaze who are waiting for bones.

"What was the matter, Max?" asked Kenneth, as soon as they were re-seated, and the breakfast once more in progress.

"That dog took hold of my leg."

"What, Sneeshing?"

"No, no. The one you call Dirk."

"He must have thought it was a sheep's leg."

"Kenneth!"

"Yes, father?"

"Go on with your breakfast. I hope you are not hurt, Mr Blande?"

"No, sir, not hurt, but it felt very wet and uncomfortable."

"The dog's play," said The Mackhai quietly. "I don't think he would bite."

"No, sir, I hope not," faltered Max, as he tried to go on with his breakfast; "but it felt as if he was going to, and it was startling."

"Yes, of course!" said The Mackhai absently, as he took up his paper, and the breakfast went on to the end, but to Max it was anything but a pleasant meal.

Chapter Fourteen
Macrimmon's Lament

"No, sir, I've asked everybody, and no one has seen them since Bridget put them to dry. She says they were in front of the fire when she went to bed."

This was Grant's reply to Max's earnest prayer that he would try and find his trousers.

"Do you think they could have been stolen?" said Max doubtingly.

"Stolen! My goodness, sir! do you think there is any one about this house who would steal young gentlemen's trousers?"

"Oh no, of course not," said Max; "but could you get a man to pick a lock?"

"Pick a pocket, sir!" cried Grant indignantly, for he had not fully caught Max's question.

"No, no—a lock. I lost the key of my small portmanteau as I came here, and I can't get at my clothes."

"No, sir, there is no one nearer than Stirling that we could get to do that."

"Oh, never mind, Max," cried Kenneth, coming in after leaving his visitor for some little time in the drawing-room; "the trousers'll turn up soon, and if they don't, you'll do as you are. He looks fizzing, don't he, Granty?"

"Yes, sir, that he do," replied the butler, compressing his lips into a thin line.

"Only his legs look just a little too white," continued Kenneth.

"You are both laughing at me," said Max sadly.

"No, no, nonsense! There, come on out."

"Like this?"

"Of course. It's no worse for you than it is for me. Come along."

Max felt as if he could not help himself, and, yielding to the pressure, he followed his young host out on to the terrace-like rock, where they were joined by Scoodrach, who came up with his eyes so wide open that they showed the whites all round.

As the red-headed lad came up, he essayed to speak, but only made an explosive sound.

"Look here, Scood, if you laugh, Max Blande will pitch you overboard. Now then, what is it?"

"Tonald—"

"Well, what about Donald?"

"She's chust waitin' for the young chentleman."

"Where?"

"In ta castle yaird."

"What does he want?" said Kenneth seriously. "Here, Max, let's go and see."

Max was not sorry to follow his young host into the shelter of the castle ruins, for there was a good deal of breeze off the sea; and, as soon as the three lads were in the shady quadrangle, old Donald Dhu came out of the ruined entry at the corner tower he affected.

As soon as the old man was well outside, he stood shading his dim eyes with one bony hand, bending forward and gazing at Max, looking him up and down in a way which was most embarrassing to the visitor, but which made the boys' eyes sparkle with delight.

Max felt ready to run back to his room and lock himself in, but, to his relief, the old man did not burst into a fit of laughing, for a grave smile overspread his venerable face.

"She wass a prave poy," he said, laying a claw-like hand upon Max's shoulder, "and she shall wear ta kilt petter some day."

Then, motioning to him mysteriously with his free hand, he beckoned him slowly toward the entry to the spiral staircase, and Max yielded, though he longed to escape.

"What does he want, Kenneth?"

"Got something to say to you, I suppose. Don't be long, and we'll have the boat ready for a sail."

"But—"

"I say, don't stop talking; it may make the old boy wild, and if you do—"

Kenneth did not finish his sentence, but made a peculiar cluck with his tongue—a sound which might have meant anything.

All this time the old man stood, with his flowing white locks and beard, motioning to Max to come; and unwillingly enough he entered the old tower, and climbed cautiously up, avoiding the broken places, and finally reaching the chamber in the top.

"She shall sit town there," said the old man, pointing to a stool set in the ruinous fireplace; and, without the slightest idea of what was going to happen, Max seated himself and waited to hear what the piper had to say.

He was not kept long in suspense, for the old man said, with a benevolent look on his ancient face,—

"She lo'es ta pipes, and she shall hear them the noo, for they're mentit up, and tere's nae music like them in ta wide world."

As he spoke, he raised the lid of a worm-eaten old chest, and, smiling the while, took out the instrument, placed the green baize-covered bag under one arm, arranged the long pipes over his shoulder, and, inflating his cheeks, seemed to mount guard over the doorway, making Max a complete prisoner, and sending a thrill of misery through him, as, after producing a few sounds, the old man took the mouthpiece from his lips, and said, with a smile,—

"'Macrimmon's Lament.'"

Max felt as if he should like to stick his fingers in his ears, but he dared not,—as if he should like to rush down the stairs, but he could not. For the old man fixed him with his eyes, and, keeping his head turned towards his prisoner, began to march up and down the broken stone floor, and blew so wild a dirge that in a few moments it became almost maddening.

For Max Blande's nerves, from the retired London life he had led, were sensitive to a degree. He had never had them strung up by open-air sports or life among the hills, but had passed his time in study, reading almost incessantly; though even to the ears of an athlete, if he were shut up in a small chamber with a piper, the strains evoked from this extremely penetrating instrument might jar.

As Donald marched up and down in a pace that was half trot, half dance, his eyes brightened and sparkled; his yellow cheeks flushed as they were puffed out; and, as he went to and fro before the window, the sea-breeze made his long hair and beard stream out behind, giving him a wild, weird aspect that was almost startling, as it helped to impress Max with a feeling of awe which fixed him to his chair. For if he dared to rise he felt that he would be offering a deadly affront to the old minstrel, one which, hot-blooded Highlander as he was, he might resent with his dirk, or perhaps do him a mischief in a more simple manner, by spurning him with his foot as he retreated—in other words, kick him down-stairs.

And those were such stairs!

Northern people praise the bagpipes, and your genuine Highlander would sooner die than own it was not the "pravest" music ever made. He will tell you that to hear it to perfection you must have it on the mountain side, or away upon some glorious Scottish loch. This is the truth, for undoubtedly the bagpipes are then at their best, and the farther off upon the mountain, or the wider the loch, the better.

But Max was hearing the music in a bare-walled, echoing chamber, and, but for the fact that there was hardly any roof, there is no saying what might have been the consequences. For Donald blew till his cheeks were as tightly distended as the bag, while chanter and drone burred and buzzed, and screamed and wailed, as if twin pigs were being ornamented with nose-rings, and their affectionate mamma was all the time bemoaning the sufferings of her offspring, "Macrimmon's Lament" might have been the old piper's lamentation given forth in sorrow because obliged to make so terribly ear-shrilling a noise.

But, like most things, it came to an end, and with a sigh of relief Max sprang up to exclaim, as if he had been in a London drawing-room, and some one had just obliged,—

"Oh, thank you!"

"She's a gran' chune," said Donald, pressing forward, and as it were backing poor Max into the seat from which he had sprung. "Noo she'll gie ye 'Ta Mairch o' ta Mackhais.'"

Max suppressed a groan, as the old man drew himself up and produced half a dozen sonorous burring groans from the drone.

Then there was a pause, and Donald dropped the mouthpiece from his lips.

"She forgot to say tat she composed ta mairch in honour of the Chief hersel'."

Then he blew up the bag again, and there came forth a tremendous wail, wild and piercing, and making a curious shudder run up and down Max's backbone, while directly after, as he was debating within himself whether he might not make some excuse about Kenneth waiting, so as to get away, the old man marched up and down, playing as proudly as if he were at the head of a clan of fighting men.

All at once, sounding like an echo, there came from somewhere below a piteous yell, long-drawn and wild, and doleful as the strains of the pipes.

The effect was magical. The old man ceased playing, his face grew distorted, and he stamped furiously upon the floor.

"It's tat Sneeshing," he cried, laying down the pipes and making a snatch at his dirk, but only to thrust it back, dart at a great stone which had fallen in from the side of the window, and, seizing it, whirl it up and dash it out of the broken opening down into the court where the dog was howling.

There was a crash, a snapping, wailing howl, and then all was silent.

"She hopes she has killed ta tog," cried the old man, as he gathered up his pipes again, and once more began to march up and down and blow.

The fierce burst of tempestuous rage and the accompanying actions were not without their effect upon Max, who shrank back now helpless and aghast, staring at the old piper, whose face grew smoother again, as he gave his visitor an encouraging smile and played away with all his might.

Would it never end—that weary, weary march—that long musical journey? It was in a minor key, and anything more depressing it was impossible to conceive. Like the pieces played by WS Gilbert's piper, there was nothing in it resembling an air, but Donald played on and on right to the bitter end, when once more Max began to breathe, and again he said,—

"Thank you."

"She hasn't tone yet," said Donald, smiling. "She does not often ket a young chentleman like yersel' who lo'es ta coot music, and she'll keep on playing to ye all tay. Ye shall noo hae something lively."

Before Max could speak, the old man blew away, and wailed and burred out what was probably intended for "Maggie Lauder;" but this was changed into "Tullochgorum," and back again, with frills, and puckers, and bows, and streamers, formed of other airs, used to decorate what was evidently meant for a grand *mélange* to display the capabilities of the national instrument.

Just when this wonderful stream of maddening notes was at its highest pitch, and Max Blande was at his lowest, and feeling as if he would like to throw himself down upon the floor and cry, he became aware of the fact that Kenneth and Scoodrach were up above, gazing down at him from the ruined wall on the side where the chamber was roofless.

Old Donald was right below them and could not see, even had he been less intent and out of his musical dreaming, instead of tramping up and down, evidently supremely happy at the diversity of noises he made.

Max seized the opportunity of Donald's back being turned, and made a sign to them to come down; but they only laughed, keeping their heads just in sight, Scoodrach's disappearing and bobbing about from time to time, as he grinned and threw up his fingers, and seemed to be going through the motions of one dancing a reel.

Max would have shouted to them to come down, but at the thought of doing so a feeling of nervous trepidation came over him. Donald had looked half wild when the dog interrupted him; how would he behave if he were interrupted again, just as he was in this rapt state, and playing away with all his might?

The lad subsided in his seat, and with wrinkled brow gazed from the piper to the heads of the two boys, both of whom were laughing, and evidently enjoying his misery.

And now for the first time it struck Max that he had been inveigled up there through the planning of Kenneth, who knew his dislike to the pipes, and had told Donald that he was anxious to hear him play.

His face must have been expressive, for Kenneth was laughing at him, and whispered something to Scoodrach, who covered his mouth with his hands, and seemed to roar to such an extent that he was obliged to bend down.

As Scoodrach reappeared, he climbed up so as to lie flat on the top of the wall, leaning his head down when Donald came toward him, and raising it again as the old man turned.

The medley of Scottish airs ceased, and at last Max thought his penance was at an end, but in an instant the old man began again blowing hard, and playing a few solemn notes before approaching quite close to Max, taking his lips from the mouthpiece and whispering sharply, —

"Ta Dirge o' Dunloch."

Then whang! wha! on went the depressing strain Sneeshing being heard to howl in the distance.

Max felt as if he must run, and in his despondency and horror, knowing as he did that if he did not do something the old half-crazy piper would keep him shut up there and play to him all day, he waited till Donald had approached close to him, and, as the old man turned, he stretched out a leg ready. Then, waiting till he had been across the room, come back, and was turning again, Max cautiously slipped off his seat, and was about to dash for the door, when there was a shout, a scuffle, a thud, an awful pipe yell, and Donald came staggering back, uttering a series of wild Gaelic ejaculations in his surprise.

The cause of the interruption was plain enough: Scood had rolled off the top of the wall feet first, clung with his hands, and in his efforts to recover himself and get back he had kicked out one leg so sharply that it had come in contact with the bag of the pipes, producing the wild yell, and sending the old man staggering back.

As soon as he fully realised what was the matter, the old man uttered a howl of rage, laid down his pipes, and rushed across at Scoodrach, who had half scrambled back.

Donald's attack altered his position, for the old man seized him about the hips by the kilt, and dragged at him to get him down, just as Kenneth was holding him tightly and trying to pull him up, Scood seconding his efforts by clinging to him with all his strength.

What followed did not take many moments, for Donald had every advantage on his side. He hauled, and Kenneth hauled, while Scood clung to his companion with tremendous tenacity.

"Pull! pull!" shouted Scoodrach to Kenneth; but the latter could not pull for laughing. And besides, he had the whole of the young gillie's weight to bear, while his foothold was exceedingly insecure.

The old piper uttered some fierce words in Gaelic, to which Scoodrach replied in the same tongue; and then, finding how helpless he was, and little likely to be drawn up while Donald was clinging to him, he drew in his legs and then kicked them out again, like one swimming, or, a better comparison, like a grasshopper in the act of taking a leap.

Scoodrach was as strong as one of the rough ponies of the place, while old Donald's days for display of muscular strength had long gone by. Consequently he was drawn to and fro as Scoodrach kicked, and was finally thrown off, to go down backwards into a sitting position.

"Now pull, Maister Ken," shouted Scoodrach. "Heave her up, or she'll hae that mad blawblether at her again."

Kenneth pulled, laughing more than ever, as Scoodrach held on by his jacket; and just then the gillie managed to get a foot in a hole whence a stone had been dislodged. Raising himself up a little, Kenneth now began to pull in earnest; but it was too late. Old Donald had struggled up and seized Scoodrach once more, giving so heavy a drag upon him that down came the young gillie, and not alone, for he dragged Kenneth with him; and all three lay together in a struggling heap upon the floor.

"Rin, Maister Ken! Rin, young chentleman! Doon wi' ye! She'll be like a daft quey the noo. I can haud her till ye get doon."

"No, no, Scood, I won't run!" cried Kenneth. "You run, Max. Get down with you."

Max obeyed, glad of the opportunity for escape; but as soon as he had passed through the door he turned, and looked in at the struggle going on.

To his horror, they more than once drew so near to the hole in the floor that it seemed as if they must go through; but they all wrenched themselves clear, and Scoodrach suddenly got free, leaped up, and drew his dirk.

"Oh!" cried Max in horror.

"Put away that knife, Scood, and run!" cried Kenneth.

"She'll niver rin frae ta auld piper!" cried Scoodrach; and, turning to the box on which lay the pipes, he caught them up, and held them with the point of his keen knife close to the skin bag.

"Noo," he shouted, "haud off an' let the young maister go, or I'll slit the bag's weam."

"Ah!" shouted old Donald.

"Ay, but I will!" yelled Scoodrach, with the point of his keen knife denting in the bag.

"Ah!" shouted the old piper again; and he made a movement toward the boy.

But Scoodrach was too quick. He stepped back, raised his arm, and seemed about to plunge the knife through the green baize.

"She'll preak her heart," groaned the old piper.

"Shall she let her go, then?" cried Scoodrach.

The old man caught hold of his hair by handfuls and gave it a tremendous tug.

"Don't cut, Scood," cried Kenneth.

"Go on down, and she shall come aifter. She'll slit ta bahg oop if Tonald ton't sit town."

The old man's breast heaved, and he gazed piteously at his instrument; following Scoodrach slowly, as that young gentleman edged round by the side of the wall till he reached the door, through which Kenneth had passed, and where he was now standing holding on by Max, both being intensely interested spectators of the scene.

"Rip her recht up," cried Scoodrach. "Noo, Maister Kenneth, are ye ready?"

"Yes."

"Down wi' ye, then. He canna catch us there. Noo, Tonald, catch."

He threw the pipes at the old man, and then darted through the narrow opening, and followed the others down the spiral stairs at such a rate that an accident seemed certain; but they reached the bottom in safety, and stood at last in the courtyard, laughing and cheering.

"Tonal'!" shouted Scoodrach; and he added something in Gaelic.

The effect was to bring the old piper's head and shoulders out of the narrow broken window opening, where he stood, hugging the pipes in one hand, and shaking the other menacingly.

Then, changing his manner, he began to beckon with his great claw-like hand.

"Nivver mind him, laddie. Come up here and I'll play ye Macrimmon owre again."

"No, no!" exclaimed Max earnestly.

"Says he's afraid you'd blow the roof off, Tonal'," shouted Kenneth. "No time. He's coming along with us;" and he led Max, to his very great delight, out through the old arch on to the broad terrace by the sea. But they had not gone many yards before they heard old Donald again piping away, with no other audience but the jackdaws, which came and settled near, and looked at him sideways, too much used to the wild strains to be alarmed, and knowing from experience that the old piper would pay no heed to them.

Chapter Fifteen
Bird-Nesting under Difficulties

"What shall we do?" said Kenneth.

Just as he spoke, Max made a jump and turned nimbly round, for Sneeshing, who had not been touched by Donald's stone, had come fidgeting round them, and had had a sniff at the visitor's legs.

"I say, Max, there must be something very nice about your legs," cried Kenneth, laughing. "Don't set the dog at me, please."

"I didn't. It's only his way. Here, what shall we do—fish?"

"Not to-day," said Max, giving involuntarily a rub of one white leg against the other.

"Well, let's go and have a shot at something."

"I think I would rather not," pleaded Max, who looked with horror upon the idea of tramping the mountain side clothed as he was. "What do you say to a sail, then?"

Max shivered as he recalled his sensations upon the ride from the steamer; but there was a favourable side to such a trip—he could sit in the boat and have a railway wrapper about him.

"Where would you go if we sailed?"

"Oh, anywhere. Up the loch, over the firth, and through the sound. Over to Inchkie Island. We'll take the guns; we may get a shot at a hare, hawk, or an eagle."

Max nodded.

"That's right. Get down, Bruce! don't you get smelling his legs, or we shall have him bobbing off into the sea."

The great deerhound, who was approaching in a very suspicious manner, eyeing Max's thin legs, turned off, and, choosing a warm, smooth piece of rock, lay down.

"Off you go, Scood, and bring the boat round. Come on, Max, and let's get the guns. You can shoot, can't you?"

"I think so," said Max, as Scoodrach went off at a trot.

"You think so?"

"Yes. I never fired a gun, but the man showed me how to load and take aim, and it looks very easy."

"Oh yes, it looks very easy," said Kenneth dryly. "You just hold the gun to your shoulder and point at a bird. Then you pull the trigger, and down comes Dicky."

"Yes. I went to see men shoot pigeons after I had bought my gun. My father said I had better."

"Oh, he said you had better, did he?"

Max nodded.

"And he thought that would do as well as shooting pigeons, for they come expensive."

Kenneth laughed.

"Ah, well, we can give you something to shoot at here, without buying pigeons; but you'll have to mind: my father wouldn't like it if you were to shoot either me or Scood."

"Oh, I wouldn't do that!" cried Max. "It isn't likely."

"Glad of it," said Kenneth dryly. "Well, then, don't make a mistake and shoot one of the dogs. I'm sure they would not like it. Where's your gun?"

"In the case in my bedroom. Shall I fetch it?"

"Yes. Got any cartridges?"

"Oh yes, everything complete; the man saw to that."

"Look sharp, then," said Kenneth; and he had a hearty laugh as he saw his new companion go upstairs.

In spite of the admonition to look sharp, Max was some few minutes before he descended. For the first thing he saw on reaching his bedroom were his two pairs of trousers, neatly folded, and lying upon a chair.

The gun was forgotten for the minute, and it was not long before the kilt was exchanged for the southern costume in the form of tweeds, Max sighing with satisfaction as he once more felt quite warmly clad.

Kenneth laughed as Max reappeared with his gun and cartridge belt in his hand.

"Hallo!" he said; "soon tired of looking Scotch."

"I—I'm not used to it," said Max apologetically. "And never will be if you go on like that."

"But I found my own things in my room, and it did not seem right to keep on wearing yours."

"Wonder where they were?" said Kenneth dryly.

"I suppose the butler found them," said Max innocently.

Kenneth whistled, and looked rather peculiar, but his aspect was not noticed by his companion, who was experimenting on the best way to carry his gun.

"Loaded?"

"No, not yet."

"Then don't you load till I tell you. I'll give you plenty of time. Come along."

"Going for a sail, Maister Ken?" cried a voice; and Long Shon came waddling up, looking very red-faced and fierce.

"Yes, Shon, and we don't want you in the boat."

Long Shon grunted, and followed close behind.

"She could go instead of Scood."

"Yes, I know she could, but she isn't going," replied Kenneth, mimicking the man's speech. "What would Scood say if I left him behind?"

"She could show you an eagle's nest up the firth."

"So can Scood. He knows where it is!"

Long Shon pulled a battered brass box out of his pouch, and took a big pinch of snuff as he waddled behind.

"She knows where there's a raven's nest."

"That's what Scood told me this morning, Long Shon."

"But she tidn't know where there's a nest o' young blue hawks."

"Yes, I do, father," shouted Scood from the boat, in an ill-used tone, for they were now down on the rocks, and Scoodrach was paddling the boat in close.

"He wants me to turn you out, and take him instead, Scood. Shall I?"

"No!" said Scood undutifully.

"Petter tak' me, Maister Ken, and she can teach the young chentleman how to hantle his gun."

"Look here, Shon, the young chentleman knows how to hantle his gun. I don't want you, and I don't want your dogs. You, Sneeshing, come back."

The ugly little Scotch terrier had waited till Scoodrach came near, and then crept down among the rocks to a crevice where he could get quietly into the water without a splash, and was paddling to the side of the boat, looking like an otter swimming.

Sneeshing whined and made a snap at the water.

"Do you hear, sir? Come back!" cried Kenneth; but just then Scood leaned over the side, gripped the little dog by the loose skin at the back of his neck, and lifted him into the boat.

Sneeshing's first act was to run forward and give himself a tremendous shake to get rid of the water, and then he performed a sort of triumphant dance, and ended by placing his forepaws over the side, and barking at his fellows on the rock.

Bruce seemed to frown at him, showed his teeth, and then uttered a deep baying bark; but Dirk answered the challenge of his little companion by barking furiously, then running up and down upon the rocks for a few moments, watching the boat, as if calculating whether he could leap in; and ending by plunging into the sea with a tremendous splash.

"Come back, sir! Do you hear? come back!" shouted Kenneth, when Dirk raised his head from the water, and uttered a remonstrant bark, which seemed to say, —

"It isn't fair. You're letting him go."

"Hit him with an oar, Scood," cried Kenneth. "Here, you Dirk, come back, sir, or I'll pepper you!"

As he spoke, Kenneth raised the gun he carried and took aim at the dog, who threw up his head and uttered a piteous howl, but kept on swimming up and down beside the boat.

"Will you come out, sir?"

Dirk howled again.

Click! click! sounded the hammers, as Kenneth drew the triggers; and Dirk now burst forth into a loud barking.

"She says she knew it wasn't loated, Maister Ken," cried Long Shon, laughing; "she's a ferry cunning tog, is Dirk."

"Hi, Dirk! look here," cried Kenneth; and he threw open the breech of his gun and slipped in a couple of cartridges. "Now then, young fellow," he continued, "the gun's loaded now; so come back and stop ashore. You're not going."

"How-ow!"

Dirk's cry was very pitiful, and, whether he understood the fact of the gun being loaded or not, he turned and swam slowly ashore, climbed on the rock and stood dripping and disconsolate, without trying to scatter the water from his coat.

"You'd better learn to mind, sir, or—"

Kenneth gave the dog's ribs a bang with the gun barrel, and Dirk whined and crouched down, watching his master wistfully as he stepped off the rock into the boat, and then held out his hand to Max to follow.

"Mind what you're doing, Scood," cried Long Shon. "Ta wint's going to change."

Scood nodded, and began to hoist the sail; the wind caught it directly, and the boat moved swiftly through the water.

"You're not going near the Mare's Tail to-day, are you?" said Max anxiously, as Kenneth laid his gun across his knees.

"No, I wasn't going; but if you want to— Here, Scood, let's go and show him the Grey Mare's Tail again."

"No! No! No!" cried Max excitedly; "and pray don't go into any dangerous places."

He bit his lip with annoyance as soon as he had said the words, for he felt that it had made him seem cowardly in the eyes of his companions.

Scood grinned, and Kenneth said laughingly,—

"Oh, I thought you wanted to go there. We won't go into any danger. Would you like a lifebelt?"

"No!" said Max indignantly; and then to himself, "I wish there was one here."

"Tak' care, Maister Ken. Ta wint's going to change."

"All right."

"You, Scood, mind you ton't mak' fast ta sheet."

Max looked round for the sheet, but he did not see it; and concluded that it was the sail that was meant.

"I do wish people wouldn't treat us as if we were babies," said Kenneth angrily. "Just as if I didn't know how to sail a boat."

He jumped up suddenly, and shouted back, —

"Hi, Shon!"

"Ay, ay!"

"Pray take care of yourself."

"You tak' care o' yoursel', Maister Ken, and never mind me."

"Mind you don't catch cold."

"Eh?"

"Tie a handkerchief round your neck, and put your feet in warm water."

"What ye mean, Maister Ken?"

"Get Mother Cumstie to come and hold your hand, for fear you should fall off the rock."

"What ye talking aboot, sir?"

"Do be careful, Shon; there's a good man."

Long Shon stood on the rock, rubbing a great red, yellow-freckled ear; and then scratched one of his brawny cheeks, looking puzzled.

"Shall I send Scoody back, to lead you with a string?"

The distance was getting great now, and the man's voice sounded faint as he put his hands to his mouth to make a speaking-trumpet.

"She ton't know what you mean."

"Ha, ha, ha!" laughed Scood.

"Go and teach your grandmother how to suck eggs," roared Kenneth in the same way; but Shon shook his head, for he could not hear the words; and Kenneth sank down in the boat, and pressed the tiller a little to port, so as to alter the boat's course slightly. "Scood," he cried pettishly, "your father's a jolly old woman."

Scood, who was half leaning back, enjoying the fun of hearing his father bantered, suddenly started up in a stiff sitting position, and tore off his Tam o' Shanter, to throw it angrily in the bottom of the boat, as his yellow face grew redder, and he cried fiercely, —

"No, she isna an auld woman. My father's a ferry coot man."

"No, he isn't; he's a regular silly old cow."

"My father's a man, and a coot man, and a coot prave man, and never wass an auld woman."

"Get out, you old thick-head!" cried Kenneth.

"I ton't say my het isna a coot thick het, Maister Ken; but my father is as coot a man as The Mackhai hersel'."

"Oh, all right, then; Long Shon is a coot prave man, but his legs are too short."

"She canna help her legs peing short," said Scood, who was still ruffled; "put they're ferry coot legs—peautiful legs."

"Ha, ha!" laughed Kenneth.

"So they are," cried Scood. "They're not so long, put they're much pigger rount than the Chief's."

"Bother! Hear him bragging about his father's old legs, Max! Here, you come and take a lesson in steering," said Kenneth, making fast the sheet, an act which made Scoodrach growl a little. "I can't steer and shoot."

"Shall she tak' the tiller?" said Scood.

"No; you stop forward there, and trim the boat. Well, Sneeshing, can you see anything?"

The dog was standing on the thwart forward, resting his paws on the gunwale, and watching the flight of the gulls. At the sound of his master's voice, he uttered a low bark.

"Whee-ugh, whee-ugh!" cried a bird.

"Look, Max, there he goes out of shot."

"What is it?"

"A whaup."

Max followed the flight of the bird eagerly as it flew off toward the shore of a long, low green island on their left.

"Now then, catch hold."

"I'm afraid I don't know how to steer," said Max nervously.

"Oh, it's easy enough. Keep her head like that, and if she seems to be going over, run her right up into the wind."

"But I don't know how."

"Never mind that. Half the way to know how is to try—eh, Scood?"

"Yes; if she nivver tries, she can't nivver do nothing at all so well as she should," said Scood sententiously.

"Hear that, Max?" cried Kenneth, laughing. "Scood's our philosopher now, you know."

"Na, she isna a flossipher," grumbled Scood. "Put look, Maister Ken—seal!"

He sat perfectly still, gazing straight at some black rocks off a rocky islet.

"Where?—where?" cried Max eagerly. "I want to see a seal."

There was a soft, gliding motion on the black rock, and, almost without a splash, something round and soft and grey-looking plunged into the sea.

"You scared it away," said Kenneth.

"Oh, I am sorry!"

"Don't suppose the seal is; but I couldn't have hit it to do any harm with this gun."

The boat glided on, and all at once, from the water's edge about a hundred yards away, up rose, heavily and clumsily, a great flapping-winged bird.

"What's that?" cried Max, whose knowledge of birds save in books was principally confined to sparrows, poultry, and pigeons.

"Heron. Can't you see his beak?"

"Yes, and long neck. What a long thin tail!"

Scood chuckled.

"What's he laughing at?"

"You mind what you're doing; you'll have the boat over. Keep the tiller as I showed you."

Max hastily complied.

"That isn't his tail," continued Kenneth, watching the heron, which was far out of shot. "Those are his long thin legs stretched out behind to balance him as he flies."

Max said "Oh!" as he watched the bird, and came to the conclusion that he was being laughed at, but his attention was taken up directly after by a couple of birds rising from the golden-brown weedy shore they were gliding by—birds which he could see were black and white, and which flew off, uttering sharp, excited cries.

"What are those?"

"Pies."

"Pies?"

"Yes; not puddings."

"I mean magpies?"

"No; sea pies—oyster-catchers."

"Do they catch oysters?"

"Never saw one do it, but they eat the limpets like fun. Now then, sit fast. Here's a shot."

Max sat fast and shrinkingly, for he was not accustomed to a gun being fired close to his ears. He watched eagerly as a couple of birds flew toward them with outstretched necks and quickly beating, sharply-pointed wings, but they turned off as the gun was raised, and, though Kenneth fired, there was no result.

"Waste of a shot," he said, reloading.

"What were those?"

"Sheldrakes. How shy they are, Scood!"

Max thought it was enough to make them, but he did not say so, and he scanned the island as they sailed on, with the sensation of gliding over the beautiful sparkling water growing each moment more fascinating as his dread wore off. They were passing a glorious slope of shore, green and grey and yellow, and patched with black where some mass of shaley rock jutted out into the sea to be creamed with foam, while everywhere, as the tide laid them bare, the rocks were glistening with the golden-brown seaweed of different species. Blue sky, blue water, blue mountains in the distance: the scene was lovely, and the London boy's eyes brightened as he gazed with avidity at the ever-changing shore.

"Is that a castle?" he said, as a square ruined tower gradually came into sight at the point of the island.

"Yes; there are lots about," said Kenneth coolly. "There's another yonder."

He nodded in the direction of the mainland, so cut up into fiords that on a small scale it resembled the Norwegian coast, and, on shading his eyes, Max could see another mouldering pile of ruins similar in structure to Dunroe, with its square mass of masonry and four rounded towers at the corners.

"What castle is that?"

"Rannage. This one on the island is Turkree. Every chief used to have a place of that sort, and most of 'em built their castles on rocks like that sticking out into the sea."

Max gazed eagerly at the ruined towers, the homes of jackdaws, bats, and owls, and he was beginning to dream about the old times when men in armour and courtly ladies used to dwell in these sea-girt fortalices, but his reverie was broken in upon by a sharp snapping bark from Sneeshing, and an exclamation from Scood.

"Oh, you beauty!" exclaimed Kenneth, as he gazed up at a great strong-winged, hawk-like bird, which went sailing by. "See, Max. Blue hawk."

"Is that a blue hawk?" said Max, as he gazed wonderingly at the rapidity with which the great bird cut through the air.

"Yes; peregrine falcon, the books call it. There's a nest yonder where we're going."

"Where?"

"On the face of that great grey cliff that you can see under the sail."

Max gazed at the huge wall of rock about a mile away, and noted that the falcon was making for it as fast as its wings would beat.

"Are we going there?"

"Yes. I want the nest. I think there are young ones in it—late couple fledged."

The rocky cliff looked so stern and forbidding, that it seemed as if climbing would be impossible.

"Then we're going on to that rock on the other side—that tall crag. That's where the eagles build."

Max gazed hard at a faint blue mass of crag miles farther, and then turned half doubtingly to his companion.

"Eagles?" he said; "I thought there were none now."

"But there are. There's one pair build yonder every year, quite out of reach; but I mean to have a try for them some day. Eh, Scood?"

"Ou ay!" ejaculated the young gillie carelessly; "why no?"

"Are there any other wild things about?"

"Any wild things? plenty: badgers, and otters, and roe deer, and red deer. Look, there's one right off against the sky on that hill. See?"

"Yes," cried Max. "I can see that quite plainly."

"Tah!" ejaculated Scood scornfully; "it's a coo."

"You, Scood, do you want me to pitch you overboard?" cried Kenneth.

"Nae."

"Then hold your tongue."

"Ou ay, Maister Kenneth, only ton't tell the young chentleman lies. Look, Maister Max, there's the teer, four, five, sax of them, over yon. See?"

"Yes, I can see them; but are they really deer?"

"No," cried Kenneth; "they're bulls."

"They're not. Ton't you belief him. She can see quite plain. They're teer."

"If they were deer they'd bolt," cried Kenneth, shading his eyes; "they wouldn't stop there."

"There they go," cried Scood, as the graceful creatures trotted over the shoulder of a hill a mile or more away, all but one, which stood up against the sky, so that they could make out its great antlers.

"So they are," said Kenneth. "Why, Max, we must go after that fellow to-morrow. How is it they've come down here?"

"Been shot at somewhere else."

"Hadn't we better go back and get the rifles?"

"Noo? No; let's come to-morrow airly, and have a coot fair try."

"Perhaps that will be best," said Kenneth in assent, as the stag disappeared, and the boat sped on.

"But may you shoot stags?" said Max rather wonderingly.

"Of course, when they are on my father's part of the forest. That's his out there."

"Forest? Where?" asked Max wonderingly.

"Why, there."

"What, that place like a great common? There are no trees!"

"Ha, ha, ha!" laughed Scood. "Who ever heard of a forest with trees?"

"Hold your tongue, Scood, or I'll pitch you overboard."

"She's always talking spout pitching her overpoard, but she never does," muttered Scood.

"Our land runs right along there for three miles. Once upon a time The Mackhai's forest ran along for thirty miles."

"How is it that it does not now?"

"Father says the rascally lawyers—I beg your pardon. He was cross when he said that."

Kenneth hastily changed the subject, as he saw his companion's flushed countenance.

"I say, we'll come out here fishing one day. Like fishing for mackerel?"

"I never did fish for them."

"Oh, it's rare sport. We have a couple of rods out each side as we sail along, and catch plenty when there's a shoal. Looks high, doesn't it?"

"Yes," said Max, as the boat glided on over the calm heaving water till they were right under a great grey wall of crag, which towered above their heads, and cast clearly-cut reflections on the crystal water over which they rode.

"That's five hundred feet if it's an inch," said Kenneth, as he threw himself back and gazed up. "Look, Max."

"What at?"

"See those two black fellows on that ledge with their wings open?"

"Yes. What are they—blackbirds?"

"Black enough. Cormorants drying their plumage."

"But it hasn't been raining."

"No; but they've been diving, and got well wet. Why, they can swim under water like a fish."

"Go on, if you like telling travellers' tales," said Max, smiling.

"Well, of all the unbelieving old Jews! Just as if I was always trying to cram you! I tell you they do. So do the gannets and dookkers. They dive down, and swim wonderfully under water, and chase and catch the fish. They're obliged to."

"Look out! there she goes," cried Scoodrach.

Kenneth raised his gun, but the bird to which his attention was drawn was out of shot.

"That's the hen bird, Scood."

"Yes; and I can see where the nest is," cried the young gillie.

"Where?"

Kenneth laid his hand on Max's, which was upon the tiller, pressed it hard, and, to the lad's surprise, the boat glided round till she faced the wind, and then lay gently rising and falling, with the sail shivering slightly in the breeze.

"Yes, that's it, sure enough, on that ledge somewhere," said Kenneth, after a long stare up at the face of the grey crag. "See, Max?"

"No."

"Why, there, about fifty feet from the top. See now?"

"No."

"Oh, I say! where are your eyes? See that black split where the rock seems to go in?"

"Yes, I see that."

"Well, down a little way to the left, there's a— Oh, look at that!"

A great sharp-winged bird came over the cliff from landward, and was about to glide down to the shelf of rock, when, seeing the boat and its occupants, the bird uttered a piercing shriek, and swept away northward.

"That's the cock," cried Kenneth. "No mistake about the young ones, Scood. Now, then, how shall we get 'em?"

Scood was silent.

"Do you hear, stupid?"

"Ou ay, she can hear, Maister Ken."

"Well, how are we to get them?"

"Aw'm thinking," said Scood, as he stared up at the beetling crag, which was for the most part absolutely perpendicular.

"Hit him on the head with that oar, Max, and make him think more quickly."

"She couldna get up anywhere there," said Scood slowly, as he scanned every cranny of the cliff face.

"Oh yes, we could, Scood."

"Nay, Maister Ken, an' ye see, if we was to tummle, it wouldn't be into the watter, but on to the rocks."

"Oh, we shouldn't tumble. You could climb that, couldn't you, Max?"

"No, not without a ladder," replied Max thoughtfully; "and I never saw one long enough to reach up there."

"No, I should think not. Look here, Scoody, one of us has got to climb up and take those young ones."

"She couldna do it."

"You're afraid, Scoody."

"Na, she isna feared, but she couldna do it."

"Well, I shall try."

"No, don't; pray, don't! It looks so dangerous."

"Nonsense!"

"She couldna clamber up there fra the bottom," said Scoodrach slowly, "but she could clamber up it fra the top."

"No, you couldn't, stupid; it hangs over."

"An' we could tak' a rope."

"Come on, then," cried Kenneth, seizing the tiller; and Max felt his hands grow damp in the palms as he looked up at the top of the precipice, and saw in imagination one of his companions dangling from a rope.

"Which will be best—forward or backward?"

"Yonder where we landed to get the big corbies," said Scoodrach; and the boat was run on for about a quarter of a mile, to where a ravine ran right up into the land, looking as if a large wedge had been driven in to split the cliff asunder.

The boat was steered in, the sail lowered, and Scood immediately began to set free one of the ropes.

"Think that'll be strong enough, Scoody?"

"Na."

"Then why are you casting it loose?"

Scoodrach gave his companions a cunning look, and made the rope fast to a ring-bolt, and then leaped out and secured the other end to a mass of rock.

"That'll hold her," he said. "Unto the ither."

"Oh, I see what you mean now," cried Kenneth, unfastening the mooring-rope from the ring in the bows. "Yes, that'll do better."

"She'll holt twa laddies hanging on at aince," said Scoodrach. "Na, na, ton't to that."

"Why not?"

"Because she'll want ta crapnel."

"Scood, you're an old wonder!" cried Kenneth; "but you'll have to carry it."

"Ou ay, she'll carry her," said the lad coolly; and, getting on board again, he lifted and shouldered the little anchor, so that one of the flukes hung over his shoulder and the coil of rope on his arm.

"She's retty," he said.

"All right. Come on, Max, and we'll send you down first."

"Send me down first?" said Max, looking wildly from one to the other.

"To be sure. You can't fall; we'll tie the rope round you and let you down, and then you can turn round gently and get roasted in the sun."

Scood laughed.

"You're bantering me again," said Max, after a few moments.

"Ah, well, you'll see. Stop back if you're afraid."

"I'm not afraid," said Max firmly, but his white face spoke to the contrary. All the same, though, he drew a long breath, and jumped out of the boat to follow Scoodrach, who took the lead, tramping sturdily over the rough rocks of what proved to be a very stiff climb, the greater part of it being right down in the stony bed of a tiny torrent, which came gurgling from stone to stone, now dancing in the sunshine, and now completely hidden beneath the débris of ruddy granite, of which a dyke ran down to the sea.

"Hard work for the boots, Max, isn't it?" said Kenneth, laughing, as he came along behind, active as a goat, and with his gun on his shoulder.

"Yes," said Max, perspiring freely. "Isn't there a better path than this?"

"No; this is the best, and it's beautiful to-day. After rain this is a regular waterfall."

"Ou ay, there's a teal o' peautiful watter comes town here sometimes," said Scood.

They climbed on by patches of ragwort all golden stars, with the ladies' mantle of vivid green, with its dentate edge, neat folds, and pearly dewdrop in the centre, and by patches of delicate moss, with the pallid butterwort peeping, and by fern and club moss, heath and heather, and great patches of whortleberry and bog-myrtle, every turn and resting-place showing some lovely rock-garden dripping with pearly drops, and possessing far more attraction for Max than the quest upon which they were engaged.

"Ah, only wait till you've been here a month," cried Kenneth, "and your wind will be better than this."

"Don't you get as hot as I am with climbing?"

"I should think not, indeed. Why, Scood and I could almost run up here. Couldn't we, Scood?"

"Ou ay; she could run up and run town too."

"Is it much farther to the top?" said Max, after a few minutes' farther climb; and he seated himself upon a beautiful green cushion of moss, and then jumped up again, to the great delight of his companions, who roared with laughter as they saw a jet of water spurt out, and noted Max's look of dismay. For it was as if he had chosen for a seat some huge well-charged sponge.

"I—I did not know it was so wet."

"Moss generally is on the mountain," cried Kenneth. "You should sit down on a stone or a tuft of heath if you're tired. Try that."

"I'm so uncomfortably wet, thank you," replied Max, "I don't think I'll sit down."

"Oh, you'll soon dry up again. Let's go on, then. We're nearly up at the top."

Kenneth's "nearly up at the top" proved to be another twenty minutes' arduous climb, to a place where the water came trickling over a perpendicular wall of rock ten feet high, and this had to be scaled, Max being got to the top by Scood hauling and Kenneth giving him a "bump up," as he called it. Then there was another quarter of an hour's climb in and out along the steep gully, with the stones rattling down beneath their feet, and then they were out, not on the top, as Max expected, but only to see another pile of cliff away to his right, and again others beyond.

They had reached the top of the range of cliff, however, and away to their left lay the sea, while, as they walked on along the fairly level cliff, Max felt a peculiar shrinking sensation of insecurity, for only a few yards away was the edge, where the face fell down to the shore.

"Don't walk quite so near," he said nervously.

"Certainly not," said Kenneth politely. "Do you hear, Scoody? don't go so near. It's dangerous. Come this way."

As he spoke, he made his way, to Max's horror, close to the verge, and, with a grin of delight, the young gillie followed him, to climb every now and then on the top of some projecting block right over the brink, and so that had he dropped a stone it would have fallen sheer upon the rocks below.

Max felt a strange catching of the breath, and his eyes dilated and throat grew dry; when, seeing his suffering, Kenneth came more inward.

"Why, what are you afraid of?" he said, laughing. "We're used to it, and don't mind it any more than the sheep."

"Tut it looks so dreadful."

"Dreadful? Nonsense! See what the sailors do when they go up aloft, with the ship swaying about. It's quite solid here. Now, Scoody, aren't we far enough?"

"Na. It's just ahint that big stane where we shall gae doon."

"No, no; it's about here," said Kenneth; and, going to the edge, he looked over.

Scoodrach chuckled.

"Can ye see ta nest, Maister Ken?"

"No; I suppose you're right. There never was such an obstinate old humbug, Max; he's always right. It's his luck."

Scoodrach chuckled again, and went on about fifty yards to where a rough block of stone lay in their path, and as soon as they were by this, he went to the brink and looked down, bending over so much that Max shivered.

"There!" he cried, and Kenneth joined him, to look over as well, apparently at something beneath the projecting rock which was hard to see.

"Yes, here it is!" he cried, "Come and have a look, Max."

At that moment the party addressed felt as if he would like to cling to the nearest stone for an anchorage, to save himself from being blown off the cliff by some passing gust, and he stood still, staring at his companions on the brink.

"Well, why don't you come? You can just see where the nest lies—at least you can make out the bits of stick."

"I don't think I'll come, thank you," said Max.

"Nonsense! Do be a little more plucky."

"Yes," said Max, making an effort over himself; and he took a couple of steps forward, and then stopped.

"Well," cried Kenneth, "come along! There's no danger."

As he stood there, with his gun resting on the rock beside him, Max could not help envying his cool daring, and wishing he could be as brave.

But he could not, and, going down on hands and knees, he crept cautiously toward the brink, and then stopped and uttered a cry, for something made a leap at him.

It was only Sneeshing, who had been forgotten, and who had been enjoying himself with a quiet hunt all to himself among the heather. As he trotted up, he became aware of the fact that his young master's visitor was turning himself into a four-footed creature, and he leaped at him in a friendly burst of greeting.

"I—I thought somebody pushed me," gasped Max. "Call the dog away."

"Down, Sneeshing!" cried Kenneth, wiping his eyes. "Oh, I say, Max, you made me laugh so—I nearly went overboard."

Max gave him a pitiful look, and, from crawling on hands and knees, subsided to progression upon his breast as he came close to the edge of the rock and looked shudderingly down.

"See the nest?" said Kenneth, as he exchanged glances with Scoodrach.

"No, no. I can see a great shelf of stone a long, long way down," replied Max, shuddering, and feeling giddy as he gazed at the shore, which seemed to be a fearful distance below.

"Well, that's where the nest is, only right close in under the rock. Lean out farther—ever so far. Shall I sit on your legs?"

"No, no! don't touch me, please! I—I'll look out a little farther," cried Max, in alarm.

"D'ye think if ye teuk her legs, and she teuk her heat, we could pitch her richt oot into the sea, Maister Ken?" said Scoodrach, in a low, hoarse voice.

Max shot back from the edge, and sat up at a couple of yards' distance, looking inquiringly from one to the other, as if fearing some assault.

"You'll soon get used to the cliffs," said Kenneth. "I say, look, Scoody!"

He pointed out across the wide sea-loch, and Max could see that two sharp-winged birds were skimming along in the distance, and returning, as if in a great state of excitement about their nest.

"There they are, Max, the pair of them," said Kenneth.

"Isn't it cruel to take their nest, supposing you can get it?" said Max.

"Oh, very," replied Kenneth coolly. "We ought to leave it alone, and let the young hawks grow up and harry and strike down the grouse and eat the young clucks. Why, do you know how many birds those two murder a day?"

"No," said Max.

"Neither do I; but they do a lot of mischief, and the sooner their nest is taken the better."

"I did not think of that. They're such beautiful birds upon the wing, that it seems a pity to destroy them."

"Yes; but only let me get a chance. Why, if we were to let these things get ahead along with the eagles, they'd murder half the young birds and lambs in the country. Now, Scood, how's it to be?"

Scoodrach grunted, and kicked away the earth in different places, till he found where there was a good crevice between two pieces of rock, where, making use of the anchor as if it were a pickaxe, he dug out the earth till he could force down one fluke close between the stones till the stock was level, when he gave it a final stamp, and rose up.

"There," he said, "twenty poys could not pull that oot."

"Yes, that will bear, unless it jumps out," said Kenneth. "Look here, Max, will you go down first?"

"I? Oh no!"

"All right, you shall go down after. Now, mind, you've got to keep your foot on the grapnel here, so as it can't come out."

"But you surely will not go down, and trust to that?"

"Trust to that, and to you, my lad. So, mind, if you let the anchor fluke come out, down I shall go to the bottom; and I don't envy you the job of going to tell The Mackhai."

"Oh, Kenneth!"

"Fact I'm the only boy he has got."

"It is horrible!" panted Max, as Scoodrach advanced to the edge of the cliff and threw over the coil of rope, standing watching it as it uncurled rapidly ring by ring, till it hung taut.

Max saw it all in imagination, and the fine dew stood out upon his face as he pressed his foot with all his might down upon the anchor, and listened to and gazed at what followed.

"There she is," said Scoodrach. "Will ye gang first, Maister Ken, or shall I?"

"Oh, I'll go first, Scood. But how about the young birds? what shall I put them in?"

Scood hesitated for a moment, and then took off his Tam o' Shanter.

"Ye'll joost putt 'em in ta ponnet," he said.

"No, no, that won't do; they'd fall out."

Scood scratched his curly red head.

"Aweel!" he exclaimed; "she's cot a wee bit of string. Ye'll joost tak' it in yer sporran, and my twa stockings. Putt ane in each, and then tie 'em oop at the tops and hang 'em roond yer neck. Do ye see?"

"That will do capitally, Scood!" cried Kenneth, seizing the socks which the lad had stripped from his feet and thrusting them in his pocket. "Good-bye, Max."

"No, no! don't say good-bye! Don't go down!" panted Max, in spite of himself; and then he stood pressing wildly down on the anchor, for Kenneth had glided over the side, and, after hanging from the verge for a moment, he gave his head a nod, laughed at Max, and disappeared, with Scoodrach leaning down with his hands upon his knees watching him.

For a few moments Max closed his eyes, while the rope jarred and jerked, and the iron thrilled beneath his foot. Then all at once the jarring ceased, and the rope hung loose.

Max opened his eyes in horror, the idea being strong upon him that Kenneth had fallen. But his voice rose out of the depths beyond the edge.

"Ask him if he'd like to come down and see."

"No, no!" cried Max huskily; "I'd rather not."

"She says she shall not come," cried Scoodrach.

"Then let him stay where he is," came from below. "Come and have a look, Scood."

To Max's horror, the gillie went down on his knees, seized the rope, and passed over the edge; Max watching his grinning countenance as he lowered himself down, with first his chest and then his face disappearing, lastly the worsted tuft on the top of his Tam o' Shanter; and there was nothing to see but the pulsating rope, and the sea, sky, and blue mountains on the other side of the loch.

And now a strong desire to take his foot from the anchor, and creep to the edge of the cliff and look down, came over Max. He wanted to see Scoodrach descend to the shelf of rock and join Kenneth. He wanted, too, to look upon the falcon's nest; for, after seeing these two descend so bravely, by a sudden reaction he felt ashamed of his own nervousness, and was ready to show them that he was not so cowardly after all.

All this was momentary; and there the rope kept on vibrating and the anchor jarred as Scoodrach descended; while, as Max pressed the stock down, and it rose and fell like a spring beneath his foot, he kept his eyes fixed upon the edge of the cliff, where the rope seemed to end, when there was a dull twang, as if the string of some gigantic instrument had snapped, and, to his horror, the rope rose from the top of the cliff as if alive, and struck and coiled round him with a stinging pain.

Chapter Sixteen
A Brave Attempt

For a few moments Max Blande stood as if petrified, and those moments were like an hour, while the thought flashed through him of what must be going on below, where he seemed to see Kenneth gazing down in horror at the shapeless form of Scoodrach lying unrecognisable on the rocks below.

All feeling of dread on his own behalf was gone now; and, as soon as the first shock was over, he tore himself free of the snake-like rope, and stepped to the edge of the cliff, to gaze down with dilated eyes.

"Well, you've done it now!" saluted him as he strained over the edge to look below, where Kenneth, instead of looking down, was looking up, while Scood was lying on the shelf of rock, rubbing himself with a hand that was bleeding freely.

"Is—is he killed?" faltered Max, whose lips formed the question he had been about to ask before he saw the gillie lying there.

"Do you hear, Scood? Are you killed?" said Kenneth coolly.

"Is she kilt? Na, she isna kilt," cried Scoodrach, with a savage snarl, which was answered by a furious fit of barking from the terrier, as he too looked down. "Hech, but this is the hartest stane! She's gien hersel' a dreadful ding."

"Then you are both safe?" cried Max joyfully.

"Oh yes, quite safe, Max. Locked up tight. Did you cut the rope?"

"Cut the rope? No, I didn't touch it. Why did it break?"

"I say, Scoody, why did the rope break?"

"Oh, she's a pad rotten old rope, an' she'll burn her as soon as she gets up again. But what a ding I gave my airm!"

"That's it, Max; the rope was rotten. Can you tie it together if we throw it up to you?"

"Na," shouted Scoodrach; "she couldna tie it together, and she couldna throw it up."

"I'm afraid I couldn't tie it tight enough," faltered Max; "but if I could, it would not bear you."

"It would have to bear us. We can't stop down here. I say, Scoody, think we could climb up?"

Scoodrach shook his head.

"Well, then, can we get down?"

"If she could get up or doon without a rope, the hawks wouldn't have built their nest."

"That sounds like good logic, Max," cried Kenneth, "so you had better let yourself over till you can hang by your hands, and then drop, and we'll catch you."

"What?"

"You wouldn't hurt yourself so much as Scoody did, because we can both help you. He nearly went right over, and dragged me with him."

"Oh!" ejaculated Max, with a shudder.

"Well, are you coming?"

"No! Impossible! What for?"

"To keep us company for a week or two, till somebody sees us. Hallo, Sneeshing! Good dog, then! Come down, we want you. Hooray, Scoody! dog for dinner! enough for three days. Then the young falcons will do for another day. Well, are you coming?"

"Oh, Kenneth," cried Max, "you're making fun again. What shall we do?"

"You mean, what shall we do? You're all right. But you had better lower down the gun, and then I can shoot Scoody decently, when Sneeshing and the young hawks are done!"

"Oh, pray be serious!"

"I am. It's a serious position. We mustn't trust the rope again—eh, Scoody?"

"Na! Oh, what a ding she gave her airm!"

"Bother your arm!" cried Kenneth. "Here, Max, what's to be done?"

"I'll run back and tell them at Dunroe."

"Ah, to be sure, that's the way! but I didn't know you could run across the loch."

Max's jaw dropped, and he gave his companions a helpless stare.

"I forgot the loch," he said. "What shall I do? Where's the nearest house?"

"Across the loch."

"Are there none this side?"

"There's a keeper's lodge ten miles away, on the other side of the mountain."

"I'll run all the way there!" cried Max eagerly. "Tell me the way."

"Well, you go right north, straight over the mountain, and whenever you come to a bog, you stick in it. Then you lose your way every now and then, and get benighted, and there you are."

"You're laughing at me again," cried Max in agony; "and I want to help you."

"Well, I want you to help us, old chap, for we're in a regular mess, and perhaps the hawks'll come and pick our eyes out to feed the young ones."

"There, now, you're laughing at me again!" cried Max. "I can't help being so ignorant of your ways."

"Of course you can't, Maxy. Well, look here, old chap, you can't get over the mountain without some one to show you the way."

"Na; she'd lose hersel'," cried Scoodrach. "Oh, what a ding she did give—"

"Bother your old airm, Scoody! do be quiet. Look here, Max: now, seriously, unless a yacht comes by, there's no chance of help, and just because we want a yacht to come by, there won't be one for a week."

"Then what shall I do?"

"Well, there's only one thing you can do."

"Yes? quick, tell me!"

"Go down to the boat and hoist the sail, and run back to Dunroe."

"But I couldn't manage her."

"All right, then. Let's all set to work and make our wills before we're starved to death. No, I tell you what: you've got the gun; you'll have to go shooting, and drop the birds over to us. You're a good shot, aren't you?"

Max was silent.

"Well, why don't you speak? Look here, take the gun and shoot a hare. You'll find one somewhere. Got any matches?"

"Yes, I have a little silver box of wax-lights."

"That's your sort! Then you can light a fire of heath and peat, and cook it, and drop it down, and we can eat it."

"But, as Mrs Glasse said in her cookery-book, 'First catch your hare.'"

"Why, you don't mean to say you couldn't shoot a hare?" cried Kenneth.

"She couldna shoot a hare," grumbled Scoodrach, rubbing his arm; and then, after looking very thoughtful and nervous, Max spoke out.

"I am going down to the boat," he said quietly; "and I shall try and set the sail, and go back to Dunroe."

"Bravo! hooray!" cried Kenneth. "That's your sort; only the wind isn't quite right, and you'll have to tack."

"To tack what—the sail?"

"No, no, I don't mean nail the sail to the mast."

"Oh, I remember; go backwards and forwards with the boat."

"There, Scoody!" cried Kenneth triumphantly; "I only wish you had got as much brains in your old red head as he has."

"Ret's a ferry coot colour for a het," grumbled Scoodrach, who was very sore, and who kept on gently rubbing the spot where he had given himself "such a ding."

"Good-bye!" cried Max. "I'll get back as soon as I can."

"That's right. Don't go to my father. Tell old Tavish and Long Shon, and they're to bring a strong rope."

"Yes; I won't forget."

"And steer with one hand, and hold the sheet in the other," cried Kenneth. "Don't do as I did. Good-bye, old chap; you're not a bad fellow after all."

"Oh, if I was only as strong and as clever as they are!" said Max to himself. "Well, what is it?"

This was to Sneeshing, who stood barking at him sharply, and then ran back to crouch on the edge of the precipice, where he could peer down at his master and at Scoodrach, who was still chafing his arm.

Max half wondered at himself, as, in his excitement, he slid and scrambled down the steep gully, getting over places and making bounds which he dared not have attempted half an hour earlier. The consequence was that he got down to the shore in a way which surprised himself, and then scrambled over the debris of fallen rocks to where the rope secured the boat to the stone.

It was no easy task to undo Scood's knot, but he worked at it, and, as he did so, wondered whether it was possible to make use of the cordage of the boat to take up and let down to the imprisoned pair, but he was fain to confess that, even doubled, there was nothing sufficiently trustworthy for the purpose; and, after throwing in the line, he gave the boat a good thrust as he leaped aboard, and then, as it glided out, found himself in a position which made his heart beat, as he wondered whether he would ever get safe to land.

Trying to recall the action of Scoodrach at starting, he seized the rope and began to haul upon the yard, to find, to his great delight, that it rose steadily and well, the line running quite easily through the block till the gaff was pretty well in its place, and the sail gave a flap which startled him and made the boat careen.

Then he stopped short, hardly knowing what to do next, but the right idea came, and he made the rope fast, crept back cautiously over the thwart to seat himself by the tiller, and, almost to his wonder, found that the boat was running easily along.

Taking the handle of the tiller and the sheet, he drew a breath of relief, for the whole business was easier than he expected, and already he was fifty yards from the face of the cliff, and gaining speed, when he heard a hail.

"Max! Ahoy!"

He looked sharply round and up, to see Kenneth waving his glengarry; and his next words sounded faint in the great space:

"Starboard! starboard! Going wrong."

To put his helm to starboard was so much Arabic to Max, but he had turned the handle in one direction, and he was going wrong, so he felt that to turn it the other way must be right. Pressing hard, then, he found that what he did had the effect of turning the boat half round, and making it go more slowly and diagonally in the direction from which the wind blew, and somewhat more toward the shelf where his friends were imprisoned, so that he could see them waving their caps, as moment by moment they seemed more distant.

And now, for the first time, as he caught sight of a pile of ruins far away to his right, he realised that he had been going away from Dunroe, which lay to the south, while now he was sailing south-east; and his spirits rose as he felt that he must be right in trying to reach that castle, which he remembered as being one that Kenneth had pointed out.

He turned his head again in the direction of the shelf, and there, high up, were the two boys, still waving their caps, either by way of encouragement or to try and give him advice by signs. But he could not tell which, neither could he signal in turn, for both hands were full; so, setting his teeth, and with a wonderful feeling of exhilaration and excitement, at which he was surprised, he devoted himself to his task.

Chapter Seventeen
A Terrible Journey

Bailing a boat is like most other things, it has to be learned, and it is a puzzling thing to grasp the meaning of the way in which it seems to act.

To sit and hold the rudder and go right away with the wind dead astern is not so difficult, but to try and sail a boat with the wind almost in your teeth, is, at the first time of asking, rather a strain upon the unaccustomed mind. The first thing which Max discovered was that, as soon as the sail was up, the boat seemed to try to take, so to speak, the bit in its teeth and run off to the north; the next, that he held in the tiller whip, spur, reins, everything for governing this strangely-mobile creature, and at the hint from Kenneth he had changed its course.

But now, as it could not go north, the boat seemed to be trying to go due east, and, with the sail well filled and careening over, she literally rushed through the water, which sparkled in her wake.

"But he said I must tack," thought Max. "Why not try and sail straight away?"

He tried to do this by turning the tiller more and more, but as he did so the speed of the boat grew less and less, and finally she stood still, with the sail shivering, and when he gave the sheet a shake, the sail gradually filled on the other side; the boat's head swung round, and he found that he was rushing due west, straight for the cliff upon which Kenneth and Scoodrach were watching his course.

For a few moments Max lost his head—metaphorically, of course, and not Carlistically. He sat, tiller in hand, gazing aghast at the great wall of rock with the rugged *débris* of fallen masses at the bottom, upon which in a very few minutes the boat would rush with a sharp crash, and then, mistily and in a chaotic manner, he realised that there would be a miniature wreck, similar on a small scale to those of which he had so often read in the papers.

"What shall I do?" he gasped; and he gazed away to the right, at where he could see the two boys upon their shelf, too far away for their voices to be heard.

There was no help or advice to be had, so he was thrown back upon his own brain for the very best help there is in the world—self-help; and, making a bold grasp, as it was hovering in a mist, he caught his lost head again, and held it tightly.

As he did this, he recalled that he held the guiding principle of the boat in his hand, pressed the tiller hard, and, to his great delight, the little vessel made a beautiful curve, ran right up in the wind, the sail flapped and shivered, there came a puff of wind that seemed to be reflected from the tall cliff, the sail filled on the other side, the boat careened over, and away he was rushing right merrily again.

It was none too soon, for, as the boat curved round, he was within forty yards of some black rocks, whose weed-hung heads were just level with the water.

But in those few minutes he had gained one splendid bit of experience in the management of a boat, namely, that he had but to keep his head and be cool, and then he could guide the craft wherever he pleased.

His spirits rose at this, as the little vessel glided rapidly on, now toward the west, and he knew that when he was close to the far side of the loch he had but to reverse the action with the rudder, and turn and come back.

There was a beautiful breeze, and he span along, his face flushed, eyes sparkling, and his heart beating fast with excitement. It was most enjoyable. He could manage the boat,—so he thought,—but by degrees he began to grasp the fact that if he kept on he would be going to and fro over the same water, and he wanted to go due south, and not east and west.

Then came back what Kenneth had said about tacking, and by degrees he more fully mastered what he had to learn, namely, that he must use the rudder, and force the boat to go south-east instead of east, and, in returning, south-west instead of west, so as to cross and recross the loch diagonally, or in a zigzag course, so that at each tack he would be farther south.

To his great delight, he found, by keeping a firm hand upon the rudder, he could do this, but it proved to be such slow work that he began to experimentalise a little more, and, instead of sailing south-east and south-west, he contrived to keep the boat's head so that he sailed south-south-east and south-south-west. Later on, when with the two lads, and Scoodrach at the tiller, he found that, had he known, he could have made more southing each tack, for the little boat could sail wonderfully close to the wind.

It was still slow work to one who was effervescing with eagerness to reach Dunroe and obtain help, and over and over again, as the distance seemed so long, Max shivered with dread lest he should have overshot the mark and passed the place.

It seemed impossible that they could have gone so far. But no; there was the castle which they had passed on the right, and there was the other that they had glided by on the left—now, of course, with the positions reversed. So, gaining confidence, and feeling wonderfully self-satisfied at the way he could sail a boat, he sped on.

Fortunately for him, the breeze was just perfect and as steady as could be, and he knew nothing of the risks to which he was exposed. He sailed on by narrow gorge and ravine—openings in the great hills—in profound ignorance of the fact that through any of these a violent squall of wind might come with a whistle and shriek, catch the sail and lay it flat upon the water, while the boat filled and went down.

Then, too, he was happily ignorant of the sets of the tide and the wild currents which raced through some of the channels, and of the hundreds of rocks which lay below the surface, ready to catch the keel or rip open the thin planks of a boat.

Max saw none of these dangers,—he did not even dream of them,—but sat with flushed face, gazing onward, as he skimmed in exhilarating motion over the sunny sea.

"I do like sailing," he said to himself, in spite of the hand which held the sheet, at which the sail snatched and tugged, beginning to ache, and the other which grasped the rudder feeling numb. For the moment, too, he forgot that the sun did not always shine, and that the sea rose angrily, and that there were such things as storms.

All went quite smoothly, however, for about three parts of the distance, when all at once a peculiar washing sound reached his ears; and, gazing in the direction from which it came, he became aware of the fact that there was some water in the bottom of the boat, gliding here and there as the little vessel gave to the pressure of the wind.

He paid no heed to it at first, only thinking that the boat must be a little leaky, and knowing that he ought by rights to seek forward a little tin can and bale the water out.

But the management of the sail and rudder fully occupied him till he made the next tack, when it struck him that the quantity of water had certainly increased, as it ran over to the other side.

But still it caused him no uneasiness. He only felt that before long he might have wet feet, and he kept on looking out ahead for Dunroe.

At the next tack, there was undoubtedly a good deal more water, and the bottom boards of the boat kept rising, one going so far as to set sail on a little voyage of its own, and floating about.

What was to be done?—to throw the boat up in the wind, and stop and bale, or to sail on as fast as he could, and get to Dunroe?

Thinking that the water did not much matter, he kept on sailing tack after tack, till the water increased so much that it brought with it a chill of horror as well as cold; for there could be no mistake in the fact that the weight of water in the boat interfered largely with its progress, and Max felt that if he delayed baling much longer she might fill and sink.

He hesitated for a moment or two, and then tried to turn the boat's head so as to meet the wind. In this he succeeded, and, as the sail shivered and flapped, he looked for the tin baler. This he did not find, because in his excitement he forgot to look in the right place, so in his flurry he took off his cap and set to work with that, dipping and pouring the water over the side. A tiring job at the best of times, and with proper implements; wearisome in the extreme with no better baler than a cap; but Max made up in perseverance what was wanting in skill, and before very long he had satisfied himself, by comparison with some paint-marks, that the water was not gaining.

At the same time he did not feel that he was reducing it much; and the difficulty stared him in the face that he could not keep on baling and make progress too.

Taking out his knife, he made a scratch at the level of the water, and, once more taking the helm, the boat gracefully bent over and sped on.

The journey now grew tediously laborious. The afternoon was passing, and it seemed to Max that he would never reach Dunroe; for at every tack he paused to examine his mark, and found that the water had gained, so that he was compelled to stop and bale once more.

He looked for the leak, but it was invisible. All he could make out was that it must be somewhere under the boards laid in the bottom of the boat.

For quite a couple of hours did this go on, with the water still increasing, and Dunroe appeared to be as far off as ever; while the lad's task was Sisyphean, since, as fast as he baled the water out, it seemed to return.

There was something else, too, for him to combat. At first he had worked with plenty of spirit, but after many repetitions of the task a deadly sense of fatigue began to grow upon him, and as it affected his body, so it did his mind, till it seemed as if a great black cloud were appearing. Despair rode upon that cloud, and, as he worked, his face burned, but his heart chilled, and in imagination he saw himself sinking helplessly, when his arms should fall down to his sides, and he could do no more.

The result was that he baled with less effect, and instead of keeping the water under, it began to master him; and he found at last, that, in spite of all his efforts, his knife-mark was covered, and the water kept inches above, and still increased.

Chapter Eighteen
How Max fetched Help

Max Blande's confidence was on the ebb. Fortunately for him, the tide was on the ebb as well, and, though he was not aware of the fact, helping him on his journey.

As the confidence failed, despair's black cloud grew heavy. The idea that the leak was growing bigger became stronger, and with it was the feeling that before long the water would come in with a rush, and down he would go.

It was very horrible; and, as he asked himself what he must do, he clutched at the first idea suggesting escape which came, and that was, that, much as he regretted being unable to get help for his two companions in misfortune, he must save his own life, and the only way to do that was by running the boat ashore. Which side of the loch should he take—west or east?

Dunroe was on the east side, but the west coast was nearer, and he steered for that; but, feeling that this was cowardly, since he might get ashore and manage to walk to Dunroe, he altered his course, after a struggle with self, and sat with beating heart, slowly sailing on, with the water rising and washing about his legs.

That last tack seemed as if it would never end, and it was only by leaning sideways from time to time that he could catch sight of the coast he was approaching, the sail shutting off the greater part of his view.

To his dismay, he could see nothing but rocks, rocks everywhere, grey, and black, and ruddy golden with the weeds. The sea, too, foamed and danced about them. No cove floored with silver sand, no smooth river into which he could glide; and he shivered as he felt, by anticipation, the crash of the boat running on to the rocks at speed, throwing him out, and the retiring waves bearing him away, and then?

It was too horrible. But there were the rocks; he was getting nearer and nearer. He could hear the splashing of the water, and he must be ready to make a bold leap on to the nearest before the waves could catch him, and then he might escape.

Nearer and nearer; and it seemed a desperate thing to do—to run that boat ashore, but it was his only chance, for she was sinking fast, he was sure.

Nearer and nearer. A few more minutes, and he would be ashore, and—

He suddenly wrenched the tiller round, the boat ran up into the wind, careened over, and bore away on the other tack.

From Max Blande's cowardice?

No; the sail had sprung aside for a moment, as his doubting hand had given way a little, slightly altering his course; and, as he gazed wildly ahead, there, half covered by the swelling canvas, and not a quarter of a mile away, the old castle of Dunroe towered up on its bold base of storm-beaten rock.

"Will the boat float long enough for me to get there?" Max asked himself.

He decided to try, and now came the most difficult part of the steering he had encountered that day, and it was not until he had made three or four attempts that he lowered the sail, about fifty yards from the rocky natural pier from which they had started, and, to his great delight, saw Long Shon and Tavish watching him, and, after a consultation, run round to the little bay, out of which they came rowing in a dinghy.

"Wha's ta young maister?" cried Tavish fiercely.

"Wha's Scood?" cried Long Shon.

Max hurriedly explained.

"Ma cootness!" exclaimed Tavish; "she tought they was poth trooned."

"Why, ta poat's full o' watter!" cried Long Shon.

"Yes; she is leaking and sinking fast."

"Ma cootness!" cried Tavish, getting in, to Max's horror.

"Don't! you'll sink her. Let me get out."

"Na, na. Why tidn't you bale ta watter oot?"

"I did, but it was no use."

Tavish gave a snort, opened the locker in the bows, and then began to toss out the water like a jerky cascade, Max watching him wildly, but, to his great relief, seeing the water begin gradually to sink.

"She's knockit a creat hole in her pottom," said Long Shon. "Tit she hit on ta rocks?"

"No, no; it came on all of a sudden."

"Why, she's cot ta cork oot!" cried Tavish, drawing his sleeve up above his elbow, and thrusting his arm down to lift one of the bottom boards beneath the centre thwart, and feeling about for a few moments before turning reproachfully to Max.

"She shouldna pull oot ta cork."

"No," said Long Shon. "She pulls oot ta cork to let ta watter oot. She's pulled oot ta cork to let ta watter in."

Tavish growled as he recommenced baling, and then smiled at Max.

"I did not touch it. I did not know there was a cork," said the latter rather piteously.

"Then she must ha' come out hersel'," said Tavish. "Ye'll know next time what to do."

"And she sailed pack all py herself?" said Long Shon.

"Yes. But do make haste. They will think me so long."

"Let's ket the watter oot," said Tavish. "You, Shon, ket the rope oot o' the poat-hoose; or shall she leave ta poys till to-morrow?"

"What! leave them all night?" cried Max in horror.

The great forester chuckled as he looked up at Max, and kept on baling away, while Long Shon rowed ashore.

"Na; she'll go ant fetch 'em. So ta crapnel line proke?"

"Yes."

"She must ha' peen ferry pad."

"Yes, of course," said Max, who sat there contentedly enough, but vexed as he found how his ignorance of a boat had caused him a couple of hours' terror.

Tavish toiled away with the baler till it would scoop up no more, and then, taking a great sponge from the locker, he sopped up and squeezed till the bottom of the boat was quite clear of water, and by this time, close down by the keel, Max had seen an ordinary wine-cork, with a piece of whipcord attached to it, stuck upright in the hole used for draining the boat when she was ashore.

Then the bottom boards were replaced, and the forester passed an oar over the side, so as to paddle the boat up to the rock where Long Shon was waiting, with a ring of new-looking rope over his arm.

"Wha's ta Chief?" said Long Shon, as they came alongside.

"Gane over ta hill."

"With his gun?"

"Na; reading a pit latter."

"Ta Mackhai gane walking with a pit latter!" said Long Shon. "What's coming to ta man?"

Tavish shook his head, and looked serious. Then Long Shon stepped in, and the boat was thrust off.

"She'll pe ferry ancry when she finds we're gane," said the forester slowly. "Put we must go and fetch ta young Chief."

"Ant tit she ever sail a poat in the lochs in Lonton?" asked Long Shon, as the boat sped away rapidly, with the wind nearly dead astern.

"There are no lochs in London," replied Max, smiling.

"Nae lochs!" exclaimed the two Highlanders in a breath.

"No."

"Why, she thought Lonton wass a ferry fine place."

"So it is; full of great streets and shops."

"There's ferry coot shops i' Stirling," said Long Shon proudly, "and so there is in Oban. She'll pe pound there's no petter shops in Lonton than there is in Oban. Put no lochs?"

"No."

"I ton't think she shall think much coot o' Lonton, Tavish," said Long Shon rather scornfully.

"Put she shall have sailed a poat pefore?" said Tavish, staring hard at Max.

"No, never. I was never in a boat alone before."

"She will never pe in a poat alone pefore!" said the forester. "Wonterful!"

Long Shon looked as if he did not believe it.

"Wonterful! It was wonterful!" said Tavish again. "She will come town here, and kill ta biggest fush; and she sails ta poat alone, and she shall kill a stag soon, and all ta hares and grouse."

"Why wass she not town py ta blue hawk's nest wi' ta poys?" said Long Shon suddenly and fiercely.

"I was holding the anchor," replied Max.

"She wass holting ta anchor, Shon. She tolt her pefore."

"Put she ought to have peen wi' ta poys!" cried Long Shon, giving the side of the boat a slap with his great hand. "She wass afraid."

"Yes," said Max, flushing slightly, "I was afraid to go down. They did want me to go."

"Put ta poy Scoodrach wass never afraid," cried Long Shon, looking hard at Max as if he had ill-used him.

"Waugh!" ejaculated Tavish slowly, his voice sounding like the low, deep growl of some wild beast.

"Ta Scoodrach wass never pe afraid," cried Long Shon defiantly.

"Waugh!" growled Tavish more loudly and deeply than before.

"Ta Scoodrach wass never pe afraid," cried Long Shon, striking the gunwale of the boat again, and his face flushed with anger.

"Waugh!" roared Tavish; and the great forester's beard seemed to bristle as he burst out into an angry speech in Gaelic, to which Long Shon kept on edging in a word or two in the same tongue, but only with the effect of making Tavish roar more loudly, till Long Shon seemed to give in, completely mastered by his big companion.

What was said was a mystery to Max, but it sounded to him as if the big forester was taking his part, and crushing down Long Shon till the latter gave in, when Tavish's face cleared, and his eyes smiled at Max, as he said, —

"She shall not do like Maister Ken and Scoodrach, or ta poat could not come and say they are on the crag."

"No, of course not," said Max confusedly, for he could hardly follow the great fellow's meaning.

Then, in comparative peace, the boat skimming rapidly over the smooth sea, they sped on, with Max wondering that the ride could be so different now that there was no danger, and he had the companionship of two strong men. But all the same he could not help feeling something like regret that he was no longer the crew and in full charge. He felt something like pride, too, in his exploit, and the day's adventure had done more than he knew towards planting him in the high road to manhood.

The castles were passed in what seemed a wonderfully short time, and the great wall of cliff loomed up on their left, but they had a long way to sail before Max suddenly exclaimed, —

"I see them! Look! Kenneth is waving his cap."

"Na; it shall pe ta Scoodrach wi' her ponnet."

Tavish uttered another low, menacing growl of a very leonine nature, and his eyes were flashing, but they softened into a smile as they encountered those of Max.

A little while after, with the two boys on high cheering them as they passed, the boat was run into the little nook and fastened, Tavish taking the ring of rope and leaping ashore, followed by Max and Long Shon, who got over the rough rocks and up the gully in a wonderful way, hopping on to stones and off again—stones which Tavish took in one of his great strides and with the greatest ease.

It was almost marvellous to Max to see the way in which the great forester made his way up the gully, so that he would have been at the top in half the time if he had not kept stopping to reach down his hand to the lad, who was at various places compelled to climb on all-fours.

"She'll do muckle petter soon," he said, smiling. "Ta legs sail ket harter. Hey, but it's a sair pity she does not wear ta kilt!"

"She hasna got ta legs for ta kilt," grumbled Long Shon, who was behind; and Max partly caught his words, and felt a curious sensation of annoyance at the disparaging remark.

Five minutes later they were on the top, when Tavish went straight to the spot where the little anchor was forced in between the rocks, picked up the broken rope, and threw it down again, before stepping to the edge of the cliff and bending over.

"She shouldna troost to a pit o' line like that."

"How did I know it was going to break?" shouted Kenneth. "It bore me right enough. It was old Scoody here who was so heavy."

"Ta rope wasna fit to bear a dog," grumbled Scoodrach. "Hech! she shall break ta rope wi' Sneeshing."

The dog, which had been ready to jump up and greet the new-comers, ran at this, and looked down, and barked at the speaker, as if disputing his remark.

"You are going to fasten the line to the anchor, aren't you?" said Max.

"Na," growled Tavish. "She sail come up wi'out ta grapnel."

He threw the coil of rope on the grass, took the end, and made a loop thereon before lowering it down.

"But you cannot bear him alone?"

"The two," said Tavish coolly, as he threw the coil back now out of his way.

"Retty?" he cried.

"Yes, all right!" shouted Kenneth; and, standing there at the very brink of the terrible precipice, Tavish bent down, and drew up the rope hand over hand till Scoodrach's head appeared, and then the lad reached out, caught at Tavish's arm, and swung easily on to the top of the cliff, when the rope was lowered again, and directly after drawn up till Kenneth's head appeared, and he too swung himself on to the top, and stood laughing at Max, whose hands were uncomfortably damp.

"Here we are!" he cried. "Thank ye, Tavvy. Why, where are the hawks, Scood?"

"She prought 'em up herself."

"No, I didn't. I left them for you to bring."

"She never told her to bring ta birds," grumbled Scoodrach, in an ill-used tone.

"I believe you went to sleep. I've a jolly good mind to pitch you overboard."

"She's always saying she'll pitch her overpoard."

"There, come along down," said Long Shon.

"No, I'm not going without my birds, Shonny," cried Kenneth. "Here, Scood, go down and fetch 'em. No; if I send you down, you'll go to sleep again, and forget them. Here, Tavvy, give us hold of the rope."

"She isna going town gain," remonstrated the great Highlander.

"Oh yes, she is."

"No, no, pray don't venture again!" whispered Max.

"What! and leave those two poor birds to starve? Not I. Here, Tav, hold tight."

The great forester stood by while Kenneth threw over some fifty feet of the rope, and then stood smiling grimly, while, in defiance of all advice, and trusting utterly to the strength of the gillie's arms, Kenneth seized the rope, and let himself glide over the edge of the rock, dropping out of sight directly, while Max held his breath, as he saw the quivering of the forester's arms as Kenneth slipped down.

Then the movement ceased, and Max exclaimed excitedly, —

"Is he down safely?"

"Ou ay! she's all right," replied Tavish, as he gazed calmly down. "Come and look."

Max shook his head. He had had shocks enough to his nerves that day, and could bear no more.

Long Shon, however, went to the edge, and stood looking down with a grim smile. Sneeshing did the same, and barked; while Scoodrach threw himself down, and lay on the edge of the cliff looking over.

"Haul away!" came from below, and Tavish drew up a pair of coarse worsted stockings knotted together and tied to the rope.

These were set at liberty, and, as they were placed upon a rock, there was a good deal of shuffling and movement inside, the occupants of the stockings trying first to ascend the legs, and then travelling back toward the toes, and remaining quiescent till there was the shadow cast by a bird, as it darted overhead, and a shrill cry, which seemed to set the young birds in a state of great excitement.

"Oh, if I'd been up there!" shouted Kenneth from below. "What a chance for a shot!"

"Retty, Maister Ken?"

"Yes; haul away."

"Now, Scood, hang on, and heave her up," cried Tavish.

"She could choost pull her up wi' ane han'," said Long Shon scornfully.

"Ay, but she's a wunnerfu' man," said the forester coolly, and he half closed his eyes, and then passed the rope through his hands as Scood took hold and walked inward, as if he had harnessed himself, Sneeshing walking by his side, and seeming to take the deepest interest in all that was going on.

A minute more, and Tavish had swung Kenneth on to the cliff, the birds were given to Scoodrach to carry, and the party descended the gully, laughing heartily at the adventure, which was talked over from all sides, and Max questioned and criticised about his sailing the boat, till they had reached within a tack of Dunroe, when Tavish said, in his broad dialect, and with one of his pleasant looks,—

"She mustn't mind what ta young Chief says. She sailed ta poat peautifully, only ta next tune she mustna pull oot ta cork."

"Eh, pull out the cork!" cried Kenneth sharply. "Why, you haven't been at the whisky, Max? No; there was none on board."

"Na, na," cried Tavish, "ta cork plug. She sailt in wi' ta watter nearly up to her knees."

"Ay," said Long Shon, gazing down at Max's still wet trouser legs; "an' aw'm thinking it shows ta creat ignorance o' ta Southron folk, to baggie up her legs like tat, when a man might wear a kilt and niver get her legs wet at all."

"All right, Shonny. Mr Max is going to have one, with a plaid that'll make your eyes ache. Now, Scoody, jump out, and take care of those hawks. Hooray, Max! just in time. There goes the gong."

Chapter Nineteen
How Kenneth was too Rash

Five days had passed—days of imprisonment, for one of the storms prophesied had come over the ocean from the far west, and there had been nothing to do but read, play chess and billiards, write letters, and—most interesting amusement of all to the London visitor—get up to an open window and watch the great dark waves come rolling in, to break with a noise like thunder, and deluge the rock with foam right up to the castle walls. Every now and then a huge roller would dash right into the bath cave, when there would be quite an explosion, and Max listened with a feeling of awe to the escape of the confined air, and wondered whether it would be possible for the place to be undermined, and the whole rock swept away.

"What!" cried Kenneth, when he broached the idea. "Nonsense! It has gone on like that for thousands of years. It's jolly! Next time we bathe, there won't be a scrap of weed left. The place will be regularly scoured out, and the bottom covered with soft shelly sand."

The outlook was most dismal. All the glorious colours of sea, sky, and mountain were blotted out, and it was only at intervals, when the drifting rain-clouds lifted a little, that a glimpse could be seen of some island out at sea.

Boom, rush, roar. The wind whistled and yelled as it rattled past the windows, and at times the violence was so great that Max turned an inquiring look at his young host, as if to ask whether there was any danger.

"Like a sail to-day?" asked the latter.

"Sail? with the sea like this!"

"Well, I don't think I should like it," said Kenneth, laughing. "Tavvy says the boat was going adrift out in the bay, but he caught her in time. It's quite rough even there. Here, let's put on waterproofs, and go out."

"Oh no. There: see how it rains."

"Yes, that's pretty tidy," said Kenneth, as the air was literally blackened by the tremendous torrent that fell. "I say, Max, this is the sort of day to see the Mare's Tail. My word! there's some water coming down now."

"It must be terrible."

"Terrible? Nonsense! Here, come into the kitchen and let's see if there's any one there."

Max wondered, but followed his young host to the kitchen, expecting to see no one but the maids, and perhaps Grant, the severe butler; but, when they reached the great stone-floored place, there were Tavish, Long Shon, and Scoodrach, the two latter seated at a table, and the great forester toasting the back of his legs at the fire, and sending up a cloud of steam, an example followed by the three dogs, who sent up smaller clouds of their own.

There was a chorus, or rather a trio of good-mornings, and a series of rappings from dogs' tails, and Max ventured to suggest to the great Highlander that it was very wet.

"Ou ay," he said; "a wee bit shoory, put she'll pe over soon."

"Pretty good spate up in the hills, Tavvy," cried Kenneth.

"Ou ay, Maister Ken; but it's gran' weather for ta fush."

"A' was thenking ye'd like to tak' ta chentleman up ta glen to see ta fa's," said Long Shon.

"Ah, we might do that when the shower's over."

"There'll pe a teal of watter coming down fra Ben Doil."

"Yes, we'll go, Max; and, say, Tav, we never went after the stags Scoody and I saw. Think we could get a shot at them to-day?"

"Weel, she might, Maister Ken, put she'd pe a wee pit wat for ta young chentleman."

"Oh, he wouldn't mind. You'd like to go deerstalking, Max?"

"Yes, I should like to go, but—"

"Oh, we wouldn't go while it rains hard; and you'd only get your feet wet."

"She couldna get over ta mountain to-day," said Long Shon decisively; "and ta glen'll be so full of watter, she couldna stand."

"Oh, nonsense! We could go, Tav?"

"Ou ay, she could go, put there's a teal o' watter apoot."

Just at that moment a weird-looking figure appeared at the door, with his long grey hair and beard streaked together with the rain, and, as he caught Max's eye, he smiled at him, raised one hand, gave a mysterious-looking nod, and beckoned to him to come.

"Here, Maxy, old Donald wants you."

"What for?" said Max, as he shrinkingly met the old man's eye, as he still kept on beckoning, and completely ignored the presence of the rest.

"He wants to give you a tune on the pipes."

Donald beckoned again in a quiet, mysterious manner, and the three dogs looked at him uneasily, Sneeshing uttering a low growl, as if he had unpleasant memories of bagpipe melodies and stones thrown at him because he had been unable to bear the music, and had howled.

"What's the matter, Tonal'?" cried Kenneth, as the old man kept on beckoning.

"She disna want onybody but ta Southron chiel'," said the old man sternly; and he continued to wave Max toward him with his long, claw-like hand.

For a few moments Max felt as if he must go—as if some force which he had not the moral courage to resist was drawing him, and he was about to rise, when the old man gave a fierce stamp with his foot.

"You'll be obliged to go, Maxy," said Kenneth. "Have a concert all to yourself for three or four hours. It will be rather windy, but the rain doesn't come in on one side of the old tower room."

"No, no, not to-day!" cried Max hastily.

"Oh, you'll have to go," said Kenneth, as the old man kept on waving his hand imperiously. "Won't he, Scood?"

"Ou ay, she'll have to go and hear ta pipes."

As if angered at the invitation not being accepted, old Donald took a couple of strides forward into the kitchen.

This was too much for Sneeshing, who leaped up on to his four short legs, barked furiously, and then, overcome by recollections of the last air he had heard, he threw up his head so as to straighten his throat, and gave forth the most miserable howl a dog could utter.

Old Donald shouted something in Gaelic, and made for the dog, which began to bark and snap at him, and this roused Dirk and Bruce to take part with him in baying at the old piper, who stopped short, as if startled at the array of teeth.

The noise was so great that Grant the butler came hurrying in.

"Turn those dogs oot!" he cried. "You, Tonal', what do you want?"

"Ta Southron chiel'," said the old man mysteriously.

"She lo'es ta pipes, and she'll play him ta Mackhai's Mairch."

Turning to Max, he waved him toward the door.

"No, no, not to-day," said Grant, who read the young visitor's reluctance to go.

"But ta chiel' lo'es ta pipes," cried Donald.

"Then you shall play to him another time."

"Yes, another time, Tonal'. Be off now, and I'll bring ye a wee drappie by and by," cried Kenneth.

"She'll pring her a wee drappie? Good laddie! She shall pring her a wee drappie, and she wass nice and try up in the tower, and she wass make a nice fire."

He made a mysterious sign or two, suggestive of his making a silent promise to give his young master all the music he had intended for Max, and went slowly out of the great stone-floored place.

"Noo, send oot the dogs," said Grant; and, to make sure, he did it himself, a quiet wave of his hand being sufficient to drive them all out into the yard behind the kitchen.

"She said she should soon pe fine," said Long Shon, as a gleam of sunshine shot through the window; for the storm was passing over, and its rearguard, in the form of endless ragged fleecy clouds, could be seen racing across the blue sky; while, in an hour from then, the sky was swept clear, and the sun shone out bright and warm.

"Now," cried Kenneth, "let's get the rifles, and go and have a stalk."

"It would jist aboot be madness," said Grant; "and the Chief would be in a fine way. Tell him he can't go."

"Oh ay! he's spout richt, Maister Ken. She's too fu' o' watter to go over the mountain and through ta glen."

"She wass saying she'd go and tak' the young chentleman to see the fa's."

"Ay, there's a gran' fa' o' watter the noo," said Tavish.

"Oh, very well, then; let's go and see the falls. Come along, Scoody. I'll get a gun. You'll take yours, Max."

"Shall I?"

"Yes, of course. We may get a good shot at something."

The two lads went back into the hall, and, passing through a swing door, they suddenly came upon The Mackhai pacing up and down.

He looked up, frowning as he caught sight of Max, and was evidently going to say something; but he checked himself, and went quickly into the library and shut the door.

"I'd give something to know what's the matter with father," said Kenneth thoughtfully. "He never used to be like this."

Max felt uncomfortable, and, being very sensitive, he turned to his companion:

"Have I done anything to annoy him?" he asked.

"You? No. What nonsense! There, come along. We haven't had such a day as this for ever so long, and I've been indoors till I can hardly breathe. Why not have a sail?"

Max looked aghast at the heaving sea.

"Perhaps it is a bit too rough," said Kenneth. "Never mind; we'll go and see the falls."

Ten minutes later they were skirting round the little bay, to turn in by the first swollen river, to track its bed up to the mountain, where the "fa's" they were to see were to be found, and, even as they went, a low, deep, humming sound came to the ear, suggestive of some vast machinery in motion; while the river at their side ran as if it were so much porter covered with froth, great flakes of which were eddying here and there, and being cast up in iridescent patches on the stony banks.

At the end of a quarter of an hour's climbing and stumbling among the wet rocks and bushes, during which the two big dogs had been trotting quietly along at their master's heels, and Sneeshing, in a wonderful state of excitement, hunting everywhere for that rabbit which he had on his mind, Max stopped short.

"Hallo! Tired?" cried Kenneth, laughing.

"Oh no! But it seems such a pity to go hurrying on. Wait a few minutes."

Kenneth laughed, and yet he could not help feeling gratified at his companion's enthusiasm.

"Here, hold hard a bit, Tawy," he cried. "Stop a bit, Shon."

The two men halted; the dogs settled themselves upon a sunny rock, Bruce with his pointed nose comfortably across Dirk's rough, warm frill, and Sneeshing curled himself up in the angle formed by the two dogs' bodies, close up to and as much under Dirk's long hair as he could; while Scoodrach seated himself on a huge block of black slate, which did not belong to the place, but must have fallen from some vein high up the gorge, and been brought down by wintry floods, a little way at a time, during hundreds of years, till it lay jammed in among the great blocks of granite like a chip in a basin of lumps of sugar. This piece of slate suited Scoodrach's eye, and he took out his big knife and began to sharpen it.

Long Shon took a little curly sheep's horn out of his pouch, and had a pinch of snuff.

Tavish filled a dumpy black wooden pipe, and began to smoke; while Kenneth, as he smilingly watched Max, hummed over Black Donald's bagpipe tune, "The March of the Clan Mackhai."

"Well," said Kenneth at last, breaking the silence, through which came a low, deep, humming roar, "what do you think of Dunroe?"

"Think!" cried Max, in a low, deep voice; "it's heavenly."

And he stood gazing up the narrow glen, with its intensely dark shadows among the rocks, through which the brilliant sun-rays struck down, making the raindrops which hung upon the delicate leaves of the pendent birches glisten like diamonds.

For it was one beautiful series of pictures at which the lad gazed: patches of vivid blue above, seen through the openings among the trees; right below, the foaming river coming down in a hundred miniature falls; silver-stemmed and ruddy-bronze birches rooting in the sides, and sending their leaves and twigs hanging over like cascades of verdure; pines and spruces rising up on all sides like pyramids of deep, dark green; and everywhere the masses of rock glittering with crystals, and clothed with mosses of the most vivid tints, and among whose crevices the ferns threw up their pointed, softly-laced fronds.

The sunlight glanced down like sheaves of dazzling silver arrows; and over the water, and softly riding down the glen, came soft, filmy clouds of mist, so fine and delicate that they constantly faded into invisibility; while every now and then there were passing glimpses of colour appearing and disappearing over the rushing torrent, as if there had been a rainbow somewhere up above—one which had broken up, and these were its fragments being borne away.

"I never saw anything so beautiful," said Max, almost wondering at his companion's want of enthusiasm.

"And do you know what makes it so beautiful?"

"It was made so."

"Yes; but it is the sun. If a black cloud came over now, and it began to rain, the place would look so gloomy and miserable that you'd want to hurry home."

"Yes; ta young Chief's richt," said Tavish, nodding his head. "It's ta ferry wettest place I know when ta rain comes doon and ta wind will plow."

"Let's go on," said Kenneth after awhile. "It gets more and more beautiful higher up."

"It can't be!" cried Max. "And is this all your father's property?"

"Yes," said Kenneth proudly; "this all belongs to The Mackhai."

"Ant it will aal pelong to ta young Chief some tay, when he crows a pig man."

Max went on with a sigh, but only to find that the place really did grow more beautiful as they climbed on, while the deep, humming roar grew louder and more awe-inspiring as they penetrated farther and farther into the recesses of the mountain. For the long and heavy rain had charged the fountains of the hills to bursting. Every lakelet was brimming, every patch of moss saturated, and from a thousand channels, that were at first mere threads, the water came rushing down to coalesce in the narrow glen, and eddy, and leap, and swirl, and hurry on toward the sea.

"Why are we climbing up so high?" said Max suddenly.

"To show you our glen, and take you up by the falls."

A curious shrinking sensation came upon Max, and Kenneth noticed it.

"This isn't the Grey Mare's Tail," he said, laughing; "and we're not in a boat."

"I can't help feeling a little nervous," said Max frankly. "I am not used to this sort of thing."

"And we are. Yes, of course. It's too bad to laugh at you. Come on."

"Is there any danger?"

"Well, of course there is, if you go and tumble in, but you needn't go near."

The humming roar grew louder as they tramped on along a sheep-track in and out among the huge stones which had fallen from the sides of the great gully. Now they were in deep shadow, where brilliant speckled fungi, all white and red, stood out like stools beneath the birch trees; then they were high up on quite a shelf, where the turf and moss were short, and the sun shone out clearly; and ever, as they turned angle after angle of the great zigzag, the roar of the water grew louder, till, after another hour's slow climbing, they descended a sloping green track and came into a great hollow directly facing them; and a couple of hundred feet overhead, a narrow rift, out of which poured an amber stream of water on to a huge block of rock some twenty feet below, the result being that the great spout of amber water was broken and turned into a sheet of foam, which spread out all over the great block, and fell sheer the rest of the distance, over a hundred and fifty feet, into a vast hollow below. Here it careered round and round, and rushed onward toward where the group were standing, while high above all floated a cloud of fine vapour which resembled white smoke, and upon which played the iridescent colours of half a rainbow, completing the picture in a way which made Max watch it in silent delight.

"Well, what do you think of it?" said Kenneth, who was amused by the London lad's rapt manner.

"Eh? think?" said Max, starting and colouring.

"Yes. What were you thinking?"

"I was wishing that it was mine—all my own, so that I could come and sit here and think."

"Well, you may come here and sit and think, but it never will be yours. It has always belonged to the Mackhais ever since they conquered the Mackalps, and took it with claymore and targe. There was a tremendous fight up above there, and, as my ancestors cut down the Mackalps, they threw them into the stream at the top, and there they were shot out over the fall, and carried right out to sea."

"How horrible!"

"Horrible? Why, it was all considered very brave and grand, and we are very proud of it. There's a sword down at the castle that they say was used in the great fight."

"And are you proud of it?"

"I don't know. I suppose so. Does seem queer, though, to chop chaps with swords and pitch 'em into the water. Rather an awkward place to come down, wouldn't it, Max?"

"Awful!"

"Well, never mind talking about it. Come up and see."

"What! climb up there?"

"To be sure. Oh, you needn't be afraid. It's quite safe. You go up that narrow path, and get round in among those birch trees, and that brings you out by the top."

"I—"

"Oh, don't come if you're scared," said Kenneth contemptuously.

Max rose from the stone upon which he had been seated.

"I'm ready," he said.

"Well, you are a rum chap, Maxy," cried Kenneth, clapping him on the shoulder. "Sometimes I think you are the jolliest coward I ever saw, and sometimes I think you've got plenty of pluck. Which is it?"

"I'm afraid I'm very cowardly," said Max sadly.

"Oh, come, now I'm sure of it!" cried Kenneth warmly.

"That I am a great coward?"

"No; that you're full of pluck. My father says that a fellow must be very brave to own he is a coward. Come on."

They started up the side, with Scoodrach following close behind.

"Going up to ta top o' ta fa's, Maister Kenneth?" shouted Long Shon.

"Yes. Coming with us?"

"She'd petter tak' care," cried Tavish. "There's a teal o' watter, and ta stanes is ferry wat."

"All right, Tavvy; we'll mind," cried Kenneth; and he plunged in among the bushes and rocks, to begin climbing upward in and out, and gradually leaving the rushing waters of the fall behind, while, as the misty foam with its lovely ferny surroundings faded from the eye, the loud splash and roar gradually softened upon the ear till the sound was once more a deep, murmurous hum, which acted as a bass accompaniment to a harsh, wild air which Scoodrach began to sing, or rather bray.

Kenneth stopped short, held back the bushes of hazel dotted with nuts, and turned round to give Max a comical look.

"What's the matter, Scoody?" he cried. "Eh? ta matter? I only scratched my hand wi' a bit thorn."

"Oh! Well, you needn't make so much noise about it."

"Noise spout it! She titn't mak' nae noise."

"Yes, you did. You hulloaed horribly."

"She titn't. She was chust singing a wee bit sang."

"Singing? Did you say singing?"

"Ay, she was chust singing ta Allambogle."

"Do you hear that, Maxy? he thinks he was singing."

"Wah!" ejaculated Scoodrach; and the little party climbed on, with Max wondering how anybody could find breath to make such a noise when climbing up so great a steep.

In a few minutes the sound of the fall began to grow louder once more, and a shrinking sensation to attack Max; but he put a bold face upon the matter, and followed close to Kenneth till the latter turned to him.

"Here we are," he said, "close to the spout." Max looked, but could see nothing, only a dense tangle of hazel stubs among the green moss, at whose roots grew endless numbers of fungi, shaped like rough chalices, and of the colour of a ripe apricot.

"I can't see it."

"No, not there; but you can here."

As he spoke, Kenneth divided the bushes, and held them apart for his companion to join him, and the next moment they were standing on the brink of a narrow rift in the rock, so narrow that the bush-tips met overhead, and made the water that glided silently along many feet below look quite dark.

"But that's not the whole of the water which goes over the fall," said Max wonderingly.

"Every drop. It's narrow, but it's fine and deep, and when it spouts out it falls on to the stones and spreads round so as to look big—makes the most of itself. Now then, are you tired?"

"Yes; my legs ache a bit."

"Very well, then, this is the nearest way home."

"I don't understand you."

"Jump in here, and the water would carry you right away down to the bathing-cave. Scood and I have sent strings of corks down here, and the stream has carried them right to Dunroe."

"I think I'd rather walk," said Max, smiling.

"So would I. Now come on and see where the water falls."

He led the way, and Max and Scoodrach followed, the latter, who was musically disposed that morning, taking advantage of the noise made by the falls to use it as a cloak to cover his own, with the result that every now and then Max was startled by hearing sounds close behind him remarkably suggestive of Donald Dhu being close upon their track, armed with his pipes, and doing battle with all his might.

"Here you are," cried Kenneth, brushing through the last of the hazel boughs, and standing out on the rock close to the edge of the great hollow into which the water poured; and the shrinking sensation increased, as Max joined his friend, and found that there was nothing to protect him from falling into the great gulf at whose brink they stood.

All this struck him for the moment, but the dread was swept away by the rush of thought which took its place. For there below, as he gazed down at the falling water arching from the narrow rift into a stony basin, to then rush over the sides and fall in a silvery veil, to the deep chasm fringed with delicate dew—sparkling greenery, amidst whose leaves and boughs floated upward a cloud of white mist, which kept changing, as the sun shone upon it, to green and yellow and violet and orange of many depths of tone, but all dazzlingly bright, one melting into the other and disappearing to reappear in other rainbow hues.

Far below them, toward where the rugged hollow opened out to allow of the escape of the water from the falls, Tavish and Long Shon could be seen, seated on the stones they had chosen, smoking their pipes and basking in company with the dogs, for the warm rays of a sunny day had of late been rare.

"There's a teal o' watter in the fa's," said Scoodrach gravely.

"Of course there is, stupid, after this rain," cried Kenneth. "Tell me something I don't know."

"Couldn't tell her nothing she don't know," cried Scoodrach. "She reats books, and goes to school, and learns efferything."

"That's just what the masters say I don't do, Scoody. Here, let's go down to the basin."

"What! get down there?" cried Max in horror, as Kenneth seated himself on the edge of the stony channel through which the water came down from the mountain before making its leap.

"Yes; it's easy enough," cried Kenneth, dangling his legs to and fro, and making them brush through the fronds of a beautiful fern growing in a crevice. "Scoody and I have often been down."

"But she shall not go pelow now," said the young gillie, looking down at the smooth, glassy current. "There's chust too much watter in ta way."

"Get out!" cried Kenneth. "Look here, Max: you can get down here to the edge of the water, and follow it to where it makes its first leap, and then get under it to the other side, and clamber on to the edge of the basin where it spreads, and look down. It's glorious. Come on."

"Na, she will not come," cried Scoodrach. "There's too much watter."

"You're a worse coward than Max."

"Nay, she shall na go," cried Scoodrach, making a bound to the spot where Kenneth was seated; but quick as thought the lad twisted round, let himself glide down, and, as the young gillie made a dash at his hands, they slid over the moss and grass and were gone.

Kenneth's merry laugh came up out of the narrow rift, sounding muffled and strange, and the two lads looked down to where he was creeping along, some fifteen feet below them, in the half-darkness of the hollow, and holding on by the pendent roots which issued from the crevices, as he picked his way along the stones, with the water often washing against his feet.

"Come down, Max. Don't be a coward," he cried, as he looked up over his shoulder at the two anxious faces, while the hiss, rush, and roar of the water nearly covered with sound his half-heard voice.

"She's coing to troon herself, ye ken!" cried Scoodrach, stamping his foot with rage. "Come pack, Maister Ken! Do she hear me? Come pack!"

Kenneth probably did not hear the words, but he looked up again and laughed, as he stood near the end of the narrow gully, with the sunny light of the great hollow behind him showing up his form, and at the same time his face was lit up strangely by the weird gleam of a reflection from the rushing, glassy, peat-stained stream as it glided on to the mouth of the gully for its leap.

"She canna stay here and see her young maister troon herself," cried Scoodrach wildly. "She must go town and ket trooned too."

"Coming, Scoody?" cried Kenneth, as he half turned round where he stood on a little block of stone, against which the water surged.

Scoodrach was in the act of seating himself upon the edge previous to lowering himself down, and, why he knew not, he hesitated and spoke, half to Max, half to himself.

"She'll go and trag her pack! she'll go and trag her pack!" Then he uttered a hoarse cry, for, as they saw Kenneth, framed in as it were by the narrow rock, gazing back at them, while the swift gleaming water swept by his legs, they suddenly noted that he started and made a clutch at an overhanging root which came away in his hands, while the stone upon which he was standing tottered over and disappeared in the rushing water.

But Kenneth was active as a monkey; and, failing in his first attempt to grasp something to support him, he made a second leap and caught at a hazel bough which grew out horizontally above his head.

This time he was successful, and, as the sturdy bough bent and swayed, the lad hung right over the rushing water.

"Chump! Swing and chump, Maister Ken!" cried Scoodrach; and then he was silent, and sat staring wildly, for he realised that he could not help his young master—that there would not be time.

Kenneth was swinging to and fro, the bough dipping and rising and dipping, so low that the water almost touched his feet. As he hung he tried to get a better hold, and made a struggle to go hand over hand to the place where the bough joined the mossy roots.

But it was all in vain. Before he could get his loosened hand past a secondary branch, the rotten root broke away from its insecure hold in the gully wall, and one moment the two spectators saw Kenneth hanging there, his form shown up by the light behind; the next, they saw branch and its holder descend quickly into the glassy water, which was momentarily disturbed by a few leafy twigs standing above its surface, then a hand appeared, then again with half the arm, making a clutch at vacancy, and then there was nothing but the water gliding onward to the opening through which it leaped down into the basin on the top of the spreading rock.

Chapter Twenty
Rival Doctors

For a few moments Scoodrach was as if frozen. He sat gazing at the rushing water, and then he sprang up and dashed past Max, shouting,—

"Come on! come on pefore he's trooned."

Max rushed after him, following the best way he could, for Scoodrach had disappeared among the low growth of hazel, and it was only by listening to the sound that he was able to make out the way the young gillie had gone.

The distance was only some fifty yards down, through a depression which led round to a kind of shelf just level with the top of the huge mass of rock on to which the water fell, and Max forgot the danger in the excitement, as he reached Scoodrach, who was standing holding on by the thin branch of a birch tree which had grown outward, and hung drooping over the great hollow below, and so near to the falling foam that its outer leaves were sprinkled with the spray.

As Max crept to his side, Scoodrach gave him a horrified look, and pointed at something in the bubbling water at the edge of the basin.

"What'll she do?" he cried despairingly; "if she climbs along the tree, she canna chump it. Oh, look, look! Maister Ken! Maister Ken!"

Even if it had been possible, there was no time to render help, for, as they gazed wildly at the basin into which the clear, smooth jet of water fell, they saw that the apparently inanimate body of Kenneth was borne nearer and nearer to the edge of the stone, and then slowly onward, to glide over in the spreading veil, and then disappear in the foam and mist far below.

"Pack again and doon to the bottom!" yelled Scoodrach, and he rushed by Max so fiercely that he had to clutch at and hold on by a sapling to prevent his own fall headlong into the watery hollow.

Max drew himself safely to the perpendicular wall, and crept back now along the rugged ledge, which had not impressed him with its risky nature before, and the perspiration stood out clammily on his temples as he reached the place where he had begun to descend.

He was here in a dense growth of nut and birch, and he listened vainly for the rustling made by Scoodrach as he ran down.

There was the dull roar of the falls behind him, and then a loud shout, and either an echo or one in answer; but that was all; and a horrible feeling of misery and despair at his helplessness came over the lad, as he thought the worst, and of how terrible it would be to go back to the castle and tell the tale.

His first instinct prompted him to cast himself down upon the earth and yield to the sensation of despair, but his second was to go on and try and do something to help.

In this intent he looked wildly round, to see nothing but a wilderness of undergrowth, and in his excitement he dashed straight on, striking the hazel stems to right and left, and, stumbling and falling again and again, he ended by rolling and scrambling down a steep slope, to drop into what might have been some terrible chasm, but only, as it happened, a few feet, and, as he gathered himself up, it seemed that he had inadvertently hit upon the rough track by which he had ascended.

At the end of a minute he recognised a peculiar-looking patch of rock jutting out above him, and recalled how he had compared it to the head of a bullock as he had clambered up.

That was enough, and the rest of the descent proved comparatively easy, till he reached a spot where he could see on his right the foaming waters of the fall, and down below, on the left, a glint or two of the torrent, as it escaped from the lower basin and hurried along the deep ravine toward the sea.

He gazed wildly at the base of the fall, in the vain hope that he might catch sight of Kenneth clinging to some projecting stone; then he scanned the wild below, but he could see nothing of his companions.

There was the spot where Tavish and Long Shon had sat smoking, but they were gone, and there was no sign of Scoodrach. Nothing but the falling water, with its deep, musical, humming roar, and the grand picture of rock and tree made dim and distant-looking by the rising clouds of rainbow-tinted spray.

He shouted with all his might, but there was only a dull echo; and, after repeating his cry, and feeling that it was drowned by the deep roar, he gave one more despairing look round, and ran on downward for a few yards, but only to turn and almost retrace his steps by the rough zigzag track, when he felt a strange catching of the breath, and stopped short, just where, some distance below, a curve of the rushing stream opened out before him, all white foam and glancing water, glistening and flashing in the sun.

He had noticed it as he climbed upward with Kenneth and Scoodrach, and a strange sensation of delight had thrilled him. But the beauty was all gone, and he could see nothing now but the scene which seemed to check his breath and fill him with despair.

For there, at the foot of a glistening curve of water which seemed to leap from amidst a pile of black rocks, stood Tavish, bending forward. Long Shon was below him, standing waist-deep, and holding on to prevent being swept away, while Scoodrach was many feet above, climbing to his right, and evidently scanning the stream.

"They think he's washed down there," cried Max aloud, "when he must be up yonder at the foot of the falls."

He shouted wildly, but his feeble voice would not penetrate to them as they stood amidst the racing water, and in his agony Max was in the act of starting to run again, when he saw Scoodrach throw up his hands, and directly after Tavish seemed to make a bound into the foam, where he fell and disappeared.

Max's mouth felt dry at this fresh misfortune, and he stood as if turned to stone, waiting to see the gillie reappear, which he did, but not where Max expected by fifty yards farther down the stream, where Long Shon stood, and, as the latter held on with one hand, he could be seen to stoop and catch at something in the water.

Max could hardly believe what he saw, as Tavish rose up high above Long Shon, when the pair slowly climbed out, the great forester with something beneath one arm.

The frozen feeling of helplessness passed off, and Max ran on down the rough slope, nearly falling again and again in his eagerness to reach the spot where from time to time he could see the group, on a green bed of moss beneath some pendulous birches; and when at last he reached them, it was to find Kenneth lying upon his back, with his head and shoulders supported against Tavish as he knelt there; Scoodrach stooping and holding his hand; and Long Shon busily binding up a cut upon the lad's head, the blood from which had trickled down over one cheek.

"Is—is he dead?" cried Max hoarsely.

There was no reply, and Max felt his heart seem to contract as he stood in the pool of water which had streamed down from the group.

"Na, na," said Tavish, suddenly thrusting away Long Shon's hand. "She'd petter let her pleed."

Long Shon looked at him wonderingly, but gave way.

"Maybe she shall. Puir laddie, ye canna dee like that."

But for a time it seemed as if poor Kenneth's race was run, so still and white he looked.

"The doctor! some one go for a doctor."

"There's nae doctor this side o' Stirling or Inverness," said Long Shon quietly. "Puir laddie! Was this your doing, Scoody?"

"Na, father; she tried to stop her," cried the boy piteously. "She wouldna stay. Is she trooned?"

"Trooned! nay, not she," cried Tavish exultantly. "Look at her een. She chust gave ane wee bit blinkie. Bide a wee, laddie, and she'll be upon her legs again."

They watched and waited in a state of the greatest excitement, all but Scoodrach, who, after giving himself a shake like a water-dog, and wringing his kilt in front and behind, began to whistle in the most indifferent manner, and ended by walking coolly away, to the astonishment of all.

But they were too busy with Kenneth to pay any heed to the young gillie's eccentricities, no one heeding his disappearance, as the half-drowned boy's hands were chafed, and Tavish gently lowered his head till he could lay it on a tuft of heath.

There had been a quiver or two of the eyelids, as Tavish had said, and from time to time there was a faint fluttering of the pulses, but after these manifestations the poor fellow seemed to relapse, and Long Shon, who had been fidgeting and muttering against the forester's treatment, impatiently dashed his bonnet on the ground.

"Ye're a' wrang, Tavvy!" he exclaimed, — "ye're a' wrang! Lat me tak' haud o' the laddie's heels, and let her hing doon my back wi' her heid close to the groon'."

"Hwhat for?" cried Tavish.

"Hwhat for?" cried Long Shon contemptuously. "Canna ye see that the puir bairn's fu' o' watter. Lat's turn her up, man, an' lat a' t' watter rin oot o' her mooth. Here, stan' aside."

"Gin ye touch the laddie, Long Shon, I'll gie ye a ding atween the een as shall mak' ye see stars for a month. D'ye think I dinna ken that it would kill the bairn at ance?"

"Na!" growled Long Shon; "I've seen 'em do it wi' the trooned men after a wrack."

"Ay, and I've seen 'em dee wi' doing that same, Long Shon. D'ye think I dinna ken what I'm aboot?"

"Ay," cried Long Shon stoutly, as Tavish kept on pressing Kenneth's ribs with mighty force and letting them go.

"Ye're glad enow to come and lat me doctor ye, though, man. Hing the puir laddie by his heels to lat the watter oot! Maun, ane wad think ye were aboot to haunle a stag, and cut her up to send to toon. Hah! see him the noo! see him the noo! Kenneth laddie—Kenneth, my bonnie chiel'! Light o' my een, my bonnie young Chief! Hech! Hech! Hech for ta Mackhai! Look at her the noo!"

Tavish had sprung up, uttering a wild yell, leaping off the ground, and waving his bonnet in the air. For Kenneth had opened his eyes, gazed wonderingly about, and then fixed them on Max, as he knelt down and took his hand, and smiled.

"What is it?" he said feebly. "What's the matter?"

Max was choking. A great ball seemed to be rising in his throat, and he had to get up hastily and turn away to hide his emotion.

"I—don't quite— What's the matter, Tavvy?"

"Matter, my bonnie laddie!" cried the great forester, dropping on his knees and placing his hands tenderly on the injured brow; "on'y a wee bit scratch on the heid. Gie's the cloth, Shon lad, and I'll bind it up. Ye had a dip i' the watter, but ye're a' richt the noo."

"Yes, I'm all right now," said Kenneth feebly; and he smiled faintly in the great forester's face, as the great rough fellow bound up his brow as tenderly as a woman.

Max had drawn back, and, as soon as the two men's attention was taken up, he crept round behind a clump of the hazels, and, as soon as he was well alone, the pent-up emotion would have vent, and, sobbing wildly, he dropped upon his knees and covered his face with his hands, repeating the prayer of thanksgiving that rose to his lips:

"Thank God! Thank God!"

Then he started to his feet, ashamed of his emotion, dreading lest any one should have seen his position and heard his words, for a low, hoarse moan seemed to come from farther in the little patch of woodland.

Was there some one else hurt? he thought; and, taking a few steps in the direction, he came suddenly upon Scoodrach at full length upon the moss, face downwards and buried in the soft green growth, while his hands were clutching his shortly-cut hair behind, and his shoulders heaved as he moaned forth,—

"She'll never hantle a poat acain! she'll never rin wi' her ower the hills! Maister—Maister Ken, she's deid, she's deid!"

"No, no, Scood!" cried Max excitedly. "He's better! He has just come to!"

Scood sprang to his feet, and a flash of wild delight darted from his wet red eyes. Then, as if recollecting himself, he dashed his hand across them and gave it a slap against his side, scowling heavily.

"On'y ta watter rin doon oot o' her hair," he said surlily. "Ta young Chief's not trooned?"

"No, no, Scood; he's—"

Max stared, for Scoodrach had turned his back, begun to whistle, and walked away.

"He was ashamed to let me see him crying," thought Max. "I'm not the only coward in the world."

He stood for a few moments gazing after Scoodrach, and then walked quickly back, to find Kenneth sitting up.

"She's a teal petter the noo," cried Tavish triumphantly. "There, laddie; ye'll get up, and we'll chust gang hame."

"Yes; I'm not much hurt, Max," said Kenneth, with a ghastly attempt at a laugh. "I say, old chap, you couldn't do that. Here, give us your hand."

Max eagerly tried to help him rise, and Kenneth made a brave effort to get upon his legs, but he snatched at the forester's arm, with his face contracting and turning ghastly pale, as his eyes looked dim and then half closed.

They gently laid him down, and bathed his forehead with water.

"Chust a wee bit dizzy, puir laddie," said Tavish tenderly. "Bide a wee, Long Shon, till he opes his een acain, and then ye shall put him on my pack, and I'll carry him doon to the shore, and we'll mak' Scood rin on and ket the poat and twa pillows, and ket him richt across to the rock."

"Ay," said Long Shon approvingly. "But she must hae a teal o' watter in her; shall she rin it oot the noo?"

"Na, na!" cried Tavish, in a low, fierce growl. "Hey, Scoody!"

"Well?" came from close by, and the young gillie showed himself, with his face half averted.

"Rin, bairn, and get ta little poat an' row her to ta mooth o' ta stream," cried Long Shon.

"Ay," cried Scoodrach, turning eagerly to run.

"An', Scoody, my laddie," cried Tavish, "ye'll chust ask Maister Crant to fling twa pillows in ta poat."

"Yes."

"And, Scoody, ye'll chust say that the young Chief is a' richt the noo, but that we're a' wat wi' sweet watter, and if she thinks a wee drappie o' whusky would pe good for ta young Chief and the rest, she can pit it in ta poat."

Scoodrach nodded, and ran off rapidly over the rugged ground, bounding across the stones like a goat, and Kenneth now tried to rise.

"Ye'll pe a pit petter the noo, Maister Kenneth," said Tavish tenderly. "She's chust sent for ta poat, and she'll kneel doon, and Long Shon will help ye to get upo' her back, ant she'll carry ye chently doon to ta mooth o' ta stream."

"Oh no, Tavvy; I can walk."

"Nay, laddie, ye canna walk. It winna pe ta first time she's carriet ye on her pack. Noo, Long Shon, chust gie ta young Chief a lift, and—that's ta way. Did she hurt ye?"

"Not—very much," said Kenneth, with a shudder of pain. "Thank ye, Tav, old chap. There, I'm like a little boy again; but it's too bad to let you carry me."

"Haud yer wheesht, Maister Ken—haud yer wheesht!" cried the big forester angrily. "What would she pe for if it wasna to help ta young Chief o' ta Mackhai? Why, Long Shon here and she would lie doon for ye to walk upo' us if it would do ye good."

"Ay!" cried Long Shon.

"Noo then, slow and steady. Come along, Maister Max; and we'll be doon to the sands before Scoodrach can get across ta bay."

The great fellow walked slowly and carefully down the gully; but, before they had gone far, Kenneth's head dropped, and they laid him down again, to revive him after a few minutes by bathing his face on the brink of the rushing stream, after which Tavish raised him as tenderly as if he had been a baby, and bore him in his arms.

They reached the shore at last, after a very slow progress, to find Scoodrach approaching fast, and tugging at the oars with all his might.

"Is ta Mackhai at hame?" cried Long Shon, as the boy came within hail.

"Na," shouted Scoodrach, without turning his head, and toiling away till he was close in, when he reversed the boat, and backed in till she grounded on the sand.

The pillows were there, so was the whisky, but no one touched it. Kenneth was laid carefully in the stern, and Max supported him, Scoodrach scowling angrily at being sent into the bows; while the two men made the water surge beneath the keel till they reached the rock, where, once more taking the injured lad in his arms as if he were a babe, Tavish carried him up the rock, and then right up to his bedroom, where he stopped and tended him as carefully as a trained nurse.

"I've been a' ower him, Maister Crant, and ye may rest easy till ta Mackhai comes pack. If she likes to sent for ta toctor, weel, let her sent; pit there's naething wrang wi' the laddie, nae banes brukkit, and naething wrang inside. She has gien her heit a gran' ding or twa, and she's verra sair, and she's been maist trooned. I've seen to manny a worse hurt than hers, so let the bairn go to sleep, and we'll see her when she wacks."

Chapter Twenty One
An anxious Time

The Mackhai did not return home till the next morning, and his first inquiry was why had not a doctor been fetched.

He nodded with satisfaction at the answer he received.

Tavish and Grant had sat up all night with their young master, and Max had been to them at least a dozen times, for a consultation to be held at daybreak, and for Tavish to agree that something must be done.

The result had been that he and Long Shon had taken the boat before sunrise, and gone off to Port Staffey, where Grant knew a medical man to be staying for a holiday, and to fish.

For poor Kenneth was quite delirious, and about midday, after going out on the terrace to scan the offing eagerly for signs of the boat, The Mackhai went back into the house, and up to his son's room, to hear the injured lad talking at random, and a hoarse sob escaped from the father's lips.

"My poor boy!" he groaned; "and am I to lose you? Well, better so, perhaps—better than to live a beggar, ready to curse your weak father for the ruin he has brought— Hah! how came you here?"

His voice had changed from a soft, appealing tone to one full of angry annoyance, as he saw Max slowly rise up from the other side of the bed, where he had been seated, hidden by the curtain.

"I came to sit with poor Kenneth, sir. I beg your pardon. I'll go now."

"If you please," said The Mackhai coldly, and there was a bitterly fierce look of dislike in his eyes, as he crossed toward the door and threw it open for Max to pass out; but the next moment he had closed it hastily, and he held out his hand.

Max looked at him wonderingly.

"I beg your pardon, Mr Blande," said The Mackhai, in a low voice, full of courteous apology. "I am in trouble, and hardly know what I have been saying."

He pointed as he spoke toward the bed, and then his countenance worked, and he wrung the boy's hand warmly, as Max caught his, and whispered in broken tones,—

"Oh, sir, you don't think he is so very bad?"

"I hope not, my lad, I hope not. Thank you, thank you. No, no, don't go. You are Kenneth's visitor and friend."

"But do pray tell me what you think of him," whispered Max excitedly.

"I cannot say. We shall have the doctor here soon."

"I should like to stay and hear what he says, sir; and then—perhaps—I ought not to—I shall be—intruding—I ought to go away."

"No, no," said The Mackhai hastily; "certainly not. My boy would not wish you to leave him—that is, if you wish to stay."

"May I?" cried Max, with such intense earnestness that his host looked at him wonderingly.

"I beg you will stay, Mr Blande," he said; "and let's hope that he will be better soon. By the way, I hope you will forget what you heard me say."

Just then Kenneth turned uneasily upon his pillow, muttering quickly the while. Now he seemed to be talking to his dogs, now his words were a confused babbling, and then the occupants of the darkened room started as he burst into a fit of laughter, and said merrily,—

"No, no, Scoody; it's too bad! Poor old Max!"

Max felt the blood rise to his cheeks and gradually pale away; and then, for quite two hours, father and visitor sat watching, the monotony of the vigil being broken by an occasional walk to a window, which commanded the sea, and at last Max was able to announce that the boat was in sight.

"Thank heaven!" muttered The Mackhai.

They had to wait for a full half-hour, though, before they could be satisfied that there was a third person in the boat—all doubt being set at rest by The Mackhai fetching his binocular, whose general use was for deerstalking, but by whose help he was able to see that the third party in the boat was a stern-looking, dark, middle-aged man, who might very well be the doctor.

The doctor it was, and, after a careful examination, he confirmed Tavish's declaration.

"Oh no, my dear sir, I don't think it is as bad as that. The boy has concussion of the brain, and he is a great deal hurt beside; but he is young and vigorous, and I think I may venture to say that we'll pull him through. It would have killed you or me, but he is a boy accustomed evidently to a rough life."

The Mackhai wrung his hand: he could not speak for a few minutes, and the doctor left him to go back to the bedside to replace the coverlid Kenneth had tossed off, but The Mackhai noted that the doctor was too late, for Max was performing this little office, and the father observed that the lad gently laid his hand upon his son's brow.

"Of course you will stay and dine, Mr—?"

"Curzon," said the doctor, smiling.

"Mr Curzon; and then see my boy again before you go?"

"My dear sir, I shall be very glad to do so; but I think, under the circumstances, I ought to stay the night."

"Will you?" cried The Mackhai eagerly.

"With pleasure. I am down here fishing, and one place is the same to me as another. If I can serve you, I shall only be too glad."

"My good sir," cried The Mackhai, "you are taking a load off my mind! Pray, pray stay, and if you care to fish, my river and loch are at your service,—tackle, boats, keepers, everything,—while they are mine," he added to himself.

"Then," said the doctor, smiling, "I am your private medical attendant for the next week; and to-morrow, if you will send your boat for my traps from the hotel at Staffey—"

"Yes, to-night," said The Mackhai hastily; and he left the room, thankful for the ray of light which had come into his darkening life, but hurrying back, to find Kenneth holding tightly by Max's hand as he kept on talking, while the doctor was letting a few drops fall from a little bottle he had brought, into a glass of water.

"There," he said, "we'll get him to take that, and I think we shall get some sleep afterwards. To-morrow we must hope for better things."

But the morrow came, and the hope was not fulfilled. Kenneth Mackhai, in spite of his youth and strength, was dangerously ill, and the doctor's face wore an anxious look.

"I have ordered my men to have everything ready for you, Mr Curzon," said The Mackhai, with enforced calmness; and Max darted an angry glance on the man who could think of sport at a time like that.

"What, to fish, Mr Mackhai?" said the doctor quickly. "No, thank you; I'll wait till I can go more at ease."

"Thank you," said The Mackhai, in a husky voice; and Max darted now a grateful look. "But pray speak plainly to me: you think my poor boy very bad?"

"Yes, sir, very bad indeed; but, please God, we'll pull him through."

The Mackhai drew a long and painful breath, and, as Max looked towards him, he thought he had never seen so sad a countenance before.

He stole out on tip-toe, for it seemed to him that he was not wanted there; but, as he reached the landing, The Mackhai touched him on the shoulder:

"Come back soon," he whispered. "Kenneth seems more restful while you are here."

Max nodded silently, and hurried down to talk for a few moments with Tavish and Scoodrach of the patient's state. Then he hurried back, thinking, as he went up to Kenneth's room, that it must be months since he came, and he wondered how it was that he could feel so much at home.

Chapter Twenty Two
The Doctor's Task done

A fortnight's terrible anxiety, during which Max rarely left Kenneth's room. Every morning, though, it grew into a custom that he should go down to the old castle yard, where Tavish, Long Shon, old Donald, and Scoody were always waiting to hear his report of the patient's progress.

"An' has she askit for the pipes?" old Donald whispered mysteriously; and, on receiving an answer in the negative, he looked reproachfully at the speaker. "She's waiting and retty," he would say; "and a good lilt on ta pipes would do her all ta petter as ta physic stuff."

At the end of a week, Donald determined to try his medicine unasked, and struck up "The March of the Mackhai" under Kenneth's window.

The doctor rang the bell furiously, and Grant, who guessed what it meant, ran out and seized the old piper, to bundle him out of hearing.

That day there was nearly murder done, for Donald drew his sgian-dhu and swore he would have the butler's "bluid," to which Grant responded by firing half a pail of water at the furious old man, who was then carried off, foaming and muttering wildly in Gaelic, and was only calmed down by Long Shon telling him it would "kill ta young Chief" if he made so much noise.

Tavish was terribly low-spirited.

"Ta pools are fu' o' saumont," he would say, "and there's naebody to catch them, for the hand that throws a flee better nor ta whole wurrld lies low. Ye'll came and catch a saumont, Maister Max? Ta Chief said she was to shoot and fush, and have ta poat when she liked. Ye'll came the morning?"

"No, Tavish; I can't leave Kenneth; perhaps he'll want me to read to him."

"Rest? wha's ta use o' reating to ta laddie? If it was na for ta toctor, wha's a clever chiel' wi ta rod, what should we do?"

For the doctor stayed on, combining pleasure with work, seeing Kenneth two or three times a day, and fishing in the intervals.

"I shall never be able to repay you for your kindness, Curzon," said The Mackhai one morning.

"My dear sir," said the doctor, "you pay me every day. I never lived better; I never had a more comfortable room; and I never had better fishing."

"You are satisfied?"

"Satisfied! My dear sir, I am congratulating myself every hour upon my luck in being able to exchange my poor services for such comfortable quarters and excellent sport."

"Kenneth owes his life to you, and I shall never be sufficiently grateful."

"Well, he owes it to me because I was the nearest doctor. Any medical man would have done the same."

"You do not make enough of your skill."

"Nonsense, my dear sir! If you are satisfied, I am."

"And you feel sure that he is mending fast?"

"Oh yes, certain. The head trouble has passed now. Poor lad! he must have had a terrible fall. I went with your forester yesterday, and he showed me the place. It's little short of a miracle that he escaped alive."

That night Max was in Kenneth's room, waiting for him to wake up before he said good-night, for the night was hot and the invalid had gone to sleep.

Max was half leaning out of the open window, gazing at the sea sparkling with light, so that it was hard to tell where the stars ended and the reflections began.

Max was thinking. He had had his regular letters from his father, one of which was in answer to an apologetic epistle on his stopping so long, and hoping that he might be allowed to stay till Kenneth was quite recovered.

Mr Blande's letter, from the old Inn of Court, told his son that he was not to think of returning, but to make himself at home at Dunroe, and do everything he could to become acquainted with the place and people, at the same time learning all he could about the fishing and shooting.

"Make yourself a country gentleman as fast as you can, and even if the Mackhais are a little stiff and distant with you, do not resent it or take any notice of the slight, but stay."

"That would be very unpleasant if they did behave slightingly," said Max to himself. "Oh, he's awake now."

He left the window and went back to Kenneth's bedside, but it was only to find that he had merely moved restlessly, and was still fast asleep.

Max did not go back, but stood there patiently watching the sleeping lad, till a faint sound made him start, and he stared at the window, feeling half paralysed, for dimly seen against the darkness there as a head visible. Then there was more rustling, and the chest appeared; a couple of arms were passed in, and their owner began to draw himself up.

Burglars! an attack upon the place! What could it mean?

The intruder's face caught the light from the lamp, as he threw one leg over the window-sill, and sat there, as if hesitating about coming farther.

"Scoodrach!" cried Max. "How did you get up there?"

"She climbed up."

"But how dangerous! What made you do that?"

"She wanted to see ta young Chief, and they wadna let her come."

"How foolish of you! you might have slipped and fallen."

"They let you see her, and they tell her she shall na come. She will see ta young Mackhai."

He said this menacingly, as if Max were one of those who kept him away.

"But he is very ill."

"Scoodrach tid not make her ill."

"No, of course not; but go now, there's a good fellow. You'll see him as soon as he's better."

"She wants to see her the noo," growled the lad sullenly; "and she tries to keep her away."

"Nothing of the kind! Why, I tell you every morning how he is."

"Yes, but she wants to see hersel'. She's going to tie, and they wadna let her come oop."

"Kenneth is not going to die; he's much better."

"She wants to see for hersel'."

"Will you go down, then, as soon as you've seen?"

"She wants to know why Scoodrach canna stay, when a strange Southron stops always in ta place."

"I am a visitor here, and was asked to stay," said Max rather stiffly; but his words were not heard, for the young gillie had dropped into the room, and ran barelegged and barefoot over the carpet to the bedside, to bend down and gaze intently in Kenneth's face.

Just then a low cough was heard on the stair, and Scoodrach darted to the window, crept out, and disappeared, just as the door-handle faintly rattled.

Max went quickly to the window, but could only see something shadowy creeping downward, and he would have stopped gazing down at the climber, whose progress had a strange fascination for him, if the doctor's voice had not taken his attention.

"Perhaps you had better shut the window. Lovely night. Has he been sleeping quietly?"

"Yes."

"That's right. Going on capitally; but do you know what time it is?"

"Yes, nearly twelve. I was waiting for him to wake up and say good-night before I went."

"Then you'll have to wait till to-morrow morning, my dear sir, for he is in a deep, satisfying sleep, and I don't suppose he'll wake again. Good-night."

He shook hands and left the room, when Max's first step was to run to the window, and open it gently, but there was not a sound to be heard but the lapping of the waves among the rocks below.

Time after time The Mackhai, whose manner seemed greatly softened to him, suggested to Max that he should go fishing, shooting, or try one of the ponies.

"The keeper will go with you," he said; "and you seem to be wasting so much time. Why, we are turning you into quite a hospital nurse."

"Oh no; I would rather not go without Kenneth," said Max hastily; and The Mackhai said no more, being in doubt in his own mind whether the refusal was from cowardice or from disinclination to leave the invalid, who grew more fretful and impatient every day that he approached convalescence.

"Why can't you go and fish, or shoot, or do something, Max? You haven't tried for the trout yet. How I do hate to see you sitting there gaping at a fellow!"

"Did I gape?"

"Yes; you're always gaping, or bothering me to take one of old Curzon's doses. I say!"

"Yes."

"See Tavvy this morning?"

"Yes."

"What did he say?"

"That he wished you to get well, and come and catch some salmon."

"Well, it isn't my fault. I want to get well, don't I? A fellow can't want to lie here always, with his back getting sore. I say, do open the window."

Max glanced at the window to make sure.

"It is open," he said.

"No, it isn't."

"Yes, it is. Look!"

"Well, shut it, then. I hate to hear the sea."

"I like it," said Max, closing the sash.

"Yes, you miserable Cockneys always do. It gives one the horrors when you can't go out. Is it high tide?"

"No; quite low."

"It can't be. Go and look."

Max went to the window and looked out.

"The rocks are bare ever so far out, and you can see all the yellow weed."

"No, I can't."

"I meant I can."

"Well, why don't you say what you mean? Phew! how hot this room is! You might open a window."

Max smiled at his companion's petulance, and opened the window.

"Now, you're laughing at a poor miserable beggar."

"No, no, Kenneth," said Max, taking his hand.

"Don't do that! I wish you wouldn't be such a molly. Can't you say 'No, no,' without catching hold of a fellow's hand?—and one 'no' is enough. How jolly hot it is! See old Tonal' this morning?"

"Yes."

"What did he say?"

"He wants to come up and play to you on the pipes."

"Did he say he would?"

"Yes; and that he'd cut his way to you if they didn't let him come. He was going to sharpen his broadsword this morning."

"Look here: if he came up and began to play, he'd drive me mad. You go down and get my double gun and some cartridges."

"What for?"

"You don't suppose I'm going to lie here and be driven mad! I'll shoot him like I would a hare."

"Nonsense!" said Max, laughing.

"Well, you go and let him blow to you."

"No, thank you; I hate it."

"So do I; only a chap who is going to be chief of a clan some day mustn't say he hates the horrible old row. Here, I shall get up."

He threw off the clothes; but Max dashed at him, and covered him to the shoulders.

"No, no!" he cried.

"There you go with your 'No, no,' again. You're just like a great girl, Max."

"Am I? I'm very sorry."

"What's the good of being sorry? Be more like a man. Oh dear! I am so tired of lying here!"

"Yes, it is very tiring."

"Well, I know that. I didn't want you to tell me. What did Scoody say?"

"He's very angry because they will not let him come up to you, and will hardly speak to me."

"No wonder."

"He says it's a shame for me to be always with you, and him not allowed to come."

"So it is. Poor old Scoody! Did he say 'she shall came'?"

"Yes, over and over again."

"So it is a shame, poor old chap! I'll bully father about it. I'd a deal rather have him here than you."

"Would you, Kenneth?"

"Yes, ever so much: hanging about one, and wanting to coddle one like an old woman! I hate it!"

"I'm very sorry. I did my best to make you comfortable."

"You don't do your best. It bores me."

"Shall I read to you a bit now?"

"No! Bother your old books! Who wants to lie here and be read to about your jolly old Hentys, and Friths, and Percy Groves? I don't want books; I want to go out on the mountain, or in the boat, and have a rattling good sail. Here, I shall get up."

Max seized him and pressed him back, for he was very weak.

"The doctor says if you get out of bed, you'll faint again, same as you did yesterday."

"All right!" said Kenneth, struggling feebly; "I want to faint the same as I did yesterday. It will be a change."

"Nonsense! you shall not get up."

Kenneth lay back panting.

"Oh, how I do hate you!" he cried. "Just you wait till I get strong again. I'll serve you out. Scoody and I will duck you, and get you on the pony, and—I know! Just you let me get a chance, and I'll send you sailing down the falls just the same as I did."

"No, you will not."

"Oh, won't I? you'll see. If you knock me about again like this, I'll wait my chance, and pepper you with grouse-shot, and see how you like that. I say!"

"Yes, Kenneth."

"Don't say 'Yes, Kenneth,' say 'Yes.' Look here: why doesn't Long Shon come to ask how I am?"

"He does, every morning."

"He doesn't! a miserable old duck's legs!"

"But he does. I told you so."

"That you didn't. You take advantage of my lying here, and— Oh, I say, you might shut that window, it does make it so hot."

Max rose to go and close the window; but Kenneth caught his hand and held it, looking up at him wet-eyed and wistful.

"Maxy, old chap," he said softly.

"Yes."

"I am such a beast!"

"Nonsense!"

"I am. Don't take any notice of what I say. I feel as if I must be disagreeable, and say all sorts of things I don't mean, and all the time I know what a good un you are, sitting in this nasty, stuffy old room, that smells of physic enough to knock you down."

"I like sitting with you."

"You can't, when you might be out with Tavvy and Scood. I'd give anything to go, and you must want to go, but you're such a good-hearted old chap, to sit there and read for hours, and talk to a poor miserable beggar who's never going to be well again."

"Why, you are getting on fast."

"No, I'm not. I'm sick of these jellies, and beef-teas, and slip-slops. I want some beef, and salmon, and grouse pie, and to get strong again. I say, Maxy, wasn't I a fool?"

Max was silent.

"You're too good a chap to say it, but you know it was just out of bounce, and to show off, and it served me right. I say, you're not put out at what I've been saying?"

"Not a bit."

"Call me a beast, and then I'll be satisfied."

"But I shouldn't be," said Max, laughing.

"Yes, do call me a beast, and forgive me. I don't mean it, for I do like you, Maxy, honour bright!"

"I want you to like me," said the lad gravely.

"Well, I do. I'm as sorry as can be that I tried to frighten you, and laughed at you. I've been sorry lots of times since I've been lying here; and you will not take any notice of what I said?"

"Is it likely?" cried Max eagerly.

"Not with you, I suppose," said Kenneth thoughtfully; "but I'm afraid I should think a lot about it."

"I shall not," said Max, "so say no more."

"Then let's talk about something else; it keeps me from thinking how miserable and weak I am. I say, old Scood always pretended to be so very fond of me; don't you think he might have come up and seen me?"

"You know he has always been trying."

"Oh, ah! so I do. I forgot."

"He climbed up to the window and got in one night."

"Scoody did? You never told me that."

"I never told anybody."

"And he got down again all safe? Why, it was more risky than climbing up a rock. You tell him he must not do it again."

"I have told him."

"I'll ask my father to let him come up and see me, poor chap. He likes me, you see, Max. I say, I am so dull and miserable, you might do one thing for me."

"Yes: what shall I do?"

"Go and fetch the dogs. I want to see them."

Max nodded, and had reached the door, when Kenneth called him back.

"What is it?" said Max, staring, as he saw Kenneth's thin white hands stretched out towards him, and a peculiar look on his face, which looked the more strange from its having a long strapping of plaster across his brow.

Kenneth made no reply, only held out his hand.

Max grasped his meaning, and caught the hand in his, to hold it tightly, the two lads gazing in each other's eyes as a strong friendship was cemented between them, one far more binding than Kenneth could have imagined in his wildest dreams.

"There; I'm going to fetch the dogs," said Max hastily, and he ran out of the room, and down and out into the castle yard, where, to his horror, the first person he saw was old Donald, looking more wild and strange than ever.

Max backed into the archway leading to the house, hoping he had not been seen, but the old man uttered what was meant for a cry of delight, and, smiling at him, began to beckon with his hand and arm.

"What shall I do?" muttered Max, as the old man came up and tried to catch hold of his arm.

"Hey, bonnie laddie!" he cried, in a confidential whisper. "She's been watching for ye. She's chust made ta peautiful new dirge, and she shall play it to you up in ta toor."

"No, no," cried Max desperately. "The young Mackhai has sent me on a message."

"Ou ay! Put she'll not pe long. It was a peautiful music, and ye— Ta Southron laddie's gane!"

It was quite true, for Max had darted back and run to the dining-room, to get round by the terrace, and so by the rocks to the other side of the ruins, in search of the dogs.

There he came suddenly upon Scoodrach, lying on his chest in the sun, and with his chin in his hands, gazing up at the window of Kenneth's room.

"Here! hi, Scoodrach!" cried Max; and the lad looked at him scowling. "Kenneth has sent me to fetch—"

Scoodrach sprang up, with his whole manner changed.

"She's sent her to fetch me?" he cried eagerly.

"No, no; to fetch—the dogs."

A savage look of anger flashed into the lad's face, and he stood with his hands working.

"Na, na," he cried hoarsely; "it's a lee! Ta young Chief sent her to fetch his gillie, and she's trying to keep her awa'!"

"I told you the truth," cried Max, almost as angrily. "Here, Sneeshing, Sneeshing!" he cried, as he caught sight of the dog a hundred yards away; and the quaint-looking little terrier pricked up his ears, looked round, caught sight of the two boys, and came helter-skelter towards them.

The effect of this dash was for a sharp bark to be heard, and Dirk came into view, with his plume-like tail waving; while, before he was half-way toward Max, Bruce came, making greyhound-like bounds and evidently in a great state of excitement.

"Good dogs! good dogs, then!" cried Max, patting them; but they received his caresses in rather a cool manner, and Bruce, who seemed disappointed, was about to turn off and go, when Max bent over Sneeshing.

The dog looked up at him curiously.

"Come along," said Max; "your master wants to see you."

The words had hardly left his lips, when Dirk made a bound, and rushed off toward the open dining-room, window, behaviour which evidently puzzled the great deerhound, who watched the collie for a few moments, and then dashed off, followed by Sneeshing, who, however, responded to a call, and, after looking inquiringly in the speaker's eyes, he followed him toward the house.

Max stopped short at the end of a few yards and turned, to see Scoodrach walking slowly away.

"Scoody!" he called to him; "you are to come up and see him soon."

"Tak' ta togs! tak' ta togs!" said the young gillie bitterly. "She can't want to see me."

The collie and deerhound had both disappeared through the dining-room window; but it was as Max suspected: when he and the terrier reached the landing, Bruce was seated on the mat at Kenneth's chamber, and Dirk lying down blinking at him, and every now and then snuffling and thrusting his nose close to the bottom of the door.

As Max raised his hand to turn the handle, Dirk could contain himself no longer, and uttered a loud bark, the answer to which was a faintly-heard call from within the bedroom.

But, faint or no, it was enough to drive the dogs half wild; and, as Max opened the door, they gave vent to a canine trio, and dashed through quite a narrow crack, Bruce and Dirk together, for the great hound bounded over the collie, while in his excitement Sneeshing went head-over-heels into the room, but only to dash up to the bed, on to the chair at the side, and then to snuggle in close down to his master, while the others leaped on from opposite sides, and began pawing at the invalid and licking his hand.

"Down! down, dogs!" cried Max excitedly, in alarm lest they should injure the patient in his weak state. But, as he ran at the bed, Dirk and Bruce set up their bristles and uttered menacing growls, while Sneeshing thrust his rough head from under the clothes and added his remonstrance in the same canine way.

"Let 'em alone, Maxy; they're only glad to see their old master again," cried Kenneth, as he began to stroke the dogs' heads. "Quiet, old boys! Friends, friends! Come and pat 'em, Maxy; they mustn't bark at you. Friends, Dirk! Friends, Bruce lad!"

"How!"

"Hooorr!"

The utterances of the two dogs, as they accepted their master's orders, and began patting the white counterpane with their tails, while Sneeshing uttered a series of short barks, shook his head, and shuffled backwards, evidently laughing dogly with delight, and ending by getting his muzzle on Kenneth's breast and lying quite still.

"Oh, I say, this is a treat!" said Kenneth, with a sigh of satisfaction, as his hands were busy pulling the dogs' ears, and drawing the skin sideways, so as to show the whites of their eyes.

"Don't let them stay long."

"Why not? Does me more good than old Curzon's dollops. I'll get up to-morrow, and have the boat for a sail."

Dirk set up his ears at this, and began to bark as if he understood, and, rising on all-fours, he pawed at Kenneth, as he would have done at a sick sheep on the mountain-side, to make it rise.

The result of this action was to make Sneeshing resent the caressing of the intrusive paw, which twice over scraped him, and he snapped at, seized it, and held on.

Dirk howled out, "Don't! you hurt!" in dog.

Bruce gave vent to an angry bark at Sneeshing, who, however, held the tighter, uttering a low worrying snarl.

"Let me send them away now, Kenneth!" cried Max.

"What? Why, it's glorious! Hold tight, Sneeshing!"

A tremendous barking began now, for Dirk was losing his temper, and in another minute he would have dragged Sneeshing out of his snug place, for he had seized him by the loose skin at the back of his neck, when Kenneth shouted at them, and the disturbance ceased.

"I say, Max," he cried, "did you ever see Sneeshing dance the fling? No, I never showed you. Here, give me those joints of my fly-rod," and he pointed to them in a corner of the room.

Max fetched them; and as Kenneth took them and let them fall over his shoulder, Sneeshing shuffled out of the bedclothes and began to bark.

"Draw out that pillow," said Kenneth.

Max obeyed wonderingly; and rather feebly, but laughing the while, Kenneth tucked the pillow half under his left arm.

"What are you going to do?" cried Max.

"Wait a moment, and you'll see. Get back, you two—get back!"

Dirk and Bruce backed to the bottom of the bed, and sat up watching eagerly, while Sneeshing threw up his head and howled.

"Quiet, stupid!" cried Kenneth; "it isn't Tonal'."

"How wow!" howled Sneeshing.

"Be quiet, sir! Yes, I will."

He threatened the dog with one of the joints of the rod, and then threw it back over his left shoulder, as he lay with his head raised, and began to squeeze the pillow in imitation of a bag with its pipes.

"Now, Sneeshing, go ahead! Give us the Hieland Fling!"

Then, in imitation of the pipes, Kenneth began, and not badly,—

"Waugh! waugh!" and went on with the air "Tullochgorum," but Sneeshing only threw up his head and howled.

"Do you want me to whack you?" cried Kenneth. "Now, then, up you go, and we'll begin again."

"Waugh! waugh!"

Sneeshing had flinched from the rod, and now he gave his master a piteous look, but rose up on his hind legs and began to lift first one and then the other, drooping his forepaws and then raising them as he turned solemnly round to the imitation music. Twice over he came down on all-fours, for the bed was very soft and awkward on account of Kenneth's legs and its irregularities, but he rose up again, and the mock pipes were in full burst, and the dogs who formed the audience evidently in a great state of excitement, as they blinked and panted, when there was a tremendous roar of laughter, which brought all to a conclusion, the dogs barking furiously as Mr Curzon came forward with The Mackhai.

"Bravo! bravo!" he exclaimed. "There, I don't think you will want any more of my physic now."

Kenneth lay back, looking sadly shamefaced; and his father half-pleased, half-annoyed, as he opened the door and dismissed the dogs, but not unkindly.

"I'm glad to see you so much better, Ken."

"Thank you, father. I was only showing Max—"

"How much better you are!" interposed the doctor. "Well, I'm very glad; only I'd lie still now. Don't overdo it. There, Mr Mackhai, I have done. Thank you for your hospitality. I can go to-morrow."

"No; you'll stop and have a few days' fishing."

"Not one more, thank you; but if I am up here next year, and you would let me have a day or two on your water, I should be glad."

"As many days as you like, sir, for the rest of your life," said The Mackhai warmly, "for you saved that of my boy."

Ten minutes after, when they went down-stairs, Kenneth said,—

"I say, Max, what a humbug I must have looked! But I am ever so much better. I hope old Curzon will come and fish next year."

While down-stairs his father was angrily walking up and down his study.

"As many days as he likes for the rest of his life!" he exclaimed fiercely. "Idiot—ass that I have been, and that I am, to offer that which at any hour may belong to some one else."

"Well," he added, after a pause, "folly receives its punishments, and the greatest of all follies is to game."

Chapter Twenty Three
The Stag Max did not shoot

"I say, Max!" said Kenneth one day, as they sat at either end of a boat, whipping away at the surface of the rippling water of one of the inland lochs, up to which the said boat had been dragged years before, upon rough runners like a sleigh, partly by the ponies, partly by hand labour. Scoodrach was seated amidships, rowing slowly, and every now and then tucking his oar under his leg, to give his nose a rub, and grumble something about "ta flee."

This was on the occasion when the fly Max was throwing came dangerously near hooking into the gristle of the young gillie's most prominent feature.

Kenneth did not finish his sentence, for just then he hooked a trout which gave him a fair amount of play before it was brought alongside, where Scoodrach, who had ceased rowing, was ready with the landing-net.

"Let me land it," cried Max; and, taking the net, he held it as he had seen Scoodrach perform the same operation a score of times.

"All right!" cried Kenneth. "He's a beauty; pound and a half, I know. Now then—right under."

Kenneth's elastic rod was bent nearly double, as Max leaned forward, and, instead of lowering the net well into the water so that the fish might glide into it, he made an excited poke, and struck the fish with the ring; there was a faint whish as the rod suddenly straightened; a splash as the trout flapped the water with its tail and went off free, and Max and Kenneth stared at each other.

"She couldna hae done tat," muttered Scoodrach.

"Yes, you could, stupid!" said Kenneth, glad of some one upon whom he could vent his spleen. "You've knocked ever so many fish off that way."

"I'm very, very sorry," said Max humbly.

"That won't bring back the trout," grumbled Kenneth. "Never mind, old chap, I'll soon have another. Why don't you go on throwing?"

"Because I am stupid over it. I shall never throw a fly properly."

"Not if you give up without trying hard. Go on and have another good turn. Whip away. It'll come easier soon."

Max went on whipping away, but his success was very small, for he grew more and more nervous as he saw that Scoodrach flinched every time he made a cast, as if the hook had come dangerously near his eyes.

Once or twice there really had been reason for this, but, seeing how nervous it made Max, Scoodrach kept it up, taking a malicious delight in ducking his head, rubbing his nose, and fidgeting the tyro, who would gladly have laid down his rod but for the encouraging remarks made by Kenneth.

All at once the latter turned his head, from where he stood in the bows of the boat, and began watching Max, smiling grimly as he saw how clumsy a cast was made, and the smile grew broader as he noticed Scoodrach's exaggerated mock gesticulations of dread.

Then there was another cast, and Scood ducked his head down again. Then another cast, and Scood threw his head sideways and held up one arm, but this time the side of his bare head came with a sounding rap up against the butt of Kenneth's rod.

"Mind what you're doing!" shouted Kenneth.

"Hwhat tid ye do that for?" cried Scoodrach, viciously rubbing his sconce.

"Do it for? Why don't you sit still, and not get throwing your head about all over the boat?"

"She tid it o' purpose," growled Scoodrach; "and she's cooard to hit a man pehind her pack."

"If you call me a coward, Scoody, I'll pitch you overboard."

"No, she wouldna. She has not get pack her strength."

"Then Max will help me, and we'll see then."

"Pitch her overboard, then, and she'll swim ashore, and she'll hae to row ta poat her ainsel'."

But Scoodrach had no occasion to swim, for he was not pitched overboard; and, as the wind dropped and the water became like glass, the rods were laid in, and Scoodrach rowed them along in sulky silence toward the shore; Kenneth, as he sat now beside his companion, returning to the idea he had been about to start some time before.

"I say, Max," he said, "I wonder what's the matter with father. I wish old Curzon was here. I think the pater is going to be ill."

"I hope not."

"So do I; but he always seems so dull, and talks so little."

"I thought he seemed to be very quiet."

"Quiet! I should think he is. Why, he used to be always going out shooting or fishing, and taking me. Now, he's continually going to Glasgow on business, or else to Edinburgh."

"When do you expect him back?"

"I don't know. He said it was uncertain. Perhaps he'll be there when we get home."

But The Mackhai was not back, and a fortnight elapsed, and still he was away.

The last few days seemed to have quite restored Kenneth, who, once able to be out on the mountains, recovered strength at a wonderful rate.

Those were delightful days to Max. His old nervousness was rapidly leaving him, and he was never happier than when out with the two lads fishing, shooting, boating, or watching Kenneth as he stood spear-armed in the bows, trying to transfix some shadowy skate as it glided as if flying over the sandy bottom of the sea-loch.

One grandly exciting day to Max was on the occasion of a deer-stalking expedition, which resulted, through the clever generalship of Tavish, in both lads getting a good shot at a stag.

Max was first, and, after a long, wearisome climb, he lay among some rocks for quite a couple of hours, with Tavish, watching a herd of deer, before the time came when, under the forester's guidance, the deadly rifle, which Max had found terribly heavy, was rested upon a stone, and Tavish whispered to him, —

"Keep ta piece steady on ta stane, laddie, and when ta stag comes well oot into ta glen, ye'll chust tak' a glint along ta bar'l and aim richt at ta showlder, and doon she goes."

Max's hands trembled, his heart beat fast, and the perspiration stood on his brow, as he waited till, from out of a narrow pass which they had been watching, a noble-looking stag trotted slowly into the glen, and, broadside on, turned its head in their direction.

Max saw the great eyes, the branching antlers, and, in his excitement, the forest monarch seemed to be of huge proportions.

"Noo!" was whispered close to his ear; and, "glinting" along the barrel, after fixing the sight right upon the animal's flank, Max drew the trigger, felt as if some one had struck him a violent blow in the shoulder, and then lay there on his chest, gazing at a cloud of smoke and listening to the rolling echoes as they died away.

"Aweel, aweel!" said a voice close by him, in saddened tones. "Ye're verra young, laddie. Ye'll hae to try again."

"Isn't it dead?" said Max.

"Na, she's no' deid, laddie."

"But I don't see it. Where is the stag?"

"Ahint the mountain yonder, laddie; going like the wind."

"Oh!" said Max; and for the next few minutes he did not know which way he felt—sorry he had missed, or glad that the noble beast had got away.

Kenneth was more successful. He brought down his quarry a couple of hours later, and the rough pony carried home the carcase for Long Shon to break up, Max partaking of a joint of the venison a few days later, and thinking it was very good, and that he enjoyed it all the more for not having shot the animal himself,—though he could not help telling Kenneth that the fat seemed to stick to the roof of his mouth.

Chapter Twenty Four
Kenneth resists the Law

Three more days glided by, spent in hunting and fishing. Max succeeded in spearing one skate himself, and was nearly pulled out of the boat by the curious fish as it made its final struggle for life. And then a momentous day came, when, after spending the morning in having a glorious sail, during which, as there was a splendid breeze, Max had felt quite comfortable, as he sat well to windward, holding on by the gunwale and helping to act as ballast to keep the boat from going over under the great press of sail Kenneth insisted upon carrying, they ran softly in under shelter of the rocks, and were approaching the castle landing-place, when Tavish came rushing up breathlessly.

"Come oot!" he roared. "Come oot, laddies!"

"What's the matter, Tavvy? Has my father—"

"Nay, laddie; he's no' come back. Come oot! come oot!"

The boat was run in, Scoodrach left to moor her, and Kenneth leaped ashore.

"What's wrong?" he cried, as he was saluted by a burst of baying from the dogs, which had been waiting their master's return.

"Wrang, my laddie? She had to gang doon to Kinlochai, and there she found ta bailies."

"What, at the farm?"

"At ta fairm, laddie, noo. An ugly, pock-faaced chief wi' hauf a dizzen loons asked me ta way to Dunroe. He's a bailie coming to tak' ta place."

"What? Nonsense, Tavvy!"

"Hey, but it's nae nonsense, laddie, for she met Dooncan Graeme, and Dooncan knew her at Glasgie. She's ta bailie, and she's coming to tak' ta Dunroe."

"Then she isn't going to have it!" cried Kenneth, flushing. "Bailiffs, indeed! It's all some stupid mistake."

"She rin on to tall ye, but ye were awa'," panted Tavish, whose face was streaming.

"They're just here, then?" said Kenneth excitedly.

"Na; she was askit ta way to Dunroe, and she sent them richt doon through ta mountains, laddie; and they'll nivver get here till some ane sets them richt."

"Bravo, Tavish! But it must be all some mistake."

"Nay, laddie, it's no meestake. Ta Chief canna pay some siller, and ta bailie's coming to tak' Dunroe."

"Is he?" cried Kenneth fiercely. "We'll see about that. Call Long Shon."

"She's in ta castle, laddie, getting ta auld gates to. She was going to shut ta gates and keep ta bailie oot."

"Bravo, Tavvy! Does Grant know?"

"Oh ay, and ivery ane's helping."

"That's the beauty of having a castle to live in, Maxy. No one can get in when the tide's up except through the old gateway; and it isn't everybody who can manage it when the tide's down. I say, you won't help, will you?"

"Help! of course!" cried Max excitedly. "But what are you going to do?"

"Do! shut up the old gates. They can't scale the rock, and they've got no boats, so we'll let them besiege us. Bah! when they find the place locked, they'll go back. Come on."

Kenneth hurried them through the house from the rock terrace, leaving the boat swinging to the buoy, and, followed by Tavish, Scoodrach, and the dogs, the two lads made for the old castle yard, whose outer entrance was the only way in unless scaling ladders were brought.

Here Grant and Long Shon, with old Tonal' to help, were busily fixing props against the old gates which had been dragged to.

"Hurray! Bravo, Grant! Well done, Shon! That's it, Tonal'! That's fast. No one can get in here."

Max entered into the spirit of the thing with the most intense enjoyment, following Kenneth through the mouldering old gate tower, and up a crumbling staircase to the broken battlements, of which there was still enough round to allow of any one walking to and fro behind the broken crenelation, between whose teeth they could look down on any one coming up the rocky path from the edge of the bay.

The old castle had never before looked so romantic to Max, and he thoroughly realised now how great must have been its strength in ancient days, towering up as it did on the huge promontory of rock, whose sides were steep enough to save it from attack when enemies approached it from the land, the one path being narrow, while from the other side only a foe provided with war galleys could have landed on the terrace, and then beneath the defenders' fire.

"We're going to have the siege of Dunroe!" cried Kenneth excitedly. "Now, Grant, and you, Long Shon, help and get up the arms, and we'll defend the place till my father comes."

"But ye mauna shute," said Long Shon.

"Who's going to, Shon? We'll fire something else;" and he gave orders which the old butler, the men, and even the maids hastened to execute, till the battlements and the broad tower over the gateway, which was furnished with the openings called machicolations, used for dropping missiles on an approaching enemy, were fairly well furnished with ammunition.

"How about provisions?" cried Kenneth, as an idea suddenly struck him.

"Ou, there's plenty, Master Kenneth," said the butler grimly, as he rather enjoyed what was going on. "There's half the deer you shot, beside the mutton, and plenty of kippered saumon."

"Oh ay; and if they try to starve us," cried Tavish, "we can catch fush from the rock at high water ivery day."

The preparations went merrily on, every one working in the old Highland spirit, and seeming indued with the idea that it was a duty to defend the home of the Chief of the Clan Mackhai against the enemy that was expected—an enemy that must be baffled at all hazards.

Old Tonal' was the most excited of all, rushing here and there, and getting in everybody's way. One minute he was hurrying off to fetch his pipes, and seemed ready to blow. Then he was off again to put them away, to come forth again and go round the castle as far as was possible on the battlements, to see whether there was a weak spot where the foe might get in.

He had completed one of these examinations, and then came to where Kenneth was giving orders.

"Whusht, laddie!" he whispered confidentially.

"Hullo, Tonal', you?"

"Ay! Whusht!"

"Ready to fight, Tonal'?"

"Ay, she'll fecht! she'll fecht for ta auld hame! But whusht, laddie!"

"Eh?" cried Kenneth; "what is it?"

"Stanes, laddie, stanes."

"Stanes! what about 'em?"

"Gin ye—but whusht!—gin ye had aboot sax hundert stanes a' retty on ta toor, she could ding them a' doon on ta caterans' heads."

"Ah, but we might break their heads, Tonal'. No, no; something softer than that. We'll have water."

"Watter? Watter, laddie?" cried the old piper contemptuously. "D'ye want to wash ta enemies o' ta hoose? Stanes,—gran' stanes,—and she'll ding them doon."

"No, no, Tonal'; that will not do."

The old man stood staring in wonder and disgust as Kenneth hurried away; but directly after he caught sight of Max, and, raising his hand and crooking one finger, he morally took the lad into custody as he approached him slowly.

"He will na hearken aboot ta stanes, laddie," whispered the old man mysteriously; "but sneeshing, laddie, sneeshing?"

"He's along with Scoodrach," said Max, pointing toward the dog. "There he goes yonder."

"Na, na, sneeshing—chust a wee pinch."

"Oh no, I have no snuff," said Max.

"Nae sneeshing!" muttered the old man, looking round; "she has nae sneeshing!"

"Hey!" shouted Scoodrach suddenly; "here they come."

Every one hurried to one or other of the openings to look at the approaching enemy, while Tavish stamped savagely on the stones.

"She's askit somebody and she's set 'em richt. She didna aught to be here for hoors and hoors, if she cam' back at a'."

"Never mind, Tavish!" shouted Kenneth; "we'll soon send them to the right-about."

"Hey, ta foe! ta foe!" yelled Tonal', throwing his hands in the air, and yelling at the group about him, before hurrying away and disappearing in the crumbling opening of the corner tower, high up in which he composed his wonderful melodies for the pipes.

"Look at auld Tonal'!" cried Scoodrach; "she's gane into her hole like a mause."

But no one turned to look at Tonal', for the enemy were approaching fast,—eight or nine sturdy-looking men, headed by a fair, round-faced fellow, speckled and splashed with freckles, so that his countenance was quite yellow, out of which peered, from under a pair of rugged sandy brows, two unpleasant-looking red-rimmed eyes, which blinked and peered and searched about as sharply as those of a monkey, waiting for the keeper with his daily quantum of carrot and dessert of nuts.

This man turned for a moment and said something to his followers. Then he took off his flat Tam o' Shanter and gave his head a vicious scratch, which seemed to have the effect of removing a little more of his hair. This, however, was not the fact, only seeming, as his head was bare in patches. Then, replacing his bonnet, he took out a greasy old pocket-book, gave it a slap, and, holding his head on one side like a magpie as he drew out the tuck, he peered in, and took out a piece of folded paper, which he held with his teeth till he had closed and replaced the pocket-book.

Next he took hold of the paper, thrust his hand into his coat tail, pulled out a ragged red cotton handkerchief, and blew his nose.

Max burst into a roar of laughter, in which Kenneth joined, for to both lads the sounding blast which followed suggested that this was the enemy's trumpet summoning them to surrender.

The man stared, and one of his followers touched him on the shoulder.

"They're haeing the laugh at ye, mon," he said.

"Haud yer gab. They'll be laughing the ither side o' the mooth sune."

He walked right up toward the gate, and then started, for Kenneth shouted, "Hallo!" in a sharp, half-menacing way.

"Mr Mackhai at home?" said the man.

"No, he is not. What do you want?"

"Mr Mackhai."

"Well, you can't see him; he's out. I'm his son."

"Then ye'll just come doon and show me the way in."

"You mean the way out."

"Oh no, I don't, my whipper-snapper. Is this the way?"

"No."

"Then which is?" said the man, looking to right and left.

"There is no way in for you," said Kenneth; and a murmur of applause followed the words.

"Look ye here, my lad," said the man, holding out his paper. "D'ye see this?"

"Oh yes, I can see it," cried Kenneth. "Here, Scoody, this gentleman wants a light for his pipe; throw him a box of matches."

"No nonsense, please," cried the man. "I come in the name of the law. Sandy, gang and ope that gate."

"Gin ye gang that gate," roared Tavish, "I'll break the head o' ye."

The man who had stepped forward, started back at this menacing warning, for Tavish suddenly appeared standing up like a giant near the gateway, with something which looked like a great stone in his hand.

"Put that doon, mon," cried the bailiff. "Ye'll be getting into trouble. Now, young sir, come doon and ope the gate, and read this paper. I take possession here in the name of the law."

"All right!" cried Kenneth mockingly. "Take away."

There was a laugh, and Kenneth shouted again,—

"Hi, Grant! you can show him how to take away."

"Are you going to open these gates, sir, and let us in?" cried the bailiff, as soon as a hearty laugh had subsided.

"No."

"Are you going to tell your men to open, then?"

"No, I'm not."

"Do you know that you are resisting the law, young sir?"

"No, but I know I'm resisting you."

"By this paper I have proper warrant to take possession of all here."

"Have you? Well, I don't care what warrant you have. My father's out, and I'm not going to let a set of ragged-looking Southroners come and do what they please in Dunroe."

"I tell you, I have a proper warrant for taking possession."

"Then put it back in your pocket, and come again when my father's at home."

"Look here, me laddie, it'll be a bad day's wark for ye, if ye resist the law."

"You be off, and come again when my father's at home, I tell you."

"I've come a' these lang miles, me laddie, and I'm no' gaeing back wi'out takking possession. Noo, ance mair, will ye open the gates?"

"No."

"Then we must break them in."

"Mind we don't break your head in, then, that's all."

"If ye daur!"

"Oh, we daur. Don't we, Scood?"

"Oh ay," roared the young gillie.

The bailiff walked back to his men, whispered a few orders, and then turned once more to Kenneth, who was standing now well in sight on the crumbling battlements, with Max by his side.

"Noo, my laddie, let's hae a' this bet o' besness settled doucely. Ye'll come doon and open the gates?"

"No surrender!" cried Kenneth.

"Ye'll hae the gates opened?"

"No; so blow your trumpet again. Defiance! There!"

He took a clean aim with a great potato; and the bailiff had to dodge the shot very sharply, to avoid receiving the blow on his cheek.

But the shot was not wasted, for a man behind had it full in the chest, and a shout arose.

"That will do!" cried the bailiff. "You've struck a blow, so you must put up with the consequences. Noo, my lads, come on!"

Chapter Twenty Five
How Donald played the War March

The bailiff turned to his men and gave them an order, whose effect was to make them shuffle together.

"You hear me, sir!" cried the bailiff. "You struck the first blow."

"You lie, you bun-faced Southroner!" cried Kenneth. "You made the first blow in that old pocket-handkerchief."

"Will you surrender?"

"No!"

"Then come on, my lads. Forward!"

"Hurray! hurray!" shouted Ken, pointing upwards; and the bailiff and his men stopped and stared with open mouths at the scene.

"Look, Max! Look, Scoody! Hurray! Mackhai! Mackhai!"

A shrill, piercing, cracked old voice echoed the cry from above, and the lads on the crumbling battlements over the gateway, where they stood ready with pails of water for sending down through the machicolations, stood gazing at a tall weird figure in full war-paint, with the front of his bonnet cocked up with its eagle pinion feathers, his grey hair flying in the breeze, his eyes flashing, tartan scarf buckled with·his great cairngorm brooch, as old Tonal' climbed slowly into sight, and stood on the narrow ledge of battlement at the very top of the right-hand tower.

"Ta Mackhai!" he yelled. "Ta Mackhai!" and, as he stood there, with scarf and kilt fluttering about his tall, lean old figure, he looked like one of the ancient fighting men of the clan come back from the Middle Ages to battle in defence of his chief.

"Ta Mackhai! Ta Mackhai!" he yelled again, in answer to a tremendous cheer from the party within.

"Come doon, ye auld idgit!" shouted the bailiff.

"Ta Mackhai! Ta Mackhai!" yelled Tonal'; and, raising an old claymore in one hand, his dirk in the other, to the full stretch of his long arms, he shrieked out,—

"Doon wi' ta caterans! Doon wi' ta Lowland loons! Mackhai! Mackhai! Fecht, laddies! fecht! Hech! hech! hech! Hurray!"

"Hech! hech! hech! Hurray!" shouted Kenneth, roaring with laughter. "Fecht, laddies, fecht!"

The weird-looking old piper waved his claymore wildly about his head, and it flashed in the sun; but in his efforts he nearly toppled off the tower headlong down to the front of the castle. He made a snatch at the ancient crenelation, and, to the horror of all, a quantity of the crumbling stone fell with a crash, and, but for a rapid dash backward, two of the bailiffs men would have been crushed.

But, active still as a wild cat, the old man saved himself; and, though one of his legs came right over the front, and he lay on his face for a few moments, he climbed back, stood erect again, planted one foot on the remaining crenele, and raised his flashing broadsword, tore off his bonnet, dashed it down, and, as his thin long grey hair streamed out in the sea breeze, he yelled once more,—

"Mackhai! Mackhai! Fecht, laddies, fecht!"

Then he disappeared.

"He's coming down with his old carving-knife, Maxy," cried Kenneth, wiping the tears from his eyes. "I shall have to go and lock the old chap up, or he'll do some one a mischief."

"Hi, there!" shouted the bailiff; and his voice was the signal for the three dogs to burst into a tremendous trio of barking. "Look here, I give you fair warning. You're resisting the law, and it'll be the worse for you if any one of my men is hurt."

"Come roond and we'll pitch ye all into ta watter!" shouted Scoodrach.

"Yes, come round the other side, you bun-faced looking bailiff!" cried Kenneth; and the defenders uttered a fresh cheer, while Grant in his excitement took off his black coat and white cravat, and rolled up his sleeves, before putting on an apron one of the maids had fetched.

"Hurray, Grant! you look as if you were going to clean the plate," cried Max excitedly.

"I'm going to take care, sir, that that scum does not touch it," said Grant, with dignity. "Well done, laddie!" he added to himself. "I'm beginning to like him after a'."

"Are you going to open this gate?" cried the bailiff, waving his piece of blue paper.

"Yes, when you are gone," cried Kenneth, stooping quickly, picking a potato out of the basket at his feet, and throwing it with such good aim that it struck the bailiff in the chest.

This was the signal for a general discharge, Max and Scoodrach hurling potatoes with all their might at the attacking party, and with more or less good aim.

"Oh, if they'd only come close in ready for the boiling lead!" cried Kenneth.

"Here, Shon!" shouted Max, whose face was crimson with excitement; "more potatoes—I mean cannon balls. Bring up a sack."

"It'll be the worse for you," shouted the bailiff. "Come on, my lads, in with you!"

There was a rush made for the gateway, but a shower of vegetable bullets came now from the whole force of defenders, Tavish throwing two at a time, and Long Shon hitting every shot.

This checked the advance for a moment, and just then old Tonal' reappeared at the front of the tower, with his hair streaming out like the tail of a silvery comet. The old man's face was puffed out and red, for now, in place of his claymore and dirk, he had his pipes in hand.

"Fecht, laddies, fecht!" he yelled; and, in spite of his being such an anachronism, there was something grand now in the wild old figure, as he stood there in full view, from crown to buckled shoon, claymore sheathed, the jewels in his dirk sparkling, and the sun flashing from his eyes as he yelled out, "Ta slogan of ta Mackhai! Mackhai! Mackhai!"

"Oh, do hold me, Maxy, or I shall go overboard," cried Kenneth, as he held his sides and roared with laughter, for the old retainer sent forth a tremendous blast from his pipes, which came echoing back from the walls within, as he marched up and down at the front of the crumbling tower about eight steps each way, blowing with all his might, his efforts being responded to by fresh cheers from the little garrison.

"Hurrah! Hech! Hurrah!" cried Tavish, who was infected by the excitement and the national music. "Hey, but we will fecht, Maister Ken! we'll die for ye. Oh, it's crand—it's crand!"

"Fecht, then, all o' ye," cried Kenneth, taking up the broad dialect; and then roaring to those in the yard, "You girls, bring up everything you can. Never mind what it is—anything we can throw."

A shrill scream of delight came from within, and, as the dogs barked furiously, the old piper still stamped up and down and played the war march of the Clan Mackhai.

"Don't stand glowering at that owd gowk," cried the bailiff. "Come on!"

The men murmured, and held back, as the ammunition kept flying, and they had to dodge the missiles, some of the younger men catching the potatoes and throwing them back.

"Stop that, some of ye," cried the bailiff. "Ye're no' playing crecket. Noo then, forward!"

This time his followers obeyed, and they made a rush, to be received by a tremendous volley, which produced first blood, Scoodrach having sent a big Dalmahoy or a Scotch Regent—this is a doubtful point in the chronicle of the attack and defence of Dunroe—and hit one of the bailiff's men full in the nose, one of Max's shots taking effect at the same time in a man's eye, and the first of the wounded staggered back to the hospital ambulance; in other words, he bolted down the rocks to the water's edge and began to bathe his face.

Another shout, though, from the bailiff, and the assaulting party charged home right up to the gateway, and began to thunder and thrust at the crumbling old gates, which were, however, held fast by the wooden props and stones.

"We can't get through here," grumbled one man. "Is there no other way?"

"No, not without a latter," said another.

"Then let's fetch a latter."

"No, no; push all together, and down the gates will go. They can't hit us here."

Squish, splash, wash, came down a perfect torrent of water through the machicolations, as what Kenneth called "the boiling lead" was brought to bear through the openings left by the old architect for the defence of the gate.

"No, no, no; don't rin!" cried the bailiff; "it's only watter."

Plosh!

Half a pailful poured down by Max came full upon the speaker's head, and he turned and headed the stampede, amidst the roars of laughter of the defenders.

"Yah! it's a' doon me back—it's a' doon me back," snarled the bailiff, stamping with fury, as he dashed the water out of his hat, and wrung his clothes, to the great delight of his men as well.

"Ye shall a' pay for this!" he shouted, as he waved the wet paper he held. "Ye'll know ye're reseesting the law."

"Come and have another shower-bath!" cried Max.

"Yes, you want it!" roared Kenneth. "Bring some more ammunition. Hi, Tonal', play up, auld mon!"

"Fecht, laddies, fecht!" shouted back the old piper, as he took the piece from his lips for a moment.

"Yes, we'll fecht!" cried Kenneth.

"Gin ye come here, ye togs, she'll slit a' yer weams!" yelled Scoodrach excitedly; and then there was a pause, for the bailiff was holding a consultation, and then he pointed down to the beach.

"What's he pointing at?" said Kenneth, as his followers placed fresh ammunition—the wet and the dry—ready.

"I know," cried Max. "That old bit of a mast."

"What, the broken topmast of the wreck?"

"Yes. They're going to fetch it, and make a battering-ram to knock down the gate."

"Then we'll half drown the beggars," cried Kenneth. "More water here! Cookie, let's have some hot."

"Hey, but ye shall have sax pots fu', Maister Kenneth," cried the woman, and in a very short time, as the bailiffs men went down to get the old spar, six kettles and saucepans of boiling water were brought up into the old broken gateway tower.

"Pour it into the pails, and soften it down, Maxy. We mustn't give it to 'em too hot," cried Kenneth.

"How much cold shall I put?"

"Half and half; that'll suit 'em. Shall I give 'em some whisky and sugar with it, Grant?"

"Nay, nay," cried the old butler; "and don't make it too cold, or there'll be no sting in it to frighten 'em."

"Now then, girls," cried Kenneth, "bring them along."

Everybody worked with a will, and plenty of missiles were carried up the broken stone stairs and stored ready, Max making himself so busy, and growing so excited, that Tavish patted him on the shoulder.

"Hey," he said softly, "'twas a gran' petty she were born so far sooth."

As for Scoodrach, he grew quite friendly, and grinned hugely at the way in which Max took to the defence.

"It's a rare game, isn't it, Maxy?" cried Kenneth, in the temporary lull of the attack.

"Game! I never enjoyed anything so much in my life. Shall we beat them off?"

"Shall she peat 'em off!" cried Tavish fiercely. "She wull peat 'em off! D'ye think ta children of ta Mackhai will let ta thieves come past ta gates?"

"Hurray!" cried Kenneth; and Scoodrach tossed up his bonnet as he shouted, and then nearly tumbled off the battlements as he tried to catch the cap, and stood scratching his curly red head as the woollen-tufted covering fell below.

"Hullo, Scood!" cried Max.

"It ton't matter," cried the gillie; "she can fecht petter withoot a ponnet."

"Look at old Donald," whispered Max.

The pipes had ceased, and they looked up, to see the old man stooping in a striking attitude, bareheaded and with his right hand shading his eyes, one knee resting on the corner crenele of the tower, his left arm grasping his pipes, while he watched the movements of the bailiff's men, as they now began to lift the spar on to their shoulders.

"Be quite ready for them when they come," cried Kenneth, after a hearty laugh at the old family retainer.

"Oh ay," said Scood, "we'll pe retty;" and, with a queer look, he drew a sgian-dhu from his belt.

"Ah, none of that, Scoody!" cried Kenneth. "Give me that knife."

"Nay; she wants it for ta togs when ta gate's knockit down."

"No, you don't. Here, Max, take away that knife."

"Nay, she will na give it up," growled Scoody menacingly; and his face grew dark as Max seized his wrist and took the knife.

"Ye daurna do that if ta young chief wasna here," he said angrily.

"Yes, I dare," cried Max, turning away, and giving Kenneth the knife, which he jerked over his shoulder into the courtyard.

At that moment the pipes struck up again, "The Campbells are coming," and old Tonal' recommenced his short march to and fro, for the bailiffs gang, after shouldering the old spar, were in full march up the steep slope towards the gateway, and as they approached they gave a triumphant cheer.

"Now, once more," cried the bailiff: "where's Mr Mackhai?"

"What do you mean with your 'once more'? You never asked that before."

"Never you mind about that, my lad; and you'll find yourself in prison for this day's work. Where's Mr Mackhai?"

"Gone to Inverness, ugly," cried Kenneth derisively.

"Then you've got to give up this place to me quietly, under an—"

Bang!

"Who threw that potato?"

"I did," cried Max, laughing at the success of his aim, and his shot was followed by a shower which disorganised the enemy so that they ducked and dodged, and ended by dropping the old spar, from which all leaped, so as to save their toes.

"Pick it up, you great fools," roared the bailiff angrily. "And you look here," he cried, shaking the paper: "all the proper legal forms have been gone through, and this is an eviction order at the suit of— Hang them! how they can throw!" cried the man angrily, as a fresh missile struck him on the cheek.

"Fecht, laddies, fecht!" yelled Tonal', stopping for a moment to shout, and then blowing again with all his might.

"You'd better go and pull that old madman down," cried the bailiff. "Now, once for all," he continued, shaking the paper, "will you surrender?"

"No!" shouted Kenneth.

"No!" yelled Scoodrach; "she'll fecht till she ties. Come on!"

"All right," said the bailiff, turning to his men, who had once more got the spar on their shoulders. "No, no," he said; "half of you get one side, half the other, and swing it by your hands. Keep step, and run with it against the gate. The rotten old wood will fly like tinder."

The men obeyed, got the spar, which was about twenty feet long, well swung between them, and stood ready.

"Now, when I say 'go!'" cried the bailiff, "off with you at a good run, down with the gate, and rush in. I shall be close behind. Ready? Go!"

The men started, but they did not keep step, and before they had reached the gate, not only were they in confusion, but, amidst the shrieking of the pipes and the shouts and cheers of the defenders, they were met by such a storm of missiles, that, after bearing up against it for a few moments, they again dropped the great spar, and ran back.

This movement was the signal for a roar of derisive cheers, the boys indulging in quite a war-dance, which was ended by Scoodrach standing on his head upon one of the creneles, as a sign of his contempt for the enemy.

It was a dangerous feat, and he would have overbalanced himself, had not his father caught hold of one of his legs and dragged him back.

"What are ye gaun to dae?" he growled.

"Here, Scood, go and fetch the dining-room—no, you go, Grant—the table-cover, and that old long spear out of the hall."

The old butler smiled grimly, and began to descend from the broken rampart to the courtyard.

"What are you going to do, Ken?" asked Max.

"Hoist our colours. I'll let them see whether we're going to surrender."

"Want any more hot watter, Maister Ken?" cried the cook.

"Yes, to be sure—coppersful. Bring it along."

For the first time in Kenneth's recollection he saw the butler run, and in a few minutes he was back, with a red table-cover and a rusty-headed old lance.

"That's right! I'll show 'em!" cried Kenneth, as he tied two corners to the lance shaft; and, amidst fresh cheering, this was stuck in a corner and fixed in position with stones, so that the colours flew out triumphantly.

"Now then, come on!" shouted Kenneth, and a roar of defiance was uttered by the garrison, as the bailiff led back his men, making them pick up the battering-ram, and organising them for a fresh attack.

"A set o' cooards!" he exclaimed; "I'm ashamed o' ye."

"Weel, ye rin too," grumbled one of the men.

"Haud yer clack," cried the bailiff. "Noo then—go!"

There was another rush, and another shower of missiles as effective as the last; but this time the men charged on, and gave a moderately effective thump on the great gate; but it was not delivered all together and with a will, for, although a little desperate, the attacking party could not help dodging the potatoes which came thudding against them, and they were confused by the shouts, yells, and the shrieking of the pipes.

But they delivered another stroke, and another, as Tonald yelled again,—

"Fecht, lads, fecht!" and then blew and stamped up and down in a wonderful state of excitement.

Hot water was poured down, potatoes, pails, pots of earthenware flew, and came down with a crash like exploding shells, and the excitement had nearly reached its height, when, in the midst of the storm of missiles thrown, the gate began to yield beneath the blows, and Kenneth was about to shout to his followers to run down and fight inside the gate, whose defenders now were the dogs alone, who barked and growled savagely at every blow.

"Don't be beaten, lads; never mind their throwing. Keep it up," cried the bailiff. "Never mind that. Go on. Another, and another, and down she comes."

Bopp!

But it was not the gate. There was a loud explosion—quite a heavy, echoing report, but the way was not open to the bailiff's men, and the occupants of Dunroe were not to be evicted that day.

For the attacking party suddenly ceased their efforts, to stand gazing in awe at something which had happened, and then they turned and fled.

Just when the wild confusion was at its height, and attackers and defenders were wild with excitement, the battering-ram threatening, the gates cracking, missiles flying, and both parties shouting with all their might, Donald Dhu was blowing his best, stamping up and down, gazing wildly at the participators in the fray, when in his excitement he stepped upon a loose stone near the edge of the tower, where the crenelation was broken away, slipped, and went headlong down, to fall in a sitting position, and cause the loud report that startled all.

"Oh, poor old Donald! he's killed!" cried Kenneth, with a cry of anguish, as all the fun of the defence passed away, and he saw himself face to face with a tragedy, whose occurrence had paralysed every one present; the sight of the falling man and the report being followed by a dead silence, which affected even the dogs.

But, to the astonishment of all, the old man suddenly sprang up, clapped his hand to his side, and whirled out his claymore from its sheath.

"Fecht, laddies, fecht!" he yelled, as he waved the flashing blade above his head. "Doon wi' t' enemies o' ta Mackhai!"

Uttering these last words as if they were a war-cry, he dashed at the bailiff, who stared wildly at the weird-looking old Highlander for a moment, and then, with his men, he turned and fled, the whole party retreating as hard as they could go.

"Hurray!" shouted Kenneth, and a burst of cheers followed, all shouting frantically as they saw old Tonal' in full pursuit.

Full pursuit?

He only went about half a dozen yards; then he limped, then he stopped short, and then he turned slowly, making his sword a walking-stick, as the gates were thrown open, and the dogs dashed out, barking savagely, and took up the pursuit, adding wings to the flight of the bailiffs men. These ran the harder as they saw the light cavalry let loose, in the shape of Bruce, followed at a distance by the heavies, as represented by Dirk, who could not go so fast, and with the infantry in support in the ragged person of Sneeshing, who hindered his advance by keeping on firing shots.

The rest of the garrison poured forth, led by Kenneth, closely followed by Max and Scood, the former running up to old Donald, who came limping on.

"Are you much hurt, old man?" cried Kenneth, taking one arm.

"Ta togs! I'd ha' slit the weam o' ivery ane!" panted the piper.

"But are you much hurt? Anything broken?"

"Proken, dear laddie, son o' my sin auld Chief—proken all to pits. Didna ye hear ta clash?"

"Let's carry him in," cried Max.

"Na, na, my bonnie Southron chiel'," said the old man, smiling at Max. "Na, na, she can walk; put, Maister Crant, she could tak' chust a tram o' Talisker or Clen Nevis, for she's a pit shakken wi' coming town sae quick."

The lads helped the old man toward the gateway while Grant ran off eagerly enough for the whisky.

"Scoody, fetch a chair," cried Max.

"Lat her carry the auld man in," said Tavish.

"Na, na, let her pe. I want to see 'em—I want to see 'em," cried the old man, waving them off impatiently; and he limped to where his instrument, with the green baize bag and pennoned ivory-tipped pipes, lay on the ground.

"Oh tear! wae's me!" he moaned, as he stooped down and picked up the instrument. "Put ta enemies o' ta Mackhai listened to ta pibroch, and she turned and fled; put," he added, looking round piteously, "it was a pran new pahg, it was a pran new pahg."

"What!" cried Kenneth and Max, as a light struck in upon them, and the circle of sympathisers pressed round; "is the bag burst?"

"Purst!" groaned Tonal' mournfully; "ant I tried so hart to haud her up, but she couldna dae it, and come doon setting on ta pran new skin. Tidn't she hear her co pang?"

Chapter Twenty Six
"Suit of Andrew Blande"

A shriek of hearty laughter rose as poor Tonal's naïve question was heard, and the old man tucked his pipes under his arm, and then took hold of the sheath and raised his claymore to return it to its peaceful state; but, as he raised the glistening basket-hilt to the full length of his stretch, it fell from his grasp with a clang upon the stones; the old man's eyes closed, and he would have fallen, had not Max thrown his arm about his waist.

"Oh, Donald, old man!" cried Kenneth piteously; "I wouldn't have laughed if I had known."

"Whisht, laddie!" said Tavish. "Lat me tak' him;" and, raising the old man in his arms, he bore him through the gates and into the servants' quarters. Here he was laid upon a bed, and the whisky Grant had brought applied to his lips.

"Oh, if we only had Mr Curzon here!" whispered Max.

"Nay, laddie, we dinna want him," said Tavish. "There's naething proken but ta pipes—nae banes. He's a bit shakkit i' ta pack. It's a coot way doon."

Just then the old man revived and looked round wonderingly, and his eyes flashed directly, as there was a loud barking again from the dogs.

"Dinna ye hear?" he cried; "dinna ye hear? Ta enemy of ta Mackhai!"

"Tavish! Scoody!" cried Kenneth excitedly. "Come on!"

"Na," said Scoodrach, grinning; "it's naething but ta togs."

"But the gates! the gates!"

"She shut 'em up chust noo, and it's ta togs that canna get in."

A watch was kept as soon as the old man had been ministered to, and Tavish seemed to be right: Donald had been terribly shaken, but no bones were broken. He displayed a good deal of solicitude at one minute, though, and looked round wildly.

"What is it, Tonal'?" said Kenneth, taking his hand.

"Gude laddie," he replied,—"gude laddie; but ta pipes—ta pipes!"

"You shall have a new set," cried Kenneth.

"Yes; I'll buy him a set," cried Max.

"Na, na. T'auld pipe is ta best. Lat 'em lay 'em here."

"Here?" said Kenneth inquiringly.

"Yes, laddie, here."

The old man's whim was gratified, and he dropped off to sleep with his arm round his instrument, cuddling it up to him on the pillow as if it had been a darling child.

Donald was left to sleep; and, under Kenneth's orders, all hands were set to work to clear away the traces of the fight, while Scoodrach was sent out to scout and bring back tidings of the whereabouts of the enemy.

The young gillie had recovered his sgian-dhu from where it had been thrown by Kenneth, and he ran off with alacrity, delighted with his task; while baskets and maunds were brought, and amidst plenty of hearty laughter the potatoes were gathered up, the women entering into the task heart and soul.

But, like Humpty Dumpty, the various earthenware pots that had fallen from the wall, even with the aid of all the king's horses and men, could not have been put together again, so Long Shon gathered the sherds into a basket, throwing one load into the sea, and coming back for another.

"I say, look here, Tavvy," cried Kenneth very innocently, after hurling a potato with magnificent aim at Max's back, and completely ignoring his inquiring gaze as the visitor turned round.

"Tid she call me?"

"Yes; we must have this old spar out of the way, for they may come back and have better luck next time."

"Hey, but they wadna daur come back," cried Tavish.

"I don't know, Tavvy. Anyhow, we'll have the spar where they can't get it. Where shall we put it?"

"She'd better pit it inside ta castle," said Tavish.

"Well, we'll all help you carry it. You'll help, Max?"

"Oh yes, I'll help," replied Max, offering the potato to Kenneth. "Do you want to throw this at any one else?"

"Eh? No. Yes, I do. I'll keep it for the bailiffs. I say, though, this is a rum game. Those people can't have any right to come like that."

"I don't know for certain," said Max; "but I'm afraid they have—if—"

He stopped short, for Kenneth flushed up.

"Oh, come, Maxy, that's too bad. Don't insult my father by saying things in that underhanded way. My father doesn't owe money, I'm sure."

Max felt uncomfortable, for he had an undefined feeling that there was something very wrong, but it was all misty and confused.

"I didn't want to hurt your feelings, Ken," he said.

"Then you shouldn't. There, never mind. Hi, Long Shon, come and help carry this old spar."

"She ton't want any one to help her carry ta bit o' wud," said Tavish contemptuously. "She could pitch it like ta caber."

He raised himself to his full height, as he strode towards the gateway where the spar lay. Then, stooping down, he lifted one end and rested it upon his shoulder, after which he kept on hitching it up and getting farther under till he had reached the middle, when he grasped it with both hands firmly, took a step back, and the far end rose slowly from the ground, the spar swaying in equilibrium slowly up and down as the great fellow stood firm till it was at rest, and perfectly horizontal, when he strode slowly and steadily toward the gate and went through into the yard.

"There, Maxy, talk about a Samson!" cried Kenneth; "what do you think of that?"

"I'd give something to be as strong," said Max, as he ran into the courtyard, followed by Kenneth, the two boys applauding loudly as Tavish gave himself a jerk, leaped aside, and the spar fell with a clang which echoed from the ruined walls.

"She's chust a wee pit heavy, Maister Ken," said Tavish, passing his arm across his brow, "and she wadna like to carry ta pit o' wood to Falkirk."

"Ta Chief—ta Chief!" shouted Scoodrach, coming running in through the gate.

"What! my father?" cried Kenneth, flushing up. "I say, Maxy, what will he say? Where is he, Scoody?"

"Chust here on ta pony," whispered the lad, with his eyes wide; and he looked round for a way to escape, as if he had a pricking of conscience as to what had been going on.

"Take the pony and rub him down. I've ridden hard. Where's Mr Kenneth?" came from outside.

The voice sounded very harsh and stern, so much so that Kenneth shrank from meeting him, but it was only for a moment.

"I'm here, father," he cried, and he went out, followed closely by Max,—who felt that he had no business to go, but that if he stayed back, it would be like leaving his friend in the lurch.

"Oh, there you are—both of you," said The Mackhai sternly; and Max noted that he was deadly pale, while the veins in his temples were swollen, and looked like a network right round to the front of his brow.

"Yes, father, here we are—both of us," said Kenneth, unconsciously repeating his father's form of expression.

"Then perhaps, sir, you will explain to me what is the meaning of that piece of tomfoolery?"

The Mackhai was evidently greatly agitated, and fighting down his anger, as he spoke in a cold, cutting tone, and pointed upward to the ruined battlements.

Kenneth and Max had both forgotten it till they glanced up, and saw the dining-room table-cover floating from the spear staff in the wind.

"That, father?" cried Kenneth, forcing a laugh, while Max felt a strange desire to beat a retreat; "that's the banner of the Mackhais."

"No fooling, sir, at a time like this," cried The Mackhai, so fiercely that his son turned pale. "And now please explain what's all this I have just learned on the way, about a party of men coming here, and there being a desperate fight. Is this true?"

"Well, there has been a fight, father. I don't know about desperate."

"Not desperate, sir! when I found two men on the road, one bruised and battered about so that he can't see out of his eyes, and his face all blood-smeared, while the other is lamed, and can hardly walk."

"Well, sir," said Kenneth boldly, "a pack of scoundrels came here with a cock-and-bull story about taking possession of Dunroe; and as you were out, and I knew it must be some trick, I called our people together, shut the gates, set them at defiance, and—there was a fight, and we beat 'em off."

A flush of pride came across The Mackhai's face, and a bright look fell upon his son, but they passed away directly, and he continued, with lowering brow.

"And you have done this, sir?" he said sternly; "and you," he added, turning sharply upon Max,—"you knew better than this stupid country boor of a boy. Why didn't you stop him?"

"I did not think of doing so, sir," said Max, hesitating; and then, speaking out firmly, "I helped him, and did my best to beat the people off. I'm afraid I was worse than he."

"What?" cried The Mackhai; "you did?"

"Yes, sir, I did."

The Mackhai burst into a wild, discordant laugh.

"You did?" he repeated mockingly. "You helped to beat off these scoundrels of the law?"

"Yes, sir."

Kenneth flushed, for it seemed to him that his father was casting a doubt on his friend's pluck.

"Yes, father, that he did; and no fellow could have fought better."

"This is most delicious!" cried The Mackhai mockingly. "You, Maximilian Blande, fought with all your might to defend my home from these people?"

"I thought the property of the gentleman who had been very kind to me was in danger, sir, and I helped his son with all my might," said Max warmly. "I'm sorry if I've done wrong. Don't be angry with Kenneth, sir. I'm sure he meant to do what was right."

"Right!" cried the Mackhai. "You young idiots, you don't know what you've done,—you do not, Kenneth. As for you, you young viper, are you as cunning as you are high, or is this childishness and—"

"Mackhai! Mackhai!" yelled Scoodrach, coming tearing into the courtyard from the house. "Maister Maister Ken, Maister Max, ta deevils have been and cot ta poat, and they've landed on ta rocks, and got into ta house."

"What!" cried Kenneth excitedly. "Come on, father. Oh, why didn't I put a sentry there?"

Taken in the rear, the boy felt, and, forgetful of his father's words, he was about to rush away to the defence, when, paler than ever, his father clapped his hand upon his shoulder.

"Stop!" he cried; and he drew himself up to his full height, as there were the sounds of feet from within, and the bailiff came through the inner archway of the castle, to stand among the ruins of old Dunroe, to proclaim the ruin of the new.

"Mr Mackhai," he said sharply, as he presented a slip of paper, "in the Queen's name I take possession here—suit of Mr Andrew Blande, Lincoln's Inn, London."

"What!" cried Max, whose jaw dropped as he grasped the state of affairs. "It is a lie! my father would not do such a thing."

"Your cursed father, sir, would do anything that is mean and base—even to sending you down here to be a spy upon us, till he could tie the last knot in the miserable net he has thrown around me."

"Oh, Max!" cried Kenneth, as his face flushed, and then turned pale.

"Be a man, my boy," said his father sternly. "Recollect that you are a Mackhai. Let this legal robber take all; let him and his son enjoy their prize. Ken, my boy, my folly has made a beggar of you. I have lost all now, but one thing. I am still a gentleman of a good old race. He cannot rob me of that. Come."

He walked proudly through the archway into the house with his son, and the rest followed, leaving Max Blande standing alone in the old courtyard, staring wildly before him, till he started as if stung. For all at once a jackdaw on the inner part of one of the towers uttered what sounded to him a mocking, jeering—

Tah!

Chapter Twenty Seven
Max asks the Way to Glasgow

"And does everything go to him, father?" said Kenneth that same evening, as he sat with his father in the study, the table covered with papers, and the wind from off the sea seeming to sigh mournfully around the place.

"Everything, my boy. Mortgage upon mortgage, interest and principal, built up and increasing year by year, till it has come to this. There, you do not understand these things. It is the worst."

"Yes, father. Well, we must meet it, as you say, like men. But it will be very hard to leave the old place. Poor old Scoody, and Tavish, and—"

"Don't talk about it, my boy, or you'll drive me mad. There, the horror has come, and it's over. We shall not be able to leave here yet for a month, perhaps. The man Blande has sent me a letter. I am not to hurry away; now he has asserted his rights, he says he wishes to be courteous to the man who has behaved so well to his son. Hah! where is Max?"

"In his room, I suppose, father."

"Fetch him down, Ken," said The Mackhai cheerfully, "and let me apologise to the poor boy. I insulted him grossly, for he couldn't have known why he was sent down here."

"Say that again, father!" cried Kenneth excitedly.

"There is no need, my boy. I am sure he must have been in profound ignorance of everything. It was a bitter blow when he was sent down uninvited; but I think we have behaved well to him till now."

"You don't know how glad you have made me feel, father!" cried Kenneth, flushing. "I couldn't have borne for poor old Max to have turned out a miserable spy."

"You like this boy, then?"

"Like him, father! Why, he is the best of fellows! When he came down here first, I laughed at him, and thought him the most silly molly of a chap I ever met. But he's so good-hearted and patient, and takes everything so well, and all the time so genuinely plucky as soon as he makes up his mind to face anything, that you can't help liking him."

"Yes; I like him too," said The Mackhai; "and, as I said, I grossly insulted the poor boy in my rage. Fetch him down, Ken, and I'll ask him to forgive me—like a gentleman."

"And he will, father—I know he will!" cried Kenneth eagerly.

"Why, Ken, my boy," said his father sadly, "you are not jealous of the new prince—the heir to Dunroe?"

"No, father," said Ken, shaking his head sadly. "I think he likes me too. Some day, perhaps, he may ask me to come down here and stay with him, and see the old place once more."

"No," said The Mackhai sternly. "You can never enter this place again except as the master, my boy. Fetch Mr Max Blande down."

Kenneth gazed for a moment sadly at his father, and then slowly left the room, when the stern look left the unfortunate man's face, and he dropped his head upon his hands.

"My poor boy!" he groaned. "My poor boy! Ruined! and by me!"

It was as if a responsive moan echoed round the house as a gust of wind came off the sea, and, starting and looking wildly round, The Mackhai rose and gazed out upon the dark sea and the dimly-seen black clouds scudding across the gloomy sky.

"It will be a bad night," he said sadly. "Ah, well, I must bear it like a man! Let's see if I can eat some dinner."

He crossed to the bell and rang.

The old butler answered the summons at once.

"Let us have the dinner at once, Grant."

"Yes, sir. Everything is quite ready, sir," said the old butler, with his eyes full of sympathy for his master in his time of trouble.

"Are those—those people in the kitchen, Grant?"

"Yes, sir."

"Treat them respectfully and well, Grant. I wish it to be so."

"Yes, sir."

The butler was retiring, when Kenneth's step was heard coming hastily along, and, as he burst into the room,—

"Father," he cried, "he's gone!"

"Gone?"

"Yes. Max has gone."

"Gone? Impossible! Where could he have gone?"

"Scoodrach saw him go, hours ago, right up the track; and he watched him till he saw him disappear."

"What! across the mountain—alone?"

"Yes, father," cried Kenneth excitedly.

"But walking—to be overtaken by a night like this—the precipices—the bogs! Good heavens, Kenneth! he could not have been so mad!"

"He asked Scood if Glasgow did not lie out there," said Kenneth hoarsely; "and he told him, yes."

"He told him that? The young scoundrel! Why?"

The Mackhai ran to the bell, tore at it, and Grant came.

"Is Scoodrach anywhere here?"

"Yes, sir; in the kitchen."

"Send him here."

There was utter silence in the room for a few minutes, and then the young gillie was ushered in.

"Stop, Grant, you need not go," cried The Mackhai. "Now, sir," he said to Scoodrach, "did you tell Mr Max Blande that over the mountains was the way to Glasgow?"

"She said was tat ta wa' to Glasgie, and she said, 'Oh ay.'"

"And you let that poor boy go out over the mountain to lose himself among the rocks and moss, knowing that he could not find his way?"

"Oh ay!" said Scoodrach coolly.

"And that he might lose his life?"

"Oh ay."

"You young villain! how dared you do this? You've murdered him, perhaps."

"Oh ay; she hopes she has."

"What!" roared The Mackhai. "You did it on purpose, then?"

"Ay," cried Scoodrach, flashing up, and, dashing the bonnet he held defiantly on the carpet, he stamped upon it. "And she'd kill any mon who tried to rob ta bonnie young Chief Kenneth of her rights!"

Chapter Twenty Eight
Lost in the Mountains

It was in a dull, half-stunned way that Max walked straight out through the castle gate, and away down the rocky slope toward the shores of the little bay.

"Is it all true?" he asked himself. "Is it all true?" And then drearily he kept on muttering, "I can't stay here now—I can't stay here now."

He had walked on for about a mile, when he turned to look back for a farewell glance at the castle, when he found Scoodrach close at his heels, glaring at him in a peculiar way, which slightly startled Max, but he returned the gaze boldly, and then, with a confused idea of walking on till he could reach some inn, when there was nothing of the kind for forty or fifty miles, he asked the young gillie if that was the way for Glasgow.

Scoodrach's face lit up with satisfaction as he said it was; and, when Max went right on, the Highland lad stopped back watching him for a time, and then, laughing silently to himself, returned to stand in the shadow and glare at the bailiff and his men; while Max trudged on, with the sense of being mentally stunned increasing, but not so rapidly as the growing feeling of misery and shame within his breast. .

Rocky path, moist sheep-track, steep climb, sharp descent into boggy hollow; then up over a hill, with a glance at the sunny sea; and then on and on, in and out among the everlasting hills, which lapped fold upon fold, all grey crag and heather, and one valley so like another, and the ins and outs and turns so many, that, but for the light in the west, it would have been hard to tell the direction in which he tramped on and on, as near as he could divine straight away for Glasgow and the south.

"I must get home," he muttered dreamily, as he tramped on. "Oh, the shame of it!" he burst out. "Father! father! how could you do such a thing as this?"

There was a wild cry close at hand, and a curlew rose, and then a flock of lapwings, to flit round and round, uttering their peevish calls; but Max saw nothing but the scene at the castle, heard nothing but The Mackhai's bitter words, and he tramped onward and onward into the wilderness of mountain and moss, onward into the night.

There are people who would laugh at the idea of an active lad being lost in the mountains. To them it seems, as they travel comfortably along by rail or coach, impossible that any one could go perilously astray among "those little hills."

Let them try it, and discover their ignorance, as they learn the immensity of the wild spaces in Scotland and Wales, and how valley succeeds valley, hill comes down to hill, with so great a resemblance one to the other, that in a short time the brain is overwhelmed by a mist of confusion, and that greatest of horrors,—one not known, fortunately, to many,—the horror of feeling lost, robs the sufferer of power to act calmly and consistently, and he goes farther and farther astray, and often into perils which may end in death.

Max Blande wandered on, looking inward nearly all the time, and backward at the scenes of the past day, so that it was not long before he had diverged from the beaten track and was trudging on over the short grass and among the heather. Then great corners of crags and loose stones rose in his way, forcing him to turn to right or left to get by. Then he would come close up to some precipitous, unclimbable face of the hill, and strike away again, to find his course perhaps stopped by a patch of pale green moss dotted with cotton rushes, among which his feet sank, and the water splashed with suggestions of his sinking completely in if he persevered.

But he kept on, now in one direction, now in another, striving to keep straight, with the one idea in his mind to get right away from Dunroe, and certainly increasing the distance, but in a weary, devious way, till he seemed to wake up all at once to the fact that it was growing dark, and that a thick mist was gradually creeping round him, and he was growing wet, as well as so faint and weary that he could hardly plod along.

Max stopped short by a block of stone, against which he struck, and only saved himself from falling by stretching out his hands.

The stone suggested resting for a few minutes, and he sat down and listened, but the silence was awful. No cry of bird or bleat of sheep fell upon his ear, and the mist and darkness had in a few minutes so shut him in that he could distinguish nothing half a dozen yards away.

The sensation of restfulness was, however, pleasant; and he sat there for some time, trying to think of his plans, but in a confused way, for the incidents that had taken place at Dunroe would intrude as soon as he began to make plans.

"How stupid I am!" he cried, suddenly starting up with a shiver of cold, for the damp mist seemed to chill him, and for the first time he awoke to the fact that his feet and legs were saturated. "I must get on to some hotel, and to-morrow make for the nearest station, and go home."

Just then, for a moment, it occurred to him that he had left everything at Dunroe; but his thoughts went off in another direction, and then in another and another, finally resting upon the idea of the possibility of getting to the nearest station.

But where was the nearest station? Stirling. The line to Oban had not been made in those days; and now Max began to grow confused, as he recalled the fact that there was only one railway line running through the Western Highlands, and whether that were to the north, south, east, or west, he could not tell.

Neither at that hour could he tell which way these quarters lay. All he knew was that he was in a thick mist somewhere in the mountains, high up or low down in one of the hollows, and that if he stirred from where he stood, he must literally feel his way.

For a moment the idea came upon him that he had better stop till daylight, but just then a peculiar muffled cry smote his ears, and a thrill of terror ran through him as he felt that it would be impossible to sit there all through the long hours of the night in the cold and darkness. So he started at once, the cry he had heard influencing his direction, for he struck off the opposite way.

He made very slow progress, but at the end of a few minutes he knew that he was descending a rapid slope, and he went stumbling on through tall heather which was laden with moisture. Every now and then, too, he struck against some stone, but he persevered, for he fancied that the mist was rather less thick as he descended.

Then he tripped, and went headlong into the drenched heather, and struggled up with the feeling of confusion increasing as he stood trying to pierce the gloom.

Mist and darkness everywhere, and he once more went on downward, but diagonally, as it had grown now almost too steep to go straight down the slope; and so on for the next half-hour, when, as he leaned forward and took a step, he went down suddenly, and before he could save himself he was falling through space, his imagination suggesting an immense depth, but in two or three moments he touched bottom, and went rolling and scrambling among loose shingly stones for quite a hundred feet before he finally stopped.

He got up slowly and painfully, half stunned and sore, but he was not much hurt, for only the first few feet of his fall had been perpendicular; and once more he stood thinking in the darkness, and fighting with the fear and confusion which like mental gloom and mist oppressed his brain.

Only one idea dominated all others, and that one was that he must not stand still.

Starting once more, it was with ground still rapidly descending, and now he went very slowly and cautiously, feeling his way step by step among the loose scree, lest he should come upon another perpendicular descent, though even here the place was so steep that the stones he dislodged slid rattling down over one another for some distance before all was again still.

He must have gone on like this for nearly an hour before he felt that he was upon more level ground, but it was terribly broken up and encumbered with great masses of stone, among which he had painfully to thread his way.

Once again he found himself walking into a patch of moss, and he felt the soft growth giving way, till he was knee-deep, and it was only by a sudden scramble backwards that he was able to get free.

Then he went on and on again amidst the profound darkness, feeling his way among stones and scrubby growth more and more wearily each minute, till he was brought sharp up by a curious, croaking cry.

The lately learned knowledge, however, came that this must be a moorhen; but the fact of such a bird being near did not suggest that he must be close to water, and in consequence he had not gone much farther before he found himself splashing along the edge of some mountain loch or pool, whose bottom where he stood seemed to be smooth pebbles.

He stooped down in a dull, despairing way, plunged his hand beneath the surface, and drew out one of the biggest stones he could find, to hurl straight before him, and, as he listened, it fell into water which gave forth a dull, echoing splash, suggestive of depth and overhanging rocks.

He tried again and again, after backing cautiously, as he thought, out of the deep direction, but only to find the water grow deeper, till, to his horror, he found it nearly to his middle. The despairing plunge, however, that he took, led him into shallows once more; but every stone he threw fell into deep water, till he jerked one to his left, and this fell on stones.

Taking that direction, he pursued his level way over a shingly beach, with the impression upon him that he must be journeying along a deep glen with high rocks on either side, and one of the little lochs which he had often seen in these narrow straths, filling up the principal part of the hollow.

Once or twice he found his feet splashing in water, but by bearing to the left he found himself again on the dry pebbles, and in this way, save for a few heavy masses in his path, he skirted what he rightly concluded was a mountain loch, though whereabouts he could not tell.

Gaining a little courage as he realised all this, he ventured once upon a shout, in the hope that it might be heard, but he did not repeat it, for he stopped awe-stricken as his cry was repeated away to his left, then on his right, and again and again, to go murmuring off as if a host of the spirits of the air were mocking his peril.

But a little thought taught him that his surmise was right, and that he was slowly making his way along a narrow glen, whose towering walls had the property of reflecting back any sound; and, though he dared not raise his voice again, he picked up the first heavy stone against which he kicked, and hurled it from him with all his might.

A terribly dull, hollow, sullen plunge was the result, telling of the great depth of the water, and this sound was taken up, to go echoing and whispering away into the distance till it died out, and then seemed to begin again in a low, dull roar, which puzzled him as he listened.

Just then it seemed to him that a warm breath of air came upon his cheek, and this grew stronger, and the dull roar more plain. Then it did not seem so dark, and he realised that a breeze was coming softly up the glen, meeting him and wafting the wet mist away.

There was no doubt of this, and, though it was intensely dark where he stood, it was a transparent darkness, through which he could see the starry sky, forming as it were an arch of golden points starting on either side from great walls of rock a thousand feet above the level of the loch. This loch, in spite of the darkness, he could plainly see now, reflecting from its level surface, which stretched away into the darkness, the bright points of the light above.

Max stood thinking, and listened to the dull roar. He had been long enough in the Highlands now to know that this was not the continuation of the echoes he had raised, but the murmur of falling water, either of some mountain torrent pouring into the lake, or by a reverse process the lake emptying its superabundant water into the rocky bed of a stream, which would go bubbling and foaming down to the sea.

The wafting away of the mist seemed to relieve him of a good deal of the confusion, and, weary though he was, he found himself able to distinguish his way, and creep along the pebbly margin of the black loch, which lay so still and solemn beneath the starry sky.

All at once, after about an hour's laborious tramp down the weird glen, with its wild crags, black as ink, towering up to right and left, he suddenly caught sight of a gleam of light, and it struck him that he had come near to the mouth of the glen, and that he could see a star low down on the horizon.

The light was to his left, and the place was so horribly oppressive, with the deep black lake on his right and the roar of water rapidly growing louder, that he gladly struck off, as he felt, to where the gorge bore round, or, as he soon made out, divided.

This led him away from the black lake, and he soon found that he was scrambling along the bed of a little stream, which came, as it were, straight from the low down star.

Then, as he walked on what grew to be a more and more painful track, it struck him that it was strange that he could only see one star in that opening.

A few minutes later, he fancied he could make out towering crags above it, and that all was black darkness where he ought to be seeing more light; and then he dropped suddenly upon his knees in the joy of his heart, for there could be no mistake about the matter: it was not a star which he could see, but a light, and, rising once more, he forgot weariness, soreness, and pain, and began to tramp slowly on toward the light.

Chapter Twenty Nine
The Mysterious Light

There were moments when Max began to feel doubtful; others when he fancied it might be some deceptive marsh light; and then a great despair came upon him, for, just as he had come to the hopeful conclusion that there really was a cottage in the glen, where he could find rest, and warmth, and food, the light suddenly disappeared, and he was in a darkness which seemed to be, from the overshadowing mountains, even deeper than the darkness of the mist.

That was but the fancy of the moment, for the stars gave him light enough to slowly continue his way, but he stopped and hesitated as to whether he should go on or go back.

The way along the edge of the loch was easy, and seemed to lead toward the entrance of the glen. This side branch grew more difficult at every step, and, as the light had disappeared, he felt it would be better to go back, and he began to descend the rough way among the stones in the bed of the stream, when, turning one of these, he happened to look back, and there was the light burning clearly once more.

That was no marsh light, it was too clear and glowing, and, feeling convinced now that it had only been hidden by some turn of the ravine or interposing stone, he once more began to ascend the streamlet, till the light, which he watched intently, suddenly again disappeared.

He stopped short and stepped back a couple of paces, when the light reappeared; and, seeing that he was right, he pressed on, with the result that at the end of a few minutes there was the light again.

Twice over it disappeared as he stumbled onward, but there it was again, and growing so much plainer as he drew nearer, that it gradually took the form of fire shining through an open door.

Convinced that it was either a little country inn or the home of some shepherd, Max's hopes rose, and he stumbled on, hoping every minute to come upon a path which should lead up to the door.

But he hoped in vain, though he had one satisfaction, that of seeing the shape of a doorway quite plainly, and the flickering of a fire, which some one must be in the act of stirring.

Directly after he saw the doorway darkened, as if somebody had passed out, and his lips parted to call for guidance to the place, when he heard a movement behind him, and, turning sharply, there was another sound, as if a stone had fallen.

This made him turn round again toward the light, when, quick as thought, something thick was thrown over his head and drawn close, a pair of sinewy arms dashed his to his sides; he was drawn backward; some one seized his legs, and, in spite of his straggles, he was lifted from the ground, and two men seemed to be carrying him over a rugged way, now up, now down.

He shouted and begged as well as his half-suffocated state would allow, for the covering to be taken from his head, but the only response he obtained was an angry shake and a tighter clasp of the arms about his legs.

All at once he could see red light glowing through the great woollen cloth which covered him, and he felt that he was thrown on the ground, and that some one was binding his legs together. Directly after, his arms were bound behind his back, he was placed in a sitting posture, and the cloth was snatched from his head.

The glowing light of a fire shone right into his eyes, dazzling them, so that for some few moments he could make out nothing but the fact that he was in a stone-built hut, before a fierce fire, and that two fierce-looking bearded men were glaring at him.

Before he could collect himself to speak, some one shouted from outside, and one of his captors replied, but the Gaelic words were quite unintelligible to the prisoner, as was also the conversation which ensued between the two men before him, though it was apparent that one was urging the other to do something from which he shrank.

"Hwhat will she want?" said the latter at last, in a harsh voice.

"I've lost my way in the mountains," said Max. "I'm tired and cold and hungry. Please undo this rope; it hurts."

The man who had not spoken said something now to Max's questioner, and it seemed that the words which had passed were translated, with the result that he burst into a torrent of harsh-sounding speech, apparently full of dissent.

This seemed to be the case, for the one who tried to speak English exclaimed sharply,—

"She shall tell her a lee."

"I—I don't understand you," said Max.

"She came along wi' ta exciseman."

"No," said Max. "I came quite alone."

"Sassenach" was the only word which Max could make out in the dialogue which followed, and this was at its height when a third fierce-looking man came in, and the three laid their heads together, glancing toward the door uneasily, and then at what seemed to be a great copper boiling over the fire.

As they stood together, with the ruddy glow playing upon their fierce countenances, it seemed to Max that he must have fallen into the hands of Scottish freebooters, and the next thing he felt was that he should be robbed and murdered, or the operations be performed in reverse fashion.

The men's appearance was wild enough to have excited dread in one of stouter nerves than Max Blande, who, faint and exhausted, lay there in so helpless a plight that he was not in a condition to do more than anxiously watch his captors, as they talked loudly in Gaelic and gesticulated angrily.

To Max it seemed as if they were debating how he should be done to death; and, in spite of the horror of the thought, he was so stunned, as it were, his feelings were so deadened, that he did not feel the acute dread that might have been expected. There was almost as much curiosity in his feelings as fear, and he began at last to wonder why they did not take his watch and chain, purse and pocket-book, both of which latter were fairly well filled—his father having been generous to him when he started upon his journey, and there having been absolutely no means of spending money at Dunroe.

The debate grew more and more angry, the men evidently quarrelling fiercely, but not a word could Max make out. Their actions, however, seemed plain enough, as they all turned their eyes fiercely upon him, and the effect was peculiar, for the ruddy firelight was reflected from them, so that they seemed to glow as they suddenly made a dart at him, two of the men dragging him unresisting to his feet, while the third, before he could grasp his intention, flung the dingy old plaid which had muffled him before, over his head, twisting it tightly about his throat.

Max uttered a hoarse cry, but it was smothered directly, and he gave himself up for lost, as he was seized once more and hurried out into the darkness. This much he knew by the absence of the light dimly shining through the coarse woollen fabric which covered his head.

He was carried in this way for quite a quarter of an hour. Sometimes they were going upwards and sometimes downwards; while he could gather that the way chosen was terribly rough, from the manner in which he was jerked about.

This went on till a dull sound came in a muffled way through the plaid, and he gathered from this that they were approaching the falls he had heard before, or else some others.

The sound of roaring water grew louder and louder, and now he knew that they were climbing more slowly evidently upward, as if the ascent were exceedingly steep. Then the sound of the water falling—a deep bass, quivering roar—grew louder and louder; while, from being hot now almost to suffocation, the perspiration gathered on his brow grew cold, and, trembling with horror, he felt that the end was near, and that the wretches who held him were about to throw him off into the fall whose waters thundered in his ear.

He uttered a few wild cries for mercy, but they seemed to be unheard, and, just when his agony was strained to the highest pitch, the roar suddenly grew fainter, and the bearers paused on comparatively level ground.

All at once one of the men unfastened the cords which confined him, after which the other grasped his wrist, and he was forced to walk onward at a rapid rate.

For some minutes he could hardly stumble along, his feet feeling numbed and tingling sharply, but by degrees the normal sensation returned, and he could feel that he was walking through short heather, and at times over soft, springy grass.

At last he was so exhausted that he stumbled again and again, recovering himself by an effort, and keeping on for another quarter of an hour, when his legs gave way beneath him, and he sank upon his knees.

A low, guttural ejaculation from his conductor now reached his ears, and he felt that the plaid was twisted quickly from his neck, the cool night air fell upon his cheek, and he could see the stars indistinctly, as if through a mist, as they suddenly grew dark, and then there was nothing.

Chapter Thirty
Dirk makes himself useful

The stars were twinkling brightly when Max Blande looked at them again, and for some time there was nothing else but stars.

But they were above him, and, as he looked up at them, they looked down at him.

He felt that it was very cold, but it did not seem to matter, so long as he could lie still there in bed with the window wide open, looking at the stars; but by degrees he became conscious that his legs ached and his arms felt sore, and the idea struck him that he should be much more comfortable if he got up and shut the window, for it was very cold.

It was a long time before he made the effort to do this, and when he did, a curious aching pain shot through him, and in a flash he knew that he was not at Dunroe, but lying there somewhere in the mountains on the wet grass, and he remembered all he had gone through.

He lay piecing it all together, and involuntarily his hand went to his pockets, to find watch, chain, purse, pocket-book, all there safely, and that he was unhurt.

Was it all a dream?

No; he felt that it was real enough, and that he must not lie there, but rise once more, and try hard, and, he hoped, with better fortune, to find some place where he could obtain shelter.

Making an effort which cost him no little pain, he turned over and struggled to his knees, but only to sink down again, feeling absolutely helpless, and ready to declare to himself that, come what might, he could not stir till morning, even if he were able then.

Looking helplessly about him, it was to see that the night was brilliantly clear, and that there was a gleam of water somewhere down far below on his right, for the stars were reflected from it. But it seemed more restful to lie there waiting, and, cold as he was, it was a dull, numbing cold that was far less painful than trying to move.

All at once he shivered with dread, for there was a rushing sound as of some creatures galloping, and he could hear faint snortings and the panting of heavy breath.

Some herd of wild animals had gone by. It could not be sheep, for the movement was too swift; but once more all was silent, and he was sinking into a half-drowsy condition, more resembling the approach of stupor than sleep, when he started back into wakefulness, for he heard in the distance the sharp barking of a dog.

This died away, grew louder, died away again, and then seemed to be coming steadily nearer and nearer, but, as it approached, so did the stupefying sensation, till the barking died right away; the stars were again blotted out, and Max knew no more till he started to himself again in alarm, as the cold, wet nose of a dog was touching his face. There was a quick snuffling about him, and then there was a loud burst of barking, and he felt that the dog who barked was standing with his forepaws on his chest. "Dirk," he said feebly; "is it you, Dirk?" The dog gave a whining cry, licked at his face, and then barked again with all his might.

Then there was silence, and from out of the distant darkness came a low hail.

The dog barked again sharply, and stopped, when there was the hail again more loudly, and this was repeated at intervals as the dog scuffled about, running a little way to bark, and then coming, back to plant his paws on Max's chest.

All this now seemed part of a dream, till he was roused again by hearing a panting sound, feeling his hand seized, and then hearing a familiar voice shout,—

"Father, ahoy! Tavvy, ahoy! Here he is!" and, as the dog whined and barked again, there were faint hails from the distance. Then these grew louder, and the next thing Max heard was,—

"Oh, Maxy, old lad!" and a warm hand was laid upon his brow.

Then there was more hailing, and barking, and an impatient muttering, and then there were deeper voices talking close by where he lay, and, as if in part of his dream, something hot and strangling seemed to be trickling down his throat.

"There," said a deep voice which seemed very familiar, "she'll ket the plaidie round the laddie when she's cot her on her pack, and that and ta whusky'll warm her."

"I'll carry him when you are tired, Tavish," said another familiar voice.

"She can carry ta puir laddie all tay an' all nicht. Maister Ken, tit ye iver see a tog wi' a petter nose than Dirk?"

"No, Tavvy; but do make haste."

"Ay, laddie; but bide a wee, till she cot her well upo' her shouthers. There. Noo, ta plaidie. Noo then, we can get there in twice twa hoors. She'll go first."

"Oh, father, are we too late?" came then in a whisper to Max's ears, as he felt himself being once more carried.

"Please God, no, my boy!" came back hoarsely.

Then there was another loud and joyful burst of barking, and then all blank.

Chapter Thirty One
An exciting Chase

"Scood! you beast!"

"Silence, Kenneth!" cried The Mackhai sternly, as he looked half-angrily, half-pleased at the flushed face of the young gillie.

"She ton't care. She'll fecht for ta Mackhai till she ties."

"Leave the room, sir!" cried The Mackhai. "You meant well, but you have done a cruel and cowardly thing."

Scoodrach hung his head, and stooped to pick up his bonnet by one of the strands of the worsted tuft, letting the soft flat cap spin slowly round as he watched it, and then he moved toward the door.

"Stop!" cried The Mackhai.

Scoodrach turned sharply and defiantly round, with his hot northern blood flushing to his temples.

"Ta Chief may kill her," he cried; "but she shall na say she's sorry."

"Go and fetch Tavish and your father, sir, and never dare to address me again like that."

Scoodrach slunk out of the room, and, as he turned to shut the door, his eyes met those of Kenneth, who shook his fist at him.

Without a moment's hesitation, Scoodrach doubled his own, and looked defiance as the door was closed.

"Never dare to address me again like that!" muttered The Mackhai. "Poor lad! there is no fear."

"What shall we do, father?"

"Do? We must all set out in search of Max, and bring him back. In my anger, Ken, I have done a brutal thing."

"But you did not mean it, father."

"How could he know that? See if he has taken his luggage. No, no; impossible! The poor lad has wandered right away into the mountains, and I am to blame. Get the ponies, Kenneth; we may do better mounted. I suppose," he added bitterly, "we may use them for the present."

Kenneth darted out of the room, met Tavish and Long Shon, and in a very few minutes the two sturdy little ponies were in the old courtyard, The Mackhai and his son mounting, and the little party starting off at once.

Before they had gone far, The Mackhai turned his head.

"Where is that boy?" he said.

No one replied, for Scood had not been seen to leave, but from where he was seated Kenneth could just see a tuft of wool sticking up above the heather, and he pressed the sides of his pony and cantered back to where the boy lay upon his face in a hollow, with his bonnet tilted on to the back of his head.

"Here, Scoody! What are you doing there?" cried Kenneth.

"Naething."

"Get up, sir, and come on."

"Na. She will gang away and be a redcoat. Naebody cares for Scoody the noo."

"Don't be a red-headed donkey. Get up, and come and show us which way Max Blande went."

Scoodrach shook his head.

"Look here, if you don't get up, I'll call father, and he'll come and lay into you with the dog-whip."

"He wadna daur," cried the lad, leaping up and glaring at the speaker.

"Yes, he would, and so would I, if I had one here."

"Gin ye daur lay a finger on her, she'll hae your bluid!" cried Scoodrach.

"There!" cried Kenneth, pressing his pony's sides, and reaching over to catch tightly hold of the lad's collar. "I daur lay a whole hand on you, Scoody. Noo, lat's see gin ye daur turn on your Chief."

"Ye know I wadna hurt a hair o' your heid," muttered the lad.

"Then come on, like a good fellow, Scoody, and help to find him."

"D'ye want to find the laddie wha's gaun to rob ye o' ta auld plaace?"

"Yes. Come on, Scood. We mustn't quarrel, and you won't be such a brute as to refuse to help me because I'm going to be poor."

"Puir or rich!" cried the lad, with the tears of excitement in his eyes, "gin ye want her to, she'll dee for ye, Maister Ken."

"That's old Scoody once again," cried Kenneth, drumming his pony's flanks; and as the little animal whisked round, Scoodrach caught hold of its long tail, gave the hairs a twist round his hand, and away they went after the others, to whom they soon caught up.

Then followed a long and wearisome search, Scoodrach pointing out the way Max had taken, when, as there was no path or even sheep-track, they divided, and went on mile after mile, only to give up at dark and return tired and faint, and with Scoodrach hanging his head as he felt how he had been the cause of all the trouble; and, seizing the first opportunity, he slipped off with the ponies, to bed them down for the night.

"We must be up at daybreak and begin again, Ken," said The Mackhai sadly. "That boy must be found. Can you form any idea which way he would take?"

"No, father. I've been trying to think, but we seem to have tried everywhere, and I don't believe he could have gone very far."

"He had a long start."

"You don't think he has come to any harm—slipped over the crags anywhere, or gone into—"

Kenneth stopped and shuddered.

"One of the boggy patches, Ken? Oh no, my boy. He has been out so much with you and Scoodrach, that he ought to be able to take care of himself by now."

"Yes, father—ought to," said Kenneth meaningly; and then, in an outburst of passion, as he stood with clenched fists, "I'll give Scoody such a thrashing as he never had in his life! I'll half kill him."

"Hush! That will do," said The Mackhai sadly. "The boy acted according to his lights. He was, in his half-savage way, fighting for the honour of our old house."

"Yes, father, but—"

"Hush, my boy! Our days are numbered at Dunroe: let us leave here with as pleasant memories as we can, and with the love and respect of those who have looked to us for bread."

"Oh, father!" cried Kenneth; and there was a great sob in his throat, and his face was contracted though his eyes were dry.

The Mackhai grasped his son's hand.

"Be a man, Ken," he said quietly. "You ought to have commenced life well, but now you will have to go forth into the world and fight your way. You must make friends, not enemies."

"It would not make Scood an enemy, father, and a good whacking would do him good."

"No, no, Ken. Now get some food, and go and lie down for a few hours to have some rest. We can do nothing till daylight."

"Very well, father. And—and I will try not to mind leaving the old place, and to be a man."

"God bless you, my boy!" cried The Mackhai, laying his hands upon his son's shoulders and gazing into his eyes. "Come, Ken, trouble has its good sides after all; it has taught me something more about the nature of my son. Now, go and get some rest; I shall not be happy till I have taken that boy again by the hand."

"Why, father!" cried Kenneth excitedly. "Oh, what an old donkey I am!"

Before The Mackhai could speak, he had rushed out of the room and across the hall, to return at the end of a few minutes in company with Dirk, who was barking, and as excited as his master.

"Why, Ken!" cried The Mackhai.

"It's all right, father. Dirk will find him. Tavvy is waiting. Don't you come. We'll have poor old Maxy back before long."

"I shall come with you," said The Mackhai, rising, and taking a flask and plaid from where they lay. "What are you going to do first?"

"I'll soon show you," cried Ken excitedly. "Here, Dirk, old boy, put on your best nose to-night, and let's show the Londoner what a Highland dog can do."

Dirk barked loudly, and followed his master as he rushed out of the room and up-stairs to Max's chamber, where Kenneth dragged some of the clothes which his visitor had worn last down upon the carpet.

"Now, Dirk! seek, laddie, seek!"

The dog dashed at the clothes, snuffed at them, tossed them over, snuffed at them again, and then uttered a sharp, whining bark.

"Come along," cried Kenneth, and he ran down to the hall, where his father was ready, and then out into the dark courtyard, at whose entrance Tavish was waiting, armed with a tall staff.

"I ken ye're richt, maister," he said. "We'll lay ta collie on chust where the laddie saw ta young chentleman last."

Very little was said as they trudged on, Kenneth holding Dirk by one of his ears, till they reached the foot of the slope, pointed out by Scoodrach as the road taken by Max.

Here the dog was loosed, and he looked up in his master's face, barking loudly, as if asking for instructions, and not yet comprehending what was meant.

"Seek, laddie, seek! Max, Max! Seek, seek!"

Dirk uttered a low yelping whine, and began to quarter the ground, whimpering and growing more and more excited as he increased the distance between him and those who followed by sound, for the dog was soon invisible in the darkness.

For quite a quarter of an hour the hunt was kept on, each minute damping the hopes of the party more and more, till The Mackhai said sadly,—

"It's of no use, my boy. You're asking too much of the dog."

"She thocht Dirk would ha' takken it up," said Tavish slowly. "She's na the dog she thocht."

"Don't give up yet, father. I feel sure."

"Hey, she's cot it!" cried Tavish wildly, as a loud baying bark came from Dirk.

"Yes, come on! He has got it now," cried Kenneth, and he dashed on at a sharp trot right into the darkness.

"Keep up with him, Tavish," cried The Mackhai. "Steady, Ken, steady."

"All right, father," came from far ahead.

"Oh ay, sir, she'll be close aifter the young Chief. Hark! d'ye hear? Dirk's got the scent, and she'll rin him doon."

Right away in the darkness the low barking of the dog could be heard, for Dirk had indeed got on the scent, and, with the wondrous faculty of his kind, he was trotting steadily on over the grass and heather, nose down, tail high, and not for a moment halting in his quest.

Hour after hour the hunt went on, no little exertion being needed to keep within hearing of the dog, who followed Max's trail right on and on—a devious, wandering trail, right along to the narrow gully where the dark loch lay. After coming to a halt several times, where Max had waded into patches of bog, and also where he had stepped over the precipitous place and fallen a few feet, to slide and scramble down some distance farther, Dirk picked up the trail again, and trotted on.

These halts gave those who followed time to catch up, and there were so many faults along the edge of the dark, narrow loch, that Kenneth and Tavish were together and pretty close behind.

"Think o' ta laddie finding his way doon here," said the forester.

"You don't think he can have slipped in anywhere?" whispered Kenneth. "It's a nasty place, even by day."

"Oh ay, laddie, and ta fush are sma' and hard to get. She'd get richt alang, though. Noo, which way wad she gang—up by ta waterfa', or awa' through ta wee bit burnie?"

"I don't know, Tavvy," panted Kenneth; "but we ought to be near him now."

"Nay; she'll be a lang gate yet, my bairn. Air ye there, sir?"

"Yes; go on," came from behind; and the rough tramp was continued, till the forester cried,—

"She's gaed up ta burnie."

"Why, Tavvy, there's a light there! What light's that?"

"Licht?" said Tavish innocently. "Hey, there's a licht!"

"What can it be?"

"Only a shepherd's bothy."

"There is no shepherd's bothy up here on the Clandougal estate, Tavvy."

"Maybe it's some Southron laird had a cot made for him to fush ta loch."

"Nonsense, Tavvy! and if it was so, no one would be having a big fire there at this time of night."

"Whush, laddie!"

"But—I know! Why, Tavvy, it's a still!"

"Whush! Here, lat's ca' back ta tog."

"Nonsense! He has gone right on. Hurray! we've found him. Max is sure to be up there by the fire."

"Ta laddies wadna lat her stop," muttered Tavish; "put we'll pe hafin' trouble wi' 'em. Hearken to ta tog!"

"Why, Ken, look," came from behind, as the dog's barking went echoing along the narrow little glen; "that must be a still. Eh, Tavish?"

"Aw'm thinking maybe it sall be a still, sir," said Tavish innocently, as his master closed up.

"Maybe?" said The Mackhai sharply; "and I'm thinking you knew it was there, and have tasted the stuff."

Tavish was silent, and they all plodded on toward the distant light, the dog's track being straight for it naturally, for the only way up the little glen was by the burn.

"Ta licht's gone," muttered Tavish. "She'll be thinking they've heert ta tog, and thrown watter upo' it, and we shall be in trouble pefore we've done."

"Hallo!" cried Kenneth; "the light's out."

The Mackhai called attention to the fact at the same moment.

"Keep close to me, Kenneth," he said. "But no they would not dare," he said to himself.

Tavish turned to his master.

"Shall she fecht?"

"There will be no need, my man. Get on. We shall find the boy has taken shelter there."

Tavish shook his head, and muttered to himself.

"What is it, Tavvy?" said Kenneth.

"If it's ta whusky they're makking aboon yonder, ta young chentleman isna there."

"Well, we shall soon see about that," cried Kenneth, pressing on in the most reckless way, and only saving himself from several falls by his activity, for he went among the broken rocks like a goat.

A loud burst of barking lent speed to his feet; and ten minutes later the party were up in front of the rough building, from which came to their nostrils the strong reek of steam, telling that water had been thrown upon the fire they had seen.

There was no answer to their calls, but Dirk was barking furiously inside, and Kenneth at once entered, Tavish following to light a match; but there was no one within, only enough visible to show what business had been going on.

"Any one about here?" shouted Kenneth, after they had satisfied themselves that Max was not to be seen.

But there was no reply, and Tavish shouted in Gaelic.

Only the echoes answered his call; and Kenneth impatiently coaxed out the dog, who seemed to think that his work was done.

"He has been here, father, and they've gone on."

"Ta loons air hiding, laddie," whispered Tavish, "and hearin' every word we say. Hey! but Dirk has it again. Gude tog! gude tog!"

Dirk had suddenly taken up the track again, and followed faithfully on, right up the side of the glen, and away over the level mountain plain, after tracking the fugitive by the side of a great fall, which made its way downward into the loch.

The rest of the hunt was easy, for Dirk took them on and on; Kenneth growing so excited, as he felt that the end of the chase was near, that he left Tavish and his father far in the rear.

Then Dirk dashed right away, and Kenneth was in turn left behind, till he knew that the dog had found, for his loud baying came from away in the darkness, as he stood barking over the spot where Max lay, half asleep, half in a state of stupor, brought on by cold.

Chapter Thirty Two
Instructions from London

"There, you jolly old scaramouch!" cried Kenneth, laughing. "Now I can serve you out."

"No, no, Kenneth; let me get up, please."

"Deal of mercy you had on me when I was ill. Now it's my turn, and I've got you. I'll serve you out."

"But, indeed, I am well enough to get up."

"No, you're not. Tavvy says you are not to stir, and you must make the best of it."

There was a scratching at the door just then, and Kenneth ran across the carpet to admit Dirk, who gave a sharp bark, and bounded to the bed to nuzzle his nose in Max's hand.

"Did you ever see such a dog as that, Maxy? There are not many that would have hunted you out as he did."

"No, I suppose not," said Max sadly and wearily, as he lay there, suffering from the chill brought on by his exposure upon the mountains four nights before. "But it was a pity you brought me back."

"That's five times you've said that to-day," cried Kenneth. "Now, just you say it once more, and I'll punch your head."

Max shook the threatened part of his person sadly, and then lay looking wearily at the window.

"Look here, old chap!" said Kenneth suddenly; "father says if you are not better by to-night, he shall send to Glasgow for a doctor to come and stop with you, and write word to your governor in London."

"I'm—I'm much better," said Max hastily. "I shall not want a doctor; and tell Mr Mackhai that I want to go home as soon as I can start."

"All right, Maxy, old chap," said Kenneth slowly and sadly; "but I say, look here—"

He stopped short, and, in a quiet, methodical way, law his hand upon his friend's brow.

"I say, how hot your head is! Wait a moment."

He placed one arm beneath his neck, lifted his head, turned the pillow, and gently lowered Max back upon the cool, soft linen.

"That's comfortable, isn't it?"

"Yes; so cool and refreshing!"

"So it used to be when you nursed me."

There was a dead silence.

"I say, Maxy."

"Yes."

"I like you now."

"Do you?"

"Yes, ever so. I didn't at first, because you seemed such a coward."

"I suppose I am," sighed Max.

"That you're not; and I'd pitch anybody overboard who said so. You were all strange to us and our ways when you came down; but you're as full of pluck underneath, though you don't show it outside, as any fellow I ever knew."

Max shook his head again.

"But I say you are. Don't contradict, or I'll hit you, and then there'll be a fight. Now, I say, look here! I couldn't help my father borrowing money of your father?"

"No, of course not."

"And you couldn't help your father wanting it back?"

"No, no. Don't talk about it, please."

"Yes, I shall, because I must. Look ye here, Maxy, if we can't help it, and we like one another, why shouldn't we still be the best of friends?"

Max stared at him.

"Would you be friends?" he said at last.

"I should think I will—that is, if you'll be friends with such a poor beggar as I shall be now."

Max gripped his hand, and the two lads were in that attitude when The Mackhai suddenly entered the room.

Max drew in his breath sharply, as if in pain, and lay back gazing at his host, who came forward and shook hands, before seating himself at the bedside.

It was not the first meeting by several, during which Max had been treated with a kindness and deference which showed his host's anxiety to efface the past.

"Come, this is better," he said cheerily. "Why, I should say you could get up now?"

"Yes, sir; that is what I have been telling your son," said Max hastily.

"Yes, father; he wants to get up and rush off at once; and I tell him it's all nonsense, and that he is to stay!"

The Mackhai was silent for a few moments, as he sat struggling with his pride, and, as he saw Max watching him eagerly, he coloured.

The gentleman triumphed, and he said quietly and gravely,—

"My dear boy, I want you to try and forget what passed the other night, when, stung almost beyond endurance, I said words to you that no gentleman ought to have spoken toward one who was his guest, and more than guest, the companion and friend of his son. There, I apologise to you humbly. Will you forgive me?"

"Mr Mackhai!" cried Max, in a choking voice, as he seized the hand extended to him.

"Hah! that is frank and natural, my lad. Thank you. Now, shall we forget the past?"

Max nodded, but he could not trust himself to speak, while Kenneth ran round to the other side of the bed.

"And he is not to think of going, father?" he cried.

"I don't say that, Ken," replied his father. "Under all the circumstances, I can readily believe that Max would prefer to return to town; but I expressly forbid his hurrying away. Oblige me, Max, by staying with Kenneth till next Thursday, when I shall return. It will be dull for him alone."

"Are you going away, father?"

"Yes; I start for Edinburgh at once, and as I shall not see you again, Max, I will say good-bye. You will be gone before I reach Dunroe in the evening."

He shook hands once more, and left the room, Max thoroughly grasping the gentlemanly feeling which had prompted him to behave with so much delicacy.

"There, Max, you will stay now?" cried Kenneth.

"Yes, I will stay now," he replied.

"Then that's all right. We'll have some fishing and shooting—for the last few times," he said to himself, as he turned away to see his father before he left the place.

Max rose and dressed as soon as he was alone, but he was not long in finding that he was not in a fit condition to take a journey; and during the rest of his stay at Dunroe there were no more pleasure-trips, for the zest for them was in the case of both lads gone.

And yet those last days were not unpleasant, for there was a peculiar anxiety on the part of both to make up for the past. Kenneth was eager in the extreme to render Max's last days there such as should give him agreeable memories of their intercourse. While, on the other side, Max felt deeply what Kenneth's position must be, and he too tried hard to soften the pain of his lot.

Max had had a business-like letter from his father, telling him that he had been compelled, by The Mackhai's failure to keep his engagements, to foreclose certain mortgages and take possession of the estates. Under these circumstances, he wished his son to remain there and supervise the proceedings of the bailiffs, writing to him in town every night as to how matters stood.

It was a cool, matter-of-fact, legal letter, written by a clerk, probably from dictation, and signed by the old lawyer. But at the bottom there was a postscript in his own crabbed hand, as follows:—

"You will be able to watch over all with more pleasure, when I tell you that Dunroe is yours. I mean it to be your estate, and you can see now why I sent you down there to learn how to be a Scottish gentleman."

Max flushed as he read this, and he exclaimed aloud— "A Scottish gentleman could not bear to be placed in such a position!" and he sat down and wrote at once to say that he had been seriously unwell, and must return to town on a certain day.

"Squeamish young donkey!" said the hard-griping old man of the world, when he received his son's letter. "Bad as his weak, sensitive mother. Know better some day. If I had been so particular, Dunroe would not be mine to leave."

Chapter Thirty Three
A sad Parting

"So you're off to-morrow, Max?" said Kenneth sadly.

"Yes. How beautiful everything looks, now I am going away!"

"Yes," said Kenneth, with a quaint glance first at the distant islands rising all lilac and gold from the sapphire sea; "how beautiful everything looks, now I am going away!"

"Oh, Ken!"

"And oh, Max! There, don't turn like that, old chap. It's the fortune of war, as they say. Good luck to you. I feel now as if I'd rather you had Dunroe than anybody else. I say, let's call Scoody, and get out the boat, and have one last sail together."

"Yes, do," cried Max eagerly.

"All right. I'll go and find Scoody. Get the lines. We may as well try for some mackerel as we go."

Kenneth ran out of the room, and Max went to the little study, got the lines, and then was about to follow his friend, when he recalled the fact that he had not been to see old Donald since he had been better.

So, going out into the courtyard, he made for the old man's quarters, knocked, was told to come in, and entered, to find the piper propped up in an easy-chair, and Long Shon and Tavish keeping him company.

The old man glared at him strangely, and grasped at something he had in his lap which emitted a feeble squeak, and Max saw that they were his pipes, about which his thin fingers played.

"I'm going away to-morrow, Donald," said Max, "and wanted to know how you were."

The old man neither moved nor spoke, but his deeply-sunken eyes seemed to burn, as he glared fiercely, and his breathing sounded deep and hoarse.

"I hope you are better?"

There was no reply.

"He is better, is he not, Tavish?"

The great forester gazed straight before him at the wall, but made no reply.

"What is the matter, Shon?" said Max uneasily.

Long Shon took a pinch of snuff, and gazed at the floor.

"Look here!" cried Max earnestly; "I wanted to thank you all for your kindness to me since I have been here, and I may not have another chance. Donald, Long Shon, Tavish—just a little remembrance, and thank you."

As he spoke, he slipped a sovereign into the hands of the two first named, and two into that of the forester. But, as if moved by the same idea, all three dashed the money at his feet, the gold coins jingling upon the stone floor.

Max's eyes dilated, and he gazed from one to the other.

"I am very sorry," he said, after a painful pause. "Good-bye. It is not my fault."

He went slowly out, and before he had gone half a dozen yards the money struck him on the back, and Long Shon cried hoarsely, —

"Tonal' sends ye his curse for blasting ta home o' ta Mackhais!"

Once more the coins fell jingling down, and, flinching away, shrinking with shame, sorrow, and indignation, Max returned into the house, feeling that he could not go boating now, and wishing that the next day had come, and he were on the road back to London.

But, just as he reached the hall, he heard the voice of the man in charge raised loudly, and, looking out, he saw the second man running along the natural rock terrace, below which lay the bathing cavern and the rugged platform from which they would take boat.

The next moment Scoodrach's voice rose in shrill and angry tones, and he could see that Kenneth was holding him back.

Max ran down with his pulses throbbing, for he felt that something was very wrong.

"I'll have the law of him," the bailiff was saying, as Max ran up. "He struck me, and drew his knife on me. I'll have him locked up before he knows where he is."

"Let her go, let her go, Maister Ken!" yelled Scoodrach, struggling furiously. "She'll hae her bluid! Let her go, and she'll slit her weam!"

"Be quiet, Scood," said Kenneth, holding the young gillie fast, but speaking in a low, despondent tone. "Here, Max, take the knife away from this mad fool."

"Nay, nay," cried Scoodrach; "if the Southron comes she'll hae her bluid too."

Instinctively grasping what was the matter, and with his cheeks flushed with indignation, Max dashed at Scoodrach, seized his wrist, and twisted the knife out of his hand.

"What does this mean?" he cried, turning angrily upon the bailiff.

"Mean, sir? My orders are to let nothing go off the premises, and this young gentleman comes doon wi' this young Hieland wild cat, and tries to get oot the boat."

"Well?"

"Well, sir, I said it was not to go, and then this cat-a-mountain struck me."

"She insulted ta young Chief," panted Scoodrach.

"Be quiet, Scoody; there is no young Chief now," said Kenneth sadly.

"Hey, but ta Mackhai will never tie!" yelled Scoodrach.

"Do you mean to say that you hindered Mr Kenneth here from taking the boat for a sail?" cried Max angrily.

"My orders air that naething is to go off the place," said the bailiff sturdily.

"Then you stopped him from taking his own boat?"

"No, sir," cried the bailiff; "it's not his boat, but Mr Blande's, of Lincoln's Inn, London."

"It is not. The boat and everything here is mine," cried Max fiercely. "Take the boat, Ken, and if this insolent scoundrel dares to interfere, knock him down."

"Hurray!" yelled Scoodrach, breaking loose and throwing his bonnet in the air. "Weel done, Maister Max! But na, na; it's no' her poat, and naething here is hers, ye ken."

"Come on, Ken."

"Well, sir, I shall report all this to —"

"Ye ill-faured loon, stan' awa'," yelled Scoodrach, as Max laid his hand on Kenneth's shoulder; and they went down together to the boat, while the bailiff and his man walked muttering back to the house.

"Jump in, Scoodrach, and cast her loose," cried Max; but Kenneth's hand closed tightly on his wrist.

"No, Max," he said slowly and sadly. "Let's get back into the house. I don't feel as if I could go for a sail to-day."

"Oh, Ken!" whispered Max; "and I said everything was mine. I did not mean it. I couldn't take a thing."

"Let's go indoors."

"But if by law the boat is mine, it's yours again now. Come, take me for one more ride."

"No, no! I can't go now."

There was a dead silence on the old grey terrace for a few minutes. The gulls wailed as they swept here and there over the glistening sea, and the golden-red and brown weed washed to and fro among the rocks.

"I ask you to go, Ken," said Max gently. "Don't refuse me this. Scood, my things are packed; fetch them down. Kenneth Mackhai, I shall go to-day; take me to meet the steamer, just as you came to meet me six weeks ago."

Ken looked at him half wonderingly.

"Do you mean it?" he said hoarsely.

"Yes. You will?"

"Yes."

An hour had not passed before the white-sailed boat was softly bending over to the breeze, and almost in silence the three lads sat gazing before them, heedless of the glorious panorama of mountain, fiord, and fall that seemed to be gliding by, till far away in the distance they could see the red funnel of David Macbrayne's swift steamer pouring forth its trailing clouds of black smoke, which seemed to reach for miles.

Then by degrees the steamer grew plainer, the white water could be seen foaming behind the beating paddles, and the figures of the passengers on deck. Then the faces grew clearer, and there was a scurry by the gangway, and almost directly after the paddles ceased churning up the clear water, the sail dropped down. Scoodrach caught the rope that was thrown; the portmanteaus, gun-case, and rods were passed up, and, not trusting himself to speak, Max grasped Scoodrach's hand, pressing a couple of sovereigns therein, seized Kenneth's for a moment, and then leaped on board.

The rope was cast off; there was a loud ting from the captain's bell, the paddles revolved, the boat glided astern, with Kenneth sitting despondently on one of the thwarts, and some one at Max's elbow said to another hard by,—

"See that red-headed Scotch boy?"

"Yes; but did you see what he did?"

"Yes; threw something into the sea."

"Did you see what it was?"

"No."

"A couple of sovereigns."

"No!"

"Yes. I saw them go right down through the clear water."

"Then he must be mad."

"Not mad," said Max to himself; "but as full of pride as of love for The Mackhai."

He made his way astern, and took off and waved his bonnet.

The effect was electrical. Kenneth sprang up and waved his bonnet in return, and, a few minutes later, Scoodrach, whose ire had passed away, began to wave his, and Max stood watching and wondering why they did not hoist the sail and return.

And then he did not wonder, but stood leaning over the rail, watching the boat grow less and the figures in her smaller, till they seemed to die away in the immensity of the great sea.

But Max did not move even then. His heart was full, and it was with a sensation of sorrow and despondency such as he had never felt before that the rest of the journey was made, boat changed for train, and finally, and with a reluctance such as he could not have believed possible, he reached London, and stood once more before his father, who met him coolly enough, with,—

"Well, Max, back again?"

"Yes, father; and I want to ask you something about Dunroe."

"Humph!" said the old lawyer, about half an hour later; "so you think like that, do you, Max?"

"Yes, father."

"Well, you'll grow older and wiser some day."

"But you will not turn them out?"

"When I want to take you into counsel, Master Max, I shall do so. Now please understand this once for all."

"Yes, father?"

"Never mention the names of the Mackhais again."

Chapter Thirty Four
Restitution

Time glided on, and Mr Andrew Blande's plans did not seem to turn out quite as he wished. The customary legal proceedings were got through, and he became full possessor of Dunroe, with the right, as the deeds said, to enjoy these rights. But he was a very old man, one who had married late in life, to find that he had made a mistake, for the marriage was hurried on by the lady's friends on account of his wealth, and the lady who became his wife lived a somewhat sad life, and died when her son Max was ten years old.

To make Max happy, his father had been in the habit of letting him lead a sedentary life, and of telling him how rich he would some day be, and had gone on saving and hoarding, and gaining possession of estate after estate.

But when he had obtained Dunroe, he did not enjoy it. He went down once to stay there, but he never did so again; and finding, in spite of all he could say, that Max would not enjoy it either, and seemed to have a determined objection to become a Scottish country gentleman, he placed the estate in the hands of his agent to let, and it was not long before a tenant was found for the beautiful old place.

As the years glided on, Max went to college, and kept up a regular correspondence with Kenneth, who, as soon as it could be managed after their leaving Dunroe, went to Sandhurst, his father contenting himself with quiet chambers in town near his club.

But Max and Kenneth did not meet; the troubles at Dunroe seemed to keep them separate. Still, there was always a feeling on the part of both that some day they would be the best of friends once more, and the money question be something that was as good as forgotten.

One day, Max, who had six months previously been summoned to London on very important business, received a letter which had followed him from Cambridge to the dingy old house in Lincoln's Inn.

The young man's face flushed as he opened and read the long epistle, whose purport was that The Mackhai had gone to Baden-Baden for a couple of months, that the writer was alone at his father's chambers, and asking Max to renew some of their old friendly feeling by coming to stay with him for a few days.

Six months before, Max would have declined at once, but now he wrote accepting the invitation with alacrity.

It was for the next day but one, and in due course Max drove up with his portmanteau, and was ushered by a red-haired, curly-headed footman to Kenneth's room.

"The maister's not in," said the footman; "but she was to—I was to say that he'd soon be pack—back, and—" "Why, Scoody, I didn't know you," cried Max. "How you have grown!"

"Yes, she's—I mean, sir, I have grown a good deal and master says I haven't done."

There was the rattle of a latch-key in the outer door, and a tall, handsome young fellow, thoroughly soldierly-looking in every point, strode into the room.

"Max, old chap!" he cried, catching his hands and standing shaking them heartily. "Why, what a great—I say, what a beard."

"And you six feet!"

"No, no—five feet ten."

"And moustached, and a regular dragoon!"

"How did you know that?"

"Know that?"

"Yes; I've just got my commission in the Thirtieth Dragoons."

"I congratulate you!" cried Max. "'Full many a shot at random sent,' etcetera."

"Then you did not know? Well, never mind that; only it isn't all pleasure. The governor says it is too expensive a service for me to go in. The old fellow's not very flush of money, you see."

"Indeed?" said Max quietly.

"Well, never mind that either. But I say, what are you going in for—Church or Law?"

"Neither. I think I shall settle down as a country gentleman."

"Yes, of course," said Kenneth hastily. "Here, let me show you your room. We'll have a snug *tête-à-tête* dinner, and talk about our old fishing days, and the boating."

"Yes," cried Max; "and the fishing and boating to come."

"Ah!" said Kenneth thoughtfully; and the conversation drifted off into minor matters, and about Kenneth's prospects as a soldier.

The *tête-à-tête* dinner was eaten, and they became as it were three boys again, Scoodrach trying to look very sedate, but his cheeks shining and eyes flashing as he listened, while pretending to be busy over his work. Then at last the young men were seated together over their coffee, and the conversation took a fresh turn.

"My father?" said Kenneth, in answer to a question; "oh, very well and jolly. I say, do you two go down much to—to Dunroe?"

"No," said Max huskily. "You do not seem to know my father has been dead these six months."

"I beg your pardon, Max, old fellow. I ought to have known. Shall you go down to Dunroe much now?"

"I hope so—often," said Max.

Kenneth was silent, and sat gazing dreamily before him, while Max watched him curiously.

"And I hope—I shall see you there often," said Max.

"Eh? what?" said Kenneth, flushing and frowning. "No, no, it's well meant, Max, old chap, but I couldn't do it. I couldn't go there again."

There was another silence, and, to Kenneth's great relief, Max rose and left the room without a word.

"Poor old chap!" said Kenneth; "I've offended him, I suppose. I did not mean to. It was very blundering and foolish of him, though, to propose such a thing."

He sat gazing before him sternly.

"Poor old Dunroe!" he said sadly. "How I can see the dear old place again, with its rocks all golden-ruddy weed, its shimmering sea, and the distant blue mountains. Ah, what days those were! I should like to see the dear old place again. But no, no! I couldn't go and stay there now."

He leaped up, and strode once or twice up and down the room.

"Here, what a pretty host I am! I must fetch him down. I've hurt him, and he always was such a sensitive chap."

He was half across the room when Max returned, with a large leather lock-up folio under his arm.

"Oh, you needn't have fetched that down," said Kenneth. "Plenty of writing materials here. But you are not going to write to-night?"

"No, not to-night," said Max quietly, taking a little silver key from off his watch-chain, and opening the folio, which was made with a couple of very large pockets. "Do you take any interest in old writings?"

"Not a bit, my boy. I've had enough to do to study up and pass my exams. But what have you got there?"

"The old mortgage and the title-deeds of Dunroe," said Max quietly.

"But—I say, old fellow, don't do that. I'm pretty hard, but the name of Dunroe always gives me a choky feeling in the throat."

"So it does me, Ken, old fellow!" cried Max, with his voice trembling.

"Then why—?"

"Wait a moment. Do you remember how we two were gradually drawn together up there in the north?"

"Yes, of course," said Kenneth huskily.

"I never had a brother, Ken, and I used to feel at last that I had found one in you."

"And I used to think something of the kind, but—"

"Why not, Ken?"—Max was holding out his hand.

Kenneth stood a moment looking in his eyes, and then grasped the extended hand firmly.

"Yes," he cried; "why not? It's the same old Max after all."

"Then you'll act as a brother to me if I ever ask you to help me in some critical point of my life?"

"Indeed I will."

"Then help me now, Ken, as a brother should, to make a great restoration, and me a happier man."

"I—I don't understand," cried Kenneth wonderingly. "What do you mean?"

"Your father's while he lives, Ken; yours after as his heir."

"Are you mad, Max?"

"Yes, with delight, old fellow!" he cried, as he forced the folio and its contents into his old friend's hands.

"But—"

"Not another word. My father left me very rich, and in a codicil to his will he said he hoped I should make good use of the wealth he left me, and that it might prove a greater source of happiness to me than it had been to him."

"But, Max—"

"I think he would approve of what I am doing now; and if you do not ask me down for a month or two every year, I'll say you are not the Ken Mackhai I used to know."

The objections to and protestations against Max Blande's munificent gift were long and continued. The Mackhai was summoned over from Baden, and he declared it to be impossible.

But all was arranged at last, and Max's fortune suffered very little by his generosity.

The Mackhais took possession of the old home once again, and Max Blande was present at the rejoicings; when fires were lit on each of the four old towers, when there was a feast for all comers, and Tavish went through the evolutions of the sword-dance, while torches were held around, and old Donald, who had to sit to play, poured feebly forth some of his favourite airs.

Max even felt that the pipes were bearable that night, as he poured out some whisky for the ancient piper, and received his blessings now instead of a furious curse.

And somehow, Max used to declare to Ken, he found ten times more enjoyment in the place now than if it had been his own.

And time went on once more.

"Remember?" said a bronzed cavalry officer to a tall, sedate-looking young country gentleman, as they sat together on the deck of The Mackhai's yacht, gliding slowly up the great sea loch.

"Do I remember what?"

"Where I picked you up from the steamer when you first came down?"

"To be sure I do, Ken, old fellow! Why, it must have been just here. Why, Ken, that's fifteen years ago!"

"Exactly, almost to a month. And I've been all around the world since then. How does it make you feel?"

"How?" cried Max, laying his hand upon the other's shoulder; "as if we were boys again. And you?"

"As if the memories of boyhood can never die."